A Sisters' Tale

SHELLEY WEINER

❧ A Sisters' Tale ❧

Best wishes —
Shelley Weiner.
March 1991.

Constable · London

First published in Great Britain 1991
by Constable and Company Limited
3 The Lanchesters
162 Fulham Palace Road
London W6 9ER
Copyright © 1991 Shelley Weiner
ISBN 0 09 470470 8
Set in Linotron 10pt Palatino
by CentraCet, Cambridge
Printed in Great Britain by
Redwood Press Limited
Melksham, Wiltshire

A CIP catalogue record for this book
is available from the British Library

The right of Shelley Weiner to be identified as the
author of this Work has been asserted by her in accordance
with the Copyright, Designs and Patents Act 1988.

FOR MYRA AND GAIL

'Will you please step this way sir. A routine procedure, you understand. Security. One can't be too careful these days.'

A loudspeaker crackled overhead and then stopped abruptly as though
a hand had been clapped over its mouth.

'Would you mind raising your arms please sir. We'd like to search
you — just routine of course.'

Obediently he lifted his arms till they were shoulder high, out-
stretched, fingers tingling. He felt a stranger's hand moving up one leg
and down the other. Embarrassed, he wondered where to look. Modestly
to the ground perhaps? Or upwards, in mute appeal to the heavens?
He had a vision of himself as a Christ-figure awaiting clearance for
take-off from the Great Air Traffic Controller above — and curbed his
smile. He didn't want people to think he enjoyed being body-searched.

'Thank you sir. You can carry on to the departure lounge.'

He followed the sign that said TRANSIT and thought of the vast
endless journeys of planets passing across the face of the sun and his
own imminent flea-hop over miniature mountains and droplets of sea.
Transit. Transitory. Transition. The passage or change from one place
or state or set of circumstances to another.

The loudspeaker crackled again. This time there was a voice.

'British Airways wishes to announce the departure of Flight 825 to
Tel Aviv. Will passengers in possession of boarding passes please
proceed to gate number 32.'

At last, he thought. At long last. He was finally on his way to put
an end to all the waiting.

❧ 1 ❧

Mia looked in the mirror and noticed that her sister was ready, waiting for her. Wasn't that typical? Somehow Gabriella always managed to finish first. Mia had led the way into the world by three years but Gabby had spent the next forty-nine straining to overtake her and usually succeeding. Suddenly, though, she was looking tired.

Mia didn't feel so fresh herself. After all, the last thing one needed in the heat of an August day in Israel was a hairdryer singeing the scalp.

'All right love? Not too hot for you?' A merciless current of fire was being directed at her roots.

'No – it's fine. Quite OK thank you.'

Someone else's perm solution thickened the still air like halitosis. Mia was stifling, perspiring, drowning in the machine-roar. But fifty-two years of habit had taught her to smile, nod obligingly, appear ever fine-thank-you. She glanced at her reflection and saw a plump stoic figure in a dusty-pink chain store sun-dress, mouth set in a pleasant arc, face decidedly sagging. Oh well. Better not to look.

'Perhaps next time we'll try a few highlights. That'll brighten things up.'

Slim-hipped Danny had paused in his agile blow-dry dance. He was considering her intently. Mia nodded uncomfortably, feeling even drabber and duller. A poor sad creature in need of highlights. She hated hairdressers.

'Yes,' she smiled. 'I'll think about it.' She waited impatiently for the moment when he'd appear with a looking glass. She'd say, 'That looks lovely – much better,' and then he'd set her free.

Mia saw with a touch of satisfaction that the mirror was as

ruthless to her sister as it had been to her. Worse perhaps. Gabby's face looked lined and gaunt in its frame of perfectly coiffed hair that had been coloured a shade of rust to blank out the grey. She sat forward tensely, thin legs tightly crossed. Listening to something, Mia suspected. Yes – overhearing some gossip, judging by the way her eyes glistened widely and wickedly.

Suddenly aware of Mia looking at her, Gabby raised her hand, wiggled two fingers conspiratorially and smiled.

At once Mia forgot her resentment, won over by Gabby's charm. She knew that they'd laugh together over the joke. Side by side they'd walk home along the dusty streets of heat-struck Kfar Tikva and they would create their own malicious magic circle walled by mockery. Just the two of them, alone after all. Here at last in the promised land.

Mia smiled. The promised land. What a laugh. Being honest with herself, really honest, it was more like the last resort. They'd come when all else had failed and now it often seemed that they were waiting, ever waiting, in this huge hot airless hole. For what? She often secretly wondered what would become of them here together. They both did. But nothing was ever said. It was better, far better, to hold on to their bond of mockery, let others be the objects of derision.

'Oh, Mims, you must hear this. It's too delicious for words.'

They were making their way to the supermarket. Steam seemed to rise from the crowded pavement. All of Kfar Tikva shopped on a Friday and most clung to the shady side of the street. Mia and Gabriella braved the sun.

'The woman sitting next to me was talking to her friend, and I couldn't, absolutely couldn't, help overhearing. Listen to this.'

'Tell me then, Gabby. Come on.' Mia felt alive all of a sudden. The heat seemed less oppressive. She was young, alert, free from the foul-smelling hell of the hairdressing salon.

'Well.' Gabby paused, savouring her power. 'It started off quite normally. You know – "Hello, how are you?" The usual sort of thing. Then they got on to husbands – and by this time I was hardly listening. "How's Boris?"

'"Not too bad." Then a long list of Boris's failings as a husband and a human being. Not very exciting. And then . . .'

'Well?'

'Boris's wife, having had her moan, asked Lily – yes, I'm sure that was her name – how her Shmulik was keeping. "Didn't he have a cold the last time we spoke?" she wanted to know.

'"A cold!" Lily exclaimed. "Did he have a cold! Rosa, do you mean to say you haven't heard what happened to my Shmulik?"'

Gabriella stood still. They had walked two blocks until they'd reached the department store with its mannequins sweating in the window. Next door was the supermarket. Everything looked yellow in the midday glare.

'And so? What happened to him? Tell me Gabby, tell me.'

It was like when they were children. Mia did the practical things, mended school uniforms, boiled eggs. Hilda, their mother, lay in bed prostrate with despair. And Gabriella made up fairy-tales.

They sat on the low wall outside the supermarket, close together in the last lingering patch of shade.

'You'd never guess. Not in a million years. Shmulik's cold, it seems, had gone on for a long time. The sniffing and nose-blowing was driving his wife crazy. Affecting their sex life too.'

'And so?'

'At last she dragged her husband off to the doctor. "Lily," he protested, "who goes to the doctor for a runny nose? Tell me?" But she wouldn't hear his arguments.

'"Enough is enough," she told him, thinking perhaps he needed his sinuses drained or, at the very least, some anti-histamine tablets. But Shmulik needed more than that. Far more.'

Gabby paused dramatically.

'What?' asked Mia, intrigued. The sun had bleached their circle of shade and bore down on to their melting hairspray. She moved closer to her sister, her conspirator. 'What was wrong with him? What did he need?'

'Brain surgery.'

'What?'

'Yup. That's what she said. His cerebral fluid had been leaking through his nose.'

'But Gabby – how awful. Surely not? A thing like that can't really happen?'

'It can apparently. Rosa also found it hard to believe. "I didn't believe it myself," said Lily. "Can you imagine? One minute

10

you think your husband's got a cold – the next you find out he has a leaking brain." Quite a shock I should imagine.'

'Hideous. Macabre. Did Rosa sound appalled?"

'Not really. They seemed to be enjoying the horror of it. Lily was quite proud – in a way. "They called in the top man," she boasted, "the country's leading expert in micro neurosurgery. Shmulik will be in hospital for weeks. You know how it is with the brain . . .?" Rosa clearly didn't. Who does?

'"But Lily," she asked after pondering for some time, "how can such a thing happen? Surely it must be very rare? Maybe your Shmulik bumped his head?"

'"Not that he was aware of," Lily replied ominously. "These things happen Rosa. These things happen."'

'Did she say he'd be all right eventually?' asked Mia. It seemed important to know.

'She didn't say. But Mims, I can tell you I'll never feel the same about having a runny nose again.'

'Nor will I.'

Mia heard her own burst of nervous laughter and wondered why the anecdote seemed so funny and then, recovering from her mirth, felt slightly uncomfortable. Why did Gabby's stories leave a nasty after-taste? What were the messages behind her myths – if they were myths? Mia often doubted their veracity. She doubted many things. But the sense of belonging to her sister's magic mocking circle was irresistible. No – she'd stop questioning. Ridiculous to analyse everything. She'd simply enjoy their exclusivity – the two of them together laughing ungently at the world.

'Let's go.'

She spoke decisively. Her big-sister voice.

'The supermarket. We'd better hurry before it closes – you know what things are like on a Friday.'

At least the crowded aisles were cool. Oppressive and gloomy, but cooler than outside. Mia steered the trolley, pausing to allow others to pass, resigned to the aggressive shoves of her fellow shoppers and suddenly acutely homesick for the calm order of England. Why had they abandoned the safe bright sterility of home for this? How dare people push her about so – grabbing things, stepping on her toes, demanding, touching? She seethed inside but smiled. Gabby forged a relentless path ahead and filled the basket with spicy eggplant salads and fancy breads and spinach pastries and exotic fruits. Their Sabbath treats.

'Come, Mims – follow me to the fish counter.'

Waiting their turn in front of the tank of live carp, they tuned themselves mentally for another well-played duet of derision. This was fun. Each Friday they would carefully select the fish that most resembled someone in their shared past. Gabby leaned forward intently and Mia, watching, waiting for the first suggestion, tried to remember how the game had begun.

Oh yes – the day her sister had studied a defeated fishy face waiting on the marble slab for the blow that would end it all and had said, 'That looks just like Joe.' Mia was stunned. Joe had been their father, gloomy, undermined, dead by his fortieth birthday.

'Gabby that's awful.' But she laughed. How wickedly evil. They were going to eat Dad for their Friday night supper. That would be sublime revenge for his leaving his little girls to the benign – and sometimes not so benign – neglect of helpless Hilda.

The following week it was Mia's turn.

'Miss Twigg,' she said triumphantly, identifying a carp that looked as though it had toothache, frowning and hating its scaly tank-mates. 'Miss Martha Twigg.'

Miss Twigg, retired much-loathed Latin teacher at a respected London grammar school, was at that moment sunning herself in the garden of her Sussex retirement home. She was blissfully unaware that her fishy *alter ego*, thousands of miles away in a Kfar Tikva supermarket, was about to receive a well-aimed death blow. That night Mia and Gabby had relished the delicate flavour of Martha Twigg lightly sautéd in butter.

Now they both studied their candidates. 'Wait a second,' Gabby said to the young executioner behind the counter, who looked at them enquiringly. 'I have it.' She turned to Mia with a satisfied smile.

'Who? Who?' Mia couldn't suppress a slight tug of apprehension. This game was fraught with danger.

'Herbert. Herbert Green. Unmistakably Herbert Green.' Gabriella was pointing at a sleek, plump specimen swimming rather clumsily round the perimeter of the tank. 'Look, he even has acne. And Herbert always did seem to be an outsider. Why they called him Hot-Blooded Herb, God only knows. Or perhaps you know, Mims? After all, he was your boyfriend, wasn't he?'

'I was young, Gabby. Hardly in my teens.' Mia suddenly felt embarrassed. With one stroke, her sister had demolished poor Herbert and returned her to clumsy, awkward adolescence. The lumpy girl again – only sought out by those at the fringes of the crowd. Herbert. Dull and boring Martin Fineberg. But then there was Seamus. Her dark handsome knight in shining armour. Mia clung desperately to the fleeting image and thought, 'Eat your heart out Gabby. You never ever had a Seamus, did you?'

Aloud she said: 'I was just doing poor Herbert a favour – agreed to go out with him out of pure compassion. And fortunately his hot-bloodedness hadn't matured beyond the odd wet kiss. Neither, thank goodness, had his acne.'

She was ashamed as she spoke. Why, again and again, did she share Gabby's nastiness to cover the discomfort that her sister constantly created? And Herbert had been such a well-meaning, gentle friend. But Mia persisted, overriding her shame.

'You're right though, Gabs, quite right. It's Herbert for the pot. I suffered plenty of humiliation for my big-heartedness.'

She indicated the blameless gormless carp to the impatient assistant, who nodded and grabbed its suddenly flailing tail. The fish gave a final slither and lurched convulsively on the marble slab as the heavy wooden club descended on its head. Mia knew that she wouldn't enjoy Herbert nearly as much as she'd savoured Martha Twigg. But she'd try to make sure that Gabby was unaware of her unease. She didn't want to spoil the fun.

Bearing food and flowers and Herbert, they squinted in the glare as they made their way up the dusty untarred road to their flat. The streets were emptying. Kfar Tikva was holding its breath till the late afternoon eased the heat. When Mia looked out on to the sun-scorched yellow desolation of the town during this hot hiatus she often felt that they'd come to the end of the earth. Was this how the post-nuclear world would look? She caught herself. Silly. It was only Kfar Tikva having its summer siesta.

Their block had no name. Just number 84. It stood on stilts like its neighbours, crouched like rows of giant jaundiced animals over shady car-parks. The entrance hall was dark and hot.

'Coffee?' Mia offered and Gabby refused listlessly. They were limp. The lift, as usual, had been out of service and they'd had to climb four floors. Humour, even the most maliciously mocking humour, was hard to retain when the temperature reached the hundreds. All one could do then was wait. Wait for evening. For something. It occurred to Mia that they seemed to do an awful lot of waiting, the two of them. They kept telling one another how happy they were, and they waited. She said nothing.

Gabby, cross-legged on the sofa, blew smoke-rings that hovered in the still air. Mia flopped down opposite her. Even breathing was an effort. She felt puffy, bloated, sticky behind her knees and under her arms. As her eyes idly followed a smoke-spiral curling torpidly upwards, Mia suddenly had an image of a helter-skelter. She saw a great tower that seemed to touch the clouds. Hampstead Heath, with its rainy Bank Holiday fairs.

❧ 2 ☙

Why had I suddenly thought of that giant cone in the sky? Nothing was further from my mind as I sat there utterly exhausted, watching her smoke and feeling my irritation rising. Bloody hell, it was hot and stuffy enough without that. And anyway it was bad for her. She'd promised.

'D'you have to, Gabs?' I couldn't stop the tiniest note of displeasure creeping into my voice. Usually I was so careful, but the heat, that choking heat – I think it was driving me crazy. The heat and the waiting. That summer the days seemed to overflow with waiting. For the cool of sunset, another tomorrow, a kinder season. I don't know . . .

She looked at me, her defiant dark-eyed look, and she tilted her head upwards and blew out a perfect floating ring. I knew then that my little sister was not about to relinquish her grip on me. Not at all. We'd laugh together, live together here in this God-forsaken place. Say that we'd chosen our joint destiny. How lucky we were to have one another after all. Chosen? Well, I suppose. But choice means freedom to leave and we were locked tight in our togetherness and neither of us was letting go. And I saw the coil of smoke and shut my eyes. And that's when I thought of the blue and yellow helter-skelter on Hampstead Heath in the rain.

There I was, eight years old again, serious, responsible little Mia, clutching the scratchy mat to my chest, my heart knocking against it as I climbed the wooden stairs to the top of the spiral slide. Ahead of me I heard footsteps, light tripping footsteps, and then her voice:

'Come on, slow-coach. *Can't* you hurry up?'

And then – 'Wheee!' A jubilant squeal that tore right through me. And she was on her way down, slithering, shrieking, pert brown little pigtails flying. And me having at last reached the top but not daring to look down. God how I hated it, forced myself to sit on the mat, gritted my teeth, let the world slip away and hurtled down, down, down. And finally stopped, my face wet with tears and the rain that usually fell on Bank Holiday Mondays. But I made myself smile when I saw her waiting there, giggling, dancing from foot to foot.

'Oh, Mimsi,' she'd say. 'You look so funny – you're all soaking. Shall we have another go? Oh please . . .'

I hardly hesitated before agreeing. Can you believe it? Hating it, terrified beyond belief – and yet I submitted. I looked beyond the wire enclosure to where the adults stood clustered under bright umbrellas, framed by the giant ferris wheel, hazy outlines in the greyness. Yes, there they were, waiting. Mum had been tired of course. Almost too tired to come along to the fair. But he'd persuaded her, said she'd enjoy it, he'd keep her warm and dry. And there he was, tending her as if she were a plump tropical plant in her cherry-red mac in the warm August rain. He took care of his Hilda and I had to look after my little sister.

'Now keep on eye on Gabriella, Mia,' he had said. 'You're my big girl, now. Don't let her out of your sight.'

'Yes Daddy.'

Why didn't I say no I won't, it's not my job, cut me out, I'm not her nanny, look after your own bloody kid. That would have lopped a couple of years off his life. But no. Not me.

'Yes Daddy,' I said sweetly.

And she knew. She knew that however many times she wanted to slide, there I'd be close behind her like a faithful little spaniel. Panting, heart pounding, dying a little each time I spiralled helplessly down into the shut-eyed blackness. But never refusing to have another go. I'm sure she got bored with it long before she consented to leave – but who could blame a five-year-old for savouring such power? And me? Why *didn't* I refuse? Oh, I don't know. It was part of the chain I suppose. Me tending Gabby, Joe tending Hilda. Such a fragile family quartet. A delicate balance that tipped and swung wildly, then fell with a thud when he went and died on us. I know it's dreadful and I shouldn't say it and I doubt if God or whoever is up there will ever forgive me for this, but I'll never forgive

Daddy for it. Anyway, that was three years later. Gabby and I had forged our bond long, long before. It stretched back to before she was born.

I hated it when my mother slept. And she seemed to do it all the time the year I was three, and her tummy kept growing and she lay on the bed and said, 'Leave me alone, Mia. Leave me alone, let Mummy rest. Mummy's very tired. Very tired indeed.' And she'd close her eyes and I'd poke at them with my fingers and I'd say, 'Mummy, open your eyes, Mummy. Please, please, please open your eyes.' And I'd cry and she would lie there, still as a china doll. Still as the one my cousin Ruth had given me – the one with the hole in the mouth and the dirty pink dress and the blue glassy eyes that were supposed to shut when she rested but always got stuck. Ugly Baba I called her, shutting her stiff lids. I couldn't bear to see her lying and staring but not seeing. It gave me bad dreams.

But Mummy wasn't my Ugly Baba. I wanted her eyes to be open, I wanted her to be watching me, loving me, holding me in her arms just as she used to do before her tummy got fat.

'Wake up,' I'd start screaming, stamping, shaking her heavy arm. 'Wake up. Wake up. Wake up.' And when she couldn't take it any more, she'd sit up and breathe deeply – in, out, in, out – and I'd stop shouting, waiting to see what would happen next. Something terrible, I knew, for I was being a bad girl.

'Get out of here, you horrible little brat,' she'd say. Not shouting, but so angry. So terribly angry that I wanted to sink into the ground, be gone for ever. 'Just get out of here and leave me alone and don't you dare come and disturb me when I'm resting ever again.'

And I didn't after a while. I'd just sit outside her bedroom door, waiting. Holding Ugly Baba, letting her sleep. And sometimes, when I had that feeling inside, making me want to scream and cry, I'd take Ugly Baba and hold her by the legs and swing her hard against my bed, bashing her blue eyes saying, 'Brat, brat, horrible little brat.' Until one day I cracked her skull. A funny sort of zigzag that parted her stiff yellow curls. And Mummy noticed and said I was careless as well. Didn't know how to look after my toys. Didn't appreciate anything. I couldn't understand what she meant but it was something bad.

17

I became very quiet then. As quiet as Ugly Baba. At night when Daddy came home from work, always so sad and tired, he'd pat my head and say, 'Been a good girl, Blondie?' and then disappear into Mummy's room. And he'd sit there for ages and I'd long for him to come out so that I could show him how still I'd been sitting and say, 'Look Daddy, look how good I've been.' Sometimes I waited for ever. But I'd learnt not to scream. I tried to fix my Baba's china head and started to call her Blondie too.

One day Mummy suddenly disappeared and Daddy went too. Aunty Rose came to stay and said, 'You're so lucky Mia – you're going to get a baby.' I nodded and sat with Ugly Baba in her room and stopped myself from crying or making any noise at all. Only brats who didn't appreciate things made a noise. Good children stayed as still as a china doll and then their mother came back and their father touched their heads and they felt warm inside. If they waited long enough . . .

They did come back.

'Mia's been an angel,' said Aunty Rose. 'A real little help around the house. Such a big, good girl.' I smiled and knew secretly that I'd magicked their return, that if I kept being quiet and good then all sorts of wonderful things would happen to me. And I rushed to Mummy, jumped up to be kissed.

But she stepped away, holding tight on to a pink bundle and said: 'Careful now, Mia. Calm down. You must be very careful not to hurt your new baby sister.'

My sister?

'Look Mia.' Daddy unwrapped the blanket and I saw the baby wrinkling up its eyes, opening its mouth and beginning to scream. And no one called it a horrible brat. They were looking at me, waiting for me to say something. Should I tell them it was a brat? Say get out of here? No, they wouldn't have been pleased. They seemed to like the silly thing, didn't mind its noise. Mummy was holding it, smiling at it.

'Her name is Gabriella,' she said.

'Oh.'

I was too frightened to say any more in case it was wrong. I had a horrible feeling that I'd made a mistake, that my being good hadn't brought them back to me at all. That this little thing, this sister thing that Mummy said was called Gabriella, had the real magic power. Then I noticed Mummy's tummy. It was smaller again, almost like it had been before she got sleepy. Maybe, if I were to be 'very, very good', a 'really good big girl', 'a help around the house' just like Aunty Rose said, they'd see I was better than this noisy red-faced sister. Surely they would.

'Why is she crying?' I had to find out.

'The little darling is hungry,' said Mummy. 'When babies are hungry, that's what they do. A baby doesn't know how to ask nicely, you see Mia. So we have to look after her . . . Oh Joe, take the child and feed her. I'm so, so tired. I just have to lie down.'

So she was still tired. The new small tummy didn't mean anything then. And Daddy was holding this Gabriella now, stroking her little head with its ugly black hair. I wanted to tell him that my hair was much nicer, I was his Blondie. But he didn't even look at me. Just looked down at the red sister and seemed very very sad. I stood back quietly and he went into the sitting-room with Aunty Rose following behind him in a busy way. She was carrying a funny curvy glass bottle with a rubber thing at the end and Daddy sat down and stuck it in the baby's mouth. The noise stopped.

'She had a difficult time Rose,' I heard him say. 'No strength to breastfeed. I'm going to have to help her a lot – let her rest, get her health back.'

The baby sucked. I could hear it. Her I mean. A noisy eater as well. Aunty Rose wouldn't like that I knew – she always told me to keep my mouth shut and eat quietly. I waited for her to say something, but no, she just sat there, frowning. Daddy suddenly noticed me standing and watching from the door.

'Mia, come here. Come and sit next to your Dad.'

I dashed to his feet.

'You're my big girl now. You must help Daddy and Mummy with your new little sister. Mummy's very, very tired and the doctor said she needs to sleep. A lot. So we mustn't disturb her. You'll help, won't you Blondie? You're such a good, sweet child.'

I held on to his knee and heard the suck-suck-suck of the sister and thought he *does* prefer me. I'd show him. Be the best helper in the world.

'Yes Daddy.'

And so it began. Aunty Rose stayed on and I hardly saw Mummy. At night after my bath I'd be allowed to go into the room and I could hardly breathe for the heat and a funny smell of dead flowers and sourness that seemed to come from the wet yellow patch on the front of her night-dress. 'She's taking a long time drying up,' Aunty Rose had explained impatiently when I'd asked why Mummy's nighty was always smelly and wet. In the meantime she lay in a lonely pool of light from the bulb over her bed and looked as if she was glued there and would never move away from the bed again.

She did. Gradually. She must have dried up enough to unglue herself from the sheets, for she came downstairs, sometimes took Gabriella from Aunty Rose, gave her a bottle of milk and then got too tired to do anything else. But I was never tired. Helped Aunty Rose, helped Daddy, so quiet, so busy. Waiting ever so patiently to hear what a good girl I was being, to hear him say 'Blondie' in that special voice and, maybe, just maybe, for Mummy to hold me as she used to before she got fat and wet. But that never happened.

And secretly in my bed I knew whom to blame. Gabriella. That noisy horrible brat who had changed everything. In the daytime I'd be the best-behaved big sister in the world and everyone would say, 'Isn't Mia sweet – so grown-up – she must be such a help and pleasure to you.' On Sundays when the other aunts came for tea, Aunty Sara and Aunty Mavis – all Daddy's sisters – I'd be allowed to have Gabriella on my lap and they'd smile and say, 'We can see that you love your little sister very much.' And I'd nod. That was clearly what good girls did.

But at night I'd have wicked thoughts. Wicked secret thoughts of taking Gabriella, stealing her away up into my room, then holding on to her tiny little legs and bashing, bashing her head against the wooden posts at the end of my bed. Bashing it until a great zigzag appeared right in the middle of that black hair. Maybe it would bleed like the time I'd slipped and bumped my head on the corner of the kitchen table and Aunty Rose had to hold a wet cloth against it for ages because the blood wouldn't stop running down my face. Yes, it would bleed just like that. Red juice pouring out of the black zigzag, all her noise and ugliness spilling out. And then Gabriella would be as quiet and still as Ugly Baba. And afterwards, of course, I'd try to fix her up so that Mummy wouldn't say I was ungrateful.

But I knew I *was* ungrateful. Ungrateful and wicked to have such thoughts about the little sister everyone said I loved so much. And I waited for my punishment. Every night when Aunty Rose had finished scrubbing me in the bath – sometimes it hurt, the way she scrubbed me so hard – she said, 'Must get you clean Mia. Must get you nicely clean.' She didn't know my bad night thoughts. And when she was through she would pull out the plug.

'Jump out quickly now,' she'd say. 'Move it or you'll be pulled down the plughole. That's what happens to naughty girls. But I know you're far too good . . .'

No she didn't.

And I stayed in as long as I dared, watching the soapy water being sucked down in a spiral. Once I put my big toe in the hole and felt how hard it was being pulled, and I jerked it away and jumped out. And I saw the water disappearing. One day I'd be too slow and it would happen to me.

Round and round I'd go, then down and down to the bottom of the earth. Like sliding down the helter-skelter. Oh God. I gripped on to the arm of a sofa in a hot space in another time and blinked away the spiralling smoke that was making me choke and my eyes water.

'Mims? Are you all right? You look sort of greenish.'

'No, I'm fine. Really. It's the heat. These endless afternoons when all one can do is wait for the sun to set. It's even too hot to sleep . . .'

'You looked like you were having a little snooze there. I was watching you.'

Why did she have to sound so accusing? I shrugged, determined not to contradict her in any way today. She was in a defiant mood and it made me very careful. I forced myself up, feeling the delicious cool of the stone floor against my feet as I walked heavily to the window. The slatted blinds were shut. That first summer in Israel we'd kept the windows wide open to invite a coolness that didn't exist. Now we knew enough to shut everything tight against the air of the scalding August daytime streets. We admitted only the cool breezes of the night. Nothing else. No one else. I parted two slats and looked out on to the deserted suburb. Another hour or so and Kfar Tikva would start waking up.

Gabby was watching me. I could feel her eyes following me across the room. 'I must tell you something, Mia.'

Oh no. I knew it. Trouble. When my sister said that, it sounded a warning bell. Must you? Are you sure you must? It was bound to be something I'd rather not hear. Gabriella was using her serious, authoritative, it-may-be-painful-but-it's-only-my-duty voice and I wanted to shout, 'Stop, you don't have to bloody tell me anything at all. Just leave everything well alone, do you hear? Leave it . . .'

But I didn't. 'What?' I asked pleasantly.

'That pink really doesn't suit you. You're much more a blue sort of person.'

'Oh.'

I suddenly felt big and gawky and so envious of the little sister who seemed to know instinctively how to knot a scarf around her neck and look stylish. I looked around the room.

'The spider-plant needs watering,' I said idly. It was drooping in a parched sort of way, green leaves brushing dejectedly against the Wedgwood bowl we'd brought from England.

'Ah, that reminds me.' Gabby uncrossed her legs, stubbed out her cigarette (how many had she smoked that afternoon?) and sat up, suddenly eager, my incompatibility with pink forgotten. What next? 'Have you seen those experimental houseplants that they're producing? On the farms where they research and grow such things – deformed-looking specimens with roots that seem to claw above the soil, all upside-down and inside-out. Grotesque, but very popular they say?'

Yes, perhaps I'd seen them. So what? I looked at her enquiringly from my post at the window. I didn't want to appear too interested. After all, she'd just made a stab at me and it was still hurting. But I never could resist the possibility of another Gabby story.

'Amazing what people will buy,' I said

'That's not the point.' Her voice had an impatient edge. Bloody hell. What *was* the point? I saw an argument looming, as certain as the coming of dusk. We were waiting for it. Something was going to happen. I shuddered, then told myself not to be silly and turned back to my watch at the window.

'Listen, Mims. It's interesting. Something I saw in an article on how they produce those things . . .'

Interesting? Agronomy bored me stupid. She knew I switched off whenever plants or flowers were mentioned. They were quite pretty to look at but the thought of tending them made me feel tired. Even the thought. I suppose I'd had to care for too many people in my life. No space for plants. Even that poor wilting spider-plant – I kept noticing its thirst but did nothing. It would die soon.

'The thing is, the thing that really grabbed me, that one of the principles they use to create strong, healthy plants (and, believe me, to survive with those deformities they've got to be strong and healthy) is to grow them under stress. Do you hear that Mims? Under stress. They keep them just a little thirsty and just a little cold. Not quite comfortable. Nothing bad enough to kill them, mind. Only to make them tougher. Survivors.'

She sat back, lit another cigarette and drew in deeply. I said nothing. Just looked at our plant and thought, 'Perhaps you won't die then. You may be suffering but it's good for you – makes you stronger all the time.' One day we'd wake up and there'd be a lush green spider-plant thrusting its muscular way into every crevice in the flat. I knew what Gabby was trying to say and it had nothing to do with plants. But I was too tired to think it through. Tired and heavy and apprehensive.

'I see,' I said at last. I could see she thought I didn't but it wasn't worth discussing. It would bring back too much. Not that I could avoid thinking about the past. It was in my mind all the time in this hot vacuum of the present. But there were things that hurt too much to talk about even then.

'Are you sure you don't want some coffee, Gabby? I'm going to make some for myself.'

She was deep in thought. I walked past her to the kitchen.

❧ 3 ❧

She didn't get it. Sometimes she was so damned slow and seemed so thick that I wanted to shake her. She put on that blankness, that blandness. Good, sweet, caring big sister Mia. That's what she wanted me and the world to think. But I knew better.

Saplings under stress. The image gripped me, tugged at my imagination. How did they prove it? With sophisticated technology to measure just the level of deprivation that would make the plant defiant? I could imagine the poor thing mustering all its sap and saying, 'Bugger it, you think you're going to defeat me but just you wait. I'll grow despite you. Tough and gnarled and strong.' The thought made me smile.

'What's so funny?' Mia asked. She'd come back from the kitchen with two brimming coffee mugs, one bearing the profile of the queen, and the other her son and daughter-in-law. A jubilee and a wedding. Family milestones just like ours but with mugs for remembrance. What mugs. They'd come a long way too, those royal mugs.

'What? Oh, thanks Mim. I was still musing about botany. Cultivation under adverse conditions. That's what the article was called. Strange how brilliant ideas can be made so boring.'

Her face closed. She gripped her coffee mug tightly, using both hands. Poor Charles and Diana must have been suffocating. Good for them – a bit of nuptial stress would make them thrive. But Mia quite clearly didn't want to talk about stress, endurance, young struggling plantlets. Nothing like that. Too close to the bone. I wasn't going to let her get away with it though. Not this time.

'Mia.' I used my serious voice. She hated it. 'Do you think *we*

24

were strengthened by what happened? Losing Dad . . . Clive
. . . Seamus? Everything?'

I suddenly had a vision of the two of us here, high up in hot
Kfar Tikva, two knotted and elderly plants sharing a brittle
terracotta pot, roots exposed and intertwined.

Mia was looking at me. The royal couple had been released
to breathe freely on the coffee table. She leaned forward
earnestly and pushed a strand of hair from her brow. It looked
as if it needed washing again, and we'd hardly stepped out of
the hairdresser. I was going to say something but decided
against it. She spoke instead:

'What about Mum? You forgot to mention her in your roll-
call.'

What *about* Mum? When had we lost her? When had we ever
had her?

'Well,' I said contemplatively, deliberately missing the point,
'one could hardly quote her as an example of someone who was
strengthened by neglect. I'd say Dad fed her so much and so
frequently that she was waterlogged.'

Did I have to be so clever-clever at all times? Well put, Gabby
– that was your mother, dismissed in a dozen pithy words. A
waterlogged weakling. I thought about her lying on her bed
(whenever I thought of Mum it was in the context of bed) and
it suddenly occurred to me that she'd been far cleverer than
anyone ever acknowledged. Her plump, limp-haired passivity
was a cover. She'd made helplessness her art – a selective
helplessness that turned Dad into her slave. Then, when he'd
died on her, she'd groomed Mia for the role. Or had big
daughter always been waiting in the wings to understudy her
father?

I looked carefully at my sister and felt an ache of compassion.
This was something I usually managed to guard myself against,
but I saw such a sad, lost look come over her that I couldn't
help it. Did she actually miss Mum? Did she not regret her
years of service? Thank goodness I'd put myself out of the slave
race. I'd made sure of that right from the start. Little Gabriella
was there to be admired, cosseted, to amuse and be amused.
But she was strictly not available for practical consideration.

*

'What a cutey-pie. Your little Gabby can twist anyone round her little finger.' That was the chorus at those Sunday afternoon family teas. Even Mum would smile when I did my weekly star turn. Once I made her laugh with an imitation of Dad coming home from work and groaning, 'What a day, what a day.' No one else laughed at that though. Dad looked sadder than ever.

Our teatime gatherings always included Dad's three sisters, Sara, Mavis and Rose. Sara arrived with Uncle Ron, Mavis with Uncle Fred, and Rose on her own. Thank goodness Aunty Rose never acquired encumbrances – we'd never have survived Mum's helplessness without her. Sara and Mavis had managed to find husbands but neither went as far as achieving children. Their darling brother Joe had made it in every way – with a wife who had money (inherited from her father the draper) and two perfect daughters. His good, clever Blondie and me, the little personality.

Yup – he really had everything, poor old Dad. While he lasted.

'So Joe. How's business?'

Uncle Fred always sat himself down in the biggest armchair, lit his pipe and boomed his voice across the room to his brother-in-law. Uncle Ron on the sofa was mostly silent. If he did venture a comment, Sara destroyed him with a scathing put-down. A scornful 'Oh, Ron . . .' She'd never forgiven him for his failure to make money and she spent each Sunday afternoon resenting him, us, her sisters, the world. 'Do you think it's natural for your Mia to be so quiet?' she'd ask my mother. And 'Isn't Gabriella slightly underweight?'

But everyone else adored us. Me. They admired Mia but they absolutely loved me. I made sure of it.

'Not too bad Fred, not too bad.' Dad, in the armchair opposite Fred, always looked doubtful when he replied. As far as I could discover later on, his wholesale fashion outlet in Great Portland Street always made a reasonable sort of profit. But even if he'd hit the big time Dad would have looked bowed and defeated and described things as 'not too bad'. 'And you?'

God, it was boring. The only good bits were the eats. Each week Aunt Sara brought an apple tart, Mavis came with a plate of éclairs and Rose arrived with a huge, round, elaborately iced chocolate cake. 'Ooh,' I'd say, wide-eyed, 'Aunty Rose, I just *love* chocolate cake.' Even at the age of four I knew instinctively how to win affection. Perhaps I lost the art along the way.

Mia sat next to me. We had tea at the dining-room table on family Sundays.

'Gabby, you mustn't eat chocolate cake with your fingers.' She used her prissiest voice, hoping Aunty Rose would notice. Mia ate neatly and consistently, her cake-fork moving up and down from her plate to her mouth and back again, never spilling a crumb. Everyone called her a good eater.

Not me. I hated proper food. Played with it, they all said. I was playing with them really – wanted them to coax me, to offer me all sorts of treats if I cleaned my plate. I kept them guessing, knew that Mia was stupid for making things so easy for them. That's why no one really made a fuss of her, silly fool. She could have got so much more by being a bit less good.

There *was* something that she got and I didn't. Most weeks Mia went for a ride in Uncle Fred's big black taxi. I remember the first time he took her.

There she was, staring out of the dining-room window. Outside, the street was cold, covered with the dirty remains of a late winter snowfall. There were no trees. The Hendon Estate was only ten years old and had yet to acquire the illusion of rootedness. Mum and Dad had bought a show house and Uncle Fred drove his taxi round the clock, day and night, only pausing to fill the petrol tank, top up his fat stomach and suck on his pipe. He was trying to earn enough to match our economic status and his dark gleaming vehicle to affluence was parked alongside our kerb. Mia was looking at it.

'How about a little ride, Blondie? I'll take you for a turn around the block.'

He'd been watching her. I didn't like Uncle Fred. He always watched Mia instead of me, and he had no right to call her Blondie. That was private – Daddy's name for her. Mia smiled. She always smiled. But I got in first.

'I'll come. I'll come. I love your black taxi Uncle Fred.'

He ignored me. 'How about it Mia? You're my big niece and sometimes you deserve a special treat. Once around the block. Come along . . .'

She stood up, looked at Mum and Dad to see if they minded. Mum was sitting at the end of the table. She also played with her food I noticed, except sometimes when Dad was at work

27

and Mia was at school and she'd go to the kitchen and make herself big sandwiches and gobble them up. I'd seen her do it. Now, when Mia looked at her, she just nodded. She didn't care one way or another. Dad shrugged and looked pleased. Well, he sort of smiled and for him that was pleased.

'That's very nice of you, Fred,' he said.

I saw them driving off. Mia was sitting in the front next to Uncle Fred, all prim and proper. He'd opened the door for her and she'd climbed in, tucking her blue-striped pinafore neatly beneath her. I watched them leave and I hated her. Why didn't he want *me* to come with him in his taxi? I'd be much more fun than my good boring sister. I'd make him laugh. I went back to my seat at the table, squashed the remains of my chocolate cake in my hands and hair and Aunty Rose's lap, and shouted my rage. They laughed and said, 'Tut tut, what a little temper the child has,' and that made me even more furious but it didn't help. Uncle Fred never took me on a taxi ride. Each week he took Mia and left me behind. I got used to it after a while. And anyway he stopped doing it after Dad died. Everything seemed to stop then.

I shivered suddenly, despite the heat. Mia noticed my shudder, the way I pulled out another cigarette and lit it greedily. Concern, then disapproval, flashed over her face. Strange how her expression, so inscrutable to everyone else, should have been like an open book to me. Or so I thought. What dark secrets lay buried in that bland blonde head? Perhaps I wasn't the only one with a secret?

'There's far more to Mia than most people imagine,' Seamus had said. He was trying to explain how it had all begun between him and her. I'd thought he meant poetic things, imagined my sister with hidden dramatic depths. After all, she could be quite perceptive – sometimes. *Did* he though?

Anyway, I certainly didn't want to start thinking of Seamus. Not then. Neither Seamus nor Uncle Fred. Nor Dad, nor that bastard Clive. My God what a line-up of men we'd had in our lives. Talk about the great and the good.

'And so,' I said suddenly to Mia, desperate to break the heavy silence. I wanted to make her laugh again, to banish my unsavoury thoughts with a little wholesome spite. 'What do you think we should do with Herbert? He's lying so patiently in the fridge awaiting his fate. The pot? The oven? Bubbling oil or a fragrant marinade? The suspense must be – uh – killing him. We'd better put him out of his misery.'

But no. She wasn't paying attention to my bantering tone. First I couldn't penetrate her defences. Now she was unstoppable.

'Funny,' she said slowly in a way that made it clear that what she was about to say wouldn't be funny at all. It rarely was. 'I was just thinking how death put Dad out of his misery. And Mum I suppose. And I was also thinking about that plant theory. It can't be so, Gabby. Not for people anyway. There are the strong and the weak, and the strong survive and the weak go under. Stress in itself is not strenghtening. I cannot believe it.'

Goodness. I'd rarely heard her so passionate. So full of conviction. And in the heat as well. Seamus had been right.

I could have responded with a slow and infuriating: 'You sound defensive, Mia. I think we should try and find out why.' After years of living in Hampstead I was well versed in psychobabble. But instead I said soothingly, 'OK, OK. It was just a passing fancy. A little thought from outside to breathe into our isolation.' Soothing but serious. We'd transplanted ourselves from England to Israel, and we might as well have moved from Mars to the moon. Here we were in the midst of a great life struggle, enormous moral dilemmas, vast confrontations. And we kept ourselves in oblivion, looking only inward and allowing only the waves of heat to penetrate our seclusion. Allowing? What control did we have? And how could we keep the world at bay for ever?

Herbert was a safer subject.

'How about deep-frying your old friend in a nice cosy batter?' I suggested. 'Then, if we don't manage to finish him tonight, we can always have cold Herbert tomorrow. That would be divine retribution for his hot-bloodedness. Such as it was. What do you think?'

She nodded.

'Cold fried fish,' she said, still in the irritatingly vague and dreamy voice. 'Makes me think of my school sandwiches on Mondays. Always filled with the mashed-up remains of Friday's dinner. Curious that, the way we had fish every Friday like a ritual that went with the Sabbath candles. In fact, the fish was more regular than the candles, wasn't it? And the sandwiches. They were as inevitable as the dawning of another Monday. Smelly and dry, until you'd finished eating them and felt the grease stuck to the roof of your mouth. I hated them.'

Such venom. I was stunned. And I'd thought she liked the fish sandwiches. I'd even thought she'd liked Mondays. I was the one who threw tantrums and hated things and cursed the world. Mia usually smiled. She walked me to school and she smiled.

I started school when Mia was an eight-year-old in Class Three.

'I hope you're going to be as obedient and hard-working as your sister,' everyone said. We walked together, down the crazy-paved path, turned left at the garden gate and then along the treeless pavement until we got to the main road. Mia took my hand then – she'd been told to – and held it tight as we crossed. I liked that. It made me feel safe. I knew that I could count on her to look after me. Funny that. I knew it and yet I had to keep putting it to the test again and again.

In the playground I noticed that Mia often sat alone. She didn't look happy or sad about it, just sat at the end of a wooden bench and organized her sandwiches on their grease-paper wrapping and ate. Then she brushed away the crumbs, folded the paper into a perfect square, placed it in the bin and waited quietly for the bell.

Surrounded by Katie and Jackie and Debs and several other best friends, I watched her and wondered how she could bear her aloneness. I wanted to go and hold her hand, just like she held mine. But I was frightened. Maybe that would make me friendless as well.

So instead I said to Jackie: 'D'you want to hear a secret about my sister?' And I told her that Mia had nits. And she told Katie and Debs and then I whispered to them that she wet the bed as well and then everyone pointed and giggled. And Mia noticed. I could see she noticed. But her face didn't change. Only when I went very close did I see there were tears in her eyes but I told myself that she wasn't really crying. It was just a speck of dust. After all, she was smiling – and no one could smile and cry at the same time. I certainly couldn't. When I cried, it was unmistakable and everyone paid attention.

But I knew I'd been nasty. And next day I waited to see if she'd take my hand. Of course she did. Again and again I tested her, and never, ever did she let me down. When we were taken to the fair, I made her follow me on the helter-skelter. Over and over and over. I knew she was scared and a part of me was ashamed. But I despised her for it. I despised her for letting me put her to the test like that, for never, ever saying no. Oh, my poor good sister.

There was a time when I didn't test her, didn't despise her at all. At night, when she was running her bath, she'd call quietly, 'Gabby, come here. Come and talk to me while I bath.' And in the steamy cubicle the two of us would whisper and laugh. I told her stories – real ones, imaginary ones. Tales about friends, uncles, aunts. 'Listen to this Mims,' I'd say – and she'd sit up in the bath, eagerly. 'Tell me, Gabby. Tell me . . .' They were usually rather cruel stories, nasty but delicious.

What a hot, safe cocoon we'd created. Strangely similar, I suppose, to our glass bubble in Kfar Tikva. But our bathtime togetherness ended abruptly one day. The devil got into me and I looked at her and her plump acquiescence made me furious and I said to her, 'Oh Mims, you do have a funny fat body – and I think you're growing titties.' This time I'd gone too far. She never invited me into the bathroom again.

On a hot June Tuesday when I was eight, I woke with a sore throat and they said I could stay at home. Mia left for school alone. I watched her marching, steadily and evenly along the crazy-paved drive and then out into the street. Holding her satchel, staring straight ahead and then disappearing. I smiled to myself, luxuriating in the day ahead. Just sick enough to stay at home, but not too ill to enjoy cool sheets and comic-books, perhaps a little treat for lunch. And maybe, just maybe, Mum would come upstairs, sit on my bed and chat to me. She sometimes did.

Dad was still sitting at the breakfast table. His porridge bowl was empty, but he sat there. Usually he left for work with the last spoonful still in his mouth.

'Are you staying at home today too, Daddy?'

I hoped he wasn't. I wanted to be the only sick one in the house. Anyway, he wasn't sick. Anyone could see he wasn't sick. He was just sad and that wasn't anything unusual.

'No, I'll be leaving in a minute Gabs. I just have a little tummyache. It'll go away though. You go upstairs and get into bed. You must keep warm if you want your throat to get better.'

I kissed him and hopped upstairs and was glad he was going. Oh, Gabriella, if only you'd known. What would you have said if you'd known? 'Daddy, don't go. Don't leave. Please, please stay and I'll try and make you happy. I'll make you laugh, I promise. Look, look at me, look how sweet and funny I am. I'll cuddle you, tickle you, make it better for you. Please don't go away . . .'

But I didn't say anything. I was glad to see him leave the house.

Mummy was upstairs in bed. Every morning he brought her tea on a tray. His offering. She took it and sighed and sat up and sipped. She was still sipping when I came into the room.

'Off to bed now, Gabriella. I'll come and see how you're feeling later on.'

She didn't want to talk. I backed out slowly, watching her place the cup in its saucer and lie down. Then I went to my room and looked at my books and waited.

Later on never happened. Everything else did. There was a sudden hammering on the door. Aunty Rose. 'Hilda, oh Hilda.' She was crying. Mummy was up, out of her bed, dressing quickly. I'd never seen her move so fast and it was terrifying. Dark gown flying like the witch in my fairy-tale book. 'Joe, Joe,' she moaned in a voice that I didn't know. I started screaming. They took no notice. I screamed louder and Aunty Rose suddenly remembered I was there and bent down and said, 'Gabriella . . . your father . . . my brother.' What? What? What was happening?

I stopped screaming and there was a sudden silence that was more frightening than the noise. So I started again. Mummy was in the big armchair, huddled up, crying in huge gulps. Rose stood over her, hands clasped together, tears like rivers down her cheeks. I'd never seen grown-up people behave like that. What had happened to my world?

Mia came home. Aunty Rose was calmer. Her sisters had arrived and Mummy had been put back to bed. I stayed in a dark corner of the sitting-room and heard them say 'heart attack', 'poor Hilda', 'poor little girls'.

'Something happened to your Daddy, Mia,' Aunty Rose told her. Mia stood still, looked up at her with big blank eyes. She didn't cry. I watched and waited and she didn't cry. I cried though. Very loudly. 'Daddy's dead, Mia, dead dead dead.' I yelled it out and took her arm, pulled it and shook it as hard as I could. She just stood there and said: 'No.' 'No.' And she pulled her arm away and went upstairs, slowly, into her room. She shut the door.

'Mia,' I screamed. 'Come out. You have to hold my hand. You *have* to look after me. I didn't really want Daddy to go to work. He could have stayed in bed with his tummyache, just like me. I told him so. I wasn't glad to see him go. I promise.'

And I banged on her door. Banged and banged and shouted, till Aunty Rose came upstairs and knocked and went in and said: 'Mia, I know you're very sad but you must take care of your little sister. You're the big one – here, let her sit next to you. You must stick together, you poor little fatherless girls.'

There. I knew she'd have to.

I went in and took my sister's stiff hand. Then after a while I went to see what Mummy was doing. She lay still on her bed. Still as a dead person. 'Mummy,' I called out, suddenly filled with new fright. Her body jerked. No, she was alive. A dark brown puddle remained at the bottom of her cup. The breakfast tea Daddy had made for her. The last one.

It was gradually growing cooler, thank God. Another hour and Kfar Tikva would be bearable. Nothing, though, could ever equal the heat of that June day when I was eight and my father died. I remember sitting on my bed and feeling as though I were ablaze. Perhaps I had a fever. Yes, that must have been what it was. I'd stayed at home with a sore throat and I had a fever.

'Mims,' I said, wanting to make sure. 'Remember the day that Dad died?'

She was still sitting with her cold coffee, deep in thought. Looked at me and frowned. 'What, Gabby? Yes. Yes, of course.'

'Did I have a temperature?'

There was a pause. Her frown grew deeper. She hated the

question. I don't know why she objected to it so much –
probably her defensiveness again – but she did.

'Yes,' she said, impatiently for her. 'I believe you did.'

'Ah well.' I stood up, stretched and started to leave the room.
I'd had enough. Her intensity was getting boring. 'I think I'll
have a quick shower. We can decide about supper after that.'

✤ 4 ✤

What a question. A typical egocentric Gabriella question. 'Did I have a temperature?' My God. There we were, all bleeding one way or another. Mum beside herself with despair, his sisters stunned and me . . . well. Me. I can't think about it. And all she could think to ask about that horrible, horrible day was 'Did I have a temperature?'

Who cared whether or not she had a temperature? And, quite honestly, I didn't remember. What I did remember – and they were branded deep into me for ever – were her screams. Those horrible strident screams. And her demands. 'You have to look after me, Mia. You *have* to.'

Yes, of course I had to. It was the only way. I was caught in a trap and she knew her power.

It was as if a great tidal wave of tears had washed over our house that day. Everyone wept. Everyone except me, upstairs on my high island where the tears couldn't reach. When Aunty Rose said, 'I know you're very sad,' I thought – you *don't* know. No one knows. And when she told me that I had to take care of my little sister, I let Gabby take my hand and first I was angry. Trapped. It wasn't fair that I should have to do this. Then I had such an ache of longing for someone to look after me that I couldn't stand it. And then I felt nothing.

Until that night. Aunty Rose was in the kitchen making tea, endlessly making tea. The other aunts stood, then sat, then Mavis said, 'I'd better go and see how Hilda's doing,' and came upstairs. Sara followed her with heavy feet and then they went down again and cried into their tea and waited.

There were long terrifying silences from Mum's room. I

thought maybe she was dead too and even that didn't seem to matter. I thought nothing would matter ever again.

Gabby kept coming in and taking my hand and feeling its heavy limpness and leaving.

Then I heard a long, low rumble from outside. It drew nearer, grew louder, then stopped with the sharp grind of a brake. I pulled my curtain aside and saw it, big and black alongside the kerb. It reminded me of a car that carried coffins. 'A hearse,' Daddy had said when I'd once asked him what that was. 'It's called a hearse and it's taking a dead person to his funeral.' I remember thinking what a short sharp name for such a large car on such an enormous journey. Had a hearse come to fetch Daddy's body? I started to shiver because I knew that *he* was gone for ever and the hearse had arrived for me. It was Uncle Fred's taxi.

'Are you cold, Mim?' She was standing at the door. 'I'm hot. I'm very hot and my throat is sore.'

I couldn't answer, I was shaking so hard. All I wanted was to curl into a small round heap on my bed and melt away. I reached for my old china doll, my Ugly Baba with the crack in her skull, still sleeping her wide-eyed sleep on my counterpane, and I held her tight with both hands to try and still my shuddering body. The front door opened. Low voices. The squeak of chairs. I dropped the doll and pressed my hands over my ears. Soon there'd be footsteps, up, up the stairs and into my room. He was coming to get me. I shut my eyes, couldn't bear to look, and suddenly smelt it. The sour-sweet smell that came out of his smooth black pipe and out of the tin with the gold writing that said 'Finest Virginia'. The taxi smell.

'No,' I cried out. Something had snapped inside me. 'Go away. Go away.' I opened my eyes but there was no one in my room. Only Gabriella staring at me from the doorway. She looked frightened and moved aside as I tore out to the landing. 'Where's my Daddy? Bring him back, you have to, have to. *You've* taken him and I hate you. I hate you all.'

They were looking up at me. Aunty Rose, frowning, already had a foot poised on one stair. Mavis watched from the door, hands clasped together. Sara, tight-lipped and red-eyed, was behind her. Uncle Fred stood like a large pillar in the middle of the hall, feet apart, arms folded above his belly, his black pipe

36

anchored to the side of his stiff sealed mouth. He knew what I was saying.

He started moving towards me, past Aunty Rose and up, up the stairs. I couldn't move, just saw him coming closer, and all I could do was breathe in big hurting gasps and wait. His hand unfolded itself and reached towards me.

'It's all right, Blondie,' he said. 'It will be all right . . .'

I felt him touch my head, his fingers against my hair. And I couldn't bear it any more. Not even me.

'Leave me alone. You dare call me that, ever again. You dare.' I pushed him as hard as I could. He staggered heavily. Aunty Rose dashed up the stairs, made sure he'd recovered his balance and then took both my arms and crouched down until she was the same height as me and looked into my face.

'It's nobody's fault, child,' she said. 'Your Daddy just got sick very suddenly and died. Now come to bed. It's late and you've had a long, terrible day. We all have.'

Uncle Fred was holding on to the banister. Watching me. His pipe was still firmly in place and his eyes were squeezed into frowning slits. I knew he knew Aunty Rose was lying. He knew whose fault it was. But he would never, ever say. And he'd never call me Blondie again. Never. Muffled voices rose from the bottom of the stairs. 'Hysterical . . . the child's over-wrought.' 'Such a good, quiet girl usually. But can you blame her? So young to lose a father.'

To lose a father. I'd lost him. I'd let someone else call me his name and I'd lost him. Gabby watched as Aunty Rose lifted the blankets and I climbed into bed.

'Will you put *me* to bed, Aunty Rose?' Her voice was very small. She'd also lost a father. Because of me.

'Yes, of course, Gabriella. Come along with me dear.'

She turned out the light. The darkness breathed blackly around me and I pulled a sheet over my head and made a cave under the pillow. It was a cave to keep the princess with the leaden body safe until the prince came to rescue her. I heard Aunty Rose leaving with Gabby. She hadn't kissed me good-night.

'I'm sure everything will seem better in the morning,' she called from the landing. She always said that and I'd stopped believing her.

'Let's go and give Mummy a hug.' Gabriella's voice was high

37

and clear. She'd forgotten her sadness already, skipped lightly out of it. I hated her for it.

'Good-night Mummy,' I heard her say. 'I'm sure everything will seem better in the morning.'

Little parrot. And Mummy would think she cared. I'd show her. Tomorrow I'd take my mother tea in her bed, just as Daddy had done. I'd do it tomorrow and tomorrow and for ever and ever. Then she'd see who really cared, which of us was truly good, truly loved her.

She might see, but she'd never know. No one would. I buried myself deeper under my pillow. Down, down into my cave where I could go numb and sleep. Here I was the beautiful, golden-haired princess who'd been turned into heavy grey lead, so heavy that there was nothing her father the old king could do but find a dark cave and put her to sleep. And wait. For if she waited long enough . . .

It didn't work that night. Usually I'd feel the heaviness and the waiting. And in the sure promise of rescue I'd drift off to sleep. I'd dream of softening as he touched me, happy ever after. Safe and warm. Loved.

But that night, that hot night in June when Daddy disappeared and Gabby had a temperature and Mummy made gasping noises from her bed and my aunts spurted tears and Uncle Fred called me Blondie for the last time ever, that night my fairy-tale failed. I couldn't even begin to tell it to myself the way I usually did.

'Once upon a time,' I tried, crushing my eyes shut, 'there was a leaden princess . . .' But the questions were like little hammers on my lids, forcing them open. When? How? Why? Especially why? And I didn't want to think why. 'Don't be stupid,' I said to the pestering questions. 'Since when did "why" matter in a fairy-tale? It simply happened that the princess turned into lead. Just sort of happened.'

But my scorn didn't stop them. They pursued me till tears started leaking out of my tightly shut eyes. You see, I knew how some people turned into lead. I'd felt it happen. I also knew that I wasn't really a princess, so there was no point waiting for anything. Except Uncle Fred, who shared 'our little secret'. And I'd told him, never, ever again.

It wasn't the princess's fault though, I told the voices. She was good. She tried so hard to be good. Only I knew she wasn't *really* good. Not deep inside. She sometimes hated her mother the queen, wanted to crush the skull of the littlest princess, was a horrible brat who didn't appreciate things. And she had secrets with her uncle. Secrets that were bad enough to kill her good, good father the king. Secrets that turned her into lead.

'I didn't want to. I didn't. I didn't.' I sat up in bed, out of my cave, my eyes wide open, staring at the blackness. 'Please Daddy, believe me and come back home. I didn't want to do it.'

That was true. Almost.

'How about a little ride, Blondie? I'll take you for a turn round the block.'

Me? He was choosing me? I'd been looking at his big black taxi through the window, imagining how it would feel to sit on its smooth leather seats, to be transported through the neighbourhood. So smart. So rich. Such a stupid dream. Gabby would probably get a ride in his taxi long before I did. She always got everything.

But no. It was me he wanted. I stole a look at my little sister. She was frowning, squashing her chocolate cake with her teaspoon, two deep lines between her brows. Her mouth was turned down at the corners. I thought she was about to have a tantrum, maybe even the kind when she'd sit down in the middle of the carpet and knock her head against the ground until they got frightened and stopped her and gave her whatever she wanted. But this time she decided to act appealing instead.

'I'll come. I'll come.'

I'd hesitated and she was grabbing her chance. But he took no notice, kept looking at me. I couldn't believe it. 'Blondie,' he'd called me. It made me feel all warm and I didn't even think it was wrong. That it was Daddy's name and that he had no right to use it. No, I just felt warm and happy and chosen.

And when I got into that cab I knew Gabby was watching me, envying me. It was so good. And I tucked my blue-striped pinafore neatly under me, just as I'd seen real ladies do. I was sure princesses did that too. That's what I was for that moment – a wonderful golden princess.

The taxi throbbed and shuddered up to the top of the street. Uncle Fred gripped his pipe with his teeth and swung the steering wheel round hard, turning left towards the High Street and then right towards the park. I breathed in the thick mixture of stale air, tobacco and leather, and thought this must be the smell of success.

'Having fun Blondie?'

He'd slowed down. His face was turned towards me. I could see the pores on his fleshy nose. There were yellow patches on the teeth that held his pipe. He was smiling in a way that I suddenly didn't like very much. I nodded.

'How about riding in the back. Then you'd feel like a real passenger, eh Blondie? How about it?'

We had stopped. In the distance I could see swings and slides. There were sounds of laughter, of children having fun. I told myself that none of them were having as much fun as me with my Uncle Fred in his big black taxi. But when I moved to the back I was secretly glad to have a glass sliding window between me and his pores and his yellow teeth. And when we started off, it *was* like I was a real passenger travelling in my solitary space. A real princess.

Then suddenly we were still, the engine silent. We were in a narrow lane, the one that cut through the park. The voices of the children could still be heard, faint and far away. Uncle Fred had stepped outside. He was opening the passenger's door.

'Mind if I come in, Blondie?'

Now I began to wish he'd stop calling me that. He wasn't Daddy after all. I said nothing but he came in anyway.

'Just a little rest – and then we can start wending our way back home. Tell you what . . .' He was suddenly breathing faster, had taken the pipe out of his mouth and was looking at me eagerly, his eyes wider than I'd ever seen them. '. . . We can pretend to be passengers together. Me and you. Uncle Fred and his little Blondie, sitting close together in a big taxi. On a really bumpy ride. A game, see?'

'OK,' I said doubtfully. It didn't seem a specially exciting sort of game. Even Gabby made up more interesting games than this. But still.

'You're a good girl, Blondie. A really good girl. I've always noticed it.'

He was sitting right next to me, had an arm around my shoulder. With the other hand he was stroking my hair. I hated it, him calling me Blondie and breathing so hard and smelling of pipe and sweat and leather seat. But I didn't want him to stop. Not really. I needed so badly to have my hair stroked. Then he kissed me. And I let him because I wanted him to keep thinking I was good. But I didn't like it when he started touching me and panting and making funny grunting noises and gasping, 'Little Blondie, little Blondie', in a strange strangled voice. I was scared. I wanted him to go away and was about to start pushing him.

But then he stopped. Moved away from me to the seat in the far corner of the taxi and was silent. His big head dropped and I didn't know what I'd done.

'You're a lovely sweet child,' he said softly. This time he didn't say Blondie. 'Do you want to come for a drive with me again?'

I nodded. What else could I do? Anyway, he did like me. There was nothing really wrong with what we did. It was just a game – quite a good game as it turned out. So why did I feel so uncomfortable inside?

'And listen.' He leaned towards me with a large red index finger across his lips. 'Let's keep our little game a secret, eh? Just between you and me. Don't tell anyone.'

'No one?' I was slightly disappointed. It would have been nice to have told Gabby, to have lured her into the bathroom and said, 'Listen – listen to this Gabs.' And she'd have leaned forward eagerly. 'Tell me Mia, tell me.' Oh, that would have been fine. I'd have told her about the Passenger Game and she'd have been so jealous.

'No – no one,' he repeated, a serious expression on his face. Then he turned away and I heard him say, 'Christ – Joe – it would kill him.'

'What?' I asked sharply, fear suddenly crawling over me. What had he said? What did it mean?

'Nothing, nothing . . . Blondie.' He'd forced it out this time. I could tell. 'Just keep it a secret. That's all.'

And I did. Played the game and kept it secret. But I didn't really enjoy it after that first time. I kept hearing Uncle Fred's voice saying 'it would kill him, it would kill him' and I knew that what we were doing must be very bad indeed. So bad that even talking about it could kill a person.

Yet every Sunday when Uncle Fred stood up with a long yawn and said, 'Time for our ride, Blondie. Coming?' I'd nod and follow him out to his taxi. Until one day I said, 'I don't really want to, Uncle Fred. I think I've had enough rides.' And he looked at me, bent down until his eyes were level with mine, until I could feel his warm tobacco breath on my face, and said: 'Oh no, Blondie. I don't think you've had enough rides at all. Anyway, you can't stop now, otherwise Daddy might suspect something. And you know what might happen if he found out . . .'

There was nothing to be done.

And that's when I started turning into lead. Heavy and grey and numb. Each night I repeated my fairy-tale to myself and that made me feel better – until the next Sunday and the next Sunday. Would I be the leaden princess for ever? After Daddy died, I believed that I would. That somehow he'd found out. It was all my fault. But at least I didn't have to go on any more taxi rides with Uncle Fred ever again for the worst had happened and he no longer had a hold on me. But he still had his taxi and his pipe and his Mavis and all I had was my dark cave and my leaden waiting. And my sister.

One evening, in the steamy safety of our bathroom, I gave my fairy-tale to Gabriella. She took it greedily and laughed and didn't even notice what it was she was taking so lightly and tossing away. She didn't see it at all.

It was the autumn after Daddy died. Five o'clock in late November and the wind was gusting down the treeless streets of the estate. Our house was silent and mostly unlit. A shadowy haven for poor widowed Hilda and her fatherless little girls. I'd just turned twelve and Gabby was nine.

Mum was in her bedroom. She'd acquired a telephone very soon after Dad died and was making new links with the outside world. 'My *old* friends,' she called them – the smart-hatted women who started coming in for coffee and then stopping for a game of cards. Mum had acquired a social life – and also a new slave. Me.

I knocked on her door. 'Mum?' Tentatively. She was talking to one of the friends, the receiver jammed between her shoulder and her ear, holding a damp towelling cloth to her head. She had a headache.

'Must go, Cecily.' She had her tired voice. 'I have such an

aching head – and I really must see to the girls' supper.' What a joke. Her see to our supper? Did Cecily – whoever she was – believe her? 'What is it, Mia?'

'Gabby and I were about to have tea. Shall I bring you some?' She nodded wanly. 'I'll come down later. Just as soon as my head feels better.'

She didn't. She hardly ever did. Sometimes Gabby and I sat on her bed or on the velvet-topped stool in front of her dressing-table and Gabby made her laugh with tales from school. 'It was so funny, Mum,' she'd squeal. And she'd release a torrent of words, tales of Gladys and Fanny and how Miss Southwood had slipped in the classroom and how Mrs Adams had long black hairs on her legs. And centre-stage in all these tales was mischievous, adorable Gabriella. I had nothing to say but I laughed with Mum and longed to have stories of my own. And I was jealous of Gabby and knew that was very wrong. She was my little sister after all.

But that evening it was different – that long dark gusty November evening when Mum stayed in bed and Gabby and I sat together in the circle of light round the brass standing lamp in the front room. I was doing my homework, frowning over my arithmetic. She was drawing. Always drawing.

'Look Mims.' She moved closer, showed me her picture of two girls – a bigger blonde girl holding the hand of a smaller one with dark pigtails and large eyes. They stood in front of a red-roofed house and in one of the upper windows she'd outlined a figure in a bed. 'That's us.' Her finger touched the spot where our hands met. I didn't hate her then. No, I wanted so badly to give her something, to share something with her. I saw that she trusted me and I wanted to trust her back.

'I'm going upstairs to have a bath, Gabs. D'you want to come and talk to me?' She always agreed. The warm steamy bathroom with its chequered green and black wall tiles was our place of togetherness, our den of laughter and secrets. Our clubhouse.

'Shall I tell you a really good story – a fairy-tale that I made up?' I was lying in the bath, water lapping over my chest. My legs were floating. I locked my ankles together and imagined I was a mermaid with a smooth floating tail. A golden-haired mermaid. That made me think of the beautiful blonde princess of my dreams – and I looked at Gabby perched on top of the cork-topped laundry box. I wanted so badly to share my dream with her.

'Yes, tell me Mims. Tell it to me.' Her face was eager. 'Is it going to be funny?'

I had to think about that. After all, anything could be made funny. Turning into lead *could* be funny I supposed – when one thought of rusty patches and magnets and being so heavy that the floorboards cracked. Gabby would have made it funny. But no. It wasn't that kind of story. She'd understand. I had a feeling she'd understand.

'It's a sad, beautiful story. A once-upon-a-time sort of tale,' I began. And at first she listened. Her eyes held on to mine and she listened. And then, when I told her about the king and the cave and the dark, dark waiting, she suddenly looked away. She didn't want to hear any more.

'Oh Mia,' she said, and there was scorn in her voice. 'Don't tell me that the silly girl lay around waiting for someone to come and rescue here – and it just happened that a prince was riding past? That's *so* stupid. Just like Sleeping Beauty. I couldn't bear her either. I thought you'd make up a better story than that.'

I tried to defend it. To tell myself that it was the story, not me, that she despised. But then she looked at me a minute later and burst out laughing and said, 'Oh Mims, you do have a funny fat body – and I think you're growing titties.' And I knew that our little bathtime club had dissolved. I never bared myself in front of my sister again. Not really.

'You are in another world today. Buck up, Mia old girl. Can't let the heat get to one you know.' She was standing in front of me, a towel tucked under her arms, water dripping on to the stone floor. 'Gosh, I feel so much better. Nothing like a brisk shower to bring one back to life.'

She lit a cigarette and sat down. I felt heavier and limper than ever in the presence of her renewed vigour.

'You know, Mims, we ought to do more.' She inhaled deeply, tugged at her towel. 'I was just thinking – eighteen months we've been here, and hardly moved from the flat. Shopping, having our hair done, cleaning – and waiting. To settle down.

44

To find our feet. To forget. And now? What are we waiting for now?'

'I don't know.' She made me so tired. No, she didn't. I *was* tired. I was also angry. She knew there was nothing to be done – and she knew why we'd come here. When would Gabby ever take heed of anyone else's needs other than her own? Yes – we were waiting, if she wanted to put it that way. I was used to it, had been doing it all my life, didn't really want to fill the space with empty activities.

'Anyway,' I shrugged, smiling at the thought, 'there's nothing new about Jews waiting. It's our heritage. We've been waiting for the Messiah for thousands of years, so what's a couple more between sisters?'

She smiled at me and it was like a cord drawing us together. 'Mims,' she said, and her voice had lost its sharp edge, 'when you talk like that, I do believe there's hope for us.'

✤ 5 ✤

The idea of the two of us sitting and waiting for the Messiah made me laugh. Once again, my plump dull sister had taken me completely by surprise. She'd seemed to be melting into the sofa, a picture of sluggish gloom. Then she'd looked up with that wonderful ironic smile and out it had come and I'd loved her. She'd given me hope and I'd told her so and she'd smiled again. But then of course I screwed it all up. I never did learn how to take care of Mia's ideas.

'The Messiah . . .' I sat back, had a good long draw on my cigarette and chewed over the concept. It suddenly made me think of a plush book-lined study in Hampstead Garden Suburb. Clive's collection of Jewish literature. He wasn't too good on the practice, my dear old ex, but he did love the theory. Not the ideas, mind you. Facts. Clive collected facts. He could never understand how Mia and I had survived a childhood in Hendon hardly touched by our heritage.

'Surely,' he'd say in amazement, 'surely Hilda sent you to Hebrew classes? Didn't you celebrate Rosh Hashana or Pesach or even Yom Kippur? Nothing at all?'

'Oh, Clive.' His questions bored me. 'You've no idea what it was like, just the two of us and Hilda. Of course, when Dad was alive, it was different. Family teas, festivals. But then everything seemed to stop. We hardly saw our uncles and aunts after Dad died. We hardly saw anyone.'

I wasn't sorry – about the Jewish bit, anyway. Who needed to learn an archaic and convoluted language? Or to sit for long hours in a synagogue counting the pages till the merciful amen and goodbye at the end of the service? Not me. I poured contempt on the whole idea.

But secretly, during the long days and endless evenings when

Clive was in the office and Vanessa busy or asleep and the house was oppressively heavy with antiques and wax polish and emptiness, I'd escape to his study and examine his books. They fascinated me – the faith, the mysticism, the Messiah. I wanted to take the ideas as far as I possibly could, explore them with someone, even – God forbid – laugh at them.

But Clive would have been shocked. He knew I wasn't a true believer (the hypocrite) and my irreverence offended his sense of propriety. And Mia and I weren't really talking. Not then. So I read and thought and smiled to myself – and then got bored and went on to something else. I've never been able to keep up an interest in anything for too long.

But now Mia's ironic reference to the Messiah had tickled something in me.

'Talking about the Messiah . . .' I saw she was getting twitchy, probably sorry that she'd mentioned him at all. 'Of course, you know it's no good simply sitting round and waiting for him. That's not the idea at all. We're supposed to be collecting merits – gold stars, good deeds, Brownie points. And they're all being fed into some heavenly slot machine until . . . Zing! The jackpot. Out he'll step, over the clouds and down, down in his golden chariot and all our problems will be over. On the other hand, if for some reason we prove slightly low on points, he'll come anyway. There's no stopping the guy apparently. But a low-budget Messiah will make a somewhat humbler entrance. Riding an ass, they say. Oh well – one can't have the glamour without the stars. Hollywood knew that.'

She was listening to me now, face rapt. 'Since when did you become such an expert on the Messiah?' she asked.

'Me? My darling sister, you'd be amazed at the things I've dabbled in. Marriage guidance, Messianic theory, monetarism, misery, the Japanese art of flower arranging. And you thought I was just a pretty face.'

She smiled knowingly. Who was I trying to fool? As if Mia wasn't aware of how it had all turned out for me. She knew everything. Almost everything. And I didn't really know her at all. Did I think I could deceive her with my dismissive witticisms, my tough-lady talk? She was gathering herself to leave. Two solid arms pushing down on either side of that awful pink dress now mottled with perspiration patches. I didn't like her seeing through me – but I didn't want her to go. I wanted her to listen. I wanted her to laugh with me.

'Stay, Mims,' I said, trying to sound as though I didn't really care. 'There's a little time yet before we have to start getting our meal together. And – listen – talking about the Messiah, I'll tell you something utterly delicious. So wicked and depraved that you won't believe it. I'm not sure I do – but it's a damn good story.'

I knew she wouldn't be able to resist. She relaxed, replaced her hands on her lap, cocked her head to the side, raised her eyebrows, and listened.

'So? Tell me then, Gabby?'

'Well.' I was back in power. Relishing it. 'You might be relieved to hear that goodness wasn't always seen as the only way to hasten the coming of the Messiah. On the other hand, since you've always been such a model of rectitude, perhaps it won't matter.'

I wasn't being sarcastic. She *was* good, had always been good. Well, her thing with Seamus hadn't been straight-and-narrow good, but that was the only deviation. And inside, who could be more righteous than my sister? But she took it badly. I could see her face closing, hands tensing. I'd lost her, said the wrong thing. Oh shit.

'But' – there was no turning back now – 'as someone with very shaky moral fibre and extremely doubtful principles' – she probably thought *that* wasn't entirely true either considering the boringly conventional path I'd followed – 'I found it most reassuring to discover the theory that the lower man sinks and the more wicked and depraved his behaviour, the quicker the Messiah will move in with his millennium.'

'And where did you come across this, might I ask?' She was interested again, thank goodness or badness or whatever.

'Some books of Clive's. Apparently, there's a most lurid description in óne of those biblical commentaries – the Mishna, I think – of the moral decay that will sweep the generation that precedes the coming of the Messiah. Corruption, the son bringing disgrace to the father and variations on that theme, the extinction of shame, all manner of perversions. People will acquire the facial features of dogs.'

I had to pause for thought. The dogs bit bothered me. Some

48

dogs were actually rather nice. Labradors, for instance. They couldn't look evil if they tried.

'Rottweilers.' I decided to amend my tale. I was sure the Mishna wouldn't mind. 'The facial features of Rottweilers.'

'And so?' Mia smiled. What was coming next?

'Logic Mims, sheer logic. Surely you can work it out? If generalized badness will precede the Messiah, then bring on the badness, boys, and down he'll come. Moral hypochondria to attract the attention of the big physician of the spirit.

'Of course, you know the way these things happen, there were some who took this learned text literally. Word has it that there was a Jewish sect, deep in seclusion in Eastern Europe, who believed in moral rot as a way of life. They saw it as their duty to act out every imaginable depravity. All in the interests of the general good, of course. Their corruption was hastening mankind's salvation.

'And boy, did they have fun. Sodom and Gomorrah had nothing on this lot. When they thought they'd reached the bottom, someone said, "Let's sink lower." And they sank, Mims. They wallowed in their wickedness and they felt not a touch of guilt.'

I looked at her and realized that, for some reason, my story had made her uncomfortable. She was sitting up as though to leave. Her smile had stiffened to a tight line across her face.

'And what happened to the Messiah?' she asked.

'Here we are, still waiting,' I shrugged. 'But Mia, at least they enjoyed themselves in a depraved sort of way. They were inventive. They were *doing* something. Unlike us. Sometimes I think we're a bit like that leaden princess you once told me about. Hiding in a cave and waiting for her prince. Remember?'

Now I'd definitely said something wrong.

'Of course I remember.' Her voice was flat. She stood up, tried to smooth the damp creases in her dress, and headed for the door. This was ridiculous. It was only a story.

'By the way, Mims,' I called after her, 'did the prince ever come? I don't think I ever did get to the end of that one.'

She stopped and, without turning back, said: 'Yes, he did finally arrive. At least I – she – thought it was him.'

Oh dear. I'd offended her. I always knew she was put out when she spoke in that particular expressionless tone. This time

I hadn't intended it at all, had merely wished to amuse. As I said, I've never been particularly adept at caring for Mia's ideas.

'What d'you mean – "she thought"? Mims? Mia?'

But she was gone. A short while later, I heard splashing sounds from the bathroom. She'd feel better after her shower – and I'd make it up to her somehow. I shivered and was suddenly aware of darkness falling and a cool breeze fanning Kfar Tikva. Thank God. Time to get dressed. I decided to choose something special to wear that night. Something really elegant. After all, there was Herbert for dinner and it should be made into an occasion. I'd tell Mia to make an effort too. If one didn't create these little celebrations, life tended to be so boring. Mia didn't seem to mind though. I listened to the splatter of the shower, heard her feet moving and the slap of her sponge.

And I suddenly remembered how it felt to be ten years old, sitting in the passage outside our bathroom in Hendon, listening to my sister splashing – and longing so hard to be asked to share her secrets again.

'Mia?' I tapped gently on the door. 'Mims – can I come in? Can we have a chat?'

'No.' The voice from the bathroom was flat and decisive.

'Please?'

'No.'

She couldn't do that to me. I was her little sister and she had to talk to me. She had to look after me and she knew it. I stamped my foot.

'Open the door or I'll bash it in. Please Mim – please, please, please can I come and sit with you?'

No response.

'Well you're a fat pig and I'll tell Mum. I'll tell her that you're not caring for me, that you're so, so nasty. Then you'll see . . .'

Silence. Then: 'Little bitch.' Mia sounded less certain. Almost as though she was crying. I was glad. She had no right to keep me away from her.

'You'll be sorry,' I called as I went to my room, sat on my dressing-table stool and studied myself in the mirror. Everyone told me how dinky I was – the smallest girl in my class, the loudest laugh, the best drawings. I made my mouth turn upwards at the corners into the cutest smile I could manage and saw that if I did it a certain way I could produce a dimple in my left cheek. I'd have to practise that.

They all loved me at school: 'Gabby, Gabby,' they called when it was time to pick teams for netball. The teachers made me class monitor, saying I was every bit as good as my sister Mia had been. So there.

But at home it wasn't like that. There was no one really to be cute for. Mia had stopped being interested in my stories. I was a baby, she said. A nasty baby. Maybe I was – but mostly when I was frightened and angry. I couldn't understand why our house was so empty. Three people inside and it always seemed empty and dark. And I'd get angry enough to want to hit and scream and kick. That's when I said nasty things to my sister. 'I hate you,' I'd say to her – when really it was them I hated. My father for going away. And Mum for never being there in the first place.

And now Mia had given up on me. She didn't want me any more. I watched tears collect round the rims of my eyes as I told myself how quite, quite alone I was. Then I heard the front door opening, jumped off the stool and rushed down, two stairs at a time.

'Mummy.' Breathlessly. 'Mia has been really nasty to me. Shall I tell you what she did?'

'Yes darling. In a minute.'

My mother didn't spend so much time in her bedroom any more. Her body didn't, anyway. Her mind was still there – or somewhere even further away. She asked us questions in a mechanical kind of way and never listened to our replies. When I told funny stories she laughed – but she wasn't really amused.

'I have the most dreadful headache,' she said, sighing and depositing three interesting-looking bags of shopping on the floor. She pulled off her coat and started making her way upstairs, her pink woollen dress clinging to her round bottom, one hand gripping the banister and the other pressed over her blonde head. I watched her from the hall and thought how much I'd rather have had a real mummy like my friend Katie's, one who would be at home, waiting in the kitchen with an apron and my tea and a smile and a soft hug. Listening to me. It wasn't fair.

I followed her upstairs. 'Mum – can I tell you what Mia did to me?'

'In a little while, Gabriella – I have to lie down. My head is killing me.' She closed her door. I stood on the dark landing, listening to the creak of her bed. No, it wasn't fair at all.

Then I heard Mia coming out of the bathroom. I'd stop her, make her listen to me. I'd tell her something so interesting that she wouldn't be able to resist.

'Mims,' I said, catching hold of a damp arm as it clutched her fluffy dressing-gown tightly around her chest. 'Mims, listen. D'you want to hear a secret?'

'What?'

'Can I come into your room with you and I'll tell you?'

'Well – all right.'

There. It worked.

She sat on one end of the bed. I perched on the other, happy again. Bursting to tell, but waiting for the right moment. I've always been a great believer in timing.

'And so?' She was growing impatient.

'Well. The other day . . .' I spoke slowly, wanting to draw this out as long as possible.

'Come on, Gabby. You probably haven't got anything to tell me at all. You're just making this up so that you can stay here with me.'

'No no, Mims. Truly I have. What happened was that I came into Mum's room and she was about to get dressed and I saw she was putting a funny cotton-wool thing round her – uh – bottom. She did. I promise. A cotton-wool thing that she hooked on to a piece of elastic round her waist.'

I looked at my sister, expecting to see amazement. Her expression hadn't changed. Oh well.

'Anyway, I asked her. "Mum," I said, "What is that? What's that thing you've got wrapped between your legs?" She didn't want to tell me, Mims. I could see she didn't want to say, she was all sort of embarrassed. Really silly. And then she told me. "It's to keep warm, Gabriella," she said. "You see, darling, Mummy has a cold in her tummy."'

Mia burst out laughing, then caught herself and smiled in a most superior kind of way. It was as though she knew something I didn't. A sudden thought occurred to me.

'D'you think that was the truth?' I asked. 'Go on. Tell me. Do you think Mum was telling me the truth?'

'It's not for me to say, Gabby. Perhaps there are things you're not old enough to know about.'

Not old enough. How old did she think I was? This wasn't the way I'd meant my story to end. I wanted her to laugh with me, not at me. It was as though she was on the other side. On the grown-ups' side. I hated to be left behind.

'I am. I'm quite big enough to know. Please tell me, Mims.'

But she wouldn't. She giggled mysteriously, but she would not say why. It was my friend Katie who whispered the truth about colds in the tummy next day at school. And how babies were made. And about being a virgin. I loved the word.

'Mia,' I said loftily that evening as we sat together over the boiled eggs she'd made, 'I know everything now – and I hope you're a virgin.'

She looked shocked. 'Shut up and eat,' she said.

I smiled.

It was after I learnt the word that I decided I wanted to be the Virgin Mary in our school Nativity Play.

'I don't think we can have you, dear.' Miss Gilmour, the singing teacher who arranged the production each year, looked doubtful. 'What usually happens is that our little Jewish children are the villagers or sometimes the sheep, if their mummies allow them. No, I don't see that it would be quite right to have a Jewish Mary.' She patted my head, thinking that would be the end of it. She didn't know me.

'Well, my sister Mia was an angel last year – and Mummy didn't mind in the least. And I'll make a good Mary, Miss Gilmour. Let me have one try at it anyway, and then you can decide.'

I gave her my cutest smile and at last she said, 'All right Gabriella, you can try. Just for today mind.'

I knew that once she had given me my chance, she'd never be able to take the part away. I'd make sure of that.

'Oh, Joseph, I'm so, so tired,' I trilled, holding on to my head the way I'd seen my mother do. 'We *have* to find an inn so that I can rest. My poor head is aching so.'

'Gabriella.' Miss Gilmour called me at the end of the practice. 'We've decided to let you be Mary after all. You did act well.'

She told me I'd need to bring a doll to school to be my baby.

53

A doll? I didn't think I had one, other than the clockwork ballerina that spun above my trinket box. She certainly wouldn't fit the part of baby Jesus. Then I remembered Mia's old doll. Her Ugly Baba. It was dirty and it had a strange jagged crack on its head but if I cleaned it and kept it cuddled closely in a blanket it would do.

'I'll bring a doll tomorrow, Miss Gilmour,' I promised.

For as long as I remembered, Ugly Baba had slept on Mia's pillow. Not exactly slept, since her eyes were usually jammed open and staring glassily at the ceiling. I could never understand why Mia liked the stupid, dirty thing. After Daddy died, though, I'd noticed that the doll had disappeared from her usual spot.

'Where's Ugly Baba?' I'd asked Mia one day. 'Why doesn't she sleep on your bed any more?'

'Mind your own business.' That was when she was just starting to act superior. It became much worse when she'd moved to the grammar school.

While she was out, I'd had a quick search for the doll. I'd been curious. Surely she hadn't thrown her out? No, of course she wouldn't. Eventually I'd found Ugly Baba, curled in the deepest recess of Mia's wardrobe. I'd said nothing.

Now, when I needed to produce my baby Jesus, I decided it would be pointless to ask Mia's permission. She'd say no just to be mean. I'd take the doll, borrow her quietly and then put her back. My sister would never even notice.

'Lovely,' said Miss Gilmour, hardly looking at my carefully renovated baby, swaddled in a white blanket with a woolly hat I'd made out of a sock to cover her injured head. 'A perfect little Jesus, Gabriella.'

'Please, please won't you come and see me being Mary in our school play on Thursday,' I pleaded at home the following evening. 'It's the main part, you know – and Miss Gilmour says I act like a real little star. I heard her telling that to one of the other teachers today. Please, Mum? Will you come? Mims?'

My mother hesitated. 'It depends . . .' she said.

'Please Mum – you have to. You'll be so proud of me.' I flung my arms tightly round her neck and felt her softening. Mia watched me and then turned away.

'All right, Gabby. We'll be there,' said my mother reluctantly.

'You too, Mims?' She was already at the door. I went after

her and whispered loudly in her ear: 'Did you know that Mary was a virgin?'

Mia shrugged me off. 'Silly baby,' she said scornfully.

Just you wait, I thought, just you wait and see me on the stage, me cradling my darling little baby and everybody clapping. You'll be so jealous.

Everyone did clap. I gave my dimple smile until my cheek started hurting and saw Mum and Mia in the fourth row, joining the applause and looking pleased. Then there was a noisy scraping of chairs and a roar of voices as shepherds and angels and sheep and wise men were praised by proud parents. The Virgin Mary remained seated on stage – a monarch awaiting her subjects.

They came. Mum first and Mia, self-consciously, slightly behind her. It was strange seeing them there, visitors from another world. Home and school life were usually kept so firmly apart. Mum looked smaller and plumper than the headache-ridden queen of her bedroom. She wore a fur jacket that smelt of mothballs. I hoped my friends hadn't noticed. Mia was clearly embarrassed by me, Mum, herself, everybody. She'd left Hendon Primary three years before and no one seemed to remember her.

They came to pay their respects and Mary received them graciously. 'Wonderful, Gabby. We were proud of you.' Mum bent down to kiss my cheek and Mia hung back. She was staring at me – no, not at me, at my baby. At my little baby Jesus. I suddenly remembered.

'Oh, Mims,' I said. 'I almost forgot. I needed a doll for my part and I didn't have one so I thought you wouldn't mind if I borrowed your old Ugly Baba. Miss Gilmour said she made a perfect baby Jesus . . .'

I couldn't think what else to say. Her face looked strange, as though she couldn't decide whether to be furious or to cry. Whatever happened, it clearly wasn't going to be fun.

'You little bitch. You little thieving bitch.' She'd moved closer, spoke softly with narrowed eyes. 'I'll never forgive you for this. Never.'

Mum was puzzled. 'Mia, darling, she should have asked you, but it's only an old doll. An old dirty doll that you outgrew years ago. Don't let that spoil her evening. Gabby was so good, acted so well.'

Mia didn't answer. Just stood – like an avenging angel. An angel who'd discovered that Mary wasn't a virgin after all. That she'd stolen baby Jesus and lied. Or done something that Katie had told me about when she explained colds in the tummy. I looked at Mia's face and was suddenly afraid. Her revenge would be terrible.

'I'm sorry Mims. I'm really sorry.'

'Can we go home now, Mum?' she asked very quietly.

It was raining when we emerged from the school. I shared Mum's umbrella, walked close to her and breathed the damp warmth and mothballs and almost forgot about Mia's anger and the silly dirty doll. Mia walked on her own. 'No thank you,' she said, when Mum offered her a space under the umbrella. She strode ahead and got wet and didn't seem to notice. Suddenly she stopped and turned round.

'Can we walk through the park?' she asked. 'It's quicker.'

'Well . . .' Mum hesitated. 'I don't know, darling.' But Mia walked towards the path anyway. She pretended not to hear. Then she turned round again.

'Give me that doll.' I'd almost forgotten about Ugly Baba, still cradled in my arm. Mia had her open palm stretched out towards me. The rain was trickling down her face and plastering her hair in a dark cast around her head. For a moment she looked like the wicked witch in my fairy-tale book who said, 'Find me Snow White,' and I was frightened of her, so black and angry in the cold wet darkness. Then I remembered it was only Mia.

'Oh Mims,' I said, trying hard to find my giggle. 'You're all wet. You look so silly. Come – come with us under the umbrella.'

She took no notice. Not this time. My arm was suddenly empty and there was Ugly Baba, dangling limply, hanging desolately from Mia's hand. Her sock hat had slipped off and the zigzag in her white-blonde head gaped. An open wound. Plump porcelain legs with bare baby feet almost touched the ground, little round toes tracing our path.

'There.' We'd reached a clearing near the gravel road that cut through the park and Mia had stopped in front of a large grey metal dustbin and was lifting the lid. Cars sometimes stopped here. In the daytime there might have been sounds of laughter, of children having fun on the swings and slides. Now there was only rain.

Steady, gushing rain and then a sudden thud. Ugly Baba was flung into the bin. The lid was replaced and I could see the words KEEP YOUR PARK CLEAN reflected from a single weak lamp near a bench in the clearing.

'Mia?' Mum spoke. Until then, she'd said nothing. Just walked through the damp deserted park watching her pointed high-heeled shoes picking a path through the puddles and allowing me to share her umbrella. 'Mia . . . why? What on earth are you doing?'

'Gone. That's it. The end of that stupid doll.' Mia was striding on again, heading for home.

'Why did you make such a fuss about me using it then?' I called out, feeling safe next to Mum and knowing home was round the corner. 'If you thought it was stupid and threw it away, why did it matter that I borrowed it? And anyway – we've got a perfectly good bin at home. Haven't we Mum?'

She'd stopped again. Her wet face glistened and her eyes looked enormous. 'You,' she said with such venom that I cowered against Mum's arm. 'You don't understand anything. Silly, hateful, thieving little show-off. I hate you.'

She'd never spoken like that. She was right – I couldn't understand. 'Mum . . .' I held on to her and cried and she patted my clutching hand.

'Come. We're almost home. She'll get over it.'

We brought our soaking wetness into the house. In the light, Mia didn't look scary at all. Just a sulky big sister with a blotchy face and stringy wet hair and shoes that trailed water.

'Be careful not to bring mud into the house.' Mum had taken her coat and shoes off and was heading for the stairs.

'Mum,' I called after her. This was supposed to have been my night. My Virgin Mary night. I'd imagined how we were going to come home, all three of us so happy, Mum so proud of her cute, clever little daughter. And now there was nothing. Not even supper. 'Mum – I'm hungry.'

'There's food in the kitchen – I went shopping today. Mia will help you. I must go and have a hot bath, otherwise I'll catch my death of cold. You too, both of you. Come upstairs and get dry.'

There was no supper that night. Later I tried to talk to Mia, caught her arm as she came out of the bathroom. Her eyes were swollen and she looked sad. 'Mims,' I said, 'I'm sorry – I didn't realize – please can we be friends? Please?'

She pulled her arm away and then looked at me and suddenly her eyes filled with tears and she nodded. I put my arms round her neck and she let me and I kissed her. Then she turned to her room and shut the door.

Next day at school everyone said what a good Mary I'd been. 'D'you think you might be an actress when you grow up?' Katie asked. 'Perhaps,' I replied. 'Or an artist. Or a great inventor.' There were so many possibilities. I'd almost forgotten about Mia's anger and the discarded baby. On my way home, though, I went through the park. The rain had stopped but everything still looked soaked and grey and bleak. The trees were almost bare. The dustbin was empty.

'Not dressed yet?' Now it was her turn to stand over me. 'What was it you said about withstanding the heat? Courage, dear sister, courage.' She was wearing white. A crisp skirt, silky top, a pearly string of beads.

'Expecting anyone?' I asked.

'Don't be silly.' Mia smiled, slightly embarrassed. 'Just Friday – you know.'

'Yes.' I knew. 'I'll get myself together in a minute. And we mustn't forget our piscatory guest of honour awaiting his dressing. I was just thinking how we ought to celebrate something . . . sometime.' My voice trailed off. What? When? We'd had all our celebrations.

'Tonight.' Mia's voice was firm. The shower seemed to have sprayed away her gloomy limpness. 'I have a feeling about tonight. Gabs, I think you're right about us getting on with things. I was standing in the bath with jets of water roaring about my ears and I suddenly thought – everything's rushing past and here we are, waiting. It's enough. We really ought to make this the first night of the rest of our . . .'

Oh God. If there was anything that irritated me more than her tendency towards sluggishness, it was this forced cheerfulness. Her smiling clichés made me wince and want to be cruel, to prick her optimism, force her back into her slow, reasonable role. It was like a see-saw. Her up, me down. Both of us frozen on to our seats, unable to dismount or to stop watching one another. Up and down. What a ludicrous duet.

'Absolutely,' I interrupted. 'I'll wear something special too. Let me see.' I surveyed my wardrobe. It had remained almost unchanged since we left England.

'Perhaps . . . yes. The black.' I lifted the slinky little old number off its hanger. 'Never failed with this one. It even used to make Clive randy. One never knows what it will do to poor old Herbert's hormones. Still, as you said, we've got to start living dangerously.' I winked at her. She kept smiling. 'But tell me Mims,' I asked, 'tell me why you're suddenly looking so pleased with yourself?'

'Who knows?' she shrugged amiably. 'I just looked at myself and for once I thought, "Mia, old lady, for a woman of fifty-two you're not looking so bad." That's all.'

'Oh. I see. So you're wearing well. Maturing nicely, hmm? Like good Cheddar cheese.'

She nodded, chuckling. 'Yup,' she said. 'If you say so.'

Did I have to carry on? My bitchiness was beyond belief. 'But Mims – ' I leaned forward conspiratorially – 'think of the smell. Don't forget how ripe cheese stinks.'

That stank. But we laughed hollowly and I knew that once again I'd blown it.

'I'm going downstairs to see if there's any mail,' she said in her flat voice. 'We didn't check the letter-box today.' She turned to leave and I called after her. The old familiar pattern.

'Mims – I wasn't serious.'

'Don't worry about it. I'll be back in a few minutes.'

I pulled my dress over my head and muttered expletives.

This is your Chief Steward speaking. British Airways would like to welcome you aboard Flight 825 to Tel Aviv. Our flying time will be approximately five hours. Soon after take-off, we shall be offering refreshments. Please do not smoke until the No Smoking signs have been switched off. We wish you a pleasant flight.'

The occupant of 14C fastened his seatbelt. He glanced surreptitiously at the passengers around him and wondered if the dark and shifty-looking traveller on 12A was a terrorist who'd evaded detection and was about to point a gun at the girl in 14B. If so, would he rise to her rescue? Or would he shrink in his seat and think, 'Thank God it's not me . . .'?

He pondered on matters of heroism and cowardice and being chosen for survival – then imagined God laughing and saying, 'Don't thank me for your deliverance. It so happened that the man in 12A has hated girls with red hair ever since his carrot-topped mother abandoned him when he was but a babe. Bad luck for her in 14B. Good luck for you.'

'Cheers,' he said to his red-headed neighbour, clinking his plastic beaker of gin and tonic against hers. 'Good luck.' She was silent. Her mother must have warned her not to converse with strangers.

'Good luck,' he repeated loudly after the voice on the loudspeaker had finally welcomed them to Israel and hoped they'd enjoyed their flight and warned them to stay seated until the aircraft came to a halt. 'At least we made it here in one piece.'

'Thank God,' she said. Relief had finally loosened her tongue. 'I always say that if He'd wanted us to fly He'd have given us wings. Flying's not natural is what I believe. Anyway, here we are.'

He smiled and wondered whether she was a natural red-head. Anyway, here they were.

And here he was at last, struck breathless by the August heat of the Holy Land. He found his voice, wiped the sweat from his brow and roused a recumbent taxi driver.

'I'd like to go to Kfar Tikva,' he said.

❧ 6 ❧

Gabriella wriggled irritably into her little black dress. Mia, angry, mortified, plodded downstairs towards the row of letter-boxes.

The sun had set. Kfar Tikva had stopped holding its breath. Block 84 stood wearily on its stilts, a dark dinosaur with a hundred eyes blinking in its belly and a heavy groan issuing from its nether regions. For there, in an ill-lit corner of the entrance porch, one of its older occupants – a certain Mrs Rosenkowitz – was sitting on a bench. Sitting and waiting.

She groaned again as she rose from her bench. Mrs Rosenkowitz had a vast vocabulary of groans to express miseries ranging from deep existential *Angst* to chronic constipation. Now she was simply stiff. Tired of being seventy-five and having aching joints. Tired of waiting.

Ida and Becky had gone upstairs long ago. She'd returned after lunch, hoping to encounter one of those strange fourth-floor sisters. All afternoon she'd imagined how she'd tell them. Casually.

'By the way,' she'd call out as they rummaged in their letter-box (they were always checking for letters), 'I thought I'd mention in case you're interested – a man came looking for you this morning.'

And then she'd watch carefully to see the reaction. Her friends had been as intrigued as she'd been when a grey-haired stranger had come ringing the bell of flat 405 above the little card marked Marks/Wiseman. Rang and rang persistently and then given up and left as suddenly as he'd arrived. There was something about him. Something fascinating. The three watching women had smelt intrigue. They'd breathed in a tantalizing aroma of scandal and shared speculations like an opium pipe.

61

At last, perhaps at last, the unnatural stillness that had hung over the sisters' flat for a year and a half was about to shatter. They couldn't wait to tell them the news and to see what would happen next.

But Ida and Becky didn't have her staying power. They'd given up. When it came to gathering or imparting gossip, no one could outlast Masha Rosenkowitz. Except Masha Rosenkowitz herself. No – even she'd had enough. Tomorrow was another day. Oh dear oh dear, the joints, the aching back, the disappointment.

Then she heard it. Footsteps descending the red stone steps. Heavy footsteps that preceded the arrival of a plump middle-aged figure dressed in white with damp blonde hair and a frown. Ah – Mia, the older one. She looked angry, which was unusual. It was the other one, the smaller dark-haired one, who was generally cross and sort of twitchy while Mia mostly wore a pleasant smile. Something or someone must have upset her today.

Mrs Rosenkowitz let out a huge groan by way of a conversation-starter. An oh-my-God-the-heat-and-my-poor-bones-and-how-do-we-take-it sort of groan. Mia ignored it and headed straight for the letter-box with a deepening scowl. The last thing she thought she needed was a Sabbath encounter with one of the three witches. More nastiness. Pure evil. No thank you.

'Oi, such heat. Such heat. You had a busy day?' Mrs Rosenkowitz was not about to let her prey escape. Not after such a long, hot wait. 'Did your visitor manage to find you?'

Mia stopped, puzzled. Her visitor? Their visitor? What was the woman talking about?

'We did tell him that on Fridays you and your sister usually went to the hairdresser, did some shopping. He hardly seemed to hear, though. Just rang and went away. Not so polite, we thought. Not polite at all.'

Him? What *him* could there possibly be? The only male in Israel who had made meaningful eye-contact – with Mia at any rate – was the young man who administered the weekly *coup de grâce* behind the supermarket fish counter. And only his victims passed through their front door.

'Was he – English?'

Mrs Rosenkowitz lowered her large pink-clad body again, produced more groans as she resettled herself for a response.

She chewed on a satisfying piece of lunch that her tongue had rediscovered in a deep place between her palate and her denture and pondered.

'Maybe, maybe,' she said at last.

She'd discussed the possibility with Ida and Becky. Becky, in her usual way, had announced with gloomy finality that the visitor, wherever he'd come from, would bring no good. 'I can feel it,' she'd said ominously. 'I've always said there was something not quite right about those two. Not that I wish them any harm – but I ask you? To live alone here, no friends, no work. And not so old either. I don't know, I really don't.'

'Oh Becky, don't talk like that.' Ida was always the peacemaker, the optimist. 'It's wonderful that two sisters can be so close. He was probably a brother or a cousin come to check that they're all right.'

Mrs Rosenkowitz had sniffed, the beak-nosed arbiter of the troika. 'From your mouth to God's ears. We'll see what happens.'

They always saw everything that happened – in the block at any rate. The entrance hall was the setting for a never-ending soap opera with a constantly changing cast. The departure of the grey-haired stranger had been followed by the arrival of the mother-baby brigade – distracted young women who spoke disconnectedly about dinner and their husbands and bedwetting, and settled in a sea of disposable nappies, rusks, plastic changing mats and writhing infants. Becky and Ida had been diverted but Masha's mind remained focused on the sisters and their plight.

Now she watched Mia's futile groping in the dark empty cave of a letter-box and the slump of her shoulders as she turned away for an empty-handed ascent to the fourth floor. What on earth was this strange woman doing here? Once, in a flash of joy after she'd come upon a picture postcard, she'd revealed that 'at last, at last' she'd heard from Joseph. 'My son,' she'd explained – and then stopped talking as though she'd said too much.

And once she'd overheard the other one – sulky, skinny, dark-haired Gabby – muttering about 'that bastard Clive'. Mrs Rosenkowitz had not dared to ask who he was. Perhaps this morning's visitor had been Clive? He was too old to be Joseph.

'I suppose,' she said slowly, wanting to keep Mia talking.

The encounter was not turning out to be nearly as satisfying as she'd imagined. Mia paused at the foot of the stairs.

'I suppose he was English. His clothing looked foreign. A nice shirt he wore – very nice. He didn't talk though, so I couldn't hear his accent. Just nodded and went away. It was about eleven o'clock.'

Mia shrugged and turned to leave. 'Thanks for telling me. Perhaps he'll call again if he really wants to see me – us – my sister. He obviously knows where to find us.'

'Wait. Wait.' Mrs Rosenkowitz made a final attempt to keep her. 'You say he knows where to find you. That reminds me. A story I must tell you, told to me by my friend Becky. Yes?'

Mia nodded, desperate to retreat but ever polite. A story? What was it about her that elicited stories? Was it a visible fairy-tale void, a fantasy gap that cried out to be filled?

'Becky is out walking the other day when she bumps into Nommi Levi, an old acquaintance she hasn't seen for some time. "Nommi," she says to her, "Nommi, how are you? I'm really surprised to see you. I heard you'd gone to stay with your children in England." "I suppose I'm all right," says Nommi doubtfully. And then she gives a bitter laugh. "Funny you should hear I've gone to England. Last week someone told me they heard I was dead."'

There was silence. Mrs Rosenkowitz smiled expectantly, anticipating a smile in response. But Mia was suddenly over-whelmed with sadness and could only manage 'How awful' as she mounted the stairs.

'Don't worry,' Mrs Rosenkowitz called after her. 'Your visitor will come back. I know he'll come back. I have a feeling in my bones.'

The climb seemed endless. A foreign-looking man in a 'very nice shirt'. A rather impolite man who nodded and went away. Someone who realized that she and Gabby were alive here in Kfar Tikva.

Mia's legs felt like jelly and this was only the second floor.

Poor, poor Nommi. Someone had heard she was dead. Did that make her dead? Mia often felt dead and wondered whether anyone in London spent much time pondering on their disap-pearance. 'Mia and Gabriella?' She could hear the vagueness. 'Oh, we'd heard they were . . .'

*

'Gabby,' she called when she finally, breathlessly, entered the flat. On the fourth floor landing there'd been the sound of bad Mozart (little Dana next door at her piano practice), the smell of good meat (another Friday night gastronomic splurge by the obese American immigrants in number 407) and the rhythmic clatter of metal against glass from the open door of 405. Gabriella, wearing a red-and-white striped apron over her dress, was beating eggs for the fish batter, frowning as she manipulated the balloon whisk and cradling the bowl awkwardly in a futile effort to contain the yellow splashes. She hated cooking.

'Any letters?' she asked without looking up.

'No. Nothing. Gabby?' Mia's voice sounded strange. Gabriella stopped beating and turned to her sister.

'Look Mims, I didn't mean to be nasty. About the cheese you know. It slipped out, a stupid joke . . .'

But Mia wasn't listening. 'Gabby, were you expecting anyone? A man? A grey-haired man?'

'Me? What on earth are you talking about?' She laughed. Then paused as though struck by a sudden thought. Then laughed again dismissively. 'Did you bump into a gentleman caller or something? How exciting.'

'I missed him. Mrs Rosenkowitz – you know, the first witch – was waiting to tell me someone had come looking for us while we were out this morning. A man, she said. A rather impolite man who nodded and left when she told him we were out. Who do you think it could have been?'

The frothy batter had subsided to a glutinous puddle. Gabby wiped her hands on her apron and a stray hair from her puzzled face. Mia leaned on the back of a chair and took deep breaths. The kitchen had suddenly become a ghost gallery, filled with hazy images of all the men that either of them had ever waited for. Then Gabriella picked up the whisk and the bowl.

'Ridiculous,' she said, taking up the rhythmic beating with renewed vigour. 'One caller – the chance of one caller – and our imagination soars. The solitude must be unbalancing us, Mims. After all, it could have been a messenger from the electricity department seeking out habitual late-payers. Or a charity collector who'd had word of the Misses Bountiful up here in the heat of Kfar Tikva. Or an insurance salesman. They find one anywhere.' She put down the bowl with an air of finality. 'There. Herbert – your dinner-jacket awaits.'

Then she turned to her sister. 'I'll tell you who it was. The prophet Elijah dressed up as a time-share merchant, come to offer us eternal salvation and a video-recorder in exchange for buying an annual fortnight in Eilat. What do you say?'

Mia smiled. Another fairy-tale. 'A distinct possibility,' she said.

'If he returns,' Gabby continued, holding up the dripping egg whisk, 'we'll ask him to join us for dinner. Some tender fish to soften him up, to persuade him to improve his terms. Salvation and the video-recorder aren't bad – but a cordless phone with direct dialling to his Boss would clinch it. A hot-line to heaven as well as two weeks a year in sun-soaked Eilat. Ever-after happiness. How does that sound?'

'OK,' said Mia. 'Not bad at all.'

She extracted a crisp white table-cloth from the cupboard. Gabriella claimed Herbert from the fridge. They moved purposefully. The heat had lifted. As she opened the door to release the fish smell and admit the cooler evening air, Mia remembered the Passover feasts of her childhood when the door would be opened for the prophet Elijah. A glass filled with sweet red wine would have been poured for him and Mia would watch the level carefully. Had he come? Was he drinking? Once she'd noticed Uncle Fred surreptitiously sipping Elijah's drink, but she'd been too timid to say anything. Mostly, though, the glass remained full. There it stood at the end of the meal, its brimming redness reminding everyone that they'd waited in vain. And no one, other than Mia, seemed to pay any attention to it at all.

Tonight she hadn't opened the door for Elijah. Not the prophet or the time-share merchant. Her sister, she noticed, was suddenly nervous. Gabriella kept pulling at the hem of her dress and casting fleeting, surreptitious glances at the door. Then she walked over and resolutely shut it.

'Draughty,' she said. 'Anyway, that's not the way to get rid of fish smells. I remember something to do with tea leaves . . .'

Tea leaves. Ah, yes, Mia recalled – she was right. One of Mum's few pieces of useful advice. She'd hated the odour that clung to the utensils after their weekly fish meal. 'I can't stand it, Mia darling. It goes straight to my head.' Then she'd suggested tea leaves. 'Soak everything in weak tea. That will do the trick.' It had worked. Odourless – if somewhat discoloured – implements were fished out of their weekly beverage-bath.

'But tea leaves won't eliminate the smell in the kitchen,' Mia observed.

Gabby wasn't listening. She was holding the door handle, deep in thought. 'Who d'you think he was, Mims? Who do you think he was?' There was no mockery in her voice now.

'Oh come on, Gabs. It's not important. Let's make supper – we don't need anyone else in our lives. In any case, he probably won't come again.'

Mia shook out the white table-cloth and thought of a mantle. Not Elijah's mantle. The flowing whiteness reminded her of the soft silk cloak worn by the rescuing knight who woke her from the leaden numbness of her dark childhood dreams. She held out the cloth, then flattened it over the table as she remembered that she'd long given up on dreams. By sixteen, the age when Sleeping Beauty pricked her finger and fell unconscious, Mia had ceased to dream.

❧ 7 ❧

I'd given up my dream of rescue by the time I turned sixteen. The leaden princess had been abandoned in her lonely dark cave. Covered with green mould, she became a solitary mound not likely to catch a passing prince's eye. Even if she did – if he noticed the curious bump once he'd entered the cave and started scratching off the mould – he'd say, 'Yuck. Lead. The metal that the ancient alchemists called Saturn. An evil planet under which to be born. What is this vile thing I'm uncovering? Far better that it lies here unclaimed in a dark silent cave. I'm off.' And he'd mount his white charger and gallop away.

Without my fairy-tale, I became foam-rubber Mia. At night in bed I'd feel myself getting lighter and lighter, so weightless and insubstantial that if I didn't hold fast on to the sides of the mattress I'd float away. I drifted into the nothingness of sleep and knew that I'd wake to another nothing sort of day. But I smiled in my rubber-doll way. Kept smiling and being responsible big sister, ever-helpful older daughter. And made sure no one noticed the bubbly void that had once been my favourite dream.

'Mims, what a treat. Such a huge box of chocolates. You must definitely get Herbert to take you out again.'

Gabriella, at thirteen, was as pert as ever. She still wore her dark hair in coquettish bunches and was skipping into adolescence with her skinny legs, a well-practised dimple and two small chest bumps that would undoubtedly grow into cheeky little breasts. No lumpy puberty for my sister. That had been my lot.

She changed best friends with the seasons and seemed quite

sure that in time she'd have an unlimited assortment of male admirers from which to pick and choose. I watched her idly dipping into the box of Dairy Milk, my ritual pre-cinema offering from faithful, spotty Herbert. Biting into a carelessly chosen chocolate, chewing and frowning and throwing it away. Then taking another without thought, and another and another – until a pile of half-eaten discards lay like droppings in the waste-paper basket.

'Hold it, Gabby. Nobody offered you the whole box.'

I spoke sharply. When I chose a chocolate, I took great pains to read the descriptions, studied the various fillings and finally, having settled on, say, Creamy Caramel, felt a sense of commitment to its cloying sweetness. Slowly, methodically, I'd nibble it away.

'You can take two more – if you eat them up,' I conceded. And I thought, 'You think life's one big Dairy Box, my charming little sister. Full of people to be picked up and tasted and then tossed away.' How different I was, safe, solid, careful Mia. That's what everyone thought and that's how I behaved. So sensibly and with such self-control.

Yes. That was how it was. Except in the deepest part of the night when I couldn't sleep and I'd quietly extract the chocolates from my bedside drawer and open the box and silently, ever so silently, unwrap a couple and eat them. Then a couple more – faster, with desperate intensity. And more and more until I felt awash in a surge of sweet brown slime and the box was empty and I'd sink into sludgy sleep. And the following day I'd hide the box and try to forget how I'd abandoned myself to the darkness. But I remembered. When I forgot to forget, I remembered everything.

This time I was taking no chances. For once, I'd invited Gabriella into my room to share that evening's Herbert pickings. Perhaps I'd let her taste and discard the entire box. Then there'd be no threat of an illicit brown tide to force open an imperfectly sealed memory. A rush of chocolate, a gush of warm pleasure, a dark, dark taxi.

No. I couldn't bear it.

Nor could I bear to remember the wet winter night when I'd buried my ugly old doll in the sodden, foul-smelling depths of the park bin. When I'd placed her in a far corner of my cupboard the night that Daddy died, I'd thought it would be for ever. I had never wanted to see her broken head or her limp dirty body again. And then she'd suddenly appeared, cradled in my sister's arms, gently cradled and covered and rocked. Her ugliness disguised and called Sweet Jesus. My Ugly Baba. I felt sick with longing, revulsion, hatred for my sister and the pain of something that felt as though it had been torn away. It was so sore, so unbearably sore, that all I could do was take that hurting, dirty creature and fling her for ever in the dirtiest and most hurtful place in the world.

Slowly, month by month and year by year, a skin grew over that sore raw patch. But it wasn't thick enough to bear much remembering or much probing from my sister. I wrote PRIVATE – KEEP OUT in big black letters on a large white card and stuck it on my door. Gabby had invaded my privacy, my shame, my dream, and I was sure I'd never forgive her.

Yet I needed her. After all, how could I be a responsible, sensible and solid good sister without a little sibling to care for? And she did make me laugh – I had to admit it.

'Tell me Mims,' she asked, wriggling excitedly as she sat cross-legged on my bed. 'Do you and Herbert hold hands in the cinema? Are you having – an affair?' An affair? Fiery passion between fat Mia and her pimply escort who only asked her out because his mother made him and, in any case, no one else would take her? Oh God. My sister was the limit. What did she know about affairs, anyway? And what *real* boy would want to have anything to do with me?

'My friend Caroline told me in secret that her mother was having an affair.' Gabby had a hand in the chocolate box and was looking at me with wide, wicked eyes. She didn't really want to know about Herbert and was fully aware of the limitations of our liaison. It was her place in my bedroom that she was reclaiming, her story-teller role. She wanted me to ask, 'Tell me more, tell me why?' I kept silent but I was listening and she knew it.

'Caroline heard her parents arguing about it. About him, a man she met at a Christmas party. Now her Dad calls him Santa Claus. Imagine, Mims – imagine her having an affair with a big, fat, cuddly Santa.'

She sighed as she bit into yet another chocolate. 'Oh, isn't our life dull?' she asked, eyes shut, dreaming of the richness of other homes, other ways. 'We don't even have a Santa to wait for on Christmas Eve. Caroline does. Not that one. Another one, with loads and loads of presents. Of course she doesn't believe in him any more. But she likes what he brings. She dreams about it.

'Her little brother too. James wishes and wishes for things. D'you know, Mims, last year he wished for a toy racing car. But he didn't get it. Instead he got a tortoise. He pretended it was a racing car, though. Played with it on the floor, holding its shell and making racing car sounds until Caroline thought its poor little feet would wear away. She told her mother and they swopped it for a miniature Ferrari.'

It was meant to be funny, but I didn't laugh. The most I could muster was a faint smile to accompany Gabby's shriek of mirth. All that waiting, the dreams of Father Christmas and his bounty. She was right. Our life was dull. No Santa. No father. Not even a poor tortoise as a consolation prize.

'Mims.' She'd stopped laughing. 'Do you think Mum finds it dull with just us? D'you think she's waiting for a Santa too?'

Mum? A Santa? Now *that* was hilarious. Our perpetually tired, plump mother in the arms of the ever-jolly, generous giver of goodies. Swept away on his sledge, pulled by flying reindeer – up, up to the great toy factory in the sky where she'd say, 'Oh, I must lie down. My poor, poor head.'

'Never,' I said emphatically. 'Mum would never look at another man after Dad. And anyway – he'd never make it into the house. The chimneys have been bricked up and if he managed to break down the front door he'd trip over the shoes on the stairs. We're safe Gabs. No one's about to spirit our mother away.'

Putting the shoes on the stairs was my nightly task. A 'Handy Household Hint' that Mum had picked up from the wireless.

'Mia, darling,' she'd said one day when I'd brought her tea after school, 'I heard such a clever idea, something to keep us all safe in the night. Three, maybe four, pairs of shoes carefully placed up the staircase to trip up an intruder. Such a clatter there'd be if anyone broke in, enough to warn anyone. Perhaps we should try it?' I suppose it made sense. And after the first few times it became a ritual. Locking the doors, checking the windows, putting out the shoes.

'Let's get ready for bed,' I said to Gabby, withdrawing the

71

chocolates. She'd had quite enough. 'Do you want to help me lock up?'

She nodded eagerly. It had been a long time since I'd asked her. We tiptoed across the landing, giggling as a breathy snore emanated from Mum's room. She'd been asleep for hours – a deep, deep sleep thanks to the tablets she took for her 'insomnia'. 'I hardly closed my eyes last night,' she'd sigh with heavy, drooping lids when I brought her breakfast most mornings. Did she have any idea how we laughed at her, pitied her, despised her? And yet I needed so badly to please her, to have her say, 'Thank you, Mia darling – what would we do without you?'

'Sh, walk quietly,' I warned, as we made our way downstairs, Gabby following obediently. It was good to lead the way. We locked and bolted and latched the doors. What treasures we were guarding in our family fortress.

'Take these.' I handed Gabby four shoes, half the nightly allocation. She took them, then looked at them. And suddenly she held out a large and well-worn size nine brown brogue. She held it away from herself as though it were a strange and potentially dangerous creature.

'Isn't this . . . ?'

'Yes. An old shoe of Dad's. Mum gave it to me. She gave me the pair and said I should use it on the stairs. It would make an intruder believe there was a man in the house, she said.'

At first I'd hated doing it, had dreamt each night that Dad was filling his shoes, walking slowly up, up, up. And then I'd started to like the dream. It was comforting really, thinking of Dad on the stairs guarding us at night.

Gabby looked doubtfully at the shoe. I pointed to the seventh step and she placed it sideways, pointing neither up nor down. Then she sprang upstairs.

'It's creepy,' she said without pausing to look back. 'I think it's horrible and creepy and I can't wait to grow up and get out of this dark, dull, horrible, creepy house.'

She turned and looked down from the topmost step. She seemed to loom over me, her bunches in disarray, red dressing-gown glowing in the half-light, no vestige of cuteness.

'Thanks for the chocolates,' she said. 'Good-night Mims.'

I stood in the hallway, Dad's other shoe heavy in my hand, and I felt the weight of my duty, my sadness and the sudden certainty that my sister would flee and leave me gasping for

72

breath under that load. She'd skip out of our lives with a cheery goodbye and I'd remain, my weightless foam-rubber form tethered to my mother's bedside. And doubtless Mum would go too, eventually. And there I'd be, tied to her empty bed.

I placed the shoe carefully on the fifteenth step, making sure that the toe faced towards my room. 'Please Dad,' I whispered, 'if you're around anywhere, in any form, please come and save me.' I imagined a golden chariot bearing a white-cloaked figure, all glitter and light. Then I thought of my father, sad and bowed and defeated by life. By death. By my wickedness. No – there was no way he could save me. No way at all.

Slowly, meticulously, I distributed the shoes and turned out the lights and went to bed. The chocolate box was empty. I dreamt that I was biting into a Creamy Caramel and came upon a small, white and rather surprised-looking worm. I felt no revulsion. On the contrary, I was sorry for the creature. He'd been safe and well fed in his chocolate home and I'd exposed him to all sorts of dangers.

'Come with me,' I said in my mellow dream-voice. 'What I really wanted was a racing car or perhaps a pet tortoise. But never mind. I'll take care of you. I'll give you a new home in which you'll be safe for ever.'

And I wrapped him in his chocolate, replaced his silver-foil shell, and placed him deep in the toe of my father's brown brogue. I heard Gabby laughing. Harsh, spiteful laughter.

'You're so silly, Mims.' Her dream-voice sounded like metal clanging against metal. 'You're silly and creepy and I'm not staying around in this dark death-place any longer. You can have your pet worm in its ghost-shoe and our mother in her ghost-bed. I'm leaving.' I looked up. She was covering her face as she laughed and floated away. I thought I heard raindrops but it was the fall of my tears on the leather of my father's shoe.

The pillow was wet when I woke. It was still dark. My mother was calling me.

'Mia, darling, I do so need some water. Would you be an angel and fetch me some? My poor legs won't carry me downstairs.' I looked at my watch. Six-thirty a.m. The first shaft of light was struggling through the tightly shut green velvet curtains. Her bedroom, as always, smelt of face-powder, stale perfume and lost hope. 'I'm sorry I woke you, my sweet. I've had a terrible dream and feel so shaken.'

'Would you like a cup of tea then, Mum?' I offered, rubbing my eyes. She was sitting up, clearly in distress. Her hair, usually so well-coiffed from its weekly set, was in dyed-yellow disarray. The satin bow designed to bunch prettily at the neck of her pyjama top hung in limp pink strands. She was wringing plump hands together, her solitaire diamond glinting in the dawn light.

'Please, darling. Yes, please.'

I turned to the door. She called me back. 'Mia, it was your father. He was there, in my dream – and he looked so sad. Even sadder than I remembered. "My little girls," he kept saying. "Hilda, how are my little girls?" "Fine, Joe, fine," I answered, but he didn't believe me. "Are you sure?" he wanted to know. "Really sure?" And I didn't know. I just didn't know.'

There were tears in her eyes. She felt sorry for herself. Life and death had treated her so unfairly. 'You've never bothered to know,' I wanted to say. Instead I sat down at the foot of her bed and murmured, 'Poor Mum.'

'Mia – *are* you all right? You never say anything. So quiet and good. It worries me.'

Worried her? After so many years it worried her? She must have been deeply upset by her dream visitation. Oh, Dad, why did you wait so long?

'Don't worry Mum. I'm fine.'

'Have you decided about school? About that secretarial college you told me about? We do have money for it, you know. Dad saw to it that I'd not be short – life insurance was always one of his priorities. What do you want to do?'

I opened the curtain. Daybreak was still hesitating at the smudgy window. I wanted to be in bed, to lie there with shut eyes and focus on the lacy patchwork patterns that seemed to drift behind my lids, blinking away the harshness of the light. Instead, I was being forced to stare at the struggling dawn, at my mother's discomfort, at the bleakness of the future.

What *did* I want to do? To climb great mountains, reach lofty peaks and proclaim my conquest? To invent epic tales, stories about people having vast dreams that turned into glorious reality, even better than the dreams? To step out of my fat Mia shell, watch my bloated foam-rubber form floating away and make good things happen?

Yes, I wanted all those things. Badly.

But I was afraid that people died climbing mountains, that reality could never, ever match the splendour of dreams and that I'd not have the courage to make things happen. And so I said to my mother in my duty-dull voice: 'The secretarial college sounds like a good idea. I'll apply for the autumn term.'

She sighed and sank back to the softness of her propped-up pillow. 'Well, that's that then. You'll have a nice, useful skill and you can stay on here at home. I'm so glad my darling.'

The future stretched ahead, a million empty shoes on a billion steps leading to nowhere but my mother's bedroom. Oh, what did it matter? I smiled and nodded. 'And now shall I bring you some tea?'

'Yes please, Mia darling, you *are* good. And the thinnest slice of toast you can manage, with some butter and strawberry jam. I need a little something for that awful head of mine. It's a miracle that I survive from day to day. Oh dear, life is difficult.'

Gabriella was sitting at the dining-room table, biting her pen and frowning over a column of figures when I returned from school the next day. She looked up.

'I hate maths,' she said. 'Maths and French and geography and Caroline Marsh, the little bitch. You're so lucky. Mum says you're leaving school in the summer.'

'Yes.'

'Secretarial college.' Her voice was scornful. She put down her pen and cupped her chin with her hand. I looked over her shoulder and noticed small outlines of birds pencilled in the margins of her maths exercise book. Swallows, eagles and doves, swooping and soaring round the rows of careful numerals. Sparrows twittering above the sum of the difference between the product of x and y. I wanted to weep.

'I suppose it's a useful sort of thing to do,' I said, trying hard to sound positive.

She'd picked up a pencil and added another feathered form to her aviary. I watched her. With bold strokes she outlined the wings, the uplifted head, the tiny beak pointed bravely to the top right-hand corner of the page. The edge of its world. 'Are you allowed to festoon your maths with animal life? Doesn't your teacher object?' I asked.

'Allowed?' Now her scorn was biting. 'Why does "allowed" matter so much to you? I don't much care what my teacher thinks. I like drawing, Mims, better than anything. And when I've finished school I won't settle for something I'm allowed or supposed to do. Oh no.' She shook her head, traced her pencil along the wings of her flying bird. 'No useful, sensible secretarial college for me. I'm going far, far away to a place where I'll paint so many pictures that one day, after I'm dead, my work will make a banner that'll stretch across the whole sky and everyone will look up and point and say, "There's Gabriella's Rainbow!"'

She laughed delightedly at the notion – then saw my face. It must have looked as crumpled as I felt. Defeated at sixteen. Beaten by obedience. Her laugh faded. She rose and took hold of my arm.

'I didn't mean to upset you, Mims,' she said. 'They're silly, my dreams. Really silly. And Mims, I'm so glad, so very glad that you're going to stay here at home with us. I don't know what I'd do without you.'

Her thin arms clung tightly round my neck. I felt her smallness, her lightness, imagined her slipping away. 'Silly dreams.' She didn't mean that. No. Tomorrow she'd be giggling and whispering to a friend (Caroline or Katie or whoever was in favour) about her fat boring sister who was going to be a dull old secretary. But now she was holding on to me. She needed me.

'I'll be around,' I told her. 'I'll probably always be around.'

I looked down at her sketches of soaring birds and tucked in a corner I saw a small stork. A cartoon stork, winking as it headed for the edge of the page with its bundle dangling from its beak. Two baby storks peeped timidly at the world. I remembered reading somewhere that a stork mother would peck, peck, peck at her offspring until she drew blood, and then soothe the wounds with her tongue. Did sisters sometimes treat one another that way? I headed for the kitchen. There was supper to think about.

'D'you fancy an omelette?' I called.

*

'Now girls, remember that you can't make omelettes without breaking eggs.' Mrs Richardson taught touch-typing, not cookery. But she was given to profound utterances, sprinkled liberally and solemnly over her lessons. She had steel glasses and metallic hair, and was frowning over thirty typewriters in three neat rows as she orchestrated the movements of three hundred hesitant fingers and thumbs into a clatter of synchronized tapping.

'Ready everybody. Sharp's the word. On your marks, get set, *go*.'

She raised one hand, holding up a wooden baton. The other fumbled with an ancient record-player. We waited, hands poised over our keyboards, for the chord that would tell us to start. It came. A mighty crash of keys. And then 'Jingle bells, jingle bells' jingled through the shabby room. Mrs Richardson shut her eyes ecstatically as her class came to the end of a line and margin bells pinged in perfect harmony.

'Ah,' she sighed to the continuing scratch, scratch, scratch of the gramophone needle in the silence. 'That was music to soothe the savage breast.'

There was a brief, relieved titter. Her satisfaction meant that we could move on to the measured rhythm of 'God save the queen'. Page sixty-nine in our typewriting manual. A lesson in tabulation. Thank goodness. 'Jingle bells' had lost something of its jollity after the two-hundreth rendition.

For me it had never been particularly jolly. 'My Method' Mrs Richardson had called her system of tuneful touch-typing. She claimed full credit for its invention. 'The *only* way,' she averred, 'for a girl to acquire keyboard confidence.' And after four months at the Richardson Academy, I suppose I'd acquired a certain level of proficiency out of sheer self-preservation. The humiliation of striking a key out of time, of handing in a piece of inaccurate text and having disapproval meted out in sharp platitudes, was more than I could bear.

'Carelessness killed the cat,' she'd intone, staring icily at the perpetrator and holding out a piece of ill-prepared work as though it were something nasty that the creature in question had brought in.

No Mrs Richardson, I'd want to say. Not carelessness. Just lack of care, of caring, of being cared for. There was nothing that I really cared about. The days switched on and off and within their measured rhythm I performed my allotted tasks.

'Good morning Mum,' as I brought in her tea with the dawn. She'd sit up languidly, take the tray. 'Morning my darling,' she'd yawn. 'Oh, you are a dear.' I needed to hear it, my daily drug. And I hated my need. I'd watch Gabby darting off to school, her mouth full of cornflakes, her head filled with dreams. Then I'd take myself to college – move dream-like but dreamless from touch-typing to stenography. There were lessons in bookkeeping, weekly lectures on deportment.

'Our product is the Perfect Secretary,' was the proud claim of the Academy, 'skilled and well-rounded, poised and polite. The pride and joy of any boss.'

I sat on my wooden seat fifth from the front in the middle aisle and waited to be turned into this mythical creature. That's what it had come to. I'd accepted that there'd be no tender prince to melt me, no gallant sire to sweep me out of the darkness. Instead there was cliché-ridden Fairy Richardson with a musical wand to magic meek Mia into a model employee.

And the magic worked. Of course it did. How supremely malleable I was. Conscientiously, I acquired the necessary skills. I'd always been well-rounded. The lessons in deportment (and a new short haircut) gave me poise; politeness – or the lack of it – had never been my problem. By the end of the year I was able to take my place in a line-up of lacquered hairstyles and lipstick-licked smiles to receive the Richardson Academy Secretarial Diploma (with merit).

My sister was there to applaud my achievement. I'd told Mum to stay at home. 'It will be a long, tiring evening.' She hadn't argued.

'Mims you look lovely,' Gabby said, touching my stiffly sprayed hair. She stepped back and studied my well-cut shirt-waister dress, looked down at my shoes and up at the band of blue shadow I'd so carefully applied to my eyelids. She shook her head. 'You seem so much older, so grown up.' I believed her and flashed my most sophisticated secretary-smile, feeling fashionable and experienced.

She clapped hard when Mrs Richardson handed me my diploma breathing a gardenia-scented 'Well done' into my ear. I looked out at the sea of strange faces and saw Gabriella and thought, 'She cares. My sister cares. Whatever happens, we'll always have each other.'

'You were the best-looking of all your class,' she declared, as we walked home arm in arm. I wanted to cry. It wasn't true – but I loved her for saying it, moved closer to her. 'You know, Mims,' she continued, her voice cutting through the darkness, 'I can't understand why you don't have any boyfriends apart from Herbert. And *he* doesn't count. I often wonder why you're hardly asked out.'

We carried on home. There was nothing more to say. Gabby hummed softly to herself and I bit back my fury, my humiliation. Silly idiot, I told myself. You allowed yourself to believe in your charm and sophistication. How could you have? In the end you're just boring Mia who isn't asked out. Why couldn't she understand that? What was there to understand? The best-looking in my class, indeed.

'Good-night Mims. Thanks for a lovely evening. I was really proud of you.' A polite recitation. She stood on tiptoe and kissed my cheek. I thought of the stork and rubbed her kiss away.

I managed to get the best job in my class. I may not have been a *femme fatale*, but I certainly turned out to be a model secretary. 'City legal practice requires reliable sec. with impeccable skills.' Oh yes. That was me.

'Goldblatt. Hyman Goldblatt.' He stood up behind an enormous kidney-shaped desk, walked round it, and came towards me holding out a huge red hand. I looked at his face and saw – Uncle Fred. I wanted to say, 'It's me – Blondie. Where have you been? Why did *you* leave me too?' I wanted to stand there and shout, 'You bastard, you nasty, dirty old man.' But of course it wasn't Uncle Fred at all. It was a fat lawyer with a pipe sticking out of his mouth and he was waiting for me to introduce myself.

'Mia Marks,' I said, stammering over the alliteration. It sounded a silly name. A plaintive squawk like the cry of an abandoned eaglet.

'When can you start? You have an impeccable report from your college and I have complete faith in Bertha Richardson. A fine woman indeed.' He sucked on his pipe and repeated, 'Yes, indeed.' My eyes were caught by the sucking of his thick lips. I cringed. 'And so,' the voice boomed, 'what d'you say?'

What could I say? Since when did I have control over the course of my life? 'Fine,' I stumbled. 'Thank you very much. I'm ready to start whenever you want me.'

The days switched on and the days switched off. And to a changed but still measured rhythm I performed my allotted tasks.

'Good-morning Mum – your tea.'

She'd sit up. 'Thank you, darling. You do look nice.' Empty praise. But perhaps she meant it? Did she? Could she? Why did I care?

'Mia, your sister's working so hard,' she'd sigh. 'All afternoon she sits doing homework. And she's looking so drawn, thinner than usual I think.' What about me, mother dear? Aren't you concerned about me? God how I hated her. I hated them both. Furious inside, I'd smile. 'Yes,' I'd murmur. 'We must look after her.'

'Goldblatt, Cohen and Carruthers. How can we help you?' Five hundred times a day in honeyed tones. Letters neatly typed. Legal briefs immaculately presented. 'Good girl Mia,' Mr Goldblatt purred. 'What a treasure you are. How lucky I was to find you.' From the other side of the office, Mr Carruthers's secretary smiled.

'I'm Hannah,' she'd announced on the first day. Her face was like the sun. Round, beaming, framed by a cloud of yellow hair. Hannah O'Reilly from Dublin. 'Isn't London wonderful? I think it must be the most exciting place in the world.'

I'd never met anyone like her before. She loved life, people, beamed out her curiosity. Coming to the big city had been her dream. 'You're so lucky to have lived here all your life – and there was I stuck with all those brothers and sisters at home.'

Me? Lucky? She thought Hendon sounded wonderfully grand, a three-bedroomed house with three occupants palatial. I laughed out loud at the thought. 'If only you knew,' I said. 'Hannah, if only you knew.' She asked so I told her – about Mum, about Gabby. Even about Herbert. 'Every second Thursday, regular as clockwork, he takes me to the cinema. A box of chocolates every time.' Hannah was fascinated. Imagine that – fascinated by me, by my boring little life. She told me about Dublin, about her three brothers and two sisters. About her

80

fathers. Three fathers. One in heaven, one in church and a third who kept her mother constantly pregnant. 'The first one's best,' she said. 'The second one hears my confession, knows all my sins. Number three's usually drunk.'

'But you don't sin,' I said, puzzled. 'Not you, Hannah. What on earth d'you confess?' She simply smiled, dismissed the question. 'Let's go out for a drink after work tomorrow,' she said.

I'd found a friend.

'Hannah?' Gabby asked when I casually mentioned the following day that I'd be late home from work. 'Hannah O'Reilly? Is she Jewish?'

'Irish. Catholic. Gabby, she's one of the warmest, nicest people I've ever met.'

'Oh.' She wasn't really interested. 'The girl who sits behind me in history is Catholic. Martha Jones. They eat fish every Friday. I told her we did too. Funny that. Why d'you think that is, Mims?'

I didn't know. Wanted to say something about things in common, all of us being the same in the end. Us and Hannah O'Reilly and Martha Jones. But she'd gathered her books and was gone.

And here we were, frying fish on a Friday night. A distant, different Friday night.

'The time of reckoning has come,' Gabby said, hands on hips, head tilted thoughtfully. 'Do we cook Herbert whole or in pieces? Consider carefully, Mims. Don't make any hasty decision.'

Think about Herbert when a dark stranger had come calling? 'Well . . .' I pondered, playing her game, 'there's the pan to be taken into account. Whole Herbert may not fit in a single pan. On the other hand, I suppose one could always cut him in half and then join him together again once he's cooked. A splodge of mayonnaise and no one will be any the wiser.'

She smiled gleefully, grabbed a knife and raised it high above her head.

'Here goes then, Herb. A divided body but a single soul.' The knife came down.

ॐ 8 ॐ

I stood there, brandishing the kitchen knife and feeling like an avenging angel bearing a blazing sword. An archangel. Yes, Gabriel's female counterpart, sister of the messenger of God, sharing his power to decree death, fire and thunder. And what was she doing? Filleting fish. But then, didn't women – even woman angels – usually end up with the boring jobs. Oh, bugger it. 'Here goes.' I put all my weight behind the knife.

A sharp blow severed the spine and Herbert was cut in two. I said something silly about a divided body and a single soul and laughed feebly. Mia was silent, staring with a sad and puzzled frown at the poor dissected creature.

'What's up Mims?' I asked lightly. As lightly as I could, for I was suddenly uncomfortable. 'It's only a fish. Just a slab of dead flesh . . .'

She raised her eyes and looked straight into mine. 'Poor Herbert,' she said. Why 'poor Herbert'? Did she know? How could she possibly know? It wasn't like me to suffer pangs of conscience, but what else could that sudden prickly gooseflesh all over my body have been about?

The air had cooled considerably, yet I was hot and perspiring profusely. Almost the way I'd felt when I was fifteen and in bed with what avuncular Dr Mitchell gravely diagnosed as glandular fever.

'At least three weeks in bed for you, young lady.' The silver-haired doctor was sitting at the edge of my bed, his hand on my wrist. He'd been taking my pulse. Before that, he'd felt behind my ears, under my arms, my groin. 'Uh-huh,' he'd said deeply and knowingly. 'Mmm.' His hands were warm and when he leaned close to me he smelt of – man. A familiar sort of smell. The smell of Daddy? Perhaps.

I breathed in deeply, trying to remember, but I couldn't even picture my father's face. This Dr Mitchell smell, though – I did like it. It made me feel warm and limp. I hoped he'd have to visit me again soon.

'But doctor . . .' Mum's voice, from the far end of the room, was loud and concerned. 'This must be serious. After all, Gabriella has glands all over her body. Surely they're not *all* affected.'

She was worried. Worried enough to dress early, call for Dr Mitchell, and watch anxiously as he examined me. She accompanied him downstairs and I heard him say, 'Don't fret too much, Hilda. It's not good for you. She'll be all right. Lots of rest and plenty to drink and she'll be fine. A spunky little lass, your Gabriella. Bright as a button.'

There was a thud as the door closed, the rumble of a motor-car engine, and Mum was back in my room.

'Poor Gabby,' she said, bending over and kissing my burning forehead. 'We must look after you, get you better soon. I'll try and telephone your sister at work and see whether she can bring home lots of fresh fruit. That's what you need.'

Gosh, this was wonderful. Both of them nursing me, a tender, delicate plant. Things had certainly improved since the night before when I'd tossed with hot ravings and sore limbs and thought the dawn would never come again and called 'Mum, Mum' and then 'Mia, where *are* you?' and no one had heard.

But now they knew I was very sick, doctor-sick and in need of special care. Three weeks in bed. I wished it could have been for ever.

Mia brought fruit and comic-books and a note from her new friend, Hannah O'Something, a real goody-two-shoes if ever there was one. 'Hannah says, Hannah does . . .' Mia would go on and on. I usually listened and pretended to be interested, but it really was boring. Such virtue, such beauty. 'It's amazing,' Mia would say. 'Hannah is never unhappy.' How sickening.

This time, to my bed of pain, she brought the news that dearest Hannah had suffered from the self-same glandular affliction in her hallowed childhood and, glory of glories, had recovered unsullied. 'Hmm,' I grunted and turned to my comic. Who cared about Saint Hannah? Anyway, there was a good chance that I'd not recover unscarred. Perhaps I'd not recover at all, with every gland in my body so fevered. That would teach her not to listen to Hannah.

She left the room, singing softly under her breath. I listened for the click of her bedroom door and threw the comic on the floor in a fury.

'Mia!' I called. No reply. Where was she? Wasn't she supposed to be looking after her sick little sister? And where was Mum, worried Mum who'd cooled my brow with her hand and said, 'We'll make you better soon, my darling' – and then disappeared to her weekly card-game, sighing that she 'couldn't possibly let Hetty and the girls down'?

'Mims,' I called again. 'I need you.'

She came. Those three magic words had never failed.

'Where are you going?' She'd put on lipstick, tidied her hair. There was something different about the way she looked. Something almost – happy. It made me scared. Mia was my safe place, my sad and rather dull sister who'd always been there. Even when she'd written PRIVATE – KEEP OUT in big black letters on a large white card and stuck it on her door, I hadn't worried. There'd always been rustling in her room and the heavy footfalls of her duty to reassure me. I could taunt her and test her but she'd never go away. Yet now her feet seemed suddenly lighter. She couldn't be testing her wings? Not Mia, my Mia?

'Why are you getting dressed again?' I asked. 'I thought you'd be keeping me company this evening.'

'It's Hannah,' she hesitated. I might have guessed. 'Hannah and her friends. I'm meeting them for coffee. I promised . . .'

'Oh. But – I'm not very well, Mims.' I hated to whine, but couldn't help my voice rising plaintively. This wasn't fair at all.

'You'll be all right, Gabby.' She bent down and kissed my cheek. 'See, you're quite cool now. I won't be long. And Mum will also be back soon. I'll bring you some supper before I leave.'

I refused to eat. I'd starve myself, not get better. That would show her.

'What about tomorrow evening?' I asked crossly when she came to say a cheery goodbye. 'Will you be staying at home with me?'

'Well – um – Gabs, tomorrow's Thursday. The Thursday that

Herbert takes me to the cinema. I have to go. He does look forward to it and it's too late to tell him I can't come . . .' She stood awkwardly, feet tightly together, white clutch-bag clasped against her chest, frowning and looking down.

'*He* looks forward to it,' I said scornfully. 'What about you? What do you want to do? And – what about me?'

She shuffled uncomfortably, frowned, then said: 'Sorry Gabby, I must go. I want to go. I know you don't think much of Herbert – and, you're right, he's not exactly Mr Universe. But he's kind and loyal and I like him. And we won't be late. And – tell you what – I'll save all my chocolates for you. The whole box.'

'Keep your rotten chocolates. And your smelly Herbert with his pimply face and silly laugh. I hope you have a perfectly horrid time – tonight and tomorrow night.'

I lay back feeling like a tragic, stricken heroine and allowed pathetic tears to slip through shut, exhausted eyes and wondered how I looked. But she wasn't watching. I heard her plodding footsteps down the stairs and a rush of wind as the front door opened and closed.

My fever spiked again that night. I had a terrifying dream in which I was in a hot, airless, lonely bubble and the people in my life passed by and ignored me. I called out and cried but no one heard. Mia was deep in conversation with Herbert. Dr Mitchell had his arms round my mother who was smiling ecstatically, breathing in his man-smell. Caroline and Katie and my new best friend, Maggie, giggled in a huddle and whispered together.

'Help me, help me,' I panted. 'It's me – Gabby – cute, funny Gabby – I'll make you laugh, tell you stories, draw you pictures. Please, please, please don't leave me alone.' But they took no notice.

I was exhausted next day. And angry. And I didn't know what to do about my anger except to call out 'Mum . . .', 'Mia . . .', sharply and sporadically and, when someone responded, to think of a request. Water. A pillow. A book. An aspirin. Anything.

'Gabs, please don't mind too much about tonight.' Mia was clearly feeling guilty. Good. 'I told Herbert you were ill and he was most concerned, said he'd come up and say hello before we went out. I told him you weren't infectious. You're not, are you? What did Dr Mitchell say?'

I hadn't thought of asking the doctor – but what the hell. 'It's not catchy,' I said confidently. They deserved to catch it, especially Herbert. Horrid, slimy toad, sneaking off with my sister. I wished he would pick up something really nasty and disappear for ever. Yes, it would be extremely satisfying if Herbert disappeared. And that pain-in-the-neck Hannah. I had a sudden thought. I couldn't get my clutches on Saint Hannah. But Herbert . . . 'Yes, do bring him upstairs to see me, Mims. I'm so bored with being sick.'

I pretended to be asleep when I heard them approaching my room. I'd combed out my hair and arranged it on the pillow to frame my face, its interesting pallor enhanced with a touch of talcum powder. When I heard the squeak of my door, I sighed hugely, opened languid eyes and saw Herbert with a big bunch of daffodils, a tightly buttoned white jacket and a toothy grin. It looked like his pimples had been buffed for the occasion.

'Isn't it sweet of Herbert to have brought you flowers?' Mia stood behind him, looking proudly over his shoulder. She *liked* the goon, I suddenly realized. Well, she deserved better. I'd be doing her a favour if I cleared the deck for someone else.

'Thanks, Herbert. Thank you very much,' I said in a small, weak voice. 'Oh Mims, won't you arrange them in a vase for me – and bring me a sandwich before you go out. I suddenly feel as though I may be able to eat a little. Cheese, very thinly cut. With tomato. You're an angel.'

She nodded agreeably. Her escort started backing from the room with her.

'Herbert, please don't go. Stay, stay and talk to me in the meanwhile.'

'Yes do that, Herb. I won't be long. It'll do Gabby good to have company, cheer her up.' Silly idiot. 'Herb . . .' God, it made me want to puke.

'All right Mia. Good idea.' He handed her the flowers and took a few hesitant steps towards me. I listened for my sister's departing footsteps, then pointed to my bed.

'Come and sit down,' I murmured. 'You'll have to sit close. I'm rather weak and it makes me tired to speak loudly. You know, this is the first time we've had a chance to chat, just you and me.'

He nodded and sat where I'd indicated, feet both firmly on the ground, grin unwavering. I could smell brilliantine and, very faintly, that man-scent again. Perhaps I was going to enjoy this more than I'd imagined. My plot had been to tell him a tale of betrayal, to humiliate him out of my sister's life. 'I must tell you this – as a friend of course,' I'd planned to whisper. 'I know she's my sister, but she's treating you badly. Using you. There are other men she really cares about.' But now, when I saw his discomfort, felt the maleness of his presence next to me and noticed how his breathing quickened when he sat on my bed, I decided to change tack. There was another way to frighten him away – and to have a bit of fun at the same time. I reached out and took his hand.

'Herb, your hand feels warm and strong. I like you. I'm sure I like you even more than my sister does – well, just as much anyway. And look.'

While I'd been fondling his hand, I'd unbuttoned my night-dress. My breasts weren't, well, large. But my friend Caroline had said when we compared shapes the week before that they were nice and pointy. Without doubt, I had superior nipples – and they were now revealed in all their perky splendour to the gawking eyes of Mia's Herbert. I pulled his hand towards my chest and he submitted without protest. He was breathing so hard I thought he might choke.

'D'you like them?' I guided his hand from one breast to the other and then downward, down over my belly. He suddenly froze.

'What – what are you doing, Gabby?' he asked in a thick voice. 'This is wrong. You're just a – child.'

'I'm fifteen. That's grown up, grown up enough, anyway. Do you want to see?' I flung aside the bedclothes. Herbert stood up sharply and stumbled from my bed like a frightened giraffe.

'No, no,' he gasped. 'It's madness. Cover yourself. Your sister's coming.'

I pulled up the blankets and exploded with laughter into my pillow. His face. His shocked face. Herbert turned to the window and stood there, straightening his jacket and struggling to control his respiration. He looked agonized.

'What's the joke, Gabs? I knew Herbert would cheer you up. Some of the stories he tells me are hilarious.' Mia had entered carrying a vase with yellow blooms in one hand and a plate of neatly cut sandwiches in the other. There was a happy smile on her face. I felt a prickle of discomfort, but it was hardly sharp enough to pop my pleasure.

'He is funny,' I giggled. 'Really entertaining. I do feel better, Mims. You two go out and have a lovely time.'

I caught Herbert's eye as he retreated from the room and gave him a meaningful wink. He looked away.

'Good-night, Gabby. Have a nice, restful sleep,' said Mia, bending down to kiss my cheek. 'Herbert, aren't you going to wish my sister better?'

'Night. Get well soon,' he mumbled from the landing.

I heard Mia coming in later that night. On the appointed Thursday a fortnight later, she stayed at home.

'What's happened to Herbert?'I asked innocently after a few weeks.

Mia shrugged. 'I don't know,' she said vaguely. 'He seems to be avoiding me.'

I'd recovered from my fever by then and was back at school. Life was full again. The game with Herbert had faded into insignificance once my friends and I had screamed with laughter over it. And Herbert himself had melted away.

'So what?' I'd mutter defiantly to the part of myself that blamed me for the disappearance of Herbert. 'He was a bore, an idiot. Mia deserves better.' And I'd blink away the image of a gentle smile and yellow daffodils – and a memory of the sudden pain that had gripped my chest when I'd smothered, with laughter into my pillow, a longing for his kindness. Such a need to be touched.

'Nonsense,' I told myself sharply and, with sharp, vicious strokes, I sketched Herbert in cartoon form. An awkward, pimply figure with huge hands gripping a bunch of drooping flowers. Then I drew him again, and this time he was looking up, an amazed expression on his foolish face. For there, soaring above his head, was a swallow. The flowers had parted and the bird had emerged with beating wings. Abracadabra. Magic. Me.

'Oh yeah,' I said cynically. For I knew there was no such thing as magic. I'd always known. Magic and fairy-stories and happy endings were things that other kids believed in. And

Santa Claus and the Bible and conjurors who made doves fly out of hats. And God.

'I'm an atheist,' I announced to my mother and Mia one evening. We'd discussed religion at school that day – me and Caroline and Martha and Maggie – and decided that, all in all, it caused more trouble than it was worth. Anyway, being an atheist sounded sophisticated.

'Really,' said Mia, not even bothering to look up from the book she was reading. I'd thought she might be interested. Not that she was actually religious herself – but there was something about her. Caroline had once described her as 'nun-like'. I didn't really know what nuns were like except that they looked serene and were meant to pray a lot and it sounded boring and I'd always thought Mia was rather boring. But she was also serene in a resigned sort of way. Always thinking, reading, imagining things. Waiting so patiently for something to happen. It occurred to me: did Mia believe in God?

I asked her. She shrugged.

'Don't talk to me then,' I said sulkily. 'You won't be able to in a few months anyway. I'm going to art school in Birmingham.'

That shocked them out of their torpor. Mum put down her knitting.

'But Gabriella darling,' she said, looking at me dazedly, 'what's this about? You never said . . .'

'I didn't think I'd make it. I applied on the off-chance and they liked my portfolio. You see, Mother dear, you have a very clever and talented daughter.' I couldn't resist the boast. After all, they *had* said I had talent – and getting into an art school was an achievement. Far more enterprising than going to Mrs Richardson's precious academy and ending up the underpaid skivvy of a slimy solicitor. I glanced at my sister. She seemed stunned.

'Didn't I tell you long ago that I was going to do it, Mims? Didn't you believe me?'

'Yes,' she said sadly. And she looked as though she was about to cry. 'Yes, you did. I did. And now – well, I suppose it'll be me and Mum left here.' Then she seemed to take hold of herself. She sat up straight and closed her book firmly. 'Gabs, I'm really, really pleased for you. I mean it. I know you're going to do well.'

She spoke sincerely. I knew my sister. Not a mean bone in

her body. I had the grace to feel a twinge of guilt for my uncharitable thoughts, my little nastinesses down the years. Only a twinge though. I've never gone in for sackcloth and ashes. Far too drab.

'Thank you, Mia. I *will* try and do well. And it's not really far away. Only a couple of hours on the train. I'll be home often and we can write. You'll see.'

She nodded and opened her book, but I saw she wasn't reading. Her lips were tight, eyes fixed ahead.

'Anyway,' I persisted, 'at least you two have one another. I'm the one who's venturing out into the cold, cruel world. Mum, you haven't said much. Aren't you proud of me?'

'Of course I am, Gabby darling. It's just that it would have been nice if you'd discussed this with me beforehand. There are art schools in London. Was it necessary to take such a drastic step? Anyway, thank goodness I have Mia here to take care of things. Oh dear, I'm not getting any younger . . . You're not thinking of leaving me too, are you darling?'

My sister shook her head, still pretending to be engrossed in her book – and I was suddenly furious at her compliance, at the way she nodded and smiled and submitted. She probably thought this had been easy for me. As easy as the endless bird pictures that flowed and flew from my pencil. As easy as waving a wand – and one-two-three I *was* a bird, winging my way to Birmingham. Perhaps she imagined I'd charmed my way in or banged my head on the floor and screamed till I got my way.

'I worked hard for this, Mims,' I said, unable to keep a note of hostility out of my voice. 'I wanted it very badly. I vowed when I was little that I was going to get away, do something. Not be caught here in a web of duty like a helpless fly, like . . .' I didn't finish. She knew though.

'Me,' she said resignedly. 'What can I do? Perhaps something will happen. All I can do is wait and see.'

Wait and see. What a pathetically stupid attitude. Did she still believe in her childish dream of a handsome prince riding to the rescue? Florimund or Moses or Jesus Christ or – God? That she'd be lying fast asleep and her saviour would release her to a happy-ever-after future? What nonsense. Sleeping princesses were usually abandoned to their dreaming and dozing, I'd decided. Eventually they stopped dreaming and carried on dozing. And finally, when they began to say things like 'Oh dear, I'm not getting any younger' it was too late to waken them.

Wait and see. Her words died away in the darkening silence. There was nothing more to say.

There was little to say at Euston Station on the day I left. I'd been woken by the drumming of rain on my window and opened my curtain to a leaden sky. There was a finality about getting up. My last breakfast. My last visit to the steamy bathroom where my sister and I had shared secrets. Nothing would ever be the same again.

'Mia, darling,' I heard my mother call. I was soaking myself in the bath. Would that be the last time I'd hear the familiar summons? 'I've managed to organize a lift for all of us to the station.' Her voice had a satisfied ring. She rarely managed to organize anything. Mia's footsteps padded across the landing.

'What?' She sounded sleepy. She'd arranged to be late for work so that she could see me off. Mum hadn't intended coming to Euston.

'Well, yesterday – quite out of the blue – I met Aunty Mavis at the shops. Goodness, I hadn't seen her in years. Do you remember Mavis – how she and Fred and Sara and Ron and Rose used to come for tea every Sunday?'

'Of course I do.' Mia's voice was sharp now. She'd woken up with a start. 'What about her?'

'Oh, she's aged. We all have. I told her about you and Gabriella – and how she was off to Birmingham and how you'd both grown up. She said Uncle Fred had retired. Bad angina or something. That man always was overweight. Anyway, he still has his taxi and Mavis said she was sure he'd adore to take us all to the station. Give him something to do. Wasn't that a good idea?'

There was a ripping sound as Mia opened Mum's curtains. 'No,' she said with surprising viciousness. 'It's a terrible idea. We've managed very nicely without them all the years. Where were they after Dad died? Gone. Disappeared. All sorts of excuses. We certainly don't need them now. Mum, how could you even think of accepting a favour from her? Anyway, I refuse to go in that taxi. I absolutely refuse.'

91

She sounded agitated, almost tearful. I wondered why. I couldn't have given a damn one way or another.

'Don't be silly darling. It's done. All organized. He's collecting us at ten. It would be bad manners to put him off at this stage. He's probably left home already.'

'Mim, you can't refuse to come and say goodbye to your only sister,' I called from the bathroom. 'What's the difference how we get to the station? You don't have to talk to stupid Uncle Fred if you don't feel like it.'

I heard her clumping downstairs.

'Don't worry about the toast today, darling,' Mum sang out cheerily. 'I haven't time to eat. Must do something about my face – seeing Mavis gave me quite a shock. Can't have Fred thinking the same about me. He used to call me "handsome Hilda" you know – "Hilda, the yellow rose of Hendon". Oh, he was funny, was Fred. He did make me laugh . . .'

Her voice faded away. Mia brought her tea wordlessly. I finished packing.

Fred didn't make anyone laugh in the taxi that day. He didn't even try. Mum attempted a few simpering reminiscences, but they echoed hollowly in the darkness of the shabby cab. Uncle Fred looked straight ahead, gripping the steering wheel with thick sausage-fingers. He was sagging with fat and kept sucking in air through a corner of his slack lips. I remembered that he used to smoke a pipe.

'Had to stop,' he said when I mentioned it to break the silence. 'Bad ticker.' That was all. Mia sat pressed into a corner of the seat looking as though she wanted to disappear. When we arrived at Euston, she got out as though ejected by a loaded spring.

'Shall I wait?' mumbled Uncle Fred.

'No.'

'Yes, please Fred.'

Mum and Mia spoke together. They looked at one another. This was becoming ridiculous. All the undertones, hidden currents. It was supposed to have been my day, my departure, my farewell. Who'd needed fat Uncle Fred?

'I'm going on to my office from here,' said Mia.

Mum, eagerly: 'Wait for me then, Fred. I won't be long.'

They walked with me to the platform and stood side by side as I boarded the Birmingham express. I noticed that they were

92

exactly the same height and stood the same way with their feet fixed at an angle of forty-five degrees. But there was little to say.

'Bye Gabby. Take care.'

'Bye Mims.'

'Goodbye my darling. Do look after yourself.'

The train moved away and they became smaller and smaller. Two small, plump women, two midgets, then two tiny specks. My nearest and dearest. Fervently, I thanked the Lord (or whoever looked after atheists) for delivering me from my dearest and nearest. Hallelujah. I was free.

Dearest Mum and Mia,

Life is exciting. Much more than I ever imagined. I have so many friends – particularly a girl called Jennifer Jameson who comes from Saffron Walden. She's asked me to come and stay with her and her family over Christmas and I've accepted – if that's all right. They are very wealthy.

My art teachers seem very pleased with me. They haven't exactly said much, but I'm almost sure they like my work. I've done several cartoons for our college magazine and everyone thinks they're funny.

I'm having a bit of trouble with Mrs Biggs, my landlady – but then, everyone seems to have problems with their landladies. So it gives us lots to laugh about.

I've been out with several boys from art school. No one special (yet). Will keep you informed.

How are you both? Mum, are you keeping well? Mims – how's the job? Do you still see Hannah etc.? I can't exactly say I'm homesick or missing you madly – I'm having far too good a time for that. But I do want to keep in touch. Please write – and let me know about Christmas. All my love,

Gabby

When did the smell of linseed oil start to hurt like lost hope? I'm not sure of the moment or even of the circumstances. One day I breathed in the familiar scent and instead of filling me with heady possibilities, a dizzying sense of potential, it burnt my chest. I coughed and tears filled my eyes.

'Gabriella Marks,' I told myself sternly, 'this is not like you. Pull yourself together and remember you're doing what you always wanted to do, having a great time . . .'

But I wasn't. It was all a huge lie. I had no real talent beyond a flair for clever caricature and in a school swimming with artistic ability I choked and spluttered out of my depth. And no one even thought I was cute or funny – not after the first few months. Not my classmates or my teachers.

'Gabriella, you must aspire to develop a more serious attitude.' The art history lecturer had called me aside to discuss an indifferent essay. Jennifer Jameson, my erstwhile best friend, overheard the reprimand with a superior smile. Christmas with her family in Saffron Walden had been disastrous. I'd felt like a creature from another planet. A lost soul.

'Hendon? How nais,' Mrs Jameson had said, the curling of her upper lip signalling that she didn't really think it was in the least nais.

'Jewish? Most interesting. And you lost your father when you were terribly young I believe?' I'd been about to nod in an appealing, orphan Annie sort of way. But she'd already turned her tinkling small talk to the more important members of the festive gathering. 'Oh, Charles,' she had gushed, 'I see you're ready for another sherry.'

After that I was ignored. Simply left to my own devices – and since I'd never celebrated Christmas before, I'd been at a loss. Followed Jennifer like a motherless lamb asking, 'What happens now, Jens? . . . What do we do next?' until she'd turned on me scornfully, saying, 'You really are a pain in the neck, Gabriella. You're beginning to bore me.'

And now she was witnessing my humiliation. I walked away from the disapproving lecturer as though I hadn't a care in the world and took refuge in a dark corner of a studio amidst drying canvases and scattered tubes of paint. I suppose that must have been the day I breathed in linseed oil and choked on despair.

But there was nothing to do, nothing to say. My letters home remained cheerful and chatty. I spent holidays in Hendon and wondered how the estate remained so stubbornly arid and treeless. And how our house hugged its gloom even in the brightest sunlight. And how Mum passed her days in languid inertia, and how long it would be before she took to her bed permanently. And how Mia endured.

But I was silent about my observations. Said nothing about my lost hope. I giggled shrilly and made jokes that faded in the perpetual twilight and longed to tell my sister how lost and lonely I was – to fling my arms round her neck and weep. But I didn't. Instead, I made scathing remarks about her lack of style, her failure to be a social success, her absence of ambition. I kept making allusions to my achievements. And I wanted to die.

I did consider it. Briefly. Imagined how pathetically appealing I'd be, a tragic heroine. 'Poor Gabriella – we had no idea she was so desperately unhappy.' Then I remembered that I wouldn't be there to enjoy the limelight of my death and abandoned the idea.

It was on an icy December morning during the third year of my course that I bumped into an alternative to suicide. Or at least he bumped into me. His name was Clive Wiseman.

'Oh, I am sorry. Oh dear. Let me help you up.'

'It's all right . . . don't worry. I'm fine.'

'Here. Here's your parcel. Oh gosh, it seems to be broken. I'm *so* sorry. Are you sure you're not hurt?'

'I told you I'm OK. Do stop apologizing, please. The vase doesn't matter. An accident. It could have been worse.'

'Yes. I suppose you're right. Anyway – let me replace it for you. It would make me feel better. Here – we're just outside the shop. This is where you bought it, isn't it?'

'Mmm. Well, yes. That's most kind of you. Really decent.'

'The least I can do. Such a bumbling idiot – and you're so little. I could have crushed the life out of you. Come . . .'

. . . And you think the Messiah will arrive in a chariot or down the chimney? Or, like the Melanesians, you believe that human fulfilment will be achieved with the arrival of a cargo of Western-type goods by ship or plane, and you build wharves and airstrips and warehouses to welcome your cargo Messiah? Or that he'll never come? Or that he was born in a stable and has been and gone?

Well, you're wrong. Quite wrong.

For it was he who walked in Birmingham in a three-piece suit with hair combed across the top to hide a balding pate and shiny shoes ill-equipped to cope with the ice of a December pavement. Sorry, so terribly sorry to have knocked down and winded poor little Gabriella Marks. Determined to make it up to her.

And she, crushed by more than a clumsy chartered accountant, wanted so desperately to be saved.

And he helping her to her feet, felt her lightness, felt so strong. Such a – man.

And she, catching hold of his arm to support herself on shaky legs, caught a whiff of his male smell and thought oh no. Oh no. Oh yes.

And God and the angels fell about with laughter. This was too funny for Words.

Clive Wiseman. Herbert Green. I looked at my sister, wiped the sweat from my brow and pointed the kitchen knife at the carp cut in two on the chopping board. Stop it, I wanted to say. Stop staring at me so. You know more than enough about me already. Sisters don't *have* to tell one another everything.

'And so, Mims,' I smiled, 'what do you pick? Heads or tails?'

❧ 9 ❧

'Heads or tails?' That's what *he*'d asked the first time we met. 'Heads or tails – Mia, is it? Ah, Mia, what a lovely name. Well, you choose then, Mia. Mia-with-the-golden-hair – will you declare my destiny?'

And he'd laughed. Not the way my sister laughed, bitterly when she looked at the poor dead fish and we knew that it was too late to choose, that everything had been for nothing. No, Seamus O'Reilly's laughter was life. A happy accident. A rainbow-wrapped surprise.

'Serendipity.'

I tossed the word at him, across the table in the corner of the smoky pub, over the hand that covered the fateful coin. He caught it and opened his fingers a little as though to trap it with the shilling. His eye caught mine. I was embarrassed. I hadn't meant to say anything. I didn't usually say anything much. What on earth had come over me? And such a silly, whimsical, Mickey Mouse sort of word . . .

'Has Hannah told you then? About the Princes of Serendip?'

I shook my head. At least he wasn't making fun of me. 'No. The word just came to me. I don't know what made me say it. What about the Princes?'

'Well – there were three of them. Just like me and my two brothers. Hannah started it, told us a story one day about the princes and their discoveries. They didn't actually set out to make them, you understand. They sort of happened. After we'd heard the first one, we started to make up more. And – I suppose I carried on. Inventing stories, believing in happy accidents.'

His sister laughed. 'And now you want my friend Mia to utter the call that will decide your future. Seamus, are you really going to base your decision to stay in London or return to Dublin on the fall of a coin?'

He nodded.

I believed him. And suddenly, with all my heart, I wanted him to stay. The pub noises babbled around us but our small round table was an oasis of silence. They were waiting for me.

'Stay,' I said to Seamus, suddenly gripped by panic, struggling to control my voice. 'If you want to stay here, why don't you do it? Why let chance decide something like this?'

'So – you want me to stay?'

He knew. What the hell. I nodded. He believed me. I could see he believed me. That he wanted to stay, to put fate back into his pocket with the rest of his change and say forget it. I'll decide. But he couldn't. Not Seamus who believed in happy accidents.

'Won't you choose? Head or tail? Please, Mia, be the voice of my destiny,' he said.

I shut my eyes. 'Heads,' I said quickly. Best to get this over with. There was the rest of my life to attend to. Mum would be wanting her tea. The curtains in the sitting-room needed washing. The gas account needed paying. Plants needed watering . . .

Slowly, slowly he removed his hand. And there was the coin, dull and dented round the edge. And I could see in the smoky half light the outline of a profile. And Seamus looked up, smiling.

'It's serendipity,' he said.

That was how it began. It. Life. My only fairy-tale. Perhaps that *was* the fairy-tale.

Once upon a time, at a small secluded table in the King's Arms, a coin fell in a space between half-full glasses of lager and an ashtray brimming with butts. A magic coin that told a handsome poet-prince that the plain young woman opposite him was a princess in disguise. 'Stay with her, cherish her,' it whispered, 'and you'll see how wonderfully she'll bloom. She's yours, your happy accident.' And the prince said, 'I will. I'll stay.' And the woman felt herself budding. She blossomed as he spoke. Everything seemed possible, even living happily ever after.

But that's not how it ended. The fairy-tale finished and the real life began.

'Mia, tell me – tell me about yourself. I want to know everything.'

'You don't. Not really. It's all terribly boring. Nothing exciting has ever happened to me.'

'You were born, Mia. Wasn't that excitement enough?'

No Seamus, I thought. Nothing was exciting. Nothing stirred me, not really. Not until you arrived with your sky-blue eyes and the words that spilt like nectar from the most perfect teeth, mouth, head, body in the world. For me. For me. And I drank them, gulped them greedily. This was better than chocolate – far, far better than the biggest box of chocolates stolen in the dark of the night.

'Well . . .'

'Mia, listen to me. You must stop putting yourself down. You've been doing it all evening. There's something about you, something special, Mia. I love saying your name, looking at you. Yes, yes I do. Why do you frown at me so suspiciously? Haven't you been told things like this before?'

'No,' I laughed. I couldn't help it. Me, Mia, being courted? Flirted with by the likes of a man who, according to his sister, had half the female population of Dublin on its knees?

Seamus, what *did* you see when you looked at me in the dimness of Hannah's flat that night, the night I'd chosen heads? Maybe you reckoned that the dull and dumbstruck female sipping coffee so correctly could be your perfect foil? Plump and blonde to your dark leanness, slow and thoughtful to your mercurial wit. Rebecca of Sunnybrook Farm to your Abelard. Romeo and Little Miss Muffet . . .

Perhaps. Perhaps. But it didn't really matter. Not then. I savoured my coffee, swallowed your words and laughed.

'Seamus, what are you going to do? In London? Where – how are you going to live?' I had to ask. Perhaps he wasn't really going to stay, didn't even exist. Maybe I was imagining him.

'What a practical bent the girl has. Where? How? I'll survive. Don't worry, I've made up my mind and I always survive. Perhaps I'll live here for a time – if Hannah will have me. I'll earn money somehow – cleaning houses, serving at tables, bearing messages. And I'll carry on writing until one day they recognize my talent. Seamus O'Reilly, Ireland's greatest living playwright. And you? Where – how do *you* live?'

His dreams. My drab reality. I could hardly bear to lay them alongside one another.

'With my mother. In Hendon. Actually – oh, gosh, look at the time – I must get home. She had a terrible headache when I left this evening and I promised I wouldn't be late. Will you excuse me?'

'I'll come with you – escort you home to your ailing parent. If you'd like me to, that is?'

'You don't have to. It's a long way and the trains aren't regular. I can manage. Really, you don't have to worry . . .' Why was I saying this when I so longed for him to be with me? Mia, speak, I told myself. Speak out. Grasp your chance for once. '. . . but – I suppose – yes, I *would* like you to come with me, Seamus.' There. I'd done it. For the first time ever I'd stated what I wanted and it hadn't even been difficult.

'Good. Excellent. Hannah – where is the girl? Ah, Hannah. I'm accompanying your friend home. D'you have a spare key so I don't wake you when I get back? Come, Mia – let's go then.'

'Hannah, thank you. Thank you for – everything. See you at work tomorrow.'

We stepped out into the night and he took my hand. We walked together and I felt him next to me. We were side by side, step by step, mile by mile. His nearness took my breath away.

'Would you like to come in?' Please, Seamus. Please come in, I prayed silently. Don't go. Don't leave. I was terrified that he'd disappear. Another lost fantasy.

'Thank you – for a while. Yes, I'd like to, Mia.'

'Sh. Here – let me put the light on. Stay here, Seamus. Sit down. I'll go up and check if Mum's asleep. It won't take long.'

Mum slept. Gentle, rhythmic snores lapped through her door on to the landing. Carefully, stealthily, I crept downstairs.

'Coffee?'

'No. Come here, Mia. Next to me. I want to talk to you, I long to touch you.'

Me? He longed for me? In a trance, I sat beside him and felt his hand gently smoothing my hair, caressing the hollow of my neck. We talked softly and he stroked me and I melted till I was soft and warm all over. Then he drew me close towards him and I prayed he wouldn't see my plainness and realize his mistake.

'Mia, look at me. Why are your eyes shut?'

I opened them, blinked at his nearness. 'Are you – sure you want to – be here – with me?' I asked.

'There's nowhere else in the world I'd rather be. Mia, do you know how lucky I was when you called heads?'

'*I* was lucky. I longed for you to stay.'

He kissed me and I thought my heart would stop. For ever. The carpet came up to meet us, clouds of maroon and gold and green, an Axminster heaven. And I clung to him, my skin touching his. Mouths, faces, everything dissolving together.

'Heads or tails?' he whispered and I felt the hotness of his breath.

'Heads, Seamus. Heads.'

We were locked together, Seamus gasping and pressing against me and into me, tearing into me, and suddenly I thought I heard a gruff panting voice. 'Blondie . . . little Blondie.' Pain, such hot searing pain. I thought I'd choke on the tears that closed my throat. A tobacco smell and tears that welled from deep, deep inside.

'No,' I sobbed. 'No, no, no.'

'Oh, Mia – oh yes.'

And it was over, all over. But I couldn't stop sobbing.

'Mia? Mia?' He frowned as he looked at me, and cupped my chin in his palm. So gently. 'What's the matter? Don't cry. Please don't cry.'

I wanted to say it's nothing Seamus, nothing at all. I'd have given anything to be able to lie that it was wonderful, he was wonderful. But I was struck dumb by tears and pain and remorse. I thought I'd never stop crying and was sure that he'd never want to see me again. Princesses didn't have swollen eyes and matted hair and shameful secrets.

I didn't believe him when he said, 'You're lovely, Mia, we'll be together again soon,' as he left. He didn't mean it. I was sure we wouldn't. Ever. I leaned against the shut front door and the grief that racked my body was almost more than I could bear.

*

Oh, the tears that I wasted. The oceans of tears that mourned his departure. Seamus came back. Of course he came back, again and again, like a ball attached to a bat with an elastic string. Like a cat to a never-emptying jug of cream.

'I love your softness, your dreamy softness,' he'd say, holding me till I felt like a limp rag doll in his arms. Cradled and cuddled like – yes, like my Ugly Baba. 'Mia, I love your sadness.'

When he said that, I knew why Seamus O'Reilly kept returning. It *was* my sadness. He was addicted to the sorrow that convulsed my body when he tore into me, time after time, saying, 'Mia – oh yes, oh yes.'

'Next time,' he'd promise afterwards, out of breath, gently smoothing my hair, 'next time, my Mia, it will be better. You'll be filled with joy – you'll never cry again – you'll see.' That's how I knew there'd be a next time, that he was captivated by the challenge. I also believed that never would he fill me with joy. Not that way. It was a part of me that I thought I had lost for ever.

But I had Seamus. In the beginning it was like a tremulous reed-tune playing hesitantly in a far corner of my consciousness. Then it grew louder, stronger – a chamber duet, a triumphant trio. A secret symphony that added a glorious silent score to the dullness of my days.

'Mia, darling.' She still called me each morning. At home, nothing had changed. 'You're off to work then, my darling?'

I nodded. 'I'll bring up your tea and toast before I leave.'

She caught hold of my arm. 'Mia, will you be in this evening? Perhaps we can watch telly together?'

I hesitated. Seamus hadn't said anything and I couldn't commit myself. She saw my reluctance.

'It doesn't matter,' she sighed. 'I can't imagine what you're up to each night with your new friends. I haven't even met them. Why don't you bring them home, Mia? This Hannah you're always talking about? Her brother, her cousins? Who *are* these people?'

I shrugged. It was none of her business. My world. Nothing to do with her at all.

'Mia . . .' her voice grew suddenly weaker. Her grip on my arm tightened. 'Mia, I went to see Dr Mitchell – about my headaches. They are getting worse. He says I have high blood pressure. Is that dangerous? Dr Mitchell says I must have plenty

102

of rest. A good diet and plenty of rest.' She sank into her pillows, overwhelmed by frightened self-pity. 'Isn't it terrible, Mia – the things that happen to me? Losing my husband, then Gabby going off like that, and now you're so busy I hardly see you. How can I possibly rest? I won't last this way. I'm not going to last.'

'Mum, you'll be all right. Lots of people have high blood pressure. I'm here to look after you – and Gabby's only gone to Birmingham. She'll be back next month for the summer holiday. Listen, I'll come straight home after work. I promise. We can spend the evening together, watch television, whatever you want.'

'You're a darling. A real treasure. I don't know what I'd do without you.'

I heard my footsteps thudding angrily downstairs. Trapped. Selfish old cow, I muttered, buttering her toast. High blood pressure or not, she'd probably last for ever, pickled in the brine of her older daughter's tears.

'Here, your breakfast.' I laid down my dutiful offering, pecked her cheek. 'Bye, Mum. Remember what Dr Mitchell said. Have a good rest.'

What a laugh, I thought bitterly. Any more rest and she'd be comatose. I shut the front door, shut her in with her grey misery and endless litany.

And as I stepped into the light, I listened for my own song, my secret refrain. My Seamus. The splash of technicolour in the dismal monochrome of my life. What did it matter if I couldn't see him that night? There'd be tomorrow and tomorrow and tomorrow. He loved me. He loved my bottomless pit of sadness.

'Mims – can I come into the bathroom for a chat? Like old times? Please?'

She was back. 'I'm fine,' she said, smiling brightly when I asked her about art school, her friends, her life. Too brightly, I thought. But I didn't pursue the thought. She didn't give me the chance.

'And you, Mims? How are you? Has Herbert surfaced again – or is there another man in your life?' She said the word 'man' with a derisory smile.

'No,' I said abruptly. If only she knew. But she wouldn't know. I wouldn't tell her. Seamus was mine.

'And how's work? Are you still friends with that Irish girl, that Hannah?'

'Everything's the same, Gabby. Yes, Hannah's still there. We're friends.'

Was it disappointment that crossed her face? A shadow, certainly, as she glanced away from me. I traced circles with my finger in the bath and watched the ripples receding. Gabby was perched in her old position on the cork-topped laundry box. She looked at me, then hesitated, then looked at me again. I tensed. Was she about to comment on my body? Would she tell me that I looked as though I'd gained weight? I sucked in my stomach.

'Mims – tell me, tell me please? Are you happy?'

Her face was pinched, eyes large and intent and focused searchingly on mine. She really wanted to know. Did she care – or was this her way of stripping me bare, gaining strength from my weakness, power from my admission of defeat? I sat up in the bath and crossed my arms over my chest. I wasn't playing. Not this time. This time I had something to lose.

'You tell me, Gabs? Are *you* happy?'

We looked at one another and I knew that we both cared. Both of us wanted desperately for the other to answer. Gabby struggled with herself and I could see she had something to say. Her mouth almost opened several times, she half-frowned, and at last she applied the brightest smile she could muster.

'Happy? Me? Why shouldn't I be?'

The moment was lost. I washed and she chattered in her old brittle way about school and social success and the terrible bore her friend Jennifer was turning out to be.

'It was deadly dull with her family over Christmas,' she sighed. 'I'll never accept an invitation there again. This year I shall definitely come home – we'll have a really cosy time together. Just Mum and you and me. Won't we, Mims?'

She looked at me appealingly. I thought of Christmas and the empty void that would be Seamus far away in Dublin with Hannah and his family. Would he miss me? A little? I knew that I'd hurt with longing for him. We'd make our annual pilgrimage to see the bright lights of Regent Street and I'd feel far away from the festivities and even further away from Seamus.

'Won't we, Mims?' she repeated impatiently, insistent on a reassuring reply.

'Of course,' I said. 'You and me and Mum. The three of us.'

She came home in December with a bone china vase and a new name on her lips. Clive Wiseman.

'He's so mature,' she kept repeating. 'Makes the people in my class seem like children. D'you know, Mims, he's thirty-two. He treats me like the most precious, delicate piece of porcelain. Makes me feel so, so special. Oh, I do love having an older man. I really had outgrown art students.'

This time her smile was less forced. She sat on the laundry basket as though it were a throne. Gabriella, princess royal of the Marks sisters, had found her Prince Charming.

'What does he do?'

I hated asking, was heartily sick of hearing about this answer to a maiden's prayer, but I was curious.

'An accountant. A *chartered* accountant. He works in partnership with his father in Birmingham. But, Mims – and this is still a secret – he's been offered a brilliant job in London. Here, in the City. Clive doesn't know what to do, but Mr Wiseman – that's his father, an absolute darling – said Clive must do what's best for himself. Opportunities like that don't arise more than once in a lifetime. They're such a – a sterling family. Clive's got an older sister too, you know. Rebecca. She's married to a Birmingham doctor, a gynaecologist. Two gorgeous children. A girl and a boy, naturally. Rebecca doesn't stop telling me how lucky I am to have caught Clive's eye. "Our family treasure," she calls him. "He's going to make some woman very happy – the best husband in the world."' Gabby shut her eyes, clasped her hands together and looked ecstatic. 'I *am* lucky. If only you could get out a bit more and meet someone like Clive, it would be so good for you, Mim.'

That did it. I'd had enough. I hadn't meant to say a word about Seamus. I'd sworn to keep him secret. But her smug condescension, her high-voiced, endless monologue of self-satisfaction and eulogy to some earnest accountant – sorry, *chartered* accountant – had been too much.

'Actually,' I said as off-handedly as I could, 'there is someone I've been seeing rather often recently.'

'*Is* there? Who?' She blinked with surprise, then laughed. 'Herbert hasn't come back on the scene, has he?'

I shook my head. 'His name is Seamus O'Reilly. A writer – playwright actually.'

'Seamus? Irish . . . nothing to do with that, what's her name, Hannah, is he?'

'Her brother.'

She was silent, frowning as she digested this information. Then she took a deep breath, assumed her most experienced voice and said, 'Mims, do you realize what you're doing? They're strange and dangerous people, the Irish – they'd easily take advantage of someone like you, so good and innocent. And Jewish. What does Mum say? I know she's absolutely thrilled about Clive. Said she's always wanted her daughters to marry Jewish men. Professional Jewish men. Not that we're about to get married – yet. After all, we've only known one another for a month. But Mims, it was like this.' She hooked her two index fingers together till they were knotted like a Chinese puzzle, stared at them, then suddenly remembered that we weren't talking about Clive any more. 'What *does* Mum say about this Seamus?'

'Nothing. She hasn't met him. I haven't told her about him. No one knows except you – and, of course, Hannah.'

'Oh.'

'Gabs – ' I couldn't help myself, I longed so much to talk to someone about him – 'Gabs, he's wonderful. The most amazing thing that's ever happened to me. And he cares for me, I know he does. We talk – about everything. His ideas, my ideas. Until I met Seamus, I never believed that I could be interesting to anyone. And – he says he loves to look at me. Imagine that? Can you imagine that, Gabby?'

'And what does *he* look like?' she asked, almost as though a man would be certain to have an unsightly defect if he could find me attractive. But I didn't notice the irony, so caught up was I in communicating my joy. My serendipity. My Seamus.

God help my naïvety.

'D'you know, Gabs, how one has an image in one's mind of a hero, an all-purpose hero, a figure who wins battles and fair princesses and holds people spellbound with his poetry and songs and dark, lean beauty. When I saw Seamus for the first time, my heart stopped and I thought, "That's him."'

There was a brief pause before she burst out laughing. 'A rogue. A handsome Irish rogue. Mims – I have to tell you this. I'm sure you don't want to hear it, but if *I* don't say it, who will? After all, what are sisters for? Mia, you're going to get hurt. Terribly hurt. People like Seamus are dangerous. After all, he must be after something more than your beauty and wit. Be careful.'

There was nothing to say. She was probably right. What indeed *were* sisters for if not to voice the things one dreaded to hear? My limbs felt heavy as I lifted myself out of the bath to end our conversation. I'd had enough. But her words continued to gather in the steam that fogged the room and misted the mirror. He hadn't tried anything, had he? Of course not. Not yet. He would, she assured me darkly. Only a matter of time. Fortunately, she didn't have that problem with Clive. He really respected her.

'Honestly, Mims, I never thought I'd meet a man so safe, gentle, dependable . . .' Then she asked off-handedly, 'And so, when can I meet this Seamus of yours?'

'You can't – at least, not this holiday. He's in Dublin with his family.'

I pulled out the plug and watched the soapy water spiralling downwards into the centre of the earth. There was a deep gurgle and I remembered Aunty Rose's warning to slow, dreamy little Mia: 'Out,' she'd say sharply. 'Hurry now. Out of the bath, else you'll be sucked down the plughole.' I remembered my terror.

'Gabby,' I asked, 'were you ever frightened of being dragged down the plughole with the bathwater? When you were a child?'

'No,' she said immediately. 'Not me. You were the one with all the fears and superstitions.'

And dreams, I added silently. And secrets. I watched the water going down, down, down and imagined it melting into the depths of a faraway ocean and then coming back with the tides. And then being lapped up by the clouds and sprinkled like tears over Dublin. Over Seamus. Soaking him with sadness, with longing to return to his Mia even though she lacked beauty and wit.

*

'It rained almost every day. I thought Dublin would drown. It's so good to be back in London – with you.'

A miracle. He'd returned. I felt my hand inside his, resting on the warm wood of the table in the smoky King's Arms, and I sipped my half-lager and wondered whether I'd been granted a taste of heaven. Slightly bitter perhaps – but I could see the attraction of an eternity in God's Arms drinking amber alcoholic nectar hand in hand with Seamus.

'A miracle,' he was saying. How could he have guessed? But no, he was talking about something else. Something wonderful he'd brought from Dublin to tell me. A fairy-tale?

'When I was about six years old,' he began, 'I was given a prize for the best attendance record at Sunday school. *The Child's Picture Book of Miracles*. I didn't think much of it. Who wanted a soppy old book with silly saints and tedious angels? I put it away. Didn't give it a thought until maybe a year later, when I had measles and nothing to do. I'd read everything on my bookshelf, except the *Picture Book of Miracles*. And it turned out to be just as boring as I'd expected, except for one picture. The only colour picture in the whole book, and I couldn't get it out of my mind.'

He paused and looked over my shoulder into the distance, as though the picture were projected on to a far wall. I followed his gaze and saw a dartboard and heard cheers. Someone had just scored a bull's-eye.

'What was it?' I asked. 'What did the picture show?'

'It was the Holy Family floating on a silver cloud. And in the centre was the Virgin Mary, so beautiful, so pure and beautiful. After I'd seen that picture, every time I went to church I'd close my eyes and try and imagine it. I never told anyone. It wasn't the sort of thing boys were supposed to think about. But it became a habit. When everyone had their eyes shut and their hands squeezed together praying, I was looking at my vision of the Holy Family, trying so hard to see the Virgin Mary's face. But I couldn't. I couldn't make it out. All I ever saw was an indistinct, glowing form.

'Until this Christmas. This time I saw her, Mia. I really saw her. Not clearly. But just enough to make out that she had blonde hair. Mia.' He gripped my hand tightly, stared at me intensely. 'I knew then – without any doubt at all – that she was you.'

108

Silence. What could I say to that? 'No Seamus. You were wrong. Mistaken identity. You see, you don't really know me, only my sadness. And sadness isn't goodness or purity. Go back to church and look again.' I might have said that, but then I'd risk losing him. I was certain that I wasn't his miracle Mary but without a shadow of doubt he was my miracle man. He'd brought me a fairy-tale from the land of the Blarney Stone, so I'd give him one in return.

'Seamus,' I said, 'I also have something to tell you. A story. Perhaps a miracle too, in its own way.' I told him about the leaden princess. And about the prince finding her in her cave. And about her melting. Softening and melting in his arms. 'I think – he was you.'

He didn't laugh. He didn't tell me, as Gabby had done, that it was a stupid, stupid story. That princesses lying around in caves didn't get woken by handsome princes. Instead he asked: 'What then? What d'you imagine happened after they left the cave? Surely they didn't stay there for ever?'

'I'm not sure. My dream always stopped there and then I stopped believing in my dream. But, I suppose . . .' I shut my eyes, tried to think beyond the happily-ever-after endings which left princes and princesses frozen in embraces in caves, before altars, out of the teeth of danger. What then? 'I suppose they travelled on together until they reached the promised land. Their promised land. Their land of milk and honey.'

'And then?'

'Oh Seamus – stop cross-questioning me. What's the difference? Does it really matter? Let's get to the promised land and we'll find out what happens after that.'

'Yes, let's.'

He meant it. Just as Seamus had tossed a coin to point the way to his future, he now wanted to follow my fairy-tale to its Never Never Land. To his land of make-believe – perhaps the Peter Pan land where grown men act like irresponsible boys and achieve eternal mothering. Was I to be his Wendy? I shuddered. More than any other story-book character, I'd always identified with ever-responsible Wendy, the girl who'd been flown to paradise under false pretences. Off I'd go with Seamus to *our* promised land only to find myself ironing his shirts, baking his bread and queuing in supermarkets for the milk and honey.

'I don't know,' I said. 'Isn't it sometimes better to leave dreams in our imagination? We may not be talking about the same sort of land. We could be terribly disappointed.'

'Mia, I'm not talking about dreams. I mean us spending a fortnight or so in the only country that has ever dared to declare itself a promised land, a Holy Land. Israel. It's to do with a play I'm working on, about an Irishman who goes on a modern pilgrimage to Jerusalem. I need to see the place and at last I've managed to save a bit of money. Mia, come with me. It's your country. Your people. Let's see it together.'

'My country? I've never felt that, Seamus – never thought of myself as having a country or a people or even a family. I don't even feel particularly Jewish – although I suppose Israel's Law of Return would mean that I could always find a home there. But go there with you? I don't know. I don't know if it would be possible . . . Mum . . . Gabby . . .' In truth I was scared to death. Tempted but terrified.

'The princess – the princess in the cave – would she have gone?' he asked softly, putting down his glass and taking hold of my other hand.

I nodded. She'd have gone to the moon with the man who melted her.

'So – you'll come.'

'I'll try.'

He nodded. He knew I'd come. How could I have resisted?

It wasn't my country. They weren't my people. I felt no sense of shared history or common heritage with the loud-voiced pedestrians who pushed me aside on pavements and buses and ate sunflower seeds and spoke a guttural language that sounded nothing like the melodious Hebrew chanted by my uncles for the forgotten festival prayers of my childhood.

'I don't think I've ever felt so alien in my life,' I said to Seamus as we walked together along the Via Dolorosa. He solemnly counted the Stations of the Cross while I cringed from the undressing stares of street vendors and the pungent smells of spices and sweat and coffee and incense.

It wasn't my country. But it was the promised land. When we'd arrived at Lod airport some passengers had kissed the hot ground and Seamus had kissed me. And something had stirred deep inside me. Something more than the melting warmth that always suffused my body at his touch. A promise.

'Mia – this is going to be wonderful. The two of us here together. I'm so glad that you managed to come.'

It had not been easy. There was Mum to entreat and placate, my guilt to assuage. 'I'm going with a few friends from work,' I'd told her. 'It's time – I need a break. Only a fortnight. I'll prepare food before I leave, lots of it. We'll ask Elsie to do some extra cleaning. You can arrange card-games, see your friends, talk to Gabby on the telephone.'

She'd agreed doubtfully. 'All right, my darling. But please do be careful. I don't know what I'd do if something happened to you. I suppose I'll manage for two weeks, but if . . .'

'Nothing will happen. I'll be back on the first.'

Once she'd accepted my impending trip as irrevocable, she suddenly wanted to talk about it. 'I nearly went to Israel once,' she told me wistfully. 'It was Palestine then. I was going to stay with an uncle who had a sort of – smallholding – in a place called Kfar Tikva. He used to write to my mother about the hardships and the heat. I longed for heat. I was always such a cold person. But then I met your father and everyone decided that it would be best for me to marry. So I never got to Palestine. The uncle in Kfar Tikva must be dead.'

The uncle in Kfar Tikva *was* dead. Long dead. We sought his smallholding and found a sun-baked block of flats steaming in the heat. I decided then that this must be the place to which people come when all else has failed. The end of the world.

'We've found it,' I said to Seamus, as we trudged along burning untarred roads in search of shade. 'The last resort.'

I'd also found Utopia. In hotel rooms and boarding houses down the length and across the narrow breadth of the land, I discovered – sex. The promise in those new deep stirrings at Lod airport had been fulfilled.

'You're not crying,' he marvelled, tracing his finger down the dry furrows beneath my eyes. I clung to him, wanted to hold on to my happiness for ever.

'No Seamus,' I said. 'It was wonderful.' I meant it.

'You're not sad any more?' he asked.

'No,' I sighed contentedly. 'The leaden princess has entered the land of milk and honey.'

*

Utopia: Sir Thomas More's island of perfection.

Cloud-cuckoo-land: a dream sky-city built by Aristophanes' birds.

Crow Airlines operates a regular direct shuttle service between these two destinations. Passengers bound for Utopia, however, should be aware that, owing to industrial action, they may experience difficulty gaining entry. There are no current landing problems in Cloud-cuckoo-land, but passengers are advised to be inoculated against an epidemic of rude awakenings and crash helmets are compulsory. These should provide some protection in the likely event of coming down to earth with a bump.

How witty we become as we laugh at our contortions and futile aspirations through the lens of the retrospectoscope. So witty. So wise. Yet if I'd had it all again – the whole thing, all the bits – what would I have chosen? Heads or tails?

'Heads,' I said to my sister, pointing to the cerebral regions of the carp who'd never had a chance to choose. 'I usually pick heads.'

❧ 10 ❧

'I always pick heads,' she said, as though she were on some winning streak. As though in the great casino of life, Mia Marks had had a glorious run of luck. Jackpot after jackpot. Indeed.

'Do you, Mims?' I asked sweetly. Why was I so angry? So what if she wanted to delude herself. 'And what good has that done, may I ask? Since when did either of us ever win anything?'

She didn't answer. She hardly seemed to hear. A remote half-smile hovered on her face and it made me furious. As long as I could remember I'd kept a scrupulous eye on the main chance. So vigilant. So careful. And now, after everything, was she suggesting that she'd been the one who'd taken it?

Oh, who cared? What was chance anyway? I used to believe that marriage was a game of chance until I read somewhere that betrothed couples tended to have earlobes of an identical length. That's when I came to the conclusion that heaven was a place where earlobes were sorted into matching pairs.

'Aha!' I could hear it. The voice of Angel Joe, dearly beloved father of Mia and Gabriella Marks, late dutiful husband of helpless Hilda. 'A 1.38-incher – a perfect partner for little Gabby.'

And he had set before her the fleshy lobes of eligible Clive Wiseman. And she'd studied them, measured their pros and cons, considered and said, 'Yes. I'll take them. What choice do I have? I may never find another pair exactly 1.38 inches ever again. But tell me, father dear . . .'

'What is it, my daughter? What would you like to know? Now is your chance.'

My chance. I should have asked about the results of the latest heavenly consumer survey into the durability of wedded bliss.

About death and the hereafter. About his Boss and the Messiah. Instead I wanted to know about all the odd earlobes that might never find matching mates. That worried me.

'My daughter,' he said thoughtfully. He'd become profound and somewhat pompous, I noticed. Perhaps the hereafter did that to one. 'Never is not a word we tend to use here. According to our most recent statistics, an overwhelming majority of earlobes last longer than the average marriage. This allows me to say with some certitude that in the end most lobes will find a way.'

His bland reassurance was like the optimism with which I used to regard the odd socks that kept reappearing in the laundry basket. 'Your mates will turn up one day,' I'd tell them repeatedly – with diminishing conviction. Until finally I despaired and threw them all away. For despite Angel Joe's sponsored message (and after all it *had* come to me on behalf of Hope Incorporated, Heaven's Limited Company), I had a strong suspicion that there was a dark nether world populated by sad single socks and odd earlobes. The hell that awaits dead sinners with a strong sense of order. Clive Wiseman, for instance. He hated untidiness. Odd socks, loose ends, his single state. Had a compulsion to sort things out.

That's why he'd leaned over and tweaked my left earlobe as I sat in the passenger seat of his new silver Volvo one Friday night. He had said: 'Gabriella, will you marry me . . .'

And I thought it was love because I'd never had my earlobe tweaked before.

'Yes Clive. I will.' I replied without hesitation. The night was still and the moon was full. And I was angry. I'd just had a postcard from the land of Israel, a majestic procession of camels across hot desert sands, with the words HAVING A WONDERFUL TIME, LOVE FROM MIA XXX on the back. I had thought about me in rainy Birmingham and wanted to kill her. And her Seamus. Her 'all-purpose hero', for God's sake. It made me think of some sophisticated robotic appliance that beat baddies, swept women off their feet and galloped off into the sunset, still squeaky-clean.

When she'd told me about him, at first I hadn't believed her.

Not Mia, I thought. Not my boring big sister who'd only half-managed to interest Herbert Green. And then I'd looked at her glowing face and known that whatever Seamus really was (and I may well have been right, he probably was a rogue), to my sister he was a prince. And I had a commoner. Clive was indeed respectable and safe and mature and affectionate, but not even in my wildest dreams could I connect him with royalty. For one thing, he had chronic hay fever and controlled constipation.

'If only I could manage a regular bowel movement without medication,' he'd said wistfully one evening not long after I'd met him and once we'd got to the point of exchanging confidences. 'Isn't it wonderful how we can talk so openly to one another? I feel I can tell you anything.'

Maybe. But no Prince Charming would have alluded to his bowels, still less to the fact that they actually moved. On the other hand, Clive was real. A real, live eligible accountant who was set to rescue me from the ignominy of art school failure and to carry me off into the bosom of his family. And I needed a bosom. I needed a family more than royalty. More than anything else in the world.

But I was angry that my need should have been so unbearably strong and that's partly why I said yes. At least I'd have something to show for it. And anyway Clive was good and suitable and I was sure I'd grow to love him.

'Oh Gabby,' he said, 'I'm so glad. I – love you.'

He waited for my response but I couldn't say it. Not yet. 'I'll be a very good wife. You'll be glad you married me.'

He kissed me and I breathed in deeply and smelt his soap and his man-smell and was reassured. It would be for the best. He'd make me feel safe and I'd make him feel special. Wasn't that what marriage was all about?

It certainly seemed that way in the Wiseman household – except perhaps the other way round. Bernice kept a constant caring eye on Eli and he told her repeatedly how wonderful she was.

'A cook – and what a cook! No one can run a home the way my Bernice does. I'm telling you, Gabriella, in all England there can't be many wives like mine.'

'Oh, go on Eli. Here, have some more liver. It's good for you. Remember what the doctor said about your anaemia.'

The dialogue on Friday nights was as predictable as the litany

115

when Bernice lit the Sabbath candles and Eli blessed the sweet red wine. At first it enchanted me. All of it. The ritual, the sense of continuity, the warmth that was dished out with the same insistent abundance as the chicken soup. The arms that enfolded me with tearful words of welcome as Clive's intended, his chosen one. Now I know that the same level of family enthusiasm greeted his choice of a new car or dinner-jacket. There was a chorus of marvel when he picked his nose. But at the time, for lonely Gabby Marks, it was all irresistible.

'Gabriella,' said Eli solemnly after he'd sipped the sanctified wine, 'I want to say how happy we were when Clive told us the news. I said to Bernice – naturally, she's a little upset about him leaving, our only son and all that – I said to her, "Bernice, we're gaining another daughter. A lovely Jewish girl. And grandchildren, please God. What more could we want?"'

And what more could I want? Did I have any right to ask for anything else? I suppressed the vague unease that stirred in my chest and smiled at my new 'sister' sitting serenely across the table. Rebecca was flanked by six-year-old Simon and four-year-old Justine. They sipped their soup without spilling a drop. Perfect children. A perfect kosher home. Richard Bloomfield, my future brother-in-law-the-gynaecologist, clearly kept strict internal order.

'I can't tell you how – glad – I am to be marrying Clive.' I couldn't manage any more. He squeezed my hand. Bernice Wiseman put her soup spoon down, picked up her linen napkin and dabbed at her eyes. It will be all right, I told myself. It will be fine . . .

'Gabby my darling, what wonderful news. I've been praying that this would happen ever since you first mentioned Clive. Oh what a relief it will be to have one daughter married and settled. Perhaps this will inspire your sister to start looking in the right direction.'

'Have you heard from her?'

'A postcard from the Dead Sea. Saying she was having a wonderful time. That's all. I do miss her. Thank goodness she's due back on Sunday and things will return to normal. I'm so pleased you're coming to London to tell her about your plans.

116

We can talk about the wedding. A family wedding. Oh, Gabriella, you *have* made me happy.'

All this spreading of happiness was making me uncomfortable. It seemed to confirm the suspicions I've always had about the motives of the Good Fairy of Pantomimeland. I always wondered what she got out of her benevolence. A house in the suburbs and a lifelong supply of chopped liver perhaps? No, I've never trusted smiling saints. I certainly wouldn't have put much faith in Saint Gabriella.

Nor did I trust my sister when she descended from the Holy Land with a face like a blissful angel. A fallen angel? Most likely with that Seamus in her host.

'Are you sure, Gabby? Are you absolutely sure about what you're doing?'

Of course I was sure. And anyway – what right had she to question my decision? What alternatives did she offer? An eternity of life with mother? A dangerous liaison with a supposedly handsome Irish playwright, who probably didn't exist since she steadfastly refused to let me meet him?

'I'd love you to come up to Birmingham and meet the Wisemans. Bernice – that's Clive's mother – has invited you and Mum to spend next weekend there. She says we must all get to know one another at once. After all, we're going to be family.'

I looked at Mia. She seemed to be in another world. Something had changed in my sister. I had a sudden thought that she'd caught hold of something – a truth, a vision of life that would for ever escape me. I'd been panting after it and she'd caught it. I was scared and then angry.

'Aren't we, Mims? Why don't you say anything? Why don't you congratulate me?'

I so badly wanted to tell her about my doubts. To explain why bold Gabby who'd flown away and soared upwards to greet the sun had retreated to the scrubland and was gathering twigs to make a nest. I longed to tell her how my poor sun-scorched wings had hurt and how desperately they'd needed soothing. And how, like a bald-headed eagle, Clive Wiseman had landed and licked smooth my feathers and shown me *his* sun. His big warm bowl of golden chicken soup. And how drinking it had made me so drowsy, so very sleepy, as he fed

117

me, sip by sip. But of course I didn't talk about any of this. How could I?

'She's an excellent cook – Bernice,' I said instead. 'I can guarantee that you'll have a great supper on Friday night. If you come.' Perhaps Mia would understand the lure of Clive's family once she'd been there.

'Of course I'll come. Mum and me, both. And I do congratulate you, Gabs. I really hope it all works out well, that you'll be happy . . .'

She said nothing about Seamus, very little about her impressions of Israel. The same irritatingly mysterious smile appeared on her face when I asked her what had happened, what she'd done and seen.

'Gabs, it was a magic fortnight. One day I'll tell you all about it.'

That was all. She was equally guarded at the Wisemans that Friday. Just sat and ate as slowly and methodically as ever and smiled. They must have thought she was retarded. Fortunately, Mum more than made up for Mia's silence.

'My Joe would have been so proud of his daughter,' she sighed. 'Of course he died many years ago as Gabby must have mentioned.' I had – but she told them again anyway. All the details of her life of loss. How she'd been a grieving widow, a lonely single parent, and now her two daughters were leaving her. Well, not Mia. Not yet. But before long she too would get married – and who was Hilda to prevent such an event? After all, wasn't that what it was all about? Life. Marriage. Children. Suffering.

There was a general groan of heartfelt agreement. My sister ate her apple strudel in silence. Eli made moves for his indigestion tablets and Bernice sent Rebecca to make coffee. 'Thankyou-for-dinner-Grandma,' chorused Simon and Justine as they folded their napkins into two neat rectangles.

'And now,' said Bernice, rubbing her hands together, 'let's talk about the wedding.'

She looked at her husband. This was his cue.

'Bernice and I have had a long chat about things,' he said. The sententious tones of his rehearsed speeches were beginning to sound familiar. I looked at his shining, slowly nodding bald head and the fingers comfortably knotted round the apex of his stomach and wondered about Clive in thirty years time and shuddered.

Eli announced that he and his dear wife had decided to pay for the best that Birmingham had to offer in the way of wedding celebrations, a tour of Europe for the honeymoon couple and a spanking new flat in London. It sounded like we'd won first prize in a game show – or, at least, like Mum had, the way she responded.

'Unbelievable,' she said, and I expected her to burst into the traditional tears of joy and excitement. 'Unbelievable generosity. Gabriella darling, you're a very lucky girl.'

Lucky? Was the beautiful young scorpion fly lucky when her suitor arrived with a nuptial gift of insect prey? Was the Kipsigis tribeswoman lucky when her intended crossed Kenya bearing the dowry? The Kenyan and the scorpion fly were paying the going rate for a young fertile virgin. In a cross-cultural survey of eight hundred and sixty human societies, a man or his family paid for a wife in almost 70 per cent of cases. So why should the Wisemans be exempt? In my calculations, Clive was getting a bargain.

'I *am* lucky,' I lied. 'Mims – will you be my maid of honour?'

She nodded.

'And I've just had a brainwave,' said Mum. 'We can ask Uncle Fred to give the bride away.'

There was a clunk as Mia put her cup into its saucer. Suddenly she'd found her voice. 'Oh no,' she said. 'You absolutely won't ask Uncle Fred. Not if you want me to be there. This time I refuse.'

She spoke loudly and defiantly. I was embarrassed. Now the Wisemans would think my sister was difficult as well as dim.

'It's OK, Mims,' I said soothingly. 'I don't care who gives me away since it can't be Dad. It certainly doesn't have to be Uncle Fred.'

'No indeed,' said Mum. 'Although I can't for the life of me see what she objects to in her uncle. We'll have to find someone else.'

'How about my grandfather?' suggested Clive. He hadn't said much either that evening, I'd noticed. 'My grandfather would be so happy to hand over my bride.'

It was agreed. Yet another joyful person in my wake. Grandpa Isaac, who'd spent his working life driving bagels and bread rolls round Birmingham, was to deliver Gabriella to his grandson. Quite fitting really.

'I'm tired,' I said to Clive. Spreading happiness was turning out to be exhausting. I don't know how good fairies kept it up.

Even the best fairy would have been daunted by the prospect of gladdening four hundred people. Three hundred and ninety-seven Wiseman supporters, two Marks women and the blushing bride. My mouth hurt from smiling and I was sure my cheeks would ache for ever.

My chest ached – a little – when the grey-bearded rabbi spoke about the voice of joy and gladness, the jubilant voice of bridegrooms from their canopies and of youths from their feasts of song.

'Blessed art Thou, O Lord,' he said, eyes shut, his prayer-shawl swaying piously, 'who makest the bridegroom to rejoice with the bride.'

It felt safe underneath the white silk canopy. The smooth ring that Clive slipped over my forefinger held the promise of an unbroken married life. My sister gazed at me steadily as she lifted my veil and offered me wine. 'I'm here,' she seemed to be saying. 'Whatever happens, I'll always be here.'

Her staying power was not matched by that of Grandpa Isaac. The old man had developed severe angina pain after treading on my gossamer train as we sailed arm in arm towards the canopy. I'd been so engrossed in my majestic appearance that I hadn't noticed the collapse of my escort.

'Don't worry,' the mentholated breath of Eli Wiseman suddenly whistled through my veil. 'He'll be fine. I'll stand in for him while he has a little rest.' I wasn't worried. Old Isaac was a survivor. On the other hand, it was a pity that the man who'd had RELIABLE DELIVERY SERVICE emblazoned on his van for fifty years had failed to make the big one. His professional pride would be dented for ever. Also, there seemed to be something not quite right about a father handing a bride to his own son. Was it illegal? Immoral? Technical grounds for an annulment? Were you watching, Lord?

But then, underneath the silk canopy, lulled by the litany, the whiteness and the wine, I stopped questioning and felt safe.

Until, with a sharp crack, an awful shattering, Clive trod on the glass to end the ceremony. Sharp splinters crunched under his heel. The cracking of a holy temple. I thought of the brittle fragility of the slim goblet under the heavy foot of my husband – and suddenly the canopy seemed to sway.

'No, no,' I whispered. 'Mims, where are you Mims? I feel – strange.'

She was there. At my side to hold me upright.

'Deep breaths,' she said softly. 'You'll be all right, Gabby. Believe me. You'll be all right.'

'Yes,' I said, catching hold of her, of myself, breathing in and out and in and out. 'I'm fine. It must have been the heat.'

Clive kissed me then. The veil was removed from my face and he bent down and his lips touched mine and everyone cheered. I smiled and only my sister suspected my panic. I danced the night away in the arms of my accountant and when midnight struck we said farewell to three hundred and ninety-eight happy people and dashed down the stairs of the Thistle Hotel. I thought about Cinderella and her glass slipper and how easily it could have shattered. The prince might have stepped on her toe – and then how would her story have ended? My slippers were white satin, easily stained and torn but unlikely to crack. Clive held on to my arm to steady me. The last thing he wanted was a fallen bride.

The Wife's Guide to Pleasing her Man in Bed. A wedding present from my husband. He'd seen it advertised in a Sunday supplement and had ordered it to be posted in a discreet plain wrapper. In the same plain wrapper it had set off with us on our honeymoon and one fine autumn night in Paris he presented it to me. We'd been married a week and I clearly hadn't quite pleased him yet. (Actually, he hadn't pleased me either, but I hadn't brought along a husband's manual. Men, I'd assumed, knew how to do these things instinctively.)

'Gabs,' he said, 'I'm happy with you. I really am. I always did plan to marry a virgin.'

'Did you? Always?' I imagined Clive in kindergarten dreaming about balance sheets, unmedicated bowel movements – and a virginal bride.

'Well, yes. As long as I can remember. It's just that – er – sex is a skill like any other, and maybe this little book will – um – teach you to be more – sensitive.'

I burst out laughing.

'That's what I mean,' he said. 'Like now. You don't seem to understand how difficult this is for me.'

It was my laughter that had got me into trouble in the first place, that first night. Our wedding night.

Clive had disappeared into the bathroom and I'd sat on the bed in my lacy nylon négligé awaiting defloration. Terrified. Listening to the rattling, brushing, flushing sounds accompanied by a whistled rendering of the Israeli national anthem, the penultimate tune played at our wedding reception. Perhaps he'd start on 'God save the queen' in time for me to lie back and think of England.

'Clive,' I called, 'when are you coming to bed?'

'In a minute.' A final flurry. A crescendo of rushing water. A gurgle. And then the door opened. 'Are you – ready?' he asked.

'I think so.' I didn't dare look at him. Was I supposed to have done warm-up exercises? Plumped up the pillows perhaps? 'What do you want me to do?'

'Umm.' He moved towards me, deep in thought. 'Relax, Gabby. That's all. You relax and I'll do everything.'

That sounded easy enough. I turned and watched him approaching the bed and saw a naked accountant with a soft white body and – my goodness, I'd never seen a real erect penis before. So this was it. The mighty phallus. And it looked like a ridiculous, quivering coat-hook.

'Gabby,' he breathed, bearing down on me. 'Gabby? What's the matter?'

I was helpless with laughter. The coat-hook collapsed. My man was not pleased. He turned over and was soon snoring and I lay on my back and stopped laughing and thought of England and felt very homesick indeed.

We made it back to England eventually. We'd done France, Spain, Germany, Italy and Switzerland. Five countries in three weeks, with a stopover in Amsterdam to buy a diamond. I learnt that I hated art galleries, cathedrals made me dizzy and Venice made me sad. That Zurich made me feel poor and Paris had bad drains and Germany gave me headaches and pleasing my man was the easiest thing in the world.

He wanted sensitivity? I gave him sensitivity. I relaxed, told him how good he was and lay very still when he stroked my body and told me he loved its firmness. 'Almost like a young boy,' he said. I didn't laugh. Every time I felt hysteria rising, I forced myself to think about the alternative to Clive, the loneliness, the sense of failure. That stopped me fast. And after a while I didn't mind it – the sex bit. In fact, by the time we got to Italy, it had become an everyday routine like doing my teeth. Anyway, as Clive pointed out, when we got home we certainly wouldn't manage it every day.

'The average married couple,' he told me over dinner on our last night in Rome, 'has sexual intercourse 3.4 times a week. So we shouldn't feel that we have to be under any sort of pressure.'

'No, we certainly shouldn't,' I said, managing to keep a straight face. 'We could perhaps limit ourselves to twice some weeks and then have a massive blow-out after a month or so without seriously disturbing the national statistics.'

He wasn't amused. Clive never did think sex was funny. Or fun. But still, we did make it back to England one way or another. And what I found there made me wish we'd stayed on the continent and tried out another few ways and then perhaps I'd have understood what had happened to my sister. She'd gone mad. Utterly off the rails. Upped and left home. Abandoned our poor distraught mother, and taken up residence with her dissolute Irishman.

I suppose I should have guessed that something like this would happen. If nothing else, I should have taken heed of my dream. That last night in the glitzy splendour of our five-star suite in Amsterdam, I'd had a vision that had made me scream out in terror.

'Gabby, what is it? What's the matter?'

'The shoes,' I'd gasped, grabbing hold of him. 'The shoes were walking down the stairs.' In my dream I'd seen my father's old brogues – the ones that Mia would put out conscientiously every night – slowly, slowly descending. And my sister standing on the landing with one hand on her hip and the other waving them goodbye. A smile on her face. The same infuriatingly secretive smile she'd had when she'd told me of her magic fortnight in Israel.

'Stop them,' I'd called out to her. 'Don't let them walk away. They're supposed to look after us. *You're* supposed to look after us. Stop them. Wait, wait, where are you going?'

She'd floated away and I'd watched helplessly. Shoes plodding downward, Mia floating upward. And I'd screamed.

Yes, I had been forewarned.

'Mum, we're back. It's us. Clive and Gabby. We're home.' My voice seemed to echo alarmingly. It rose to a squeak and then faded into heavy silence. The house was dark and felt empty. Where was she? Why wasn't she at the door to welcome The Couple? Where was my sister? Were the dashing groom and his glamorous blushing bride to be cheated of their heroic homecoming? This wasn't fair.

'Mum? Mia!' angrily.

And then I saw the shoes abandoned on the stairs. Weary brown brogues, one on its side revealing a worn heel and rubbed-away sole and its mate, five steps below, poised upright as though awaiting a foot and about to walk away. I remembered my dream.

'Mia! Mum!' fearfully.

'Gabby darling . . .' Her plaintive call was like a siren wailing through thick fog. 'I'm here, here upstairs. In my bedroom. Something terrible has happened.'

'Clive, come with me.' I needed his support, held tight on to his hand as I stepped over the shoes and crossed the landing. Her room smelt of stale perfume and perspiration and the red roses that drooped in the bone china vase on her dressing-table. I recognized the vase. It was the one I'd brought from Birmingham, the shattered vessel restored by my Clive. I moved closer to him for protection.

'What is it, Mum?' I asked. I knew. By then I'd guessed. But I wanted her to tell me – and even then I found it hard to believe. 'How could she?' I repeated. 'Mum, how could she do this to you – to us?'

My mother was sobbing deeply. 'She came home with roses,' she wept. 'There – those red roses. A week ago. "Mum," she said to me, sweet as ever, "Mum, I've got something to tell you." Oh, Gabby – I should have known. I should have been so watchful. That Seamus. Those dangerous Irish friends of hers.

But I trusted her. Not Mia, I kept telling myself. My Mia would never do anything silly. Such a sensible girl. I trusted her. And look how far that's got me? Gabby my darling, what *am* I going to do?'

I moved closer to Clive (as though to say I have a husband now and naturally my first duty lies with him, so don't start making demands on me) and said soothingly: 'We'll talk to her, Mum. Me and Clive. Try and get her to see reason. And we'll stay here with you until our flat is ready. Don't worry, it will all be for the best.'

Brave, consoling words. Concealing words. My fury was so strong that I thought it might burst through the solicitous smoke-screen like a fireball with blazing tongues to lash my helpless mother and lick my silly husband standing speechless at my side and leap over London to consume my selfish sister and her Irishman. They all deserved to burn and turn to ashes.

'Don't worry,' I repeated. 'We'll look after you Mum.'

Clive nodded. 'Of course we will, Hilda,' he said. 'Of course we will.'

He nodded wordlessly, squeezing my hand, when I said what I had to say to Mia. She'd finally telephoned from her love-nest in the murky depths of Cricklewood.

'And so?' I asked self-righteously. 'Do you feel pleased with what you've done? Are you happy with yourself? Your mother might have died. We came home to find her beside herself with worry and grief – and you know as well as anyone else how precarious her health is. Honestly, Mia, I am surprised at you. It might have been understandable if you'd been having a proper, open relationship with someone. But this – this sort of underhand behaviour – it's just – sordid.'

The line crackled. This was high-voltage moral indignation and I fully expected a gasp of shocked remorse. Instead I heard a laugh, a joyous ripple of mirth that came pulsing down the wire. I held on to Clive disbelievingly, shaking my head. What had happened to my dutiful sister?

'My goodness, Mims,' I said, struggling to keep my voice steady. 'You *have* changed.'

'Gabs, please understand. It was something I had to do. We'll talk about it properly one day – soon. We'll meet, the four of us. You'll like Seamus, you really will. Everyone does.' She wasn't laughing any more. My brave runaway sister was asking for my approval. Like hell.

'If that's the way you want to conduct your life . . .' That sounded hollow, even to me.

'Did you have a good – honeymoon?' She was clearly determined to worm her way back into my affections. 'I – thought about you – often.'

Oh, how I longed to be able to say dreamily, 'It was a magic time Mims, a trip to Wonderland. Some day I'll tell you about it.' I wanted to illustrate the five-star advantages of being a fully paid-up wife with tales of luxury suites with bidets and boxes at the opera and shopping sprees and champagne. But I'd never quite worked out what to do with a bidet, the opera had been boring, champagne had made me sick and continental shops were confusing. As for the rather overrated joys of the nuptial bed, I suppose there were times when I thought there just might be some fun to be had out of the contortions, and undoubtedly it was all very necessary for the continuation of the Wiseman line. But on the whole . . .

'Yes,' I said cheerfully. 'We had a great time.'

'Gabs, I'll be in touch soon. We'll get together.'

'Bye Mia,' I said, managing to sound cool, then adding, 'see you – soon.' There was a wobble in my voice. Disappointment, for she'd spoilt my homecoming. Loneliness. I so wanted to talk to her, to laugh with her, to be in the bathroom with her, saying, 'Mims, listen, listen to me – I have something to tell you.' I suppose it was love. Longing. Damn that wobble.

'Goodbye,' I repeated firmly, replacing the receiver and turning to my husband. 'This is going to end badly. Mark my words, Clive. It's not going to end well.'

He nodded darkly and I felt slightly better. 'Come,' I said. 'Let's make a shopping list for the flat.' He agreed enthusiastically. In those days, he agreed with most things I said and gave me just about everything I wanted. Together we were creating what the estate agents would later describe as 'an ideal first-time buy for the upwardly mobile young couple'. The finest in Finchley, with wall-to-wall carpeting, avocado bathroom fittings and gold dralon curtains that matched the three-piece suite. The biggest and best-equipped kitchen I'd ever encountered. And the biggest bed.

'Gabs,' he'd said to me soon after our return to London, 'when it comes to doing up the flat, I'll leave it to you. After all, women have more of a feel for that sort of thing. And anyway, I'll soon be starting my new job and won't have much time for shopping etcetera.'

He coughed importantly. He'd be balancing the books of the high and mighty while I'd be booking delivery appointments for the balance of our furniture. But I didn't mind. It was part of the marriage contract. A deal was a deal.

'Of course,' I said agreeably.

'There are just two little things I – well – insist on. If I may . . .'

'Of course.' What were two small things in an ocean of new assets?

'I'd like us to have a king-sized bed and a kosher kitchen.'

The first was easy. Make the bedroom somewhat crowded, but what the hell. The second requirement, though . . . was that part of the deal?

'I don't know very much about keeping a kosher kitchen,' I hesitated.

'My mother will help you. We've spoken about it already. She'll come here and stay with us and set it all up for you. It's not difficult, Gabs, just a matter of separating the milk from the meat. You'll get the hang of it. After a while, it will run itself. My mother assures me it will.'

'Well – if that's what you want.'

'I do. She does. It's what we've always done in the Wiseman family. It will turn our flat into a home.'

'Who are you?' wide-eyed Cinders asked the figure in the sensible suit and set grey hair who'd appeared in the centre of her gleaming new kitchen.

'Bernice Wisewoman, your fairy godmother. I've come to teach you the magic spells that will turn pumpkins into fritters, potatoes into latkes, your husband into a mouse and your flat into a home. Everything – all the spells and incantations I know – I am handing down to you.'

'But fairy godmother, I don't think I want to learn your spells. I've never liked latkes or pumpkin fritters. I'd rather not be married to a mouse. To be honest, fairy godmother, all I long for is to go to a ball. I thought *that*'s what fairy godmothers arranged.'

'Silly child. Balls end at midnight but marriages last for ever. Be sensible now and let's get on with it. First of all, I want you to bring me your new stainless steel meat pot and the plumpest chicken you can find. And then we'll need half-a-dozen carrots and an onion . . .'

At last our flat had been fully transformed. The kosher kitchen beamed contentedly at the reproduction *Mona Lisa* over the mantelpiece. Bernice, in the spare bedroom, had been persuaded to stay 'just for another couple of weeks – please' by her son who adored her cooking. Adored her. Adored me.

'Oh Gabs,' he said, 'I never imagined that marriage could be so good. Here I am, with the two women I love most in this world. It's wonderful. Mum, the meatloaf is excellent. As ever. I hope you've given Gabby the recipe.'

I said nothing. I suppose I could have reminded him that despite the king-sized bed we were not keeping up with the national average. The previous week we'd sunk to an all-time low of 1.2. But then, as he admitted, having a mother in earshot was inhibiting. On the other hand, here he was inviting her to prolong her stay. Who cared? I was feeling nauseous anyway. All this rich food was giving me indigestion.

'Excuse me,' I said as I left the table and went to the bathroom. A framed scroll hung over the lavatory. The sort of parchment print that might have said 'Home Sweet Home'. This one didn't though. It was Clive's treasure, his favourite quote from Hippocrates, ornately inscribed: 'It is best when the stools are soft and formed and passed at an hour customary to the patient when in health.'

Talking about chance, tossing coins, drawing lots. The excitement of a run of luck. A flutter. A fluke. A flash of good fortune.

'Since when did either of us ever win anything?" I'd asked my sister bitterly.

That's when I thought of the print, the wise words of Hippocrates that followed us from lavatory to lavatory on our pathway through suburbia. From the low-level avocado model in Finchley to the pastel pink in Muswell Hill and ultimately to the square-bowled oak-seated throne in Hampstead Garden Suburb. No luck. No lottery. Just dogged persistence and unswerving faith in the gods of regularity.

Perhaps that was the answer. Maybe Clive had been right all along.

❧ 11 ❧

No, we hadn't won anything. Not either of us. Ever. I'd once been runner-up in the All-Barnet Challenge Cup for the Most Helpful Brownie of 1955. And I'd almost had my number drawn in a school raffle. We'd have won a week in Scarborough if I hadn't missed by one digit, but I suppose Mum would have been too tired to go anyway. Yes, Gabby was right. Calling heads had got me nowhere. I didn't even win Seamus in the end. But the losing of him was like – oh, like a voyage through violet tropical seas scented with musk and wild roses. Like leaping with a comet and dancing with a meteor and having a moon-rock picnic on Mars. While it lasted, it was the adventure of my dreams.

Funny how I can say that now, without it hurting. I'd never have believed it possible. Not then. Not when I woke up and realized that Cricklewood wasn't part of Utopia but a far-flung outpost of Cloud-cuckoo-land. It was a tree-top pseudo-paradise that was rocking perilously in howling high winds. That's when I knew I had to climb down, to get off fast. But until that day I believed I'd found heaven.

'A magic fortnight,' I'd said to my sister. I couldn't say any more for I was afraid it would disappear. Even then, in those heady early days, I would think of Seamus and think of fairy-dust, and fear that if I breathed too hard it – he – would blow away.

I did breathe too hard and, yes, in the end he did blow away. But I still kept breathing. And that was a miracle more amazing than any fairy-tale. It was life.

*

130

'I'm sorry I'm late.' He was waiting for me at our usual table in the King's Arms. It was the first time we'd met since our return from Israel. I looked at this stranger, a smallish dark-haired man with wrinkles at the corners of his navy-blue eyes and a torn red jumper. My lover. My lover. At any rate, he seemed glad to see me.

'Mia, sit down. Have a drink. What happened?'

'You'll never guess. My sister – my little sister – is getting married. An accountant, he's a thirty-two-year-old accountant. And she's just nineteen, leaving art school. And getting married. Oh Seamus, they're all happy, and I'm so upset.'

'Why? It's always seemed to me that your sister Gabriella knew exactly what she was about. I'm sure you don't need to worry yourself about her.' He took a long sip of his lager and frowned when he saw that I was shaking my head.

'It's not a matter of need. She's – mine. And she – well, she sort of does things and I'm never sure what she's feeling, thinking. I thought she was – fine – at art school. Now she seems almost too bright, too chirpy. Seamus, she – we – had no father . . . I can't help worrying. Our family's like a flimsy tripod on unstable ground. It would be impossible for me simply to step away and see it collapse and then deny responsibility. I've never even wanted to until – us. Not really.'

I looked at him trying to make sense of what I'd said and suddenly I didn't care any more about the weight of my duty – as a daughter, a sister or anything else. There was only him. Seamus. Nothing else mattered. I held my breath and knew that at his touch, his summons, I'd follow blindly to the end of the earth. To the end.

'Seamus . . .' I couldn't help it. 'I do love you – so much.'

'That's it then, the whole point.' He put down his glass with a thud. 'Mia, it's our time now. Your family will survive without you. Everyone does in the end. Think, think of what we have. Come and live with me – you can, now that I have the flat. After all, we're not children. We shouldn't have to meet in pubs, sneak – times – together. We've known better in Israel. You and I should be with one another whenever we want. All the time.'

I shut my eyes and imagined – tried to imagine – the paradise of life together. The two of us in a vast Elysian field savouring a million-course banquet. An Eden without end. Then I caught myself. Told myself not to be an idiot. Didn't everyone know that Eden ended and million-course banquets made one sick? The whole idea was impossible – as impractical as any Utopian dream.

'It's impossible,' I said firmly. 'Especially now that Gabby's leaving. My responsibility is at home – for now, anyway.'

'And what happens when *you* want to get married? Are you going to be denied even that? Are you supposed to stay at home and care for mother for the rest of your life?'

'Ah, *married*.' I smiled ironically. 'Now that's another story. Married means settled. It means a good match, a nice Jewish boy with a profession and a stable income. A husband. I'm afraid that you, dear Seamus, don't qualify on any count. An impecunious Catholic playwright, a dangerous foreigner with a dubious reputation, is not my mother's idea of a son-in-law.'

'Sorry,' he said lightly, and shrugged. 'Well then, this Clive, your sister's Clive, he sounds absolutely perfect. You'll have to find one like that for yourself. In the meantime though . . .' He took my hands and looked at me hard. 'Come and live with me.'

'No, no.' I couldn't bear saying it. He'd go away, find someone else, and there I'd remain, alone with Mum. So good, so dutiful. And so unhappy. But there was nothing to be done. Was there? 'No, Seamus,' I repeated as firmly as I could. 'There are some things I simply cannot do.'

'You'll consider it though? Won't you?'

I thought about it. Day and night there were voices that crowded my head until I was sure that I must be going mad.

The righteous tones of Duty: 'Your family: your sister, your mother. They need you and count on you. Don't forget to leave the dinner in the oven and a note for the milkman. You promised. You promised . . .'

Good Sense: 'Don't be naïve. There are no princes in the real world. It's all a fantasy, a delicious fairy-tale. Get on with your life, Mia. Look for someone real . . .'

Temptation: 'Yes, leave it all behind you, Mia. Leave it and run for your life. You've paid your dues. Your mother will survive – and your spirit will survive. Like a parched plant that is watered, it will uncurl and bloom. Remember the numbness, the old interminable heavy numbness, and compare that with even a single minute of happiness with Seamus. Does it matter how long it lasts? Nothing lasts, Mia. Take what you can and enjoy, enjoy . . .'

No. Yes. Beware. Dare. The voices sounded incessantly. 'Isn't your sister sensible – so fortunate – doing the Right Thing?' they demanded of me as I spooned soup into my tight mouth round the Wisemans' dinner table. I tried to smile supportively at my sister, engagingly at Clive, appealingly at the rest of the gathering – and then wondered why I was trying so hard and imagined their faces if they could hear the conflict in my head and resumed smiling despite myself.

'A wonderful family,' Gabby had said, 'a sterling family.' She'd wanted me to join the Sabbath meal in the belief that I'd be charmed by the magic circle created by flesh and blood and money. 'Aren't they great?' her constant glances in my direction seemed to be asking. 'Don't you wish you could be part of this too?' She probably thought my silence was to do with envy, but this family circle had failed to cast a spell over me with its particular brew. I saw pounds and pounds of excess flesh and the blood that had been shed to provide liver and chicken soup and slabs of roast beef. And the money that was buying my sister.

'Unbelievable,' Mum exclaimed breathlessly when overfed Eli had declared his hand. 'Gabriella darling, you're a very lucky girl.'

Lucky? Was a white wedding, a holiday and a luxury flat worth a lifetime with clean-living Clive and his manicured nails and monogrammed mind? He held up the hand of his bride-to-be as though to say, 'Didn't I do well?' And I wanted to catch Gabby, to hold her back, to hold her. 'Not so fast, he's not the last. There is something more Gabs. I may have found it. Not perfection perhaps. Not safety. But something, something that stirs a vast pool brimming with all the fairy-tales ever invented and creates multicoloured ripples that take my breath away. Oh Gabby, please please wait . . . don't sell your soul.'

My unspoken words provoked mocking laughter from the voice of Temptation. 'See? See how you hate the alternative? Take what you have, Mia. Take it and run.'

And I looked at my sister and was about to put a hand on her shoulder and whisper, 'Let's talk, we need to talk,' when I saw that her face was fixed in a tight ironic smile. And I knew that Gabriella was quite aware that she was speculating in securities. She was laying down her assets – youth and innocence – in the firm anticipation of long-term gain. A sterling profit. A good investment. Perhaps she was right and my 'something more' was a myth . . .

'Never!' Temptation was gaining the upper hand. 'Look at him, her Clive with his smug face and eyes that keep darting to his mother for approval. Listen to his platitudes. He acts as though he'd bought her already, like the proud owner of a sleek new car. There *is* something more Mia. You know there is.' There were no sounds of dissent from the other voices in my head. They were strangely subdued in this house of Duty, this bastion of Good Sense. And they were silenced altogether when Uncle Fred's name came up. Friendly, jolly Uncle Fred, deliverer of the innocent, the perfect person to give away a virgin bride.

'Oh no,' I said, appalled. 'You absolutely won't ask Uncle Fred. Not if you want me to be there. This time I refuse.'

That was when I made up my mind. It was the thought of Uncle Fred, the revival of his memory, that shocked me into a decision to take my chances with Seamus. There was a hush in the room like the stillness between the last crashing chords of a symphony and the first wave of applause. But no one started clapping. Instead my sister said soothingly, 'It's OK Mim. I don't care who gives me away since it can't be Dad . . .' And my throat suddenly closed with a surge of longing for my father, for a hand that might have stroked my head and said, 'Blondie, my little Blondie.' For the safety of home, a real home, with size nine feet to fill the shoes on the stairs. Seamus wore size eight.

'I've been thinking about it, Seamus. About us – me coming to live with you.'

'And?'

'It might – just – be possible.'

'Mia that's wonderful. When? When can you come?'

We were on a rug beside an electric heater in the larger of the two rooms that comprised his Cricklewood abode. The rug was worn, its geometric pattern obscured by wine stains and coffee blots. The flickering efforts of the single-bar heater to penetrate the winter chill were futile. Yet on that small shabby carpet alongside the weak rays of warmth I'd been transported to kingdoms filled with flowers and eternal sunshine. Holding tight on to my King Solomon, we'd flown high with the wind, soared with the birds of the air, and landed in Utopia. By then I'd become quite familiar with the place and was beginning to recognize some of the landmarks, to avoid some of the tourist traps.

My familiarity with Utopia was not nearly enough to breed contempt. But it did seem to have bred something else. Waves of nausea, the non-arrival of my period. No, it was impossible, unthinkable. Seamus had said to trust him to be careful. 'I've never got it wrong,' he'd sworn. 'Never.' I'd believed him, still believed him, and chose to ignore the persistent symptoms.

'Soon,' I told him, stroking a silky patch of skin I'd discovered in the small of his back. 'After Gabby's wedding. I'd hate to cause a stir before her big day, to take away her limelight. As soon as it's over, I'll come here to you, and we can be together – all the time.'

I looked around, beyond the rug and the heater to the dullness of the walls that had once been painted cream and the small window with a floral cotton curtain to keep out the squalor of the high street. There was a poster on the wall, an advertisement that shouted the joys of WEEKEND CRUISES FROM HARWICH CALLING AT CONTINENTAL PORTS. It pictured languid travellers in nautical white elegantly arranged on the deck of the SS *Vienna*. Beneath the poster was a wooden table inelegantly cluttered with Seamus's old typewriter, his half-completed manuscript, a jar of strawberry jam and a cracked butter dish. Through the half-open door I could see the bedroom. A single bed, a small cupboard, a solitary crack of light that seemed to say this is a one-person place. I was suddenly uneasy. Would there be space for me? He noticed my frown, followed my appraisal of his flat.

'Mia, come as soon as you can.' He turned my face to his, searched it with his eyes and then kissed my eyes till I closed them and stopped looking and only felt, felt, felt . . . 'We'll manage. Anything is possible. You'll see how happy you'll be – here. With me. I'll make you happy.'

135

I *am* happy, I wanted to say. With you Seamus, I'm happy. But that's not what he wanted to hear.

'You'll be all right, Gabby. Believe me. You'll be all right.'

The splintering sound of breaking glass beneath the bridal canopy had pierced my fiercely held composure too. I'd wanted to grab my sister, to pull her away from the bald-headed investor who'd just clinched his deal and was about to kiss his new asset on her ripe mouth – to say, 'Gabby, let's run. Let's run away together.' As the wedding goblet cracked, I saw with sudden stark clarity that I'd had my sip of joy and my sister would never taste it with Clive and I wanted to sob with sadness – and the nausea and fear that were intensifying day by day.

But then I saw her pallor, her lips forming the words 'no – no . . .' and I knew that it was too late for her to escape. Her die was cast. I had to prop her up as long as I could and then run for my life.

We had a moment together in a corner of the banqueting suite in the Thistle Hotel. Herman Harris and his Birmingham Big Band had been crooning and strumming with relentless enthusiasm. The bride's bunch of orange blossom lay wilting on a chair as she took the floor in the arms of her satisfied swain. He danced her round the polished patch. She looked small. He looked pleased. I hated him.

'You'll be all right,' I repeated to her in a lull between brassy numbers. I had to say it. She took my hand.

'Yes, Mims, Clive will take care of me.' She spoke forlornly as though she didn't quite believe it. Then she braced herself and smiled till the old dimple appeared on her cheek. 'Isn't this fun?' she chirped. 'I do believe that being a bride is even better than acting the Virgin Mary in the school play. Remember, Mims?'

'I remember.'

'Go on, go and dance. Enjoy yourself. Look at the feast the Wisemans have provided. Everyone else seems to be tucking in. Mum is happier than I've ever seen her – look at her Mims, she's dancing with my father-in-law. Arm in arm with Eli. Bernice had better watch out. Oh, there's Clive. I'd better go and join him.'

'Wait, wait a second, Gabby. There's something I must tell you.'

'What?' She stopped in mid-flight and turned to face me. 'What is it?'

The band struck up a rousing tango. 'Hold her tight,' crooned Herman Harris. 'Tight, tight, tight,' chorused his Big Band in earnest discord. She was waiting to hear what I had to say. I couldn't do it. My mouth wouldn't form the words. I embraced her instead. 'Whatever happens,' I managed to whisper, 'I care about you. Very much. Remember that, Gabs.'

At midnight she disappeared down the stairs. I followed her out, almost expecting to find a slipper abandoned on the landing, and remembered how Cinderella's sisters were supposed to have mutilated their feet trying to squeeze them into her dainty shoe. Blood poured from their toes and their heels. But it didn't help. Nothing helped. I leaned on the banister and thought of Gabby and Clive and their wedding night and wept into the limp bunch of orange blossoms she'd thrust into my arms as she'd left. 'Take these, Mims,' she'd said. 'You'll be getting married next.' Oranges for fertility. White blossoms for purity. What a joke, I thought, drenching the blooms with salty tears. What a bloody joke.

Ten days later I came home with a dozen red roses for my mother. The sweet-smelling flowers nestled serenely in their tissue-paper cornet. I'd already taken my books and clothing to Seamus's flat.

'Mum,' I called. 'It's me – Mia. Are you upstairs?'

'Darling – yes, I'm here. Do you feel like bringing a pot of tea upstairs with you? I'm exhausted . . .'

The wedding had drained her last small drops of energy. For ten days she'd complained of a lassitude so great that even lifting a teacup was an effort. Mitchell had ordered bed rest and she'd responded with her usual relieved compliance.

'There's nothing to be done, Mia darling,' she'd sighed, sinking back into her pillows. 'He says that with my health the way it is, I can't be too careful. Oh, I do miss my little Gabby. I wonder how she is. So far away. I'm sure Clive is taking good care of her though – such a responsible man. If you could find yourself a husband like that, I'd be more than happy to lose you too . . . although God knows how I'd manage.'

'You would, Mum. Everyone does.' I spoke off-handedly, as though the idea of Mum managing were purely theoretical. But my chest tightened and my innards knotted alarmingly. I shuddered as a tide of nausea rose through my body and demanded to be released.

There was no denying it any more. I was pregnant. Every single book that I consulted provided confirmation. At work, Hannah looked at me strangely. I'd told her of my intention to live with Seamus. But not this. No one knew this. In the dark nights, I imagined something growing inside me – someone, a child, a boy, Seamus's boy. And I held myself tightly, held on to this tiny being and felt myself filling with warmth and wanting to open out my arms to hold Seamus and his baby, our baby. And then I imagined him pushing me away, saying, 'My baby? Our baby? That wasn't part of the plan.' And I shivered. I was suddenly so cold, so very cold.

In the dark nights I held myself tightly and shook with chilly foreboding. But no one knew about it. Not yet.

'Mum, I brought you some flowers.' First things first.

'How sweet of you, Mia darling. Why? It's not my birthday is it?' She smiled complacently from her pillow, so sure of the attentions of her older daughter.

I shrugged. 'I just felt like it. Thought they'd cheer you up. Wait – I'll go down and fetch the tea and put the roses in a vase.'

In the kitchen the voices that had been silent for several weeks rose in such tumultuous cacophony that I was sure she'd hear the noise upstairs. 'Don't do it,' screeched Duty and Good Sense. 'Have courage Mia. Courage. Think of tonight in bed with him – all night long . . .' said Temptation; then, trying a different tack, '. . . and think of the baby.' At this, even Good Sense was silenced. 'You have to do it,' it admitted. 'There's no alternative.' I went upstairs with the flowers and the tea and the heavy certainty that there was no other way.

She watched me, set-faced and silent, as I stumbled over my words, trying to explain. 'I do love you, Mum,' I faltered. 'It's just that – this is something I've got to do. I've thought it over very carefully . . . I'll come and see you. Often. I'm sure Elsie will look after you, just as she did when I went to Israel . . .'

For a few seconds the room was so quiet I thought I could hear the roses breathing in their bone china vase. Then I saw she was rising, getting out of her bed and coming towards me. I shut my eyes and I was three years old again, shaking her awake and waiting for her to shout, 'Get out of here you horrible little brat. Get out.' I stepped back, blinking as I tried to see her approaching, but my eyes were blinded by tears. Then her hands were on my shoulders and her voice rasped into my ear.

'Bitch. Bitch. You great clumsy whore – how could you? How could you?' And she shook me till I staggered limply to the door and down the stairs to the entrance hall where I stood, overcome by huge convulsing sobs. I heard a thud and saw a shoe come hurtling towards me. Then another. Daddy's brown brogues. I sank to the parquet floor and thought I'd cry for ever.

'Get on with it then.' Her voice from upstairs was hard and relentless. 'Get out of here and go to your lover. And don't come crying to me when he gets tired of you.'

'Never,' I gasped. 'Never, never, never.' A gust of wind took hold of the front door as I opened it. It slammed behind me and I heard the smash of glass as I ran whimpering down the rain-soaked path.

He lay next to me and stroked me from the top of my head to my heaving shoulders, over and over again. 'Don't cry, my Mia. Don't cry. It will all seem different in the morning. I promise you it will.' And he turned my face to his and kissed me and said, 'You're beautiful when you cry.' I was about to say, 'Seamus, I had to come to you. There was no other way. You see . . .' But when he touched my breasts I couldn't say anything at all. I loved him so much that little else mattered.

In the morning nothing seemed different. The same tears resumed their course down my cheeks and the same rain wept outside in sympathy. It rained inside too, into a metal bucket that Seamus had placed in the centre of the living-room. Lying alone in the bed, I heard steady dripping and the syncopated clicking of his typewriter.

'Seamus,' I called, 'what's the time?'

'Sh Mia, sleep. It's only six o'clock. I always get up early to write.'

I lay in bed, curled into a tight ball, and listened to the sounds of water and words and wondered whether Mum had woken and called, 'Mia darling' before she'd remembered. And I watched the grey dawn soaking up the darkness and thought of the light bright mornings of Israel and hugged my foetal secret and moved my head to make a new damp patch of tears.

'What is it, Mia? Why are you crying so? We're here – together. This is what we wanted . . .' He'd left his work and was sitting at my side.

'I don't think I can go to work today, Seamus. I don't feel – very well.' The rain drummed on the window and I worried about whether it would carry on for forty days and forty nights. Seamus's ark was not even watertight. Like Mrs Noah, I'd hesitated before climbing on board. Had she cried? They'd quarrelled violently, Mr Noah and his wife. Would we argue too, me and my peace-loving Seamus? Would he throw me to the flood when I told him the secret? The night before he'd said he loved to look at me as I lay naked on the bed and he'd traced his hands down my body and told me it felt like the purest silk. For the first time ever, I'd withdrawn from his touch – recoiled like a frightened animal, so scared that he'd feel the difference. That he'd guess. I *had* to tell him.

'Seamus, stay here a moment. There's something I have to say.'

He held my hand, sat very still as I spoke. Then he rose slowly, walked very slowly to the living-room and started tapping sporadically on his typewriter. I curled back into my tight ball and felt myself adrift on the floodwaters. Abandoned. My fears fulfilled.

'Mia.' He'd come back. 'We'll manage. We'll take care of it. Are you sure you don't want to . . ?'

'No. I couldn't bear to – kill – our – child.'

'Well then.' He sat down, gathered me in his arms and rocked me as though I were – our child. 'It's not what I – we – would have chosen. For now. But there's nothing to be done. We'll manage.'

'Are you sure, Seamus?'

'I'm sure.'

It was as though the sun had burst out and a great rainbow spanned the sky. I shut my eyes and saw bright colours and heard the beating of dove's wings and felt him next to me, into me – and it was paradise regained. We'd manage, he had said. We'd be all right. He'd said nothing about loving me – but I believed implicitly that my love would be enough for both of us. For all three of us. The rain battered down and dripped into the dingy flat – and I put my faith in rainbows and blue skies and turtle-doves and love.

Did I feel pleased with what I'd done? Was I aware that my mother might have died? Was I happy with myself? Her voice shrilled on relentlessly. Gabby, I wanted to say, Gabby please stop. Wait. Let me explain myself. Let's talk. I can't bear to hear your self-righteous disapproval. Leaving Mum to live with Seamus was something I had to do. But she didn't give me a chance.

'Honestly Mia.' Her tones reached new heights of moral indignation. 'It might have been understandable if you'd been having a proper, open relationship with someone. But this – this sort of underhand behaviour – it's just – sordid.'

What could I say to that? From the faraway land of Finchley, where there were household sprays to wipe away doubt and everyone paid homage to the sanctity of The Family, my defection was a supreme act of betrayal. Yes, Gabby, it was sordid to say the least. I couldn't tell her how sordid it really was, so I laughed. A bitter laugh that must have burnt along the telephone wire like a fuse and exploded in a cloud of bile in her ear.

'My goodness, Mims,' I heard her say, so sadly, so very sadly. 'You *have* changed.' And I managed to stop laughing and tried to talk. But it was no good. She refused to listen.

'I've lost my sister,' I said softly to Seamus when our conversation had ended with a few polite formalities and brittle farewells. 'She's settled for suburbia and it's a million miles from Cricklewood. I've lost a sister and a mother. Now there's only – us.'

'Did you tell her?' He put a tentative hand on my belly. Seamus had been most subdued since my revelation. We'd had fewer trips to Utopia and I'd put it down to the pressure of finishing the play or . . . oh, I was too tired to ask questions. My days had grown heavy with tiredness.

141

'No. I didn't dare. Perhaps next time we speak. Or the next time.'

'It's *your* sister,' he shrugged. 'Have you told my sister?'

I hadn't spoken much to Hannah since I'd moved in with Seamus. We'd sat behind our desks at opposite ends of the office and exchanged pleasantries and the sun seemed to have gone out of her smile. She didn't like what I'd done and I squirmed under her unsaid disapproval even more than Gabby's scorn. Several times I'd raised my eyes from my work and she'd been looking at me carefully, studying me with a puzzled frown.

'I haven't said anything, but I think she knows. She's guessed.'

'We'll have to tell people – sometime,' he said thoughtfully. There was no mention of marriage or the future or a proper home for a child. 'Sometime,' he'd said. And the word trailed off into a void that was like the vacuum following a fairy-tale ending. The prince having kissed the princess and they having made wonderful love and he having said 'Come with me to the promised land,' and she having come. And then? There they were, cramped in Cricklewood, she watching him making up his tale of an Irishman who finds Jerusalem, watching him dreaming of another Jerusalem. And praying that whatever love he felt for her wasn't turning to obligation. For she knew that passion never spoke in a still small voice.

'Perhaps we won't need to say anything. Eventually they'll see for themselves.' I was determined to pretend that the baby wasn't happening. Told myself that if not for this thing growing inside me everything would be perfect. If only it would go away. I hated it – and longed for it. For I knew that it was the only piece of Seamus that would always be mine.

'Gabby, let's get together sometime soon. I want to talk to you.'

I'd phoned her again, eventually. My need to see her, to be close to her, had been stronger than the fear of her scorn. Through a lens clouded with sentimentality and nostalgia and loneliness, I looked back on our times together in the steamy bathroom and saw bliss. How I missed her.

'I miss you,' I said, and she must have heard the wobble in my voice.

'Funny, Mims – I was just about to phone you,' she responded brightly after the briefest possible pause. 'I wanted to tell you about the flat and everything. It's all so exciting. Bernice has been staying with us, helping us to settle in, organizing things you know. Anyway, she's gone back to Birmingham now. And I thought it would be really nice if you and – Seamus – would come for dinner. Next Friday.'

Her voice tripped ever so slightly over Seamus's name. It faltered over the invitation, the peace-offering. It wasn't easy for her. Gabriella was offering to share the Sabbath candles with her errant sister and a dangerous stranger. She was declaring a truce.

'Thank you,' I said, suppressing a sudden desire to giggle at the vision of Seamus in a skull-cap sipping his sanctified wine. Of me, a Sabbath bride big with illegitimate child. Of Clive smacking his lips over stocks and shares and the fragrant meal, and Gabriella – my little sister Gabriella who'd flown away to become an artist – feeding him chopped liver and indigestion tablets. 'We'd love to come.'

By the sixth day God had completed all the work he had been doing. He'd created man and woman in his own image and told them to be fruitful and multiply and rule over the fish in the sea and the birds of heaven and every living thing that moved on the earth. He looked at everything he had made and was rather pleased with himself. On the sixth day he added the finishing touches and on the eve of the Sabbath he gave himself a well-earned rest.

On the eve of the Sabbath a few thousand years later, the new Mrs Wiseman looked at all she'd created – the wax-polished dining-table, the gleaming formica kitchen, the chicken sizzling behind the glass-doored oven. And she saw that it was good. And she said to her husband (with whom she had multiplied but not yet been fruitful): 'Tomorrow we'll have a good rest. Preparing for guests is so tiring . . .'

And on the eve of the Sabbath several hundred miles away and a mere micro-second later in terms of eternity, two sisters looked at the haven they'd created in a pocket of heat in the Holy Land – a stone floor, a spider-plant and a battered carp sizzling in the pan. And they swore that it was good. And the older sister said to the younger (both of whom by then had multiplied and borne fruit): 'Perhaps we should start eating. Whoever it was is probably not coming back. Tomorrow we'll have a good rest. Preparing for the Sabbath is so tiring . . .'

'Out. They're always out on a Friday morning. The hairdresser, shopping. You know what it's like?'

He hadn't. But the ancient crone seated with her buddies in a dim corner of the foyer had seemed to know everything. The three had reminded him of harpies: evil, winged monsters with the heads and breasts of women. But perhaps, he thought, trying to be charitable, they were the Graces in disguise. For beauty and charm were not always apparent to the beholder. That was a lesson he'd learnt well. Still, the last thing he'd wanted was to be trapped in conversation. So he had shrugged indifferently and turned to the door.

The noon heat rose from the yellow path and beat down from the bleached blue sky. 'I'll have to wait,' he thought. And he remembered how the children of Israel had waited in the wilderness for forty years before they were allowed to enter the promised land. They'd been pacified with hot bread from heaven and their parched throats soothed with water that gushed from a rock – and they'd waited. He didn't have forty years.

'Orange juice, please,' he said tersely to the Arab waiter in the small restaurant set back from the shady side of the main shopping street. He'd chosen a secluded table – just in case. It wouldn't do for him to be seen. Not yet. He wasn't quite ready and he wondered whether she was ready – and doubted it. Would they ever be?

He raised the glass to his lips and felt the liquid slipping down his throat like cool nectar. Would it give him immortality? Just a touch?

Deep in thought, he hardly noticed the emptying of the street. Suddenly it was still. Kfar Tikva had retreated indoors to make way for the Sabbath. Would the sisters be preparing? Cooking fish perhaps?

'I can't go through with this,' he said to himself. 'Perhaps I should go home.' Then he lifted his eyes to the darkening sky and saw a single bright star and he knew there was no going back. The time had come.

❧ 12 ❧

When God kindled the first star on the Sabbath eve, there was a hush in heaven, and then a great rush of wings as the angels came down bearing souls of every shape, size and colour. 'Take advantage of our special weekend bargain,' they whispered into earth-bound ears. 'We're offering an extra soul on free twenty-four-hour loan in exchange for peaceful contemplation on the day of rest.'

And millions of God's people – those who'd always meant to fill in coupons for football pools and ignored invitations to take part in lucky draws and lost the money-off vouchers they tore out of newspapers and never expected to win anything anyway – thought, 'Why not? What have I got to lose?'

And they picked out a soul and placed it alongside their old one to wear for a night and a day.

And God looked down on them and smiled. He knew that the night before Sabbath was like human life on the eve of the world to come. That the day of rest was the hereafter. And that with two souls and a breathing space, his people would taste paradise.

'Not bad,' he thought, 'not bad at all.' It was always satisfying to orchestrate a good deal.

'Perhaps we should start eating,' said Mia. 'Whoever it was is probably not coming back.' She sighed as she turned over the fish in the steaming oil and it seemed to sizzle sympathetically. Herbert had always made all the right noises. 'Tomorrow we'll have a good rest. Preparing for the Sabbath is so tiring. Isn't it, Gabs?'

Her sister had left the kitchen and was standing at the living-room window staring out into the night.

'I can see a star,' she said. 'Oh Mia, I feel so strange.'

No, thought Mia fiercely, giving the frying pan a shake. This was not what she'd planned for their Sabbath eve. Not at all. She hated the tension, the feeling that they were on the edge of an abyss. For eighteen months she'd thought they'd found a refuge in Kfar Tikva. Peace. A kind of forgetfulness.

It was what they had wanted when all seemed lost and the two of them were holding on to one another in the Hendon house with its ghosts of shoes and secrets in a steamy bathroom and a weak voice that had called, 'Darling . . .' and been silenced.

'Kfar Tikva?' Gabby had asked when the letter had arrived. 'Where the hell is that?'

Who cared? Mia took the envelope listlessly. Nothing had mattered much then. It was as though all her caring had been poured into those around her – her child and her mother, and the last drops wrung out to restore her shattered sister. All needing her. Draining her till she drooped like the plants she now pointedly ignored in the dark deathlike house. Kfar Tikva? Ah, yes.

'I remember now,' she'd said. 'Mum once mentioned an uncle who had a smallholding, a little corner of Israel. I went to see it when I was there with – Seamus.' She still found it difficult to say his name. 'But there was nothing. Only a block of flats that seemed to have been baked yellow-brown in the sun. I remember the heat. And I remember seeing it as the place to which people came when all else had failed. The end of the world.'

'Sounds ideal,' Gabby had laughed bitterly. 'The perfect spot for two screwed-up sisters.'

Mia read the letter. A descendant of the aforementioned uncle had died intestate and after many years his closest living relatives had been traced. The daughters of Hilda Marks had inherited his fortune – a two-roomed apartment in a sun-scorched block perched on ground that had once been his smallholding in the promised land.

'We're heiresses,' she said in a flat voice. It all seemed so remote. Nothing to do with her at all. What difference would it make, owning a flat in faraway Kfar Tikva?

146

'How about it, Mims?' Gabby spoke more animatedly than she had for months. A course of electroconvulsive treatments had hardly touched the frightening depression into which she had sunk. Medication hadn't moved her. Psychotherapy had failed. Yet the idea of an escape – the promise of heat and light at the end of the tunnel – had captured her imagination. Suddenly there were echoes of the little girl who had pictures to paint, stories to tell, an adoring world at her feet.

'Why don't the two of us simply pack up and go? Please, Mims – let's think about it?'

It was the old Gabriella talking. The sister who'd held out the tantalizing promise of closeness, comfort, companionship. 'The two of us.' Mia was captivated despite herself. A part of her knew that closeness usually meant dependency, that comfort rarely went two ways and that her sister had always found her companionship dull. Experience told her that it would never work. And yet . . .

'Mims, listen.' Gabby used her most persuasive tones. 'Don't you think it was fate that we should be offered the place now, just when we're at a – crossroads? It's like a story. A happy accident. You know the word – serendipity?'

'Yes,' she'd said quietly. 'I know the word.'

It was the babes in the wood all over again. Sisters lost in the forest, cowering together in fear of serpents and storms and evil witches – until there, far in the distance, they see a bright patch of light. Their legacy. Their happy accident. A magic talisman from their mother to help them to fight the terrors of the night. Hand in hand they make their way to claim their birthright and in the fierce glow of their togetherness the forces of evil are struck blind and helpless. And they reach their place of safety, their magic patch of light and there they live for ever more. The two of them.

Fantasy, thought Mia. Would she ever be cured of seeing her life in fairy-tale terms? Dreams, dreams, dreams, she muttered crossly. You're too old for them now. Children chase rainbows and best friends and bright bubbles, and think they can make things happen. You should know better by now.

So she told herself. Yet Gabby's promise had been irresistible. She'd finally agreed and they'd loosened their ties with England and set sail for the promised land. The two of them. And for eighteen months Mia had waited in vain for the closeness and comfort and companionship with which her sister had enticed her away. And meanwhile Gabby had been waiting too. For what?

'I can't understand why we're both so edgy today,' Mia said sharply. 'All afternoon, and then this man coming and going. And now you say you feel "strange". What's up?'

'I don't know. It's an odd sensation. Like when you're watching the final act of a long and tedious play and expecting the curtain to fall. And you don't know if you really want it to end because it's a cold and rainy night. Much cosier to stay in the dark theatre. But the play is so boring and it goes on and on and on . . .'

Gabriella turned to face her sister. She was about to cry. Her brittle composure seemed to have shattered and she looked little and crumpled in her black designer dress.

'Oh Gabs.' Mia left the spatula in the pan and crossed the room. Her little sister felt like a fragile bird in her arms. A sharp-winged bird who struggled away.

'You're right, Mims.' No, Gabriella didn't want to be comforted. Mia stepped back sadly for she knew that whatever Gabby thought, however long she wanted to stay in the dark auditorium, the curtain was dropping. They'd have to face the cold.

She imagined herself stepping out into a biting wind, being buffeted but not falling. Refusing to accept numb shelter in a warm secluded cave but walking on and on towards her own magic patch of light. Alone. And suddenly Mia knew it was possible. It was as though something had burst into bud inside her. Perhaps her soul had sprouted its own sister.

'But Gabs, it doesn't have to be . . .' she began. She badly wanted to share this with her. It was important. But Gabriella had reassumed control. Her voice had regained its edge.

'Whoever it was is not coming back,' she said testily. 'I agree. We may as well start eating.'

There was a pause. A thought. A ripple of little Gabby almost imperceptible over her fixed frown. 'How about lighting some candles tonight, Mims?' she asked in a voice that seemed not to care one way or another. 'Shall we?' She *did* care. 'Let's do it Mims – for old times' sake.'

*

Clive Wiseman was otherwise engaged when spare souls were being offered on the chilly night in January that his sister-in-law and her lover had been invited for a meal. Constipation. General irritation.

'Leave me alone,' he muttered to the persistent angel as he strained on the lavatory and looked to Hippocrates for inspiration. He'd been pestered all day. Clients wanting financial accounts. His mother demanding accounts of his health, wealth and marriage. A beggar on the tube. Next door's bulldog who felt a fatal attraction for his balls.

He'd beaten off the bulldog and brushed away the angel. As if the prospect of an evening with that pudding-faced Mia and her Irishman wasn't enough to cope with. One soul would be quite sufficient, thank you very much.

'A ridiculous idea,' he'd said to Gabriella. 'I can understand your wanting to see your sister. After all, family is family. Nobody knows that better than me. But, honestly, to entertain that – Seamus – under our roof. And on a Friday night. I don't know what came over you.'

It was their first real disagreement. He'd read about tiffs in early marriage and wondered when they'd start having them. At least he knew now that they were behaving normally in that respect even though their rate of conjugation appeared to be somewhat below par. Clive had tried his best to dissuade her, but Gabby had stood firm.

'Please Clivey,' she'd said (he loved it when she called him that). 'This is something I really want – very badly. I couldn't bear to have a permanent rift with my sister. And now that she's living with this man, we should try and accept him.'

He hadn't been convinced but there'd seemed to be no point arguing and so he'd agreed. And now the fateful evening had come and he regretted his compliance.

'Fuck!' he said furiously as, in rising from the lavatory after futile endeavours, he hit his head on the sloping ceiling. 'Fuck, fuck, *fuck*!' He didn't normally go in for expletives, particularly hated it when women swore, but things were really getting him down. 'Piss off,' he said to the angel, who'd been hovering by in hope. She fluttered nervously away. Perhaps the man's young wife would be more open to an offer.

*

149

Gabriella in the kitchen was exceedingly nervous.

'An all-purpose hero coming to Finchley for food,' she marvelled. Then laughed at herself. After all, it was only Mia, her boring old sister. Mia and a man she'd picked up somewhere. And everyone, absolutely everyone, had been scornful and said she was sordid and the man must be a bastard and she didn't deserve to be asked for dinner anyway. Not after she'd left her poor sick mother in the lurch and abandoned her sister.

'They're extremely lucky to have been invited,' she said primly, smoothing her daisy-print apron over the simple navy-blue dress she'd put on for the occasion. She'd spent ages deciding on her image. Should she be the innocent child-bride in soft pastels? Woman of the world in chic black? Serious in sober navy? And the menu? Should it be heavy on cholesterol and Jewish tradition, just to show Mia what she was missing? Or wholesome healthy fare with plenty of fibre – the product of a caring wife? Or perhaps a touch of haute cuisine? After all, she had travelled the . . . well, Europe. Some of it anyway. Eaten in the best hotels . . .

Gabby bent down to check on the chicken, its golden-brown skin gleaming through the glass door of the oven. Crisp potatoes nestled beneath its breast. The soup simmered on the hob, fragrant memorial to another late fowl. Small egg-yolks bobbed on the surface alongside a scrawny brown neck and a grey gizzard. The kosher kitchen bubbled and sizzled and steamed its aromatic epitaph to the henhouse, and the angel (having entered) praised Godmother Bernice for her thorough teaching.

'A nice solid meat meal,' thought Gabby, standing up, satisfied, smoothing her hair. 'Stability. That's what she'll envy more than anything.' And him? Sir Galahad-from-Dublin? What would impress him? 'Who cares?' she asked defiantly. 'Why on earth should I care what *he* thinks?'

'Why indeed?' whispered the angel, who'd overheard and knew everything. And into Gabby's ear came the offer of a second soul for a night and a day. 'It will double your capacity for food, drink, thought, enchantment. You'll be twice the woman you are.'

'Oh, well,' she shrugged, 'I may as well take it. A good deal. Nothing to lose . . . not that his opinion of me really matters.' She placed two candles on the elegantly set table and gave a last glance at the food. The angel winked and flittered away, leaving Gabriella (with an extra soul and a few added dabs of Chanel in various places) awaiting her guests.

'Clive,' she called. 'Are you ready. They'll be here any minute.'

Mia regretted having accepted her sister's invitation. She was nauseous and nervous and reluctant to expose herself to Gabriella's scrutiny. It was only Seamus's eyes that she wanted. She longed to bask in the orbit of his vision, in the field of his touch, all day and all night long.

'Do you still like – to look – at me?' she asked, praying that her body wouldn't change too much, too fast. Her breasts were already heavier and she tensed when his hands lingered on her thickening waist. He'd tire of her. She knew he would.

'Of course I do. Mia, you're beautiful. If only you'd believe me.'

If only. She ran her hands down the leanness of his back and shut her eyes and tried to engrave the feel of his body into her memory. Another keepsake from Cloud-cuckoo-land. One day when she was much, much older, she'd take out her overflowing box of mementoes and show them one by one to the child growing inside her. 'Long ago,' she'd begin, 'very long ago, I went on the most wonderful journey imaginable. I travelled to a country that most people only visit in their dreams.'

But now their journey was to Finchley. Friday night supper with Gabby and Clive was hardly the stuff of heady fantasies. Why on earth had she agreed to go when they could easily have stayed at home and gone to paradise instead?

'Are you almost ready, Seamus?' she called. 'Gabby said to be there at seven and I have a feeling we ought to be punctual. Clive's not the sort to tolerate latecomers. His digestion is – rather delicate.'

There was a gurgle of mirth from the bathroom, where her lover seemed to be going to inordinate lengths to smarten himself for the Sabbath. He'd trimmed the dark stubble he'd decided to cajole into the beginnings of a grainy beard and was enthusiastically lathering his legs.

'I can't wait,' he shouted above energetic splashing sounds. 'Clive sounds an utter delight.' An explosion of laughter and

151

then a lull as he closed the tap. His face appeared round the door, scrubbed and gleaming and eager.

'And your sister, Mia? You say she doesn't look anything like you?'

'No, we're not at all alike.' She'd described Gabby several times. His endless questions were beginning to be irritating.

'I won't be long. Just pulling on some pants and a jumper.'

He seemed so keen for this confrontation. Mia sighed tiredly and sat at the table and tried not to listen to his cheerful whistling as he combed his hair and dressed noisily. She noticed a half-full sheet of typescript still in place in his typewriter and started reading it. 'Jerusalem. Act III. Final scene.' Gosh. She hadn't known that he was so close to the end. 'Final scene.' Wasn't it awesome, the power of a writer to decree the end of a chapter, the end of a book, the end of it all? She ran her eye down the page.

> BRENDAN. It's not real – this place that we've found. I think we're chasing a dream. (A long silence) D'you know, my darling, I don't think there is a Jerusalem. Not here. Not on earth.
>
> CUR

'CUR'? Couldn't he bring himself to complete the word? Had he been interrupted – or overwhelmed with the might of his power? Was God ever overwhelmed with the might of His power to create – endings? Mia was suddenly dizzy with the immensity of all the endings made by man and God and weak with her helplessness to create her own endings or new beginnings. She put her hands over her ears to shut out the complacent tuneless whistling of this man who'd half-dared – and was deaf to the voice of the angel whispering its ware: 'A soul, a soul. A nice fresh soul for the Sabbath. Take it, Mia, enjoy, enjoy.'

But she didn't hear. And even if she had, she'd probably have refused. Her own soul felt like a vast ocean in which she feared she would drown. The last thing she needed was another. Double the feelings? Double the pain? No. Certainly not. One was quite enough.

Rebuffed, the angel flew listlessly to the bedroom where Seamus, still whistling, was lacing his shoes. He was thinking

152

about the fun he'd have teasing pompous Clive and being ever so polite to prissy Gabriella, about how he'd almost finished his play and if only the milkman hadn't knocked at the door he'd have finished completely and that would have been that. About . . .

'What?' He stopped whistling. Something, someone, was whispering in his ear. 'What's that you're offering? A soul? An extra soul for the Sabbath? But I'm not even Jewish.'

'No matter,' said the angel wearily. Selling was exhausting, particularly since the bottom seemed to have fallen out of belief. People were more interested in capital gains than spiritual growth. 'We're now extending the deal – for a limited period only you understand – to interested others and since you're on your way to sanctify the Sabbath, I have you on my list. You're my last customer, so please decide quickly. I'm tired.'

'Fine. I'll take it.' That was Seamus. A man of decision.

'What? No questions? No quibbling? You'll just – take it?' The angel, astounded, handed over the soul. 'Must fly,' she said – and was almost back at the gates of heaven when she realized that she hadn't collected her half of the bargain from that handsome Irishman. She'd forgotten to take from him the pledge that he'd spend his Sabbath in peaceful contemplation.

Damn! Oh God – now she'd sworn as well. And just when she'd finally made it to the marketing department. Now she'd be back in the cleaning squad, hoovering heaven and endlessly ironing cloaks for that fussy Elijah who was waiting till things were better before taking a trip down to earth. Well, he'd be waiting for ever. She could tell him that for sure.

'Come on in, come on in. I'm Clive. Very pleased to meet you.'

'Seamus O'Reilly.'

'Hello Seamus. This is Gabby, my wife.'

'Well, hello Gabriella. We meet at last. You don't look like your sister at all.'

'I told you she didn't. Hi Gabs – it's lovely to see you.'

'Mims, you look – wonderful. Hello, Seamus. I'm glad you could come.'

'Sit down everyone. Make yourselves comfortable. Seamus, a drink? It's whiskey that you – your people – like, isn't it?'

153

'No thank you, Clive. I'll stick to – er – kosher wine tonight. That's what – your people prefer. Not so?'

(Polite laughter. A long pause during which throats are cleared and sentences half-begun.)

'Well then, since we're not drinking, perhaps we should start dinner. Gabby, are we all ready? Good. Mia, you'll be amazed at what an excellent cook your sister's turning into. Come, let's move to the table.'

There were six souls side by side round the dinner table when Clive Wiseman recited the Kiddush over a cup of wine. Six souls and four people heard the sanctification. A man and a woman with two souls each. Two high-octane spirits that sparked across the expanse of starched white linen and ignited, and almost outshone the two candles glowing in their silver sticks.

'Amen,' said Clive, and took a token sip. Red wine gave him headaches but on Sabbath eve it was a duty to imbibe – a little.

'Amen,' said Seamus and sipped voluptuously. His two souls sang a sensuous duet. 'Cheers,' he said mischievously, tilting his ruby glass towards Gabriella who sat opposite him. She looked away. Her souls were strangling her. She swallowed and told herself to breathe.

'Seamus, honestly, that's not what you're supposed to say.' Mia was embarrassed. She felt Clive's accusing eyes on her, as though she were responsible for desecrating the sanctity of his Sabbath. He's not mine, she wanted to say. He doesn't belong to me. I wish he did.

Clive shut the prayer book and sat down. There was something amiss about this gathering and he didn't like it one bit. 'Have a piece of chollah,' he said to Seamus. 'It's special bread to remind us of the manna sent down to save the Israelites in the desert from starvation.' Perhaps the Irishman would be impressed with the significance of it all. Add a bit of dignity to the occasion.

'Ah, manna,' said Seamus. He took a bite and frowned, thinking. '"The taste of it was like wafers made with honey . . .",' he quoted dreamily. 'Have you ever heard of the Manna of St Nicholas of Bari, Clive? Some called it Aqua Tofana. Ever come across it?'

'No,' said Clive doubtfully. Of all the subjects in the world, he'd chosen one about which the Irishman knew something he didn't. Clive hated to be caught out. 'What about it?'

'It was the name of a poisonous liquid containing arsenic – used by young wives who wanted to get rid of their husbands.' Seamus looked at Gabriella and smiled, and her chest tightened again and she rose to fetch the chicken soup. There was a long uncomfortable pause. 'Of course,' he added lightly, 'this was long ago – in Italy. Young wives today are generally most happy with their husbands.'

'Yes, they are,' said Gabby as firmly as she could, returning with the brimming silver tureen. 'Would you like some soup?'

Seamus watched her dipping the curved ladle into the golden liquid. Her wrist was tiny and perfectly formed. Her little-girl body was moulded into navy-blue severity and her child-face set into young-wife conformity. He saw a small wild creature trapped and afraid in the claw of domesticity. Longing to be rescued. And his two souls swelled and soared at the thought of Seamus, the gallant knight, releasing the trap. Setting her free. Adoring her.

'I'd love some soup,' he said. His voice was not quite steady.

'I can honestly recommend it,' said Clive. 'My mother's recipe you know. It's been in the Wiseman family for ages.' He spoke with complete authority. There was nothing anyone could tell him about chicken soup.

It was going to be a long evening, thought Mia, as she lifted a spoonful to her mouth. She tried to smile, to say something amusing, but it was as though her body were made of mirrored glass and her mind kept bouncing back into itself. Into the small secret place where there was fear and a baby and an empty space where there should have been a mother.

'How's Mum?' she asked suddenly. She had to know.

'Fine. Getting along well.' Gabby forced her attention away from the disturbing presence opposite her. This man who'd suddenly made her remember she was – a woman. 'Elsie's working there full-time now – cleaning, cooking, looking after her,' she said meaningfully. 'And Clive and I are there as often as we can manage. She asks after you.'

'Give her – my love.'

It was going to be a long evening, thought Clive, as he lifted a spoonful to his mouth. And they hadn't even got to the main course yet. Roast potatoes – mmm, that should be worth waiting for. And then apple crumble. They always had apple crumble on Friday nights. Wasn't it wonderful the way they were establishing their own family traditions? And then, after coffee, they'd leave at last. The guests. What a misery that Mia was becoming. Worse than ever. And what a coarse bumpkin she'd got for herself.

And after they'd gone, please God, he could get to grips with his bowels and then perhaps have a little sex. On the other hand, it was Friday and he was tired and he was sure Gabriella was tired and it was supposed to be a night of rest, so perhaps they'd go to sleep and worry about sex another time. Now Saturday night . . .

Yes, it was going to be a long evening. It *was* a long evening. For Clive. For Mia.

And for Gabby and Seamus, blinded and breathless in the flare of four incandescent souls, it was an eternity.

'Hello – Gabriella?'

'It's you. I knew you'd phone.'

'I'm glad you answered. Where's Clive?'

'Out. On Saturday afternoons he usually visits his Aunty Bubbles in Edgware. And Mia?'

'Out. She didn't say where she was going. Gabriella, I have to see you. I hardly slept all night.'

'Where? How? It's impossible. You know it's impossible.'

'Nothing is – if you want it badly enough. Tell me, does Clive usually stay out – long? On a Saturday when he visits his Aunt – er – Bubbles?'

'Till around six.'

'It's only three. Ages still. May I come and see you? Please?'

'Oh – Seamus. I don't . . .'

'Please. Gabriella, please. I need to see you. You need me too. Don't say no.'

'How can . . . oh, I don't know. I don't know what to do. Perhaps if you came for – coffee – we could have a good – talk. Would you like to do that? Have a – chat?'

'Yes – yes. I'm leaving now. Be with you in no time at all.'

*

156

As the shadows began to lengthen on Sabbath afternoon, the pious prepared to mark the ending of the day of rest. 'Havdalah', they called it. The ceremony of division. They brought out boxes filled with sweet-smelling spices and candles to be lit.

And as the sun sank, they blessed the flames that danced on their tables and thanked God for his gift of fire.

And as the angels descended to gather in the Sabbath souls, the pious breathed in the scent of cinnamon and ginger and cloves and mace to nourish the single soul they retained. And they thanked God again. They appreciated everything.

And back in heaven, the angels counted their souls and tried to balance the books. (Naturally they waited until the Sabbath was quite over before starting on their paperwork. God was terribly fussy about rules.) But somehow, no matter how many times they re-counted, there was one soul missing.

They looked accusingly at a certain colleague who'd been demoted to the ironing board. But she stared back blankly. It was bad enough to be punished for blasphemy, she'd decided. Admitting the loss of a soul would be fatal.

For she hadn't collected the soul lent to Seamus. One by one, she'd gathered the others, until she came to a certain Finchley address to retrieve the item borrowed by one Gabriella Wiseman (Mrs). When the angel entered, fully expecting Mrs Wiseman to be inhaling spices or – at the very least – her husband, she came upon her deep in the aromatic scent of Seamus O'Reilly.

Profoundly shocked, and feeling rather responsible (after all, this O'Reilly chap had got away without signing the placidity clause), she'd shut her eyes and grabbed the first soul that came to hand and jetted away, hoping fervently that the error wouldn't be spotted.

And so a new week dawned. Evening came, and morning came, the first day. And Seamus, feeling the weight of two souls and reeling under the wondrous memory of an afternoon of ecstasy with liberated Mrs Wiseman, wanted her. Wanted her so much it was unbearable. And Gabriella, her single soul deprived of the holy smell of cinnamon etcetera, felt the weight of her guilt. And reeled as she tried to expel the memory of such sensual pleasure she'd never have believed possible. And regretted it. She felt such remorse it was unbearable. Never would she be able to look her sister in the eye again.

🌿 13 🌿

Never would I be able to look my sister in the eye again. Never. I didn't know it was possible to feel such remorse.

'I have an awful headache, Clivey. I think I may be getting flu,' I told him weakly, and buried myself in the blankets and blamed Seamus for my betrayal. He'd led me on. Blasted his way into my kosher bastion, my formica fortress in Finchley, stripped me of my apron and my oven-gloves and my Maidenform bra and . . .

Oh, it was wonderful. Our king-sized bed had never seen such contortions, never heard such moans of ecstasy. The *Wife's Guide* proved quite redundant. I knew how to please him. I knew, I knew. And God how he knew ways to make me gasp at the great pyrotechnic display that whooshed and sprayed and sparked luminous colours in the pastel-pinkness of our marital suite. He showed me fireworks and stroked me and soothed me and filled me with such supreme contentment that I was sure I must have entered heaven.

Until I heard the tinkling sound of Seamus peeing into Clive's throne and his mocking voice. 'Hippocrates, eh?'

'That's my husband's,' I said, sitting up.

And I knew this wasn't really heaven at all. It was the heart of suburbia and I'd chosen to dance to its beat. Any more fireworks with Seamus and someone would have a coronary thrombosis. Already I suspected a clot.

'I feel terrible,' I said, holding my chest which had suddenly begun to ache.

'Gabriella, don't. Please don't.' He came back and put a warm hand on the soreness and I felt myself swimming – and forced myself back to the surface. I'd drown. I knew I'd drown and be dead in a blackness that was a long, long way from heaven. 'I

love you,' he was saying. 'Truly, truly I do. I've never told that
to anyone before.'

Anyone? What about . . .

'No. Not even your – sister.'

'But . . .?' I began. But I didn't want to know. I was suddenly
afraid – for her, for me, for everyone. What was I doing? What
had I done? I dressed. Panties. Bra. Tights. The neat skirt and
blouse that Clive liked me to wear on Saturdays. The cameo
brooch Bernice had given me pinned at my throat. Everything
back in place. Forget. Forget.

'I love you,' he said again, coming up from behind me and
turning me round and dropping the softest lips imaginable on
to the pulsing place just above the cameo brooch. My breath
stopped. I became a giant heartbeat, pounding, pounding, oh –
I was going to. I caught myself. Clenched my jaw, my fists, my
stomach and my knocking heart, and said, 'It's five-thirty. We'd
better – straighten things out. Clive might come – early.'

He nodded. Tidied the bed with me, followed me obediently
downstairs.

'Goodbye,' he said at the door. He didn't touch me. His eyes
touched me.

'Goodbye.'

I was alone in the kitchen with two half-empty mugs of cold
coffee. Slowly I tipped them into the sink and watched the
brown liquid and off-white slimy skins slipping down the drain.
Dead skins gone for ever while mine still tingled from his touch.
I hadn't known that skin could feel so. I rinsed the mugs and
placed them upside-down on the draining rack and then
decided to dry them and put them away. No traces. No visible
sign at all that I'd had coffee and – a chat – with my sister's
man. Only a fiercely gnawing ache that I decided must be guilt
and remorse. It was a new pain. A sort I'd never ever felt
before.

For Clive I labelled it as the worst headache of my life, the
beginnings of the most dreadful flu.

'Have you taken anything?' he asked. He was a great believer
in the efficacy of patent medicines and worshipped them in
tandem with the gods of regularity. Well then, I'd worship
alongside him or underneath him or upstairs in the synagogue
gallery where the women were kept. Anywhere, anything to
make up for what I'd done.

'What d'you suggest?' I asked, with just the right amount of respect due to a high priest of hypochondria. 'This is the third day I've been feeling like this. All of yesterday and now this morning.'

He mulled over my malady, medicated me, made me tea and gave me sympathy. I groaned from under the bedclothes and he squeezed the sheets and said, 'I'd better get going, Gabs. I'll be late for work.'

'Bye,' came my muffled tearful voice. I felt so sorry for this pitiful creature who'd been pushed from her chosen path of righteousness. It wasn't fair. She'd never really meant to stray. There she was with her basket of kosher goodies, skipping happily along and Doing the Right Thing when along came a wicked, wicked wolf.

How I wished Seamus were dead. Had never been born. I wished – oh, damn it, what I really wished was for him to be with me in bed.

The phone rang.

'Gabriella? Are you alone?'

'Yes. Look, Seamus. I'm sorry about what happened. Let's forget about it. OK?'

'You're *sorry*? I can't believe you're sorry about something so – wonderful. Gabriella, I meant it. I did. I've never said it before. I love you. We have to talk.'

'No.'

'Please. Why not? I simply don't understand.'

'Seamus, no. It's impossible. I can't – do it any more. I'm feeling – so bad about it. You have to understand. There's – Clive. And – my sister. I can't do this to my sister.'

'Can't we just talk about it? I'll meet you somewhere. Talk – only talk. I promise you.'

'That's what you said on Saturday. No. Please, no. Goodbye.'

I put down the receiver, my virtue rating slightly higher, my libido soaring and my spirits down to nil. How was I to keep resisting him? Would he persist? Would I eventually succumb? No Gabriella no, I told myself sternly. Hold firm. I would, but I didn't want him to give up. Not yet. Not so easily. He'd said he loved me. Had he told my sister that too? I was sure he had. But there was a tiny little part of me that thought perhaps not and an even smaller part that was – glad. A micro-corner of me

160

that was pleased about the possibility that maybe I'd taken something of hers that she'd never even had.

A wave of pain washed over me and I pulled the sheets back over my head and wished that he'd leave me alone, never pester me again. Would he?

He did. Tenaciously. And I held firm equally tenaciously. And I stayed in bed for the week and Clive brought me flowers and a huge jar of multicoloured vitamin pills.

'These will pep you up,' he said, holding out two pink ones with a glass of water. I swallowed them. He drew up a chair alongside the bed and took my hand and fondled it. In a rush of warmth – and guilt – I flung out my arms and pulled him towards me and crushed my mouth against his. He turned his face away.

'You might be infectious,' he explained, straightening the limp locks of hair over his bald patch. 'It's silly for us to take chances.' I looked at this man whom I'd – chosen. And I couldn't help comparing him with Seamus. And I didn't even find the comparison funny. I buried my face into the pillow and broke into painful sobs.

'Gabs?' He patted my shoulder, frightened. 'Gabs, are you all right? I've never seen you like this . . .'

No, no, no, I wanted to scream. I'm not all right at all, you great oaf. I'm going to have to stick with you for the rest of my life just because I made up my mind that you were going to give me security and a family, something to belong to, and I can't go back on my decision now. And I'd rather be with anyone – no, someone – else. And I can't. You've bought this king-sized bed and I'm going to have to lie in it. I cried and cried till there weren't any tears left. Then I slept.

And Seamus kept phoning and still I said no but waited for him to try again. Until one morning, about ten days after the fateful Sabbath, the phone rang and it was Mia.

'Gabby, I have to speak to you. Can I come over?'

'Of course . . . what – about? When – do you want to come?'

'Any time. I'm not at work. I wasn't – feeling well.'

'Oh – I'm sorry. Actually I'm also stuck at home. I haven't been feeling – too well – myself. Flu I think.'

'Oh. Is it all right if I come today, this afternoon perhaps?'

'Come for lunch. I'll warm up the bagels Bernice sent me. We can have them with some soup.'

161

What on earth did she want? Surely he hadn't said anything to her? She sounded desperate. He'd sounded desperate.

'Gabriella,' he'd said pleadingly the day before, 'this is unbearable. I can't live like this. You have to agree to see me.'

'No, Seamus. No. No. No.'

Perhaps he'd gone to her and told her all. What would I say? What could I say? 'I'm sorry, Mims. I'm so sorry. I didn't mean it to happen at all.' That wouldn't be enough.

'Have a bagel,' I'd try. 'Bernice's bagels always make one feel better. You know, she gets up at six in the morning to roll the dough. I'm going to start doing that. It's good for the soul. Here, have one with some chopped liver. She made that too. A real saint, my mother-in-law. I don't know what I'd do without her.' No. That wouldn't be enough either.

It turned out that nothing was enough. There was a knock on the door at one o'clock and there she stood, looking like – well, exactly the sort of woman Bernice would have described as having 'let herself go'. Her hair was greasy and uncombed. There were dark pouches under lost eyes. Her grey smocked dress would have been rejected by Oxfam and she'd have been turned down for the part of 'before' girl in the beauty ads. Charity shops and make-over cases existed on hope. And Mia seemed hopeless.

'What is it? What's the matter Mims?'

I hadn't meant to burst out with that. I'd dressed carefully as the innocent child-bride with lightly applied lipstick and a touch of mascara to add drama to the eyes. The department store consultant had taught me exactly how to do it. 'Mia!' I was going to exclaim. 'It's good to see you. Come and sit down. The bagels are in the oven, and while they're warming you can tell me all about it . . .'

But I hadn't counted on the way I'd feel. The catch in my throat. The longing to throw myself into her arms. To comfort, be comforted. Oh Mia, what had happened to us?

'Gabby . . .' she started. Tears welled up. She couldn't go on.

'It's OK. Come, come inside. Mims – what's the problem?'

She allowed me to lead her into the living-room where she sank into one of the fully upholstered chairs and her head sank into her arms and she sobbed with despair.

'What is it?' I asked again. There'd been so much crying in that flat recently it was a miracle it hadn't fogged up with galloping damp. But was my sister as moisture-resistant as my flat?

'It won't feel so bad once you've spoken about it,' I said with crossed fingers.

'It will,' she hiccupped. Then it all came out in a rush – that she was pregnant, she was losing Seamus, she was afraid.

That was it. Phew. No mention of me at all. Now I could be truly supportive.

'Oh, Mims – you'll have a beautiful child,' I said. She would. Any child of Seamus's would be beautiful. 'I'm sure you're imagining it – about Seamus. He's probably just getting used to the idea of being a – father. You have told him, haven't you?'

She nodded. I gave her a tissue. She wiped her eyes and blew her nose loudly and I brought her a bagel.

'He must be in a state of shock,' I said as confidently as I could. 'Men are like that, you know. Not as resilient as we are.'

'And there's Mum,' she said after a while, much calmer now. I was doing a fine job. 'I'm so upset about what's happened with her. I thought she'd have accepted – things – by now. D'you think she ever will?'

I thought about it. Mum seemed less angry than oblivious. Spoke about the ever-worsening deficiencies in her health, the flaws in Elsie's housekeeping and the tendencies of her friends to cheat at cards. I'd have said she was almost happy. Almost likely to be receptive to the idea of a reconcilliation.

I'd do it. I'd play the good fairy and bring it about. It was the least I could do for my sister. For myself. For my redemption.

'Mims – I'm going to have a word with her. I've a feeling that she might be coming round. Don't bank on it. But I'll see what I can do.'

She'd stopped crying completely now. For the first time I saw a hint of hope in her bearing. She looked at me and almost smiled. 'I think I'd – like you to do that Gabs. I've – missed her.'

Her eyes met mine, and now she smiled properly. And the dark pouches and greasy locks and raw nose seemed to fade behind something that lit her from within. Something that had caught the imagination of Seamus – perhaps something finer than the Little Red Riding Hood he'd ravished on the six-foot bed. I turned away. I couldn't bear to see it. It felt safer to focus on the grease and the pouches and the raw red nose.

'Mims,' I said, using my know-it-all voice. I couldn't help myself. 'I really ought to tell you that perhaps you shouldn't make your – er – insecurity so visible. You know, in terms of your concerns about Seamus staying interested. You mustn't let yourself go. When you make an effort, you can look really attractive. Mims, I'm telling you this for your sake. Because I – care.'

The light went out. I stopped feeling pleased with myself. I'd speak to Mum on her behalf, I vowed. And I'd hold firm in my refusal to see Seamus again. It would be my penance.

There'd have been something deliciously satisfying about tut-tutting with Clive over the scandal of my sister's pregnancy. He'd have sat back, his smug smile peeping from behind a curtain of earnest concern, saying, 'Predictable. Absolutely predictable.' 'Wasn't it?' I'd have sighed. 'I could have told her this would happen when she first mentioned that Irishman. Honestly, Clivey, the problem with Mia is that she's totally inexperienced. Anyway, now that this Seamus has got her pregnant, he'd better stand by her. After all . . .' But I couldn't do it. I didn't have the gall to pontificate. Not even me.

'Mia was here,' I said when he came home that evening. He'd stopped at the deli on his way and was armed with smoked salmon and pickles and a half-pound of herring. I'd told him I was still too weak to cook.

'Uh-huh.' He groaned as he lowered himself into an armchair. 'And so? What did she have to say? You're looking better, by the way. Much more like the old Gabs.'

'I'm feeling better. A little. She's – upset about Mum. I said I'd try and fix things up.'

'Good girl. Shall we eat? I'm famished.' And that was that. He suggested sex that night. Tentatively. As though he expected me to refuse, half-hoped I would. I did. I couldn't face it after – Seamus. Perhaps in time I'd forget how it was and how it could have been. After all, it wasn't important. Not really. Even Clive said so.

'All the books tend to overestimate the significance of – er – the sexual side of a relationship,' he announced, chewing on a pickle. That was a climbdown. He'd sworn by the books. Maybe his appetite for sex wasn't as hearty as that for the pickle he was swallowing with such gusto. Aiming for 3.4, he may have bitten off far more than he could chew. He coughed. 'There are other things – like mutual support, understanding, friendship, family. They're what really matter. Aren't they Gabs?'

He wanted reassurance and I gave it. No skin off my teeth. 'Absolutely. We'll always have – those – other things. Won't we, Clivey?'

He nodded hard. Reached out and squeezed my hand in a relieved sort of way. His honour had been saved. I held tight on to his fingers. They were damp with pickle juice.

'Clivey,' I said, producing my tired-and-submissive voice. 'This bug I've had really seems to have knocked me out. I need a break so badly. I know you're dreadfully busy at work, so it would be pointless suggesting that the two of us go away. Even though I'd love that more than anything. As a second best, though, d'you think it would be possible for me to go to Birmingham for a – while. D'you think your mother would have me? It's just that – I'm feeling so – weak. And I can't really take care of myself properly when I have – the flat to worry about.'

He leaned forward anxiously. 'You're not . . .'

'No, no.' We hadn't had sex for two weeks and before then I'd had a period. He'd lost count. And he generally kept such a careful eye on my menstruation pattern. He was slipping, most definitely slipping. 'I don't think so,' I added. Just in case. I was sure Seamus had taken precautions but there was always a risk. 'I just need a break. Do you think it would be possible?' 'Of course,' he said. 'I'll give my mother a ring right now. There shouldn't be any problem.'

There wasn't. What were fairy godmothers for if not to spirit stricken heroines away from dangerous places? She waved her wand and a few days later I waved to Clive as I boarded the Birmingham express. He'd hugged me so intensely, one would have thought I was going to Outer Mongolia. I wished I were.

'Bye Gabs,' he'd said, almost tearfully. 'Make sure you have a good rest.'

I needed it after all my efforts to tie up loose ends before my departure. First, a call to my mother: 'Mum, I wish you'd try to understand what happened to Mia. She's missing you. Won't you talk to her?'

It was no pushover. Mum had dug in her heels and discovered she could survive without her big daughter. She'd found 'resilience' among the lexicon of medical symptoms she was tirelessly assembling. It came after hyperventilation and before dyspepsia. Next she would hit upon 'self-sufficiency' and that would be the end of Mia. But she hadn't got there yet. And although Elsie was a paragon among housekeepers, she wasn't one's own flesh and blood. I pointed this out.

'I suppose Elsie could let me down,' she finally conceded. 'Yes, I do feel Mia's absence.' Reluctantly she agreed that if her older daughter were to telephone, she'd try and 'talk things over'.

I conveyed this message to my sister. 'Do it, Mims,' I urged. 'She really does want to make it up. I know she does.'

'Did you tell her . . .?'

'No. Only that you wanted to speak. You didn't want me to, did you?'

'No – no. I'll do it myself.'

She thanked me three times 'for everything'. I had the grace to feel ashamed. A little. After all, hadn't I redeemed myself by playing the go-between, healing the breach between mother and daughter? And wasn't I removing myself from the danger of temptation? Holding fast to my resolve not to see Seamus again? Burying myself in Birmingham so that he could forget me and tend to the needs of my pregnant sibling?

'Mia – um – told me,' I said with difficulty when he called the last time with his pleas for me to reconsider. It was the day before I was due to leave.

'About . . .?'

'The baby. She also said you'd promised to look after her. That you'd said to her – several times – that everything would be – all right.'

'I did. I said – we'd manage.'

'Seamus, I'm going away. I don't know when I'll be back.' This was wonderful. Straight out of the script of one of the movies Mia and I had wept through at the Hendon Odeon. I'd always wanted to be the virtuous object of the charismatic villain's adoration. The beauty who tearfully tore herself away. I tried to cry.

'Gabriella, don't do this. You don't seem to understand. I

love you. I can't carry on unless I see you. I'm like a man possessed.'

'Please, Seamus – please give this up. Forget about me and take care of my sister. I'm asking you for the last time. Please. I have to go.'

I put down the phone with a sense of finality. No – I didn't start sobbing, for I believed I didn't love him. But I had a feeling that I wouldn't be talking to Don Juan O'Reilly again. When I told him I had to go, I meant away from the fireworks and back to the kitchen. It was my way of saying, 'Seamus, pyrotechnics scare me stupid.' It was my declaration (more fool me) that the aroma of chicken soup was safer than the smell of gunpowder. It was also my way of saying to Mia, 'I'm sorry.'

'Gabby, my dear Gabby, you look tired. We'll feed you up.' She hadn't brought her wand when she came to Birmingham station to meet me. But one could always count on Bernice to carry her full range of incantations.

Like: 'I'm so glad you felt able to ask us to look after you – you're one of the family you know.' And: 'Eli and I just knew we had another daughter the minute Clive brought you through the door.' And: 'Tomorrow we'll go shopping, you and me. And then we'll pop into the hairdresser. Oh, I can't wait to show you off to my friends.'

I didn't resist as she cast her spell over me, lulled me into the ideal state of filial gratitude stipulated in the code of the Jewish Mothers-in-Law Guild. Drowsy with regular doses of appreciation and gefilte fish and fresh fruit and family feeling and a statutory side-helping of guilt ('Have some,' she insisted. 'Believe me, it goes with everything'), I hardly noticed the days slipping by.

'You seem much better, Gabs. Ready to come home now?' asked Clive eagerly when he arrived on the Friday to spend Sabbath with the family. With us.

'Not yet,' I said weakly. 'I think I need a little longer.'

By the following week, he was somewhat less acquiescent. 'The flat feels – a bit – empty,' he said with more than a hint of a whine. 'And it's not all that easy to clean.'

When he whispered into his mother's ear something about a trace element deficiency, that was that. 'Gabby,' she said sweetly – but there was steel in her voice, 'you mustn't forget that your duty lies at your husband's side.'

I wasn't sure how I was going to cope with being side by side or beneath him or in any other position his manuals suggested. But I sensed Bernice meant business. A daughter-in-law was a daughter-in-law. But a son . . .

'Next week,' I promised. 'One more week and I'm sure I'll feel well enough to go home.'

The following Friday, they took me to the station. 'Look after yourself, dear Gabby,' said Bernice. Her final incantation. 'Look after yourself and mind you take care of my Clive.'

I opened the door to the smell of disinfectant. The flat was spotless. In the kitchen a single cup, saucer and plate had been left to drain on the rack. Everything appeared to have been wiped – from the counters and appliances to the glass coffee table in the living-room. Even the satin-covered bed, which had all the cosy enticement of a marble sarcophagus, seemed to have been rendered completely germ-free.

I could well understand the reluctance of bacteria to hold sexual orgies on our kitchen units or sterile sheets when other breeding grounds promised so much more excitement. As for me, though, I'd left myself no choice. I was a wife. Clive's wife. And this, I reminded myself sadly as I lay back on the perfectly plumped pillow, was our home.

'Welcome back Gabby.' A note from my husband left on my bedside table. Ever concerned about our catering arrangements, he'd written clear instructions for the preparation of our supper. It was set out like a profit-and-loss account. 'Everything you need can be found in the fridge.' How thoughtful.

'PS I can't wait to see you this evening – and to have you with me in bed tonight. It's been lonely.' Oh dear.

'PPS Your sister wants you to call her as soon as possible.'

My sister. I'd spoken to her twice from Birmingham.

'I'm going to see Mum on Saturday,' she'd said the first time. On the second occasion she'd announced she felt 'better', was working hard, Seamus had finished his play and was trying to sell it. Things were all right. More or less. I filled in the hesitant gaps with chatter about the improving state of my strength, the wonders of Bernice's cooking, the deficiencies in Eli's digestion

168

and a few observations about the relevance of Israel for the Jew of today (the Wisemans were ardent Zionists – not for themselves of course – and I'd picked up a lot from their zealous discussions).

I'd spoken to her twice and we'd managed to say nothing. And now? 'As soon as possible' had an ominous ring.

'Mims, I'm home.'

'Oh, it's you. Gabby I'm so glad you're back. I – missed you.'

'Clive left a message for me to call you urgently. Is there anything wrong?'

'Not really *wrong*. I didn't say urgently. As soon as you could. I was a bit – lonely, that's all. You see, Seamus had to go away. To Dublin. To negotiate with someone about his play . . .'

'Is he back?'

'No.'

'When . . .?'

There was a sharp intake of breath. The sound of nose-blowing and throat-clearing. Mia was struggling to control herself. What a pointless, heartless question. But then, heart had never been my strong point.

'He didn't say. He paid the rent – six months in advance. Just in case he was held up, he told me. He had to go, Gabs. His writing's important to him. I couldn't let my – needs – stand in his way.'

I made a non-committal soothing sound and felt close to tears myself as I heard her suddenly give way to woeful sobs.

'He will come back though.' She blew her nose again. 'I'm quite sure he'll be here for – the baby.'

'Me too,' I said as confidently as I could. 'Tell you what, Mims – I'll come over tomorrow afternoon when Clive goes to visit his Aunty Bubbles. We can talk more then, and perhaps go and see Mum. Together. The two of us. How does that sound?'

'Fine,' she said, giving a final blast into her handkerchief.

'Fine,' I said to Clive when he appeared a few hours later with daffodils for my arms and a wet kiss for my lips. 'I'm feeling fine.'

I'd opened the door to the flowers and his happy smile and my stomach had lurched. I'd seen this somewhere before.

169

Somewhere, sometime. Long, long ago. A young man called – Herbert Green. How ridiculous to have thought of him now. I ignored the unpleasant goose-bumps, put Herbert firmly back into history and returned my husband's smile.

All afternoon I'd fought off the echo of my sister's hopeful voice saying, 'He will come back – I'm sure he'll be here for the baby.' Would he? Did he care about his baby, about Mia? 'I can't carry on unless I see you,' he'd told me. Had he meant it? Had he left because of – me? The thought had scared and revolted – and secretly delighted – me. No, no, no, how could I possibly be glad? It was simply better this way – a practical solution after what had happened. He'd be out of temptation's reach. And then, after a while, he'd come back to my sister and his baby. He would. She was probably right. He'd come back – to us.

'Supper's ready,' I said, burying my face in the flowers and breathing in their spring scent. 'Oh, I *am* so much better Clivey. It's amazing what three weeks of tender loving care can do for one.'

He agreed emphatically. No one knew about mother-love better than my Clive.

We dined by candlelight. Two candle flames that winked at me like beacons over the same white linen sea that had made my head swim seeing Seamus. Tonight my head was steady. Stop winking, it's not funny, I told the flames as I sprinkled salt on the table-cloth. My husband had spilt a drop of red wine and that was the way the Wisemans always treated wine spills. Salt worked wonders, as long as it was rubbed in well, according to my wise old fairy mother-in-law.

'D'you like it?' I asked Clive. I was talking about the fish. He'd left the ingredients for sole meunière in the fridge.

'Mmmm,' he nodded. 'Delicious, Gabs.'

'D'you like it?' he asked me later. He was talking about the foreplay. He'd clearly done some reading while I was away.

'Mmmm,' I nodded. 'It's wonderful, Clivey.'

A while before, he'd announced his decision to stop using Protection.

'I think we're ready to start a family now,' he'd said. 'My career seems established, we've got a foot in the property market and you're nice and strong again. How about it, Gabs?'

'OK,' I said with as much enthusiasm as I could muster. 'That sounds fine.'

And so Clive went about his task of impregnating me – with a new sense of purpose and the most advanced techniques modern manuals could provide.

'Lie this way,' he directed. 'It's the way to make a boy.'

'Don't move for at least ten minutes afterwards,' he suggested. 'One has to give the – er – process a little – time.'

I went along with his instructions. Moved myself into the required positions. Made all the right noises. I'd have hung upside-down from our Laura Ashley lampshade if he'd asked. Anything, anything. And as I waited the recommended ten minutes for Clive's sperm to kick and splash towards my ova (even his mother had admitted he was a lousy swimmer – his seed probably still needed water-wings), I blinked away sudden tears. I was suddenly sadder than I'd ever felt before. So sad that I wanted to die.

The sadness lingered like last night's perfume when I knocked on my sister's door the following afternoon. I hoped she wouldn't smell it. I wanted to be cheerful and encouraging and optimistic.

'Buck up old girl,' I'd planned to say. 'It will all turn out for the best. I know it will.'

The first thing I saw when she let me in was a pair of brown shoes neatly placed side-by-side in the hallway. Shabby lace-ups. I couldn't help staring. She noticed.

'Seamus's,' said Mia – almost apologetically. 'He left them behind. I put them here – for when he gets – back.'

She looked at the shoes and then looked at me. And I couldn't manage the cheerfulness. I couldn't. She came towards me and my huge sadness welled up and we rocked one another and cried and cried.

'Come,' I said after a while. 'D'you still want to go and see Mum? I told her that we might be coming.'

She disappeared into the bedroom. I looked around at the dark shabby flat and imagined Seamus sitting at the empty table. Imagined him studying the bright poster offering carefree cruises to continental ports. Imagined him on deck, waving goodbye . . .

'Do I look – all right?'

She'd powdered her nose and tidied her hair. But her nose still shone red and her limp hair seemed to have turned beige. A large checked overcoat failed to hide her emergent bulge. She looked awful.

I turned away, nodding. 'Come Mims. Let's go.'

We went home through the park and up the road along which we used to go hand in hand to school. The sun appeared briefly and cast two shadows at our feet. Mia's spread wide and long and grey on the pavement. Mine looked stick-like and insignificant. I took her hand and we walked behind our shadows until we reached the familiar front door.

❧ 14 ❧

She'd taken my hand as we'd walked towards the house. It was like when we were kids and she'd catch up with me, out of breath. 'Mims,' panting with the excitement of it all, 'Mims, you'll never guess what happened.' But this time she said nothing and I said nothing for it was no fun guessing any more. Everything had happened.

Together we stood on the doorstep. It had been polished bright red and the brass knocker shone. She nudged me forward.

'Go on then. She's expecting us.'

My feet felt like great clods of clay, pushed into the ground by the weight of my swelling body and Seamus's old woollen overcoat. The feet that had carried me back from Eden – such a heavy, plodding burden. But now they were stuck. I couldn't move them any more. Two steps, I pleaded. Only two more steps and you're home.

I lifted my arm and knocked twice as firmly as I could. Straightened my shoulders and raised my head and told myself that I had no need to be penitent. No need to return like the prodigal daughter. No need for guilt or regrets or contrition. No regrets. None. So I told myself.

'Mia darling. Gabby . . . come inside.' The door opened and – thank goodness – her familiar voice released my feet. I stepped inside, holding the coat buttoned firmly around me.

'Hello Mum,' I said. 'Hi Mum,' said Gabby. She stayed close to my side.

The house looked tidier than I'd ever seen it. Not a thing out of place, not a shoe in the hallway or on the stairs. I looked up towards the landing and felt sick as I remembered the thud of brown brogues hurled at me in the wake of her shrill invective. 'Bitch, bitch. You great clumsy whore . . .'

But now she was speaking in the old faded way. 'Don't you want to take your coat off, Mia darling. Come inside. Elsie has prepared a lovely tea for us all. Doesn't she look after the house beautifully?'

The question was addressed to me. A rebuke. I nodded. 'I'd rather keep my coat on – for the moment,' I said. 'You look – very well, Mum.'

'Look well?' she repeated, sitting down with a sigh. 'If I do that's a miracle. No, darling – as your sister will tell you – I've been far from well. But one has to struggle on.'

Her pale blue eyes scanned Gabby approvingly – tailored skirt, cream silk blouse, cameo brooch at her throat, hair carefully groomed, prim wifely demeanour – and then rested on me. I squirmed and felt my lumpen disarray.

'And you? How are you?' she asked with some difficulty. Mum had never been in the habit of enquiring about my well-being. This time, as ever, she expected me to say, 'Fine thank you,' and give her another opening to enlarge upon her ailments. Gabby sat sedately opposite me, awaiting her turn to be asked. She really had turned into a model daughter.

'Fine . . .' I began. And then, as I looked at the two of them arranged so correctly in the neatened room that smelt of Elsie's furniture polish, a sudden spasm of anger caught at me and made me gasp, unable to continue. I had to breathe in deeply. And I wanted to scream, to shatter the tableau. 'Stop pretending,' I wanted to shout. 'Cheap scent can't disguise stale sweat – and furniture polish won't hide the stink of heartache and lies in this room. It's time for some truth.'

'Actually Mum,' I said, in a cool controlled voice, 'I'm pregnant. Expecting a baby in five months. Seamus's baby.'

I stood up. Raised myself through the thick silence and took off his heavy checked coat. Their eyes followed me. I could feel Mum studying me, her wayward daughter. Her erstwhile dutiful daughter. She put her hands over her face and then removed them, frowning, puzzled.

'Oh.'

'Well?' I asked rather aggressively. 'Is that all?'

'Don't be unfair, Mims.' Gabby had found her voice. 'Give her a minute to get over the shock.'

174

I sat down. Mum sighed hugely. 'Well, this is all rather a lot for me to cope with,' she said. 'Gabriella darling, I think you'd better go and bring the tea. I don't know . . . I don't know what to say.' She looked across at me, still frowning. 'What does *he* say? Him – the – Irishman?'

'Seamus? He says – it's fine. That we'll be all right.'

'He's not – marrying you?'

I shook my head. 'He's in Dublin at the moment,' I said quickly. 'Just for a while. He'll be back for – the baby.'

'Oh,' she repeated. This time I didn't push her to elaborate. What more was there to say? Gabby came in with the tray.

'Don't these scones look delicious?' she exclaimed. And I knew that the subject was closed. Truth time was over and it had hardly even begun. But the tableau had regrouped and with whiffs of home baking and the aroma of tea to reinforce the furniture polish, not even I could smell the sadness any more. Well – hardly.

The talk lapped gently over Mum's blood pressure, Clive's virtues, Gabby's housewifery and the vagaries of the weather. It touched upon the possibility of 'the Wisemans' starting a family soon, and then retreated hastily to safer ground and trickled away altogether as Mum produced a 'dreadful headache' and we accompanied her upstairs and saw her into bed. At last we shut the front door and Gabby said, 'That's that,' like a final gurgle followed by our footsteps in retreat down the path.

'And so, what d'you think?' she asked as we waited for a bus.

I didn't know. I hadn't thought. Had this been the visit I'd been dreading for so many weeks? Afternoon tea with a stranger? Yet somehow, having re-entered the house, having walked up the stairs again, having put her to bed, I didn't feel quite so alone. I'd kissed her cheek and our touch seemed to confirm the continuation of my life out of hers. Whatever she was, whatever became of me, I was her continuation. At least there was that.

'It wasn't – what I expected,' I replied after a while.

And as I spoke, I had the feeling that our exchange was familiar. I'd heard the same words before. Where? It puzzled me all the way back to Cricklewood until I remembered the

175

conversation that had followed the dinner with Gabby and Clive.

'And so, what d'you think?' I'd asked Seamus, expecting a barrage of barbed wit, a hearty laugh at the expense of my self-righteous sister and her pompous spouse. But there was a long silence.

'It wasn't – what I expected,' he'd said at last.

He'd pulled off his shoes and collapsed on to the bed immediately we got home that Friday night. Shut his eyes as though the sixty-watt bulb were blinding him.

'What is it?' I asked. 'Aren't you feeling well?' I'd never before seen his energy depleted. For some reason it frightened me.

'Exhausted,' he said. 'I've been working hard.'

'She's a good cook, my sister,' I said vaguely. I had to say something – to keep him, his attention. His shut face and slumped body seemed to be excluding me. I sat down and stroked his arm. 'They have a very nice home.'

He grunted. I couldn't manage any more pleasantries, just lay alongside him with my hand on his arm. He didn't move. I felt the heat of his flesh and thought if I couldn't have all of Seamus I'd settle for an arm. Only an arm, and perhaps a hand to touch me with tenderness. To warm the small child-part of me that had never been allowed to be a child.

I drifted into a sleep filled with dreams of Sabbath candles and hands that came towards me to save me from falling into the flames. And I looked for the face that belonged to the hands and expected to see Seamus. Instead I saw my father. 'Daddy,' I said in horror. 'Daddy, where have you come from? You're supposed to be dead.' And the hands moved right past me, allowing me to fall, fall, fall, and stretched out to save my sister.

'Gabby my darling.' Hold on, this wasn't Daddy's voice. It belonged to Seamus. 'Gabby, come with me.' And I grabbed at the hands, clutched on to the arms and held on for my life. 'No,' I screamed. 'No, no, you're mine. You're mine.' I woke up, still gripping his arm. He was muttering something incomprehensible, still fast asleep.

'Seamus,' I said, waking him gently. 'Don't you think we ought to get undressed and go to sleep properly?' But he didn't respond. Turned over and carried on mumbling. I thought I

176

heard him say my sister's name, but I could have been mistaken.

I probably was mistaken, for he didn't mention my sister at all after that Sabbath meal. I tried to talk about her.

'Weren't you surprised to see how very different me and my sister are?' I asked chattily over coffee the following morning.

Seamus looked dazed. He nodded and rose from the table. 'I think I'll try and do a little work,' he said. 'There's a scene I must redo.'

'Oh.' I tried to hide my disappointment. We usually went shopping on Saturdays and then came home and drew the blinds and melted together in the dusky heat of languid afternoons. That's what we usually did.

'So – um – shall I go off to the supermarket on my own then?' The last thing I wanted was to be a nag.

'Please Mia, if you would. I'm not feeling too good.'

I returned at midday laden with parcels and watched for the smile that usually spread across his face when he saw me. 'I'm back,' I said hopefully. He turned round, disorientated. He'd been in another world. The page in his typewriter was blank.

'Hi,' he said. And there was no gladness at all in his voice or on his face. I paused and waited for it but I knew it wasn't coming. Something had changed in Seamus, something profound and I couldn't understand it. I lifted the bags of food on to the table and they felt very heavy. As though they were filled with rocks and stones. Rocks with sell-by dates and stones with built-in obsolescence. Nothing lasted for ever.

'I think I'll take myself off somewhere this afternoon,' I said. 'A film, a museum perhaps. I feel like wandering around on my own for a change.'

The words hurt as I expelled them. He looked relieved. I wanted to cry.

'Fine,' he said. 'I'll do some more work. And then perhaps I'll also go out for a while.'

He wasn't home when I returned at six. I'd pulped a pocketful of tissues watching *Brief Encounter* for the seventh time and comforted myself with a pound of Black Magic which I subsequently brought up in the ladies' loo on Cricklewood

Broadway. I curled on the bed in the dark empty flat and felt sick and drained and miserable. Where was Seamus?

His lips woke me. Lightly, on my forehead, kissing me to consciousness. I sat up. It had all been a bad dream. He loved me as much as – ever. I smiled and opened my arms and the smile froze on my face as I saw him backing away.

No, I told myself sadly, it hadn't been a dream. It was real. Something in Seamus had died. But the child in my body, his child in my body, still squirmed and grew.

'Gabby, I have to speak to you. Can I come over?'

I'd put off calling her for days. In a trance, I'd gone to work and come home and watched him each evening in a world of his own. He'd sit in front of his typewriter and stare ahead blankly. 'I'm going for a walk,' he'd say and return ten minutes later. When the telephone rang, he'd jump.

'What is it?' I kept asking. 'Seamus, what's wrong?'

But he'd shake his head irritably. 'Stop watching me all evening, Mia. Leave me alone, will you.'

I left him. Gave up. Lay on the bed and was sixteen again. A numb princess in a dark cave waiting. But I wasn't sixteen. The prince had come and gone. I was twenty-two and pregnant and my life seemed over. I stopped eating, stopped caring how I looked – and at last gave up caring about loss of pride in front of my sister. Phoning Gabby was my final humiliation.

She offered me bagels and coffee and commonsense and compassion and some valuable advice – for my sake, naturally – about making an effort to look good for Seamus. That really boosted my morale. She also agreed to help patch things up with Mum.

I thought it would help – visiting Gabby, talking to Mum. I thought Seamus would somehow matter less, that I'd see him more in perspective. That if I re-established my family bonds, I'd see that the chains tying me to my 'dangerous Irishman' were made of paper.

But paper chains are stronger than one imagines and when they're covered with tinsel and coloured foil and delicate tissue they can bring magic to the dullest room. And I decided I'd gladly swop paper chains in Cricklewood for all the family links that duty could buy.

'I spoke to Mum today,' I told him. 'I think she'll eventually come to terms with my leaving. With – us.'

'That's good Mia,' he said. 'I'm pleased.' He didn't sound particularly pleased. He didn't sound particularly anything. He was revising his play for the umpteenth time.

'I also spoke to Gabby.'

Now he looked up, interested. I was pleased to catch his attention and burbled on animatedly. She hadn't been well and was going to Birmingham to stay with her in-laws and had Seamus any idea how dreadful they were and Bernice and Gabby would probably spend hours making liver and disapproving noises about wicked Mia and her evil man . . .

Then I noticed he wasn't listening. As I spoke, he'd slowly withdrawn and was now sitting with his head drooping on his chest. He looked ill.

'Aren't you well Seamus?' I asked. Perhaps his indifference was due to failing health? He looked up.

'Probably not,' he said wearily. 'I think I need some fresh air. I'll take a little walk. Be back soon.'

That's when I decided he needed a tonic. I asked for 'something strong' at the chemist's the next day, something that had a little of everything. And I bore my elixir home with the fervent belief that this would be the answer.

It worked. I was sure it was working when two weeks had passed and life with Seamus hadn't stopped. He'd even made love to me (once) with a desperation I'd never seen before. It was a good tonic, I decided. Things would be all right. Better than ever. I believed in the elixir as though it were my philosopher's stone, my fountain of eternal life, creator of perpetual motion. After all, how was a simple legal secretary expected to understand the absurdity of alchemy or the unyielding laws of thermodynamics?

I held on to my incautious optimism right to the end. To the day he said, 'Mia, let's go out tonight. I have some news.'

'Good news?' I asked eagerly. I knew he was waiting for responses to his play.

'Maybe,' he said. But he didn't seem excited. 'Where would you like to go?'

I didn't need to think. There was no question about it at all. 'The King's Arms,' I said immediately.

*

He was waiting for me at our usual table. This time there were no coins to toss, no promised lands to dream about.

I sneezed as I settled myself into my usual seat. I hated being pregnant. It made me feel clumsier than ever. Had there really been a time when Seamus had sworn he loved to look at me? I sneezed again.

'Bless you,' he said. It came out automatically.

I remembered when he would look into my eyes and offer each word like a caress. I nodded, blowing my nose. 'Your news,' I reminded him, trying to sound full of anticipation. 'What's your news?'

'Well, as you know I've been hawking my play around.' He took a sip of lager.

'And?'

'There's a fringe theatre company in Dublin that's – very interested.'

'How wonderful. Let's drink to their – interest.'

'It's actually more than that. They'd like to do the play – but they want me to come and help them direct it. I've – agreed.'

'You've agreed.' He'd agreed. Just like that. No discussion. No possibility that perhaps I might want him with me, that since I was carrying his child he had an obligation . . . Oh, God, hadn't I known all about obligation? I suppose I could have exploded in fury, thrown a tantrum, banged my head on the wooden table in the middle of the King's Arms, the same table on which he'd tossed a coin and I'd called heads. I could have said Seamus you bastard what about me?

But I didn't. There'd have been no point. I wanted to be a partner, not a liability. If he felt free to leave, perhaps he'd come back. Perhaps.

'How long are you going for?' I asked, keeping my voice carefully modulated. There was no danger of weeping. I'd shed a million tears into the lap of my lover, but now that he was leaving my eyes were bone dry.

'Six months,' he said quickly. Too quickly. 'I've paid the rent in advance, all the money they sent me for the play. If there's any problem, I'll send – more.' He looked away. Ashamed?

'The – baby?' I hesitated.

He took my hand, gripped it tightly. 'Mia, I am coming back, remember? I will do it. I won't let you down. I care about you

180

and – the baby. You'll see. Just give me six months and I'll be back.'

I nodded and felt dreadfully tired suddenly. 'When?' I asked quietly. 'When do you plan to leave?'

There was a short pause.

'Tomorrow. They want me to be there as soon as possible.'

Why the hurry? The urgency? I could understand that he'd grown weary of me, that the magic had worn off, but why did he have to run so fast? Was there anything or anyone else? I was about to ask, but it didn't seem to matter. He'd gone already. My Seamus had gone.

We lay alongside one another that night. On our backs, staring at the ceiling. I took his hand and he gave it up limply and I imagined myself looking down upon our bodies. Two deceased lovers lying side by side in state. Wouldn't it be appropriate to shower them with rosemary?

I didn't sleep that night. Just remembered.

I remembered all the next day as well. And the next. And the next and the next. I couldn't stop. It was like after someone has died and you keep finding unbearable tokens of a life that's been lost. I cried for two hours when I found Seamus's plastic dice under the bed. The single grey sock abandoned behind the washing basket affected me more profoundly than our brief goodbye at the door. And when I saw that he'd left his brown lace-up shoes in the cupboard I thought my heart would break. Choking on tears, I placed the shoes carefully in the hallway. There was still some wear in them, I thought. Seamus would be glad to find them when he returned – home.

I saw my sister staring at them when she finally came to see me and I knew what she was thinking and we held one another and cried for everyone and everything. Then we saw Mum and there was the reassuring thought that, whatever happened, I was her continuation. That I had our continuation – mine and Seamus's – growing inside me. Ever growing.

And eventually as the weeks passed I knew that I'd live. We'd live. That life went on.

'How are you keeping Mia?' Hannah's friendship seemed to have returned with her brother's defection. She tried to beam her old warmth across the office, to melt the chilly disapproval that surrounded me. Goldblatt, Cohen, Carruthers and other new partners in the burgeoning practice were solidly against sex outside marriage, the careless kind represented by my ringless finger and visible bump. Their estimation of me had plummeted.

I appreciated Hannah's concern but now I'd grown wary. 'Fine thanks,' I nodded. 'The doctor says the – baby – is coming along nicely.'

'How long?'

'About twelve weeks more. I'll try and keep working as long as possible.'

And then? She didn't ask but I knew she wanted to.

'Seamus says he'll be back round the time of the birth.' I spoke as convincingly as I could. I wanted to believe it too.

'Oh – good,' she said, sounding relieved. Perhaps she felt responsible?

'I'm fine Hannah, truly,' I repeated. I didn't want to be Hannah's liability either. I was determined to be self-sufficient. Like a mother bird, I'd gather twigs and soft feathers and choice bits of food and make a home for a baby out of our love-nest in Cricklewood. I'd manage. I was sure I would.

'Mims – *are* you managing? I've been worrying about you. We hadn't heard . . .'

'Yes. Of course Gabby. Everything's – fine.'

'Oh good. Have you heard from – him? From Seamus?'

'Not . . . well, a couple of weeks ago he sent a note to say that the play was coming along nicely. And that he'd see me – soon.'

'Oh. Nothing else?'

'That was all. But I *am* well Gabs, really. You must come and see what I'm doing to the flat. It's going to be a paradise for a baby. Full of colour and light and warmth . . .'

'Mims, I have something to tell you. Wonderful news.'

'What?'

'I'm pregnant too. The tests came back yesterday. Can you imagine – both of us. I wasn't sure . . . I'd been feeling strange for weeks. But I didn't think – so soon. Clive and I had only been – trying – for such a short time. And now they say I'm

182

three months gone. Three months, Mims. That means my baby will be born two months after yours. Isn't it amazing?'

'I – don't know what to say. I can't quite – believe it. You – a mother . . . Are you pleased, Gabby? Really pleased? And Clive? What does he say? And Mum? Have you told her? Gosh – I'm stunned.'

'Clive is absolutely beside himself. Can't get over his virility. Mum's delighted. And Bernice is on her way to London right now. The doctor says I need lots of rest and she's going to stay with us for a – while – to make sure I get it. She offered immediately. Aren't I lucky to have in-laws like the Wisemans?'

Why wasn't I unequivocally delighted at the idea of my sister joining me in pregnancy, at the prospect of the two of us in baby-shops and clinics, pushing prams along pavements, comparing notes about nipple care and nappy services, strained carrots and sleepless nights? I should have been thrilled, truly thrilled.

But I wasn't. There I'd been, building another nest in Cloud-cuckoo-land. A tree-top haven for a mother and her continuation. Yes, the shrine to Eros had blown away, but I was industriously replacing it with another temple for two. This time it was being dedicated to the Goddess Maternity.

And now she'd brought her reality to my illusion. Her 'beside himself' husband, her ever-nurturing mother-in-law, her mother who was no doubt thrilled to be acquiring a *legitimate* grandchild . . . admit it Mia. You were furious.

Don't be mean, I told myself sternly. Where's your generosity?

But I looked around at my sanctuary, at the walls I'd painted white, the picture of a bluebird that had replaced CONTINENTAL CRUISES, the small wicker cradle I'd found in a charity shop. And it suddenly seemed so little. So empty. Such a small puny shrine compared with the huge temple to The Family in which my sister and her offspring would be worshipped. And I couldn't find it in myself to be generous.

I put down the phone and sat forlornly on the bed that had seen love and conception and dreams and their dying and tried to be happy – for Gabby and for my child who'd have a cousin. For us all. I tried hard.

183

The weeks passed and I kept trying and I carried on building my nest. Another feather. Another piece of fluff. The softest lamb's-wool blanket imaginable, given to me with all sorts of wishes from the partners and staff of Goldblatt, Cohen and Carruthers.

'We'll be happy to have you back as soon as you feel – able,' said Mr Goldblatt as he handed me the parcel. I mumbled my thanks and wondered whether he meant it and if I'd ever feel able again.

And the weeks passed more slowly and I carried on trying and everyone thought I was doing 'amazingly well'. Until at last my nest was as complete as any nest without eggs could be, and all I had left to do was to keep trying to be happy and to keep waiting.

'I'm well,' I told Gabby, again and again. 'And you? How are you keeping, Gabs?' Perhaps my solicitude would make up for my lack of true fellow feeling – which, thank goodness, she didn't seem to suspect. 'Are you taking good care of yourself?'

'I've been told to stay in bed as much as possible – high blood pressure or something. But don't worry Mia, I'm being well looked after. Has Mum spoken to you yet?'

'About what?'

'Oh – I don't know whether I was meant to say anything. Well, I suppose it doesn't matter. She was with me yesterday and we were talking about you on your own and she mentioned that Elsie was leaving – retiring to Spain or something, I don't know how she'll afford that on what Mum's been paying her, but anyway . . .'

'And?'

'And Mum said – *she* said, honestly Mims I didn't put her up to it or anything – how – um – nice it would be if you came back. With the baby. If – er – Seamus doesn't . . .'

'Thank you very much, Gabby, but I don't think . . . Seamus is coming back. He is. He won't let me down. Anyway, I've made a lovely home here for the baby. There's no point even thinking about it. You can tell Mum.'

I phoned him that night. He'd given me a telephone number but I hadn't used it before. Every time I'd been on the point of dialling, I'd restrained myself. Reminded myself not to pester him. That he'd come when he was ready. In truth I was terrified that his voice wouldn't sound glad when he heard it was me.

But that night my need to speak to him was stronger than the fear.

'I'm coming home soon, Mia my darling,' he said. The same voice. The lilt. The 'darling'. My heart skipped a beat. Oh – hadn't I *known* that he cared? I didn't want to ask when.

'The baby's due in two weeks,' I said.

He mentioned something about a delay, a production hitch, a hiccup, a temporary setback . . . but I wasn't listening. He'd called me darling. He'd said 'home'. He'd be back. I lay on the bed and put both hands on the mound that squirmed as though it wanted to kick its way into the world. 'Daddy's coming soon,' I said happily. 'Your daddy's coming home.'

Thursday's child has far to go. So they say. Vanessa Wiseman, who came into the world on a hot Thursday in August, had almost two months to go before her expected delivery date. But then, hadn't her mother always been impatient?

The excited Wiseman family gathered to pay homage to their newest princess, a wiry five-pounder with the tiniest limbs imaginable and the most enormous navy-blue eyes. Secretly – well, perhaps not that secretly, but one didn't want to make the little one feel unwelcome – they'd longed for a prince. But, they kept saying as they all touched wood, as long as she was healthy.

And they drew their chairs up to the bedside of good Queen Gabriella, who lay in flowery splendour in the best suite of the most expensive private clinic in Finchley, and helped her choose her meal from the fifty-item supper menu.

'Have the salmon,' insisted Eli. 'We may as well try and get our money's worth.'

'The liver,' said Bernice. 'It's good for the milk. The baby will thank you one day.'

'The schnitzel,' put in Hilda. She wasn't going to be left out. It was her grandchild too. 'There's nothing as digestible as good crumbed schnitzel.'

The good queen decided on salmon (after all, her father-in-law *had* paid the bill), but the little princess had to sup on hope. She'd pursed her rosebud mouth and sucked with all her might but nothing seemed to come. 'You'll have to wait my darling, won't you?' said grand-godmother Bernice. 'Just a little patience and your mummy's milk will flow.'

More than a little patience was being called for in the faraway kingdom of Cricklewood, where breastmilk flowed more abundantly than fat-pursed fathers-in-law and five-star nursing homes. The good queen's older sister, normally rather a pleasant young woman, was reaching the end of her endurance.

It was typical, she thought furiously, the way Gabriella had succeeded once again in pipping her at the post. Wasn't there anything in which she could come first?

And while she lay thus, seething with uncharacteristic bitterness and bemoaning her singleton state, young Joseph decided he'd had quite enough placental nourishment. It was time to see what the world would offer in the way of mother's milk and chicken soup and other gustatory delights. Within minutes, his mother had summoned an ambulance – and within hours she'd accomplished a 'perfect birth', according to the ecstatic junior house officer at the local teaching hospital. It had been his first solo delivery.

'Have the savoury mince,' suggested Hilda the following day, running her eye down the supper menu with not-so-good Queen Mia who'd received one bunch of carnations (with best wishes from the Wisemans) and a single visitor. From King Seamus of Dublin there'd been – nothing.

'Or perhaps the ox-tail.' Supper was a safe subject. All this excitement gave Hilda such a headache. It was a miracle she'd made it to the hospital. 'You need lots of nourishment for little Joseph,' she continued. After all, this was her grandson – her first grandson – which was more than the Wisemans had. 'A boy is a boy.'

Mia lay back to ease her heavy breasts. At least – and she had to admit that this did give her a certain measure of satisfaction – at least she'd been the sister to produce a son . . .

Yes, I was the one with the son. But it didn't seem to cheer me. Nothing did as I waited for a cab to take me and my blue-blanketed bundle to our solitary abode. I shut my eyes in the shuddering car and held on to little Joseph and tried to forget I was in a taxi, tried to imagine the wonder if . . . oh, I could hardly bear to think about it . . . if I were to open the front door of our flat and see Seamus. 'Imagine,' I whispered to the child, 'imagine if Daddy were there, waiting for us.'

Of course he wasn't. Silly idea. But perhaps he was on his way. Perhaps he'd lost track of time. Maybe I should give him a call, just a quick one, to remind him. About his baby. Not to pester him. Just a brief reminder.

I dialled with unsteady hands. Joseph whimpered on the bed beside me. He was hungry.

'Sh my darling,' I said, 'I'll feed you just as soon as I've spoken to your daddy.'

It rang. I held my breath. It rang and rang. Finally someone answered. A woman. 'Seamus? Seamus O'Reilly? Yes, he did stay here. He's moved though. A couple of weeks ago. No, he didn't leave a forwarding address.'

I put down the phone and picked up my baby and cried into his blanket. We cried together. And cried and cried. 'He'll be back, he'll be here – any day,' I said to Joseph, over and over again. But deep inside I knew that he wouldn't. That any day was flimsier than 'sometime' and trailed like an endless gossamer ribbon into the never-never.

'Hello, Mum. It's me – Mia.'

'Hello my darling. How are you? How's – er – Joseph?'

'Mum, he's wonderful. Only three months old – and such a little person. Daddy would have been so proud.'

'Yes, he would. Of you and Gabby, both. You should see our Vanessa – the sweetest thing.'

'I have. She's – lovely. Mum, I'm thinking of going back to work.'

'That sounds very enterprising darling. Any news of – your – Seamus?'

'No. Mum, I was wondering . . .'

'What?'

'Remember – you mentioned quite recently to Gabby – about Elsie leaving? About me perhaps – moving back? Can we – talk about it?'

*

Don't think, don't think. Keep walking – that's it. Left, right, left, right. Hold the baby. Hold him tight. The front path seems endless. Backwards, perhaps I should try walking backwards. Maybe she'll be waiting for me, waiting at the door and saying, 'Shut your eyes Mia darling. Shut them and turn round and I'll tell you when you can look. I have a surprise for you. Someone's here . . .'

But of course Mum has never gone in for surprises. A fixed sum of money for birthdays. No balloons. No Christmas crackers. No fairy-tales. No happy endings.

I keep my eyes open and turn the key in the door. Joseph tucks his head into my neck and I feel his softness, breathe in his baby-smell and call out to announce my arrival. It seems as if I've never stopped calling.

'Mum, it's me. Mia. We've come home.'

🍃 15 🍃

'Welcome home my dear Gabriella. Here, let me take the little one. Come darling, come to Bobba Bernice. I have a lovely bottle of milk for you all ready and waiting. Gabby, you take a rest now. Remember what the doctor said about not overdoing things.'

I relinquished Vanessa into the arms of her number one grandmother (self-decorated with the Jewish title to avoid confusion with number two) and blinked at the brightness of our home. My fairy godmother had certainly been busy. Steel pots simmered on the sparkling white cooker and the floor tiles beamed at the light leaping through perfectly polished window panes. I did my best to beam at Bernice.

'Thanks Bee,' I said. That's what she'd decided I should call her. B for Bernice and Bobba. And Be grateful. And Be one of us. And Be the Best little Jewish wife and mother money can buy. I'd agreed – to all of it. And as I obediently slid between the crisp sheets that covered our king-sized bed, I reprimanded myself severely for suddenly thinking of fireworks.

'Stop Gabriella – forget, forget. What was one afternoon compared with all this? The security, the child, the family. Everything. And Clive is safe – he'll never let you down. Look what happened to your poor lonely sister.'

And I lay in the cotton coolness and smelt the pine-scented air freshener from the *en-suite* bathroom and heard my daughter gurgling at her Bobba and the soup bubbling on the hob and the busy voice of Bobba Bernice.

'Clivey my sweetheart,' she was saying, 'can you bring the flowers in? The ones from the hospital. They're in the car. Bring them in and we can arrange them round the flat.'

I shut my eyes. Rest, rest, I told myself. Remember what the doctor said. Rest in peace. Surrounded by a flatful of flowers – carnations and roses and chrysanthemums and irises, all half-dead from the hospital.

I slept, still as a corpse. I woke, numb and still corpse-like. For months now, even before the pregnancy had been confirmed, ever since that fateful Sabbath, I'd passed the days and nights like a sleepwalker. An agreeable, compliant sleeptalker. Model wife, exemplary daughter. A sweet smiling puppet.

'You chose this. It was your choice,' I'd remind myself, as I lay like an overturned snail with my feet in the air for the obligatory post-coital ten minutes. At least after we'd had evidence of Clive's spermatic success I was allowed to move off the bed as soon as I wanted. But I'd had few occasions to use my new liberty. Once Clive had impregnated me *he* seemed to stop wanting it. Much. Naturally he turned his indifference into a virtue.

'Sexual intercourse,' he told me, 'is not generally advisable in early pregnancy, particularly with someone as delicate as yourself Gabs.'

'Oh – fine,' I said. I hadn't known that I was particularly delicate but if that's what the books said. And anyway, they would take better care of me if they thought I was fragile. Hadn't my mother used selective helplessness all her life?

Vanessa came early, which confirmed their suspicions that I wasn't quite rugged enough to cope with the stresses of childcare, lactation and Clive's nutritional needs. Bernice grabbed hold of her grandchild with such compassion that I was sure I'd already failed as a mother by expelling her from the womb too soon. But the doctor – a private obstetrician with long slim fingers and bedroom eyes – said Vanessa was 'surprisingly mature for a prem baby'. He examined my breasts (for the milk that never came) and for a moment I emerged from my trance. Just for a moment.

But by the time we'd got home I was asleep again. I remembered the story about a Greek poet who was supposed to have slept for fifty-seven years and eventually awoke to find that he possessed all the wisdom of the world. What would I know when I finally came to? The thirteen principles of the Jewish faith? The date of the coming of the Messiah? The secret of Bernice's matzah balls? The true mean rate of sexual fulfilment among the married population of south-east England?

'Wake up Gabs, it's time to feed Vanessa. My mother's left everything ready for you – she's gone to the hairdresser.'

Perhaps, I thought dazedly as my husband tried to rouse me to fulfil my maternal obligations, perhaps the Wiseman sort of wisdom would hardly be worth waking for. Maybe I should carry on sleeping for ever and ever and ever.

'Mims, are you well? How's the baby?'

'Fine. Very well. How are you?'

I asked her and asked her and each time she said, 'Fine,' and each time I wondered whether her 'fine' was as hollow as my automatic echo. A sick feeling gnawed at my stomach every time I thought about her – and that was often. I'd imagine her in the Cricklewood flat – her and baby Joseph. His baby. Mother and child in their cosy nest.

And first I'd be quite envious, picturing her placidity and self-sufficiency and how needed she was by her child. The little Mia had seemed so much more than my fitted family and kosher kitchen. Then I'd think of Seamus – how she'd lived with him, made love with him, over and over again. And I hated her for it. And I remembered that Mia had brought him to me and I hated her even more for that. And loved her. And thought about her obsessively since I couldn't bear to think about him. And telephoned constantly.

'I'm fine,' I replied. As ever.

'Gabby – ' Her voice had changed suddenly. There was a note of urgency. My chest tightened. Seamus? (I couldn't help it.) Had something happened? 'Gabby, I haven't said anything until now. I've been trying so hard to carry on. Hoping. Each day I've been hoping to hear from him – something. But I can't any longer . . .'

I heard Joseph wailing in the background and my sister's despair and I wanted to take the telephone and hurl it against the wall to stop the sound of her hopelessness. I couldn't stand hearing it.

'There's the rent to pay,' she was saying, 'and I'm going to have to go back to work and – I've spoken to Mum and – well, that's it. We're going to live in Hendon, me and Joseph. With Mum.'

Her voice faded away. I wanted to reach out and stop it. Her voice, her soul. To say Mia don't die, don't give up, I need you. Let's care for one another, hope together. But she was still in Cricklewood and I was in Finchley and there was fish to be fried for Clive's supper and Vanessa to feed and Bernice to phone and a memory to suppress. So much to do. No time to talk . . .

'It will be for the best,' I said in my most reassuring voice. 'I'm glad you've decided. Mum will be pleased. We'll speak again soon.'

We spoke – several times. And finally, on a blustery November afternoon, I took my immaculately dressed little daughter to visit Grandma Hilda, Aunty Mia and Cousin Joseph in Hendon. 'Don't you dare cry,' I whispered, wiping her nose and trying to fluff up her sparse black hair. Vanessa grimaced and wriggled in my arms. Even then, she had what her Bobba described as an 'independent spirit'. I called it bloody-minded.

Mia opened the door wearing a deep plum suit that I recognized from years before. She'd clearly just returned from work and seemed thinner and somehow more self-assured. Her hand reached out to touch mine and the voice that said 'Gabby' was soft and – peaceful.

'Hi Mims,' I said in the old light way. 'Vanessa, say hello to your aunty.'

Vanessa squirmed and Mia took her into her arms and all at once the child was still, moulding her small body into the warm neck and deep plum chest of her aunt. I'd never seen her so relaxed.

'Well,' I said with somewhat forced good humour, 'you certainly seem to have a way with her. She probably senses you're – family. Bernice Wiseman says it's the strongest instinct we have.'

As I prattled on nervously (she was making me nervous – I couldn't handle that air of composure), we moved into the living-room. A teenage girl, kneeling on the carpet, was making cooing noises to the fair-haired baby in her arms. He looked up at her adoringly.

'Thanks so much Jane. I think you can go home now,' said Mia, in full control. 'Remember, tomorrow at twelve. I'll pay you at the end of the week.'

'Where's Mum?' I asked after Jane had left and Joseph had been strapped into his seat, smiling contentedly. Vanessa's sporadic whimpers carried threats of an imminent downpour. 'Isn't she at home?'

'She is. Upstairs. She didn't feel very well this morning but said she'd come down when you arrived.'

'You're lucky you have that girl Jane. To help with the baby. She seems very nice.'

'Yes. I am lucky.'

Was it a note of irony I detected in her voice? No, I was sure not. Mia didn't go in for that sort of thing. I must have imagined it.

Mum eventually appeared lamenting how difficult it was for her to sleep soundly with the cries of a baby at all hours of the night and how much importance Dr Mitchell had always placed on her having an uninterrupted eight hours but what could one do . . .

'Honestly Mum,' objected Mia – and for the first time her composure slipped. Slightly. 'Joseph hardly wakes. He must be the most placid baby in the world.'

We watched him, deeply intent on a brightly coloured rattle which he gripped with both hands. His cousin had stopped whimpering (temporarily) and lay quite still staring up at his face as though waiting for Joseph to decipher the meaning of existence from the object he was examining so minutely. We all waited.

'They do look like cousins.' Mum broke the silence. 'Even though they have dissimilar colouring, there's something . . . let me see. It's the eyes I think. That dark – I'd say almost navy – blue. Yes, look girls – Vanessa and Joseph have identical eyes.'

'We are sisters after all,' I said quickly – and was about to quote more of Bernice's genetic theories to cover my sudden discomfort when Mia disappeared to fetch the tea and Vanessa's storm erupted and Mum developed a headache and there was feeding and winding and crying and consoling and changing and disposing. And the visit was over.

'She's managing well – my sister,' I said to Clive that evening as we swallowed our supper during a lull between Vanessa's outbursts of rage that the doctors had diagnosed as six-o'clock colic.

'Keep calm, Mrs Wiseman,' had been their considered opinion. 'A tense mother makes matters worse.'

'I am calm,' I'd repeated through gritted teeth as I'd paid the fees and reported to Vanessa's Bobba that first, second and third medical opinions were in complete agreement about the superior physical and mental equipment of her granddaughter.

'I'm sure,' Bernice had said happily. 'The Wisemans are a sturdy breed. Just keep an eye on her movements, though. There's a slight familial tendency to constipation. Clive . . .'

'Yes – I know.'

I knew. I knew everything about Clive – or thought I did.

I watched him savouring his meatloaf (the last of the foil-wrapped dishes left in the freezer after Bernice's extended post-natal visit). I waited as calmly as possible for Vanessa to resume screaming and made interested responses to the woes of an overworked chartered accountant and astute observations about Mia's management skills and thought – this can't be real. I'm in the middle of a dream.

Had I really spent the afternoon with a cool composed sister who was once again dutiful in a house in Hendon with toys on the stairs instead of worn brown brogues? Where we'd sat on the floor holding babies with identical navy-blue eyes? And where a voice from above had called out its familiar refrain: 'Mia darling, I'd love some toast. The thinnest slice you can possibly manage.'

A dream, a dream. My life was a dream. And again I prayed fervently that I'd never wake up. Unless perhaps I could return to being ten-year-old Gabriella, the dimpled Virgin Mary with all sorts of wondrous possibilities ahead. But of course none of us can possibly be ten again. And so I carried on sleeping. And sleeping.

The amazing thing was that no one suspected I was asleep. Unwittingly I'd hit upon the perfect drug-free solution to suburban stress and the pain of a life that seemed to have lost its way. I should have marketed it: 'Are you ever troubled by the nagging aches of what might have been or the lingering odour of nostalgia – a smell that not even your best friends will tell you about? Try GABRIELLA'S SLEEPWALKING CURE and fool them all. You'll smile through suburbia without feeling a thing.'

I might have made my fortune. Gone public. Established a

Sleep Shop in every station in the country. Diversified into T-shirts and video-cassettes teaching Sleepy Sex and a pheromone-suppressant lotion called Stun. I might have become a multi-millionairess and taken my profits in used bank notes on ships and planes to faraway places. Left my sleeping partner and my anaesthetized self and gone in search of the biggest fireworks display in the world. I might have done so many things.

Instead I kept my stupor to myself and fooled everyone. Well, almost everyone. Vanessa knew. Even as a baby she would watch me with those disconcerting eyes and I could see her fury mounting as she made effort after unsuccessful effort to rouse me. When she learnt to talk, one of the first things she said was 'wake up'.

'Wake up Mummy!' she'd shriek in a high angry voice as she stamped and shook my limp heavy arm. 'Open your eyes! Please, please, please open your eyes.'

She would poke my lids with sharp little fingers and I'd sit up and breathe deeply and try to control the rage I was feeling towards this intrusive creature who was puncturing my secret.

'Nessa,' I'd say as calmly and reasonably as I could, 'Mummy's very tired so I want you to go to your room and play quietly for a while and then later we can go for a walk.'

'No. I won't.'

'The park. I'll take you to the park.'

'No.'

'Well then, maybe if you're very good we can go and visit Aunty Mia.'

That did it. It never failed. Vanessa adored her Aunty Mia. All the pent-up anger that seemed to vent itself with every cry she'd ever uttered melted at Mia's touch. She'd take her hand, snuggle against her aunt's soft chest and find peace. It hurt to see it – but not enough to waken me. 'Sleep, Gabriella, sleep,' was my self-addressed lullaby. 'You're doing fine. Absolutely fine.'

Clive thought so too.

'I knew you'd settle into an excellent little wife and mother,' he said in a self-satisfied way, as though he'd personally picked the elements and shaken them up and could now enjoy the predicted compound created by his well-tried formula. 'My mother always says she saw your potential the second she set eyes on you.'

'She's been such a help,' I recited. 'I don't know how I'd have managed without Bee.'

We were eating chicken à la king in our quiet and spotless flat. Vanessa had finally dropped off – calling, calling to the last. 'Mummy, what are we going to do tomorrow . . . Mummy can you take me . . . buy me . . . kiss me . . . Mummy, Mummy, why don't you listen?. . . Mummeeee.'

'Shut up, will you,' I said at last, unable to contain my fury. 'Daddy's had a hard day at the office and needs to eat his dinner in peace. And anyway, I'm sick to death of hearing your voice. Absolutely sick of it.'

'Well done Gabs,' he said into the stunned silence that followed my outburst. 'Children need to be taught that their parents need time together too.'

We needed the time to keep a careful and consistent inventory of our steadily mounting assets. Another rung up the property ladder to a house in Muswell Hill, Oriental carpets, promising paintings, prestigious cars. The fruits of Clive's diligence. Those with diminishing returns – such as our decreasingly satisfactory sexual congresses – were ignored.

'We really ought to start thinking about another child,' he'd said dutifully when Vanessa turned three. I'd agreed and obligingly returned to the upturned-snail routine and various recommended male-sperm-enhancing positions. But this time nothing happened and Clive developed migraine and I developed thrush.

'I'm so tired Clivey,' I started saying, 'so desperately tired.'

'Go to sleep then Gabs.'

I needed no second bidding.

'Why is this night different from all other nights?'

I hadn't really noticed. I'd been dozing through the nights and the days and the months and the years and suddenly it was Passover and we were in our biggest house yet. We'd arrived in the heart of Hampstead Garden Suburb and Clive had said, 'It's about time we had a seder, Gabs. My mother really needs a year off after all this time.' And of course I'd said, 'Yes darling' – I usually did – and Bernice had arrived with her best suit and brightest wand to make matzah out of bread and a grey nutty paste called charoset out of the mortar the enslaved children of Israel had used to build the mighty pyramids of Egypt. It tasted vile.

'And so Gabriella, who's coming tonight?' she'd asked. She was mixing salt-water to serve with hard-boiled eggs and bitter herbs and a charred shankbone and other ingredients she'd conjured out of tears and pain and the toughness of life. So as not to forget, she said. My fairy godmother was never one to let bygones be bygones.

'Just us,' I replied. 'Us – and of course my mother. And my sister and Joseph.'

'And will Vanessa be asking the four questions this year?'

'She says she will.' Who could tell? The last seder had almost ground to a halt when Vanessa had gone on strike. She'd sat cross-legged on the floor and utterly refused to ask the questions. And since the whole Haggadah, the entire story of enslavement and exodus and freedom, was devised as a response to the curiosity of the youngest of the gathering – and this one clearly had none – Eli (who was conducting the seder) had almost downed his prayer book.

Until I'd convinced him that even adults could be curious and perhaps we should all ask the questions together – and anyway we could smell kneidlach and turkey and potato kugel and other enchantments from the kitchen and knew that if we didn't get on with the tale we'd never be allowed to eat.

This year, despite bribery and threats and entreaties, Vanessa refused again.

'Do it,' I whispered through clenched teeth. 'You're six years old. Don't be such a baby.'

'I won't,' she said resolutely. 'I won't, I won't, I won't.'

'I will,' said Joseph Marks. He looked up at his mother for affirmation.

Mia nodded. 'He'll manage,' she said. 'He wanted to know all about the Passover and why we ask the questions. I – tried to explain. He can ask them in English – I couldn't remember the Hebrew.'

And so it was Joseph's high voice that rose above the seder table. Why *was* this night different from all other nights? And Eli looked at this child who really wanted to know and he forgot his emergent ulcer and incipient angina and the aroma of the tzimmes steaming in the kitchen as he spoke to him about the people of Israel and the promised land.

'In every generation, one ought to regard oneself as though one had personally come out of Egypt,' he said solemnly.

And Joseph listened with matching solemnity, his large blue eyes fixed on his cousin's grandfather who seemed to know all the answers. And I noticed that Vanessa, who'd been sitting next to me in silence, had suddenly moved round the table and snuggled behind her Aunty Mia with both arms round her neck. 'Me too,' I wanted to plead. 'Can't I come and hold on to you as well? Me, your little sister Gabby . . . don't leave me out.'

She looked at me across the table and her eyes seemed to say 'I'm sorry' and suddenly I was furious. She'd come to my palace in Hampstead and should have paid homage to Queen Gabriella and her court. She ought to have been overcome by my splendour, overwhelmed by my might. Instead she'd arrived like a smug Mother Earth with her sickeningly virtuous pretender to the Wiseman throne and cast a spell over my daughter, the real princess. And even my mother, the same mother who'd once said Mia was wicked, a terrible disappointment, a bad bad girl, now smiled upon her with fond pride. And worst of all Mia now seemed to be – sorry for me. It wasn't fair. It just wasn't damn fair at all.

I wanted to turn to my fairy godmother. 'Bee, tell me honestly – who's the fairest between my sister and me?'

'You are, Gabriella dear,' she'd say. 'Of course, Mia does have a certain something . . .'

Bloody hell. I'd try Clive. 'Clivey darling, give it to me straight – don't you think Mia's rather overweight?'

'I suppose so. On the other hand . . .'

Who cared what he thought anyway? These days he was barely interested in my accounts of the trials of Vanessa, gave me little credit for my cooking and had ceased to take stock of our marriage. He was far too busy with the rising fortunes of an accounting practice that needed all his interest and credit and stocktaking skills. Clive's own little fortune often failed to rise during his conscientious weekly entries in our double bed – but his double-entries to the lavatory each day were clearly productive. Mornings and evenings, he'd mount his new oak-seated throne – and emerge forty minutes later with the look of a man who has made a good deal.

No – I swore I didn't care what he thought. But I knew I still needed him badly. His soothing words about the perfection of my housekeeping skills, my immaculate grooming and unparalleled mothering were the top-up doses of the drug that was keeping me soundly asleep. I depended on his words and the safety of his presence.

And so, when Mia's look of compassion threatened to stir all sorts of awakenings, I moved to my husband. 'D'you think we're almost ready to eat yet, Clivey?' I asked with a caressing hand on his smooth bald head.

'Just about Gabs. We're almost there. The food smells absolutely delicious.'

Later when we'd supped and were sipping the fourth cup of wine and Eli was deep into his antacids and Mum was telling Bee how much worse her headaches were becoming and Vanessa was showing her latest acquisitions to her cousin, the front door was opened to admit the prophet Elijah who traditionally came calling on Passover eve.

'I'm not sure about the wisdom of this,' frowned Clive. 'After all, this is Hampstead Garden Suburb and you know what the burglary rate is like . . .'

But his sensible caution about exposing his possessions to the lawbreakers of England was overruled by the fervent lawkeepers of Moses. 'A seder isn't a seder without Elijah,' muttered Eli – and flung open the french windows and tried to lure the good prophet inside with a goblet of wine.

But no one came. It just happened to be the annual general meeting of the Hampstead and District Burglars Association followed by an *Antiques Roadshow* that was lasting longer than expected. And Elijah – judging by the wine that remained untouched – was otherwise engaged.

No. Nobody came and the guests went home and Clive's 'Lovely seder, you were wonderful Gabs' sent me to sleep. And I dreamt about Elijah, the strangest dream about him having been unable to leave heaven this Passover due to the inefficiency of an angel who was ironing his cloak. She'd been at it for the past six years and it was still far from ready.

'I understand exactly what you're going through,' I commiserated with the frustrated prophet. 'It's getting harder and harder to find good help these days.'

'She was sent down to me from the marketing department,' sighed Elijah. 'Apparently she'd been grossly inefficient there as well. But honestly, I don't know why I should have to put up with it. I'll give her another five years or so, then they can have her back. After all, people are waiting for me. They won't hang around for ever.'

I tried to wake Clive, to tell him about my amazingly vivid dream. To tell him I'd been to heaven and seen Elijah and knew exactly what was keeping him there. But he turned over and suggested I went straight back to sleep. So I did.

And slept. And slept.

And when we celebrated a decade of wedded bliss I was still serenely slumbering. I snoozed through the Bar Mitzvah ceremony which proclaimed thirteen-year-old Joseph Marks a Jewish man and pretended not to hear the praise lavished on the boy and his mother by Eli Wiseman (who made the speech) and swallowed my bitter disappointment and furious jealousy and pride.

'Congratulations, Mims.' I kissed her in the synagogue. 'It's great that Joseph has found an – identity. Isn't it strange that Vanessa refuses to have anything to do with being Jewish? One would have thought . . .'

She shrugged and said something bland like 'One never can tell' and we couldn't talk about it any more. There seemed to be so many issues we avoided. My marriage. Her real feelings about life with Mum. And Seamus. Never ever did we mention Seamus.

On the other hand, who wanted to revive old hurts, old hopes? No, better to stay in a suburban stupor. And I can't say I hated it all the time. I rather enjoyed the sense of achievement when I picked up bargains in the sales and discovered brilliant new hairdressers and qualified as a bereavement counsellor and Clive bought me another new car.

And so I hardly noticed the years slipping by. Until suddenly Vanessa was turning eighteen and it was to be on a Friday and Clive was saying, 'Wouldn't it be nice if we had a special dinner in her honour – you know, the whole family Gabs – after all one's daughter doesn't have such an important birthday every day.' And of course I said, 'Yes darling,' since I still usually did. And Bernice arrived with her latest best suit and her ever-shining wand (everyone said she was quite amazing for her age) and tried to turn noodles and eggs into lokshen pudding and her rebellious navy-blue-eyed granddaughter into a perfect Jewish princess.

God himself hardly noticed the years slipping by. Until suddenly it was the Friday of Vanessa Wiseman's eighteenth birthday and he'd lit the first star in heaven and was sending forth his Sabbath eve marketing team with the weekly celestial offer of a second soul.

'This is your last chance,' he warned one of his angels, a particularly troublesome member of his host who'd been reprimanded by Elijah for imperfect ironing and had begged to be restored to the sales force. 'Another slip and I'll have no choice but to let you fall.'

She nodded and, determined to make amends for earlier lapses, flew straight down to Hampstead Garden Suburb in search of a certain Clive Wiseman. For during her long years of service to Elijah (where she'd done little ironing but much creative thinking), she'd decided that the only way she could make up to him for that dreadful business with Seamus O'Reilly was to insist that he accept an extra soul for free.

'Take it with my compliments, Clive,' she'd say. 'Wear it in bed with your wife tonight – and I can guarantee fireworks.'

But there was no sign of Clive Wiseman in his listed Hampstead address. The angel thought perhaps he'd moved again (up the property ladder to Chelsea perhaps), until she recognized the voice of his wife Gabriella. An angry voice. Furiously shouting at a stubbornly resentful eighteen-year-old who'd locked herself in her bedroom.

'Bobba and Gramps are here. They've come specially for your birthday. I spent all day bloody cooking for you, so you'd better come out of your room immediately and put a smile on your face and be pleasant.'

'No. I won't. I don't feel like it. Who asked you to cook for me anyway? You don't really care about me and I refuse to spend another single evening being criticized by you and Bobba. I won't come out – so you can tell them all to go away.'

'Ungrateful little bitch. Just you wait till your father gets home from the office.'

Ah. So that's where he was. She unblocked her ears as she left the Hampstead sound zone. Family quarrels were so unset-

201

tling. Well, she'd soon put this one right. It was amazing what a little extra soul could do to a marriage.

A single light burned in a tall office block in Victoria. In the luxuriously appointed suite leased by Wiseman and Partners (Chartered Accountants), there was a last-minute panic to complete the annual accounts of a prestigious client. Mr Wiseman, now the revered senior partner, had asked a fresh-faced articled clerk to stay on and help him.

'I'd be most appreciative Ronald,' he'd said. 'You see, it's my daughter's birthday and we're having a slight – er – family do. And I'd like to get home as soon as possible.'

'Of course sir,' had been the obliging response. Ronald was ambitious – and anyway he had rather a crush on Clive Wiseman. He'd always had a soft spot for older men, had Ronald.

And so when the angel flew in, exhausted from her earnest do-gooding, her quarry was seated at his desk, deep in the profit and loss figures of Smith & Son Ltd.

'What is it?' he asked absent-mindedly. 'A soul? Free? You mean I'd owe you nothing? Go ahead then, quickly. I have to get home.'

That was easy. A cinch. The angel was hugely relieved – and in a flush of euphoria she offered a soul to young Ronald as well. What the hell. And Ronald, eager as always for the main chance, accepted with alacrity.

And the angel flew off, rather pleased with herself. She turned back for a last look at two satisfied customers thinking there's nothing in the world like making a good sale when . . . oh dear. This was not what she'd planned. Not at all. She didn't even know such things were possible. What was she to do?

For the four souls and two bodies of the respected accountant and his fresh-faced clerk were no longer focused on money matters. They'd locked together amongst the ledgers, clung passionately to one another between a multitude of sheets and bills and, balanced precariously atop piles of books, they swore eternal devotion.

Shocked beyond measure, the angel watched as Clive repaired to the Gents to – collect himself for the evening ahead. He looked at his watch anxiously. Gosh, he was terribly late

202

and his mother was coming. Well, she'd have to wait a few minutes longer. When a man had to go . . .

Ten minutes later, she watched him emerge with an exalted smile.

'Ronald my dear fellow,' he was saying, 'this is a momentous occasion. I've just achieved a lifelong ambition. At last, at long long last, I managed to produce a natural and perfectly formed motion. Ronald, tonight I am a happy man.'

'I don't get it – and I don't like it. Not one bit,' whispered the angel as she prepared for take-off and wondered how it would feel to fall and fall and fall.

Vanessa's birthday dinner was a disaster from start to finish. Bee burnt the lokshen pudding. Then Mia phoned to say Mum wasn't well and they were waiting for the doctor. Then Clive called to announce he'd be late. Then the birthday girl barricaded herself in her bedroom and refused to come out and I had to contend with Bernice's mounting irritation (the child is completely without gratitude, she kept saying) and Eli's sinking blood sugar (he'd developed diabetes).

Then Mia called again to say that Mum seemed worse and there was still no sign of the doctor.

Then Clive: 'I'm ready to leave the office now Gabby darling. The work took much longer than I expected.'

Me: 'Fine, fine. Come as soon as you can.' Why had he suddenly called me darling?

Mia again: 'The doctor's finally here. Mum seems to be unconscious. Oh, Gabby. It's awful.'

Me: 'I don't know what to say . . . ring me again when the doctor says what's wrong.'

Bernice: 'What's happening? What's going on? Where's Clive? He's never been this late before. Do you think we ought to notify the police?'

Me: 'No, no, Bee. He's on his way. He told me so.'

At last, at last, the sound of the key in the door. Never have I been so happy to see him. He seemed happy too. Unusually happy.

But the moment of contentment came and went. Clive went upstairs to deal (unsuccessfully) with his rebellious daughter. Mia phoned for the fourth time to say that Mum had been medicated and the doctor would return in the morning. 'He thinks she's had a stroke,' she sobbed.

'Don't cry Mims,' I said, feeling helpless. 'People do recover from strokes you know.'

And I put down the phone and burst into tears. And Clive ate supper with his parents. And Vanessa went to sleep.

A few days later another framed quotation appeared beside the hallowed words of Hippocrates on the lavatory wall. This time it was taken from the Song of Solomon: 'My beloved put in his hand by the hole of the door, and my bowels were moved for him.'

I didn't quite understand it and was about to ask Clive what it meant. But then Mum became worse and was taken to hospital and Vanessa took it into her head to leave home and – well, Solomon's song on our lavatory wall seemed somewhat irrelevant. Especially after I'd answered the phone to Mia's hysterical voice late one night about a week later. Clive was working overtime again.

'Gabby,' she was saying, 'I've just had a call from the hospital. Mum's dying. We'd better get there fast.'

❧ 16 ❦

'Miss Marks? Is that Miss Mia Marks?' A voice that never slept. It waited, cool and businesslike and ever alert, to bring bad news into the dark of night. I'd heard the telephone and dreamt it was a dream but it rang and rang relentlessly and I knew and woke and, heart pounding, lifted the receiver to let out the voice. There was no stopping the messenger of death.

'Yes, it's me.'

'This is the sister speaking. Your mother seems to have taken a turn for the worse. We – don't think she has long to – live. Perhaps you'd better come here – as soon as you can.'

'Oh – yes – I will. Thank you.'

I'd thanked her. She'd tinkled a death bell in my ear and I'd said thank you. Ever, ever grateful Mia – to the man who'd deserted her because he'd shown her paradise, to the world that was taking her son because it was giving him belief, to the mother who'd done nothing – for being there. But not for long, the brisk voice in the night had said. Not for long. Thank you. Thank you so much for telling me, sister.

'You don't have to thank me,' she might have said. 'Isn't this what a sister is for – to tell you the things that you'd rather not hear?'

Was that it? If so my sister Gabriella had been slipping of late. She'd almost stopped telling me anything, and I suppose I'd done the same. But now I'd have to fulfil my duty. Would she rather not hear? Would she care? Would the self-consciously sociable and stylishly unconscious Mrs Wiseman mind that her mother was drawing her final breaths? I hardly knew any more.

'Gabby, it's Mum. She's dying. We'd better get there fast.'

'I'm coming Mims. I'll meet you at the hospital.'

She minded. She wiped away a tear as we stood on either

side of the bed looking down on the wraithlike figure of the woman who'd borne us. With the sister, we'd walked quietly through grey shapes and deep groans in the darkened ward to a far corner where her bed was curtained like a shroud. White light blanched the last touch of colour from a face that had always looked faded. Her pale eyes were open but seemed to see nothing.

'We've done all we can. Her breathing's very weak. The doctor said there's nothing more . . .'

I touched the sister's arm. 'It's OK,' I whispered (why was *I* comforting *her*?) 'Can you leave us with her – for a while?'

She slipped out soundlessly and Gabby moved round the bed and we watched over her side by side, hand in hand. Breathing together and waiting for each breath of hers.

'Mum,' I said, 'Mum, it's us. Mia and Gabby.' I put a tentative hand on her cheek, stroked it gently, afraid that her flesh would crumble at my touch. It looked as though it had been carved out of fine white powder.

'Mum,' said Gabby in a little voice. A small lost child. 'Mum, don't die, I don't want you to die.' She pulled me towards her, burying her head in my shoulder and crying, and I suddenly saw that my mother's eyes were shut.

'Gabs.' We held our breath. But hers continued. In . . . out . . . in . . . out. She seemed to be sleeping. Perhaps she'd get better. Maybe she'd live. 'I'll call sister.'

'No, wait.' Gabby held me back. 'Look.' Mum's eyes were opening. She was frowning, trying to lift her head, gazing intently at me as though she were about to say something. We waited, afraid to breathe, to move. But the words wouldn't come and her frown went away and a shadow seemed to cross her face as she surrendered to her final helplessness.

'What – d'you think she was – trying to say?' asked Gabby, holding on to me, trembling at this soundless snuffing of a life. Already Mum had joined the past tense.

'I don't know,' I said, looking at my mother now resting in her last-ever bed. 'Perhaps she was wanting a piece of toast.'

There was a small shocked silence. Then my sister flung her arms round me and we laughed and cried and our tears splashed over our poor dead mother who would never ask me for the thinnest slice of anything again.

*

206

'It was the end,' I said, sitting at the edge of his bed as dawn broke on my first motherless day. I hadn't slept. All the things I'd never said to her ran through my head. The truths I'd never told her, those I'd never demanded from her. Why? Why?

'Joseph,' I told my son, averting my head to hide the ravages of my grief, protecting him as ever and suddenly sad about the truths I'd hidden from him, 'your grandma is dead.'

He took my hand and held it and his seemed solid and strong. Not a boy's hand any more. 'I'm sorry Mum. I'm so terribly sorry.'

Rays of morning light slid in between the curtains and under the door and melted together and the room that had once been Gabriella's was no longer dark. But Joseph and I didn't move. I wanted to stay there for ever, sitting at the edge of his bed with my hand in his.

'Do you remember?' I wanted to ask, 'do you remember the day we came here to live with Grandma? Do you remember – before? Do you remember Utopia?'

But of course he didn't. How could he? He'd arrived in my arms, four months old, with his world in the soft warm neck and breasts of his mother. I'd been his Utopia and he'd been my memory, his navy-blue eyes my memento. That night, that first night of the rest of my life when I'd brought my Joseph to Hendon, I'd sat alongside his small crib and mourned the drabness of the life I was offering him. Streets that were ever treeless, an arid house devoid of cheer. Such emptiness.

'I'll make it up to you my darling Joseph,' I promised my son. 'I'll make you a multicoloured dreamcoat even finer than the one worn by your namesake in the Bible. I'll cut it out of the rainbow, weave into it the richest legends I can find, the most fantastic fairy-tales, knights in search of truth and honour, glorious stories of love and conquest. It will be my gift to you, my favourite, one and only son.'

And there, in the very room that had once been Gabriella's, I'd drawn close to Joseph night after night after month after year and wrapped him in dreams of every imaginable hue. For more than a thousand and one nights I'd been his Scheherazade and now we'd come to our final story. 'The end,' I'd said, 'it was the end.'

'Mum,' he said suddenly after a long silence. The room was now quite light. Through a crack in the curtains I could see the sky was blue. Mum was missing a fine day. Not that she'd gone out much – but she'd always been interested in the daily weather reports I'd brought her. Vaguely interested, as in everything. 'Will you manage, with me going to college and now Grandma – gone? This wasn't how it was meant to be. I don't like leaving you here alone. Shall I stay on – for a while?'

'No,' I said emphatically. Never ever did I want Joseph to feel bitter about any sacrifice he'd made for me. 'We must carry on as planned. You must leave, after – the funeral. And don't worry about me. Please Joseph. I'll be all right. I always am.'

'I'll be all right.' How many times had I repeated these words down the years? Until they'd stopped asking. I'd convinced them all. The first time Gabby came to see me after I'd moved back with Mum, I was sure she'd packed charitable compassion with the spare nappies and bottles and cuddly toys and teething biscuits she'd brought in a huge pink plastic holder for her cross little daughter. When I opened the door to her, I could feel her judging the age of my old plum-coloured suit and mustering all the sympathy she could for her poor deserted sister.

'Gabby,' I said. I couldn't manage anything else. If I sounded too emotional it would confirm her suspicions.

'Hi Mims.' As though nothing had happened. 'Vanessa, say hello to your aunty.'

I opened my arms to my little niece with her white smocked dress and scowling face and expected the squirming body to resist with yells of anger. Instead her small face looked into mine and her eyes widened into deep pools of longing and then shut peacefully as she nuzzled against me. 'Hello Vanessa,' I whispered. We'd fallen in love.

'You certainly seem to have a way with her,' Gabby said with rather forced jollity. Her daughter's contentment with me seemed to irk her. She liked it even less when Mum made a remark about Vanessa and Joseph having identical eyes. I dismissed it as one of those rather meaningless proud-grandma statements, but Gabby was quite defensive.

'We are sisters after all,' she said sharply.

Yes, I suppose we were. And after I'd kissed her goodbye and given Vanessa a last hug and looked into her huge eyes and felt a shiver at the base of my spine which I attributed to

208

the November air, I smiled and waved and decided that on the whole it had been a successful visit. Gabby would probably go back to her Clivey with the rather disappointing news that poor old Mia was managing well.

I shut the front door and returned to the living-room where Mum was prostrate with an aching head and demanding to be helped upstairs and Joseph was wailing for food and attention. And I sat on the sofa with my own throbbing head in my hands and wondered who the hell I'd been trying to fool with my studied air of containment, all that determined self-possession. I imagined my sister going home to her attentive husband with her supportive friends and efficient mother-in-law – and felt very alone.

But feeling lonely didn't help. And so I placated my mother and picked up my sobbing son and held him on my lap, rocking him gently till he calmed.

'Shh – listen Joseph,' I said softly. 'Listen very quietly and I'll tell you a story. A fairy-story that opens with the words "Once upon a time" and ends . . . I'm not quite sure yet. The truth is, Joseph – and you'll find this out in the way children always find their parents out – I'm better at beginnings than endings. But have patience my little boy. Our ending will come. It's inevitable. And perhaps, if we don't lose hope, it might still be "They lived for a good time afterwards, happy and in pleasure." For that's the best of all possible endings, for a fairy-story. Let's call ours the Tale of Two Sisters.'

'Once upon a time there were two sisters whose father died when they were quite young. And their mother, although she fed them with all the best food that the kingdom could provide and clothed them in the finest garments available in the chain stores of the day, failed to nourish their spirit. She wasn't a bad woman, not in the way of Snow White's wicked stepmother or Cinderella's evil parent. The thing was, she'd been starved of fairy-tales herself and simply didn't know any better.

'And so the two sisters grew up with a huge hunger, a longing for something that they couldn't quite define. Big Sister thought it might be love, but she wasn't sure what this was since she'd trusted the love of a father who'd left her and an uncle who'd tried to steal her innocence. But it hurt, this longing, until she couldn't bear the pain. And so she put herself to sleep, a deep deep sleep, even deeper than that of Sleeping

Beauty. And in her slumbers she dreamt of a prince who would wake her and answer her longing for this thing she suspected was love.

'"Stuff and nonsense," scoffed Little Sister, who was sure that her hunger was for success and excitement. What, after all, was love? And she made herself wings of wax (she'd heard of a Greek who'd done that, but never bothered to reach the end of his tale) and flew towards the sun. And of course her wax wings melted and she started falling, falling to the ground.

'Far below, someone had noticed her descent. A man rich in possessions who'd been about to acquire a pretty songbird to make his home complete. And when Little Sister with her useless wings came tumbling to the ground he helped her up and saw that her feathers were fine and her voice was worth training and offered her a golden cage in which she could sing all day and all night and never risk falling again.

'And Little Sister, whose eyes were still blinded by the glare of the sun, thought the rich man was a prince and a golden cage would bring the glitter of success and excitement she craved. And she agreed. And when her fairy godmother came to teach her all the songs that caged birds were expected to know, she proved an apt pupil and sang beautifully for her supper in the safety of her cage, and wondered why her hunger never quite went away.

'Meanwhile Big Sister's patient sleep turned out not to be in vain. A prince came by and woke her and took her to a magic country far away where love and beauty were granted to all who lived there. And Big Sister, who'd always been quite plain, became suddenly so lovely that the sun and the moon were quite taken aback when they cast their light on her.

'So was Little Sister.

'"Perhaps my golden cage is a size too small," she thought. "Not that I begrudge my sister her happiness – but fair's fair. I want to visit her magic country as well." And she tried to reach it. Perhaps, perhaps she did manage a brief visit. She certainly begged her fairy godmother to cast every imaginable spell on her in an attempt to achieve her sister's sudden beauty and she preened herself in her cage and sang louder than ever. She even produced a little princess.

'But then it didn't seem to matter any more after Big Sister's prince disappeared. Once again the golden cage was a safe place – and Little Sister decided to dull her persistent, gnawing hunger by putting herself to sleep as well. And such a well-taught songbird was Little Sister that she could carry on singing in her sleep without anyone really noticing.

'Except Big Sister, who heard the songs getting thinner and sadder but couldn't say anything because she was trying so hard to sing her own song of hope, to nourish her own little prince with some of the magic that their mother had withheld from them. And she didn't have the strength to feed Little Sister as well.

'And so, there they were. Little Sister asleep in her cage, bravely singing her weak warbling song, and Big Sister, who'd once been woken and could never go to sleep again, singing to her small son the short rich song of her awakening. But was that the end of the tale? Two voices in a waste land, for ever and ever?

'Possibly. On the other hand, my dear little Joseph, there are other options. What if, for instance, the sisters learnt to sing together? To combine their voices in a powerful two-part harmony that would soar through the darkness and create a magic world of music and light?

'No? Not likely? You think they'd never stop trying to outsing one another?

'Well, perhaps a knight might come and rescue – well, one of them. Two passing knights might be rather a lot to expect. But mightn't one, a single armoured nobleman on his quest for the Holy Grail, perchance be crossing the waste land and happen to hear the song of a maiden in distress?

'No? Too far-fetched? And you don't think a nobleman on a dangerous mission would encumber himself with a distressed and helpless maiden?

'Joseph, you are difficult to please. That's it then. I can't think of any other ending, unless the sisters redeem the waste land within themselves. And that's asking a great deal.'

When Joseph was old enough to understand the tales I told him, he insisted I gave them real heroes and proper endings. Not silly helpless sisters who didn't know if they were coming or going. He wanted heroes like Jack the Giant-Killer and Sinbad the Sailor, who would overcome great hurdles, carry out seemingly impossible tasks, do battle with the most evil villains imaginable and end up living happily ever after. And when I said the concluding words, he'd sigh with relief, and I knew that they made my fatherless son feel safe.

That's perhaps why he was so intrigued with the story of Passover. It had all the ingredients. A collective hero (the children of Israel), oppression, danger, a mighty battle, the magic parting of the seas – and a happy ending. The vision of a promised land.

'Tell me about the plagues, Mum. Tell me about the Angel of Death. Didn't she kill any Jewish children by mistake?' He seemed obsessed by the tale.

'When we go to Aunty Gabby's on Wednesday night you'll hear it all. That's what the seder is about, to tell the story of Passover.'

Joseph was the child who asked the four questions that night. His cousin Vanessa couldn't have cared less about the answers but Joseph desperately wanted to know.

'In every generation, one ought to regard oneself as though one had personally come out of Egypt,' preached Eli Wiseman to my son, who suddenly realized that he, too, could be one with the children of Israel. He could be a hero who'd escaped from Egypt. He, Joseph Marks, could even end up living happily ever after. I saw him watch the old man with widened eyes and I understood the possibilities that were suddenly shining out in front of my son. And I wanted to take his arm, to hold him back and say 'Joseph, it's a fairy-tale like any other. Don't believe it too much. You might be hurt.'

But I couldn't. I'd given him dreams but no substance and now he was trying to make them real. And Vanessa, who had suddenly appeared behind me and was almost choking me with the might of her need, had been fed plenty of substance but so very few dreams. It was sad. One of the saddest Passovers I'd ever experienced. When they opened the door for Elijah (after a lengthy debate on the security risk) I saw Joseph waiting with baited breath. And I knew that the prophet was just as likely to come calling in Hampstead as – as Seamus O'Reilly was to return from Dublin. And I'd given up on Seamus long ago. Well, almost.

*

212

A single letter. A hundred and fourteen handwritten words in all the years. It had arrived when Joseph was six months old in the days when I'd still sung to him at night about his Daddy's return.

My dearest Mia,
I haven't forgotten you. Hannah told me about the baby. That he's beautiful and you've named him Joseph after your father. I'm glad. Your father sounds as though he was a good, kind man. I'm not good, Mia, not nearly good enough for you. Please try and put me out of your mind. It would be better for you – and for Joseph. I heard that you'd moved back with your mother and were managing well. I'll send money when I can – at the moment I'm broke as all plans for my play have fallen through. I start work with a construction company tomorrow. Best love, Mia. I think about you often.
Seamus

I'd read it over and over, extracting all its juices till finally, when I'd put it aside, it was like an exhausted piece of chewing gum. The highly flavoured additive-laden kind that thrills the taste-buds at first, then gets rather bitter and then – nothing. He had no wish to see me again. No desire to see his son. 'Please try and put me out of your mind. It would be better for you – and for Joseph.'

How the hell could Seamus have begun to know what was good for me – or for the son he'd never bothered to meet? Suddenly furious, I'd picked up Joseph and held him very tightly and remembered a small doll that I'd once squeezed and cried into, then smashed against the wooden bedpost until its head had split. And I'd pressed my face into the blond curls of my boy baby, the unbattered head that I was to fill with a million dreams, and sobbed and sworn never to mention his father to him again.

I tried not to. To pretend that Seamus had never existed. It was easier after Hannah had left London.

'I'm going back to Ireland Mia,' she'd told me one day. It was quite soon after I'd returned to work. We'd tried to resume our friendship but it had been no good. Too much had happened. 'My father's very ill.'

'I'm sorry.' Such an empty and meaningless expression of a

213

sympathy that I couldn't even begin to feel. Her father. Seamus's father. Joseph's grandfather. So what?

'Would you like me to – say anything? Take anything?'

'No. Thank you.'

She had kissed me goodbye and I'd smelt lavender. Hannah hadn't changed her perfume in all the years I'd known her. 'I'm sorry – so terribly sorry – about the way things have turned out. It's been like a weight on me. I've felt so – responsible. But honestly Mia, please believe me, there was nothing I could do.'

'I know. It's OK. Best, best luck Hannah. Please let me know how you are.'

'I'll write.'

She had from time to time. About the death of Mr O'Reilly Senior, the activities of the various siblings and finally, around the time Joseph turned six, about the marriage of her brother Seamus.

I thought it would be best for you to know that he was married last week to a lovely young girl called Mary who belongs to our church. He'd been seeing her for some time.

It had happened. Seamus had found his virgin bride. I felt neither anger nor sorrow. Just a sense of the inevitable. This had been his destiny ever since he'd opened his *Book of Miracles* after that Sunday school prize-giving many many years before. And now his son, his Joseph whom he'd never seen, was poring over his own *Book of Miracles*, the story of Passover. Joseph was searching for his own destiny.

And that, God help me, was when I decided I had to lie to him. I believed with all my heart that there was no other way.

'Joseph, come and sit next to me. I have something to tell you,' I said the next time he asked me why he didn't have a dad like all the other kids at school. And I explained to him that he'd once had a father, a good, kind father who'd have been so proud of him. A father who'd lived for him. And died for him. For us.

'He died loving us, Joseph.' I meant it. I honestly meant it. For that's the way the Seamus in my head had died and was still dying – with a grace that, even if I'd invented it, I needed so badly to believe in. And one of the reasons why I'd made no real effort to contact him, to demand his return, was that I

214

couldn't bear to confront his littleness, his frailty. His reality. And that was why I'd always refused to discuss him with my mother or sister. I was frightened that the image of my Seamus would not withstand their scorn.

Joseph seemed to understand. Now that he'd been assured of once having had a father, he was satisfied to put yet another mythical figure into his hero-crowded head.

'D'you think he's gone to heaven?' he asked.

'If there is a heaven, that's where he belongs.'

'Congratulations Mims,' she said to me, brushing her ruby-red lips over mine. It was Joseph's Bar Mitzvah. Gabriella wore a little red dress to match her lipstick and mascara that seemed to open her glazed dark eyes unnaturally wide and a smile that was even wider and emptier than her eyes. I wondered whether she was on tranquillizers. There was something about my sister that made me think of a sleepwalker.

'It's great that Joseph has found an – identity.' Even her voice sounded prerecorded.

I mumbled something inconsequential as we took our place in the synagogue gallery to witness the emergent manhood of my thirteen-year-old son. Mum sat on my left and Bernice Wiseman on Gabby's right and I thought about the strange word that had issued from her perfectly painted lips.

Identity. Meaning either absolute sameness or individuality. What sort of identity was Joseph supposed to have found? What identity had Gabriella sought? And me? Was the legend I'd created out of my life too fanciful to be considered an identity?

Joseph's voice rang out, high and clear. Eli Wiseman stood close to him in place of his father. Both wore white prayer shawls and black skull-caps. Identical. Eli's hypochondria had lifted, symptom by symptom, as he'd scoured the Talmud, sifted through the Midrash and relearnt the Laws of Moses, finding answers to the endless questions posed by this curious child of his daughter-in-law's sister. A bond had grown between the old man and the seeking boy. An identity?

'There's an old Jewish story I want to tell you,' Eli told the guests who'd gathered in the synagogue hall for chopped herring, whisky, exchanging hardships and enduring a speech or two in honour of the Bar Mitzvah boy.

'While a child is in the womb, they say that it is not only able to see from one end of the world to another, but it learns the entire Torah. Off by heart, word for word. But then, when it finally enters the world, an angel comes down and strikes it on the mouth and causes it to forget everything it has learnt. I've always wondered why. Why should God send his angels to batter newborn babes? I used to imagine a world in which everyone came equipped with knowledge of the Torah and think surely it would be a better place. That's what I thought – until I met young Joseph Marks and he helped me discover the joy of relearning. Now I understand.'

There was scattered applause and they all toasted my son and the hall quickly emptied and I wondered if, while I'd been losing Utopia in Cricklewood, embryonic Joseph had been learning the Torah and whether I'd ever been taught it and if my sister with her kosher kitchen had ever really wanted to know it. And Vanessa? Where was Vanessa?

'Isn't it strange that Vanessa refuses to have anything to do with being Jewish?' Gabby had remarked in her walkie-talkie doll voice. 'One would have thought . . .'

'You never can tell,' I said, not knowing what to say. Vanessa had developed a sore throat on the day of her cousin's Bar Mitzvah. 'I hate my parents,' she'd told me vehemently after school one day. She often came to talk to me.

'D'you mind if I – tell you – things, Aunty Mia?' she'd once asked hesitantly. 'No one else seems to understand me.'

'Of course not, Nessa. You can come whenever you like.'

She slipped in frequently, seeking my arms and ears but carefully avoiding her cousin. When Joseph started to become close to her grandfather, she stopped referring to him altogether.

'It's not fair,' she'd once burst out. 'He should have been their child and I yours and then everybody would have been happy.' Then she saw my face. 'I'm sorry, Aunty Mia. You'd never want to swop Joseph for anyone, would you?'

'No. I couldn't. But I do love you, Nessa darling. I really do.'

'What's love?' she asked bitterly, turning away.

And I knew then that it wasn't something one felt but something one did and kissed the tear that crept down her cheek and saw that Vanessa, the child with everything, believed she belonged to nobody. While Clive made money and Gabriella moved in all the right circles and made a perfect Hampstead home and all the correct parental noises, their daughter was lost and lonely. Did they know? Should I tell them?

I tried.

'Gabs, it's Vanessa. I'm worried about her. She doesn't seem to be happy. Perhaps you should – try and talk to her.'

'Oh, Vanessa. She's always been unhappy – from the minute she was born. I think she's been spoilt. Bernice believes that too. She'll grow out of it though. We both think so.'

'And Clive? What does he think?'

'What a ridiculous question. Since when did Clive ever think? He agrees with his mother, of course. But don't worry about it Mims. Listen, I've just discovered the most marvellous hair-dresser in Golders Green. Perhaps you can come with me sometime. The last time I saw you I thought your hair looked as though it could do with a decent cut.'

It was no good. I tried again once or twice as time passed and we all got older and Mr Goldblatt shed a few partners and most of his hair and Mum acquired more ailments and Gabby and I grew further and further apart. Sometimes we tried to reach one another. But we were balanced so precariously, she propped up by the myth of suburbia and I by the fragile strands of my mythology and the waste land stretched below and if we leaned over too far we'd fall.

And so we hardly noticed the years slipping by. Until suddenly Vanessa was turning eighteen and it was to be on a Friday and Gabby's brisk telephone voice was inviting us – me, Mum and Joseph – to a special dinner in her honour.

'As Clive said last night, we ought to celebrate. After all, one's daughter doesn't have such an important birthday every day.'

Of course I accepted. And the next day there was a hammering at the front door and it was Vanessa and she was furious.

'I told them and they don't listen to me. I don't want a bloody birthday party. I refuse to endure another family meal ever again. Aunty Mia, I can't bear to live in that awful house with them a minute longer.'

'Come – come inside and sit down Nessa. Here, next to me. Now tell me. What's the problem?'

217

Everything. Her mean-spirited mother, spiritless father, the soulless home in which she'd cried alone for almost eighteen years. The grandparents who seemed to disapprove of every breath that she drew and whom she never wanted to see again. Ever.

'She – Bobba, Bernice, or whatever I'm supposed to call the old cow – told me last week that she was sure they'd mixed me up with someone in the hospital where I was born. That's the only way she could account for me being so dreadful and rude and unlovable. Not like a Wiseman at all. Why should I have to endure their meaningless happy birthday wishes?'

I stroked her dark hair and tried to reassure her and she told me – after she'd sworn me to strictest secrecy – that she had a boyfriend. A forbidden Christian boyfriend. His name was James and they were planning to set up home together.

'After I turn eighteen,' she said defiantly, 'there's nothing they can do.'

'Oh Nessa,' I said sadly and remembered everything but could tell her nothing. For the things I remembered were never spoken about and there was the tale of Joseph's hero-father to protect. And so all I could say was: 'Please, please think about – things – before you – do anything.'

Such a lame piece of advice. A dry bit of biscuit offered to someone tempted by exotic fruit. And I could have told her so much. I could have held my niece and said, 'Nessa, listen and I'll tell you how it really was.' She nodded, flicking away my crumbs. But I did finally persuade her to attend her own party.

'On one condition,' she said. 'I'll be there if you're there.'

'I will be,' I promised. 'We can sit together.'

I meant it. Of course I did. How was I to predict the sudden collapse of my mother? After a seventy-three-year decline, did she have to choose the morning of her granddaughter's eighteenth birthday for her fall?

'Gabby, it's Mum. I don't think she's very well at all.'

'What's new? Bee, the lokshen pudding smells like it's burning. You'd better take it out of the oven. We'll be seeing you tonight then Mims?'

'I told you, Mum seems ill. Really ill. I came up with her breakfast this morning and she could hardly talk. She says she can't move. Gabs, this time I'm scared. I called the doctor. I've told them at work that I'll be late. I'd better wait and see what he says.'

'I'd offer to come and give a hand Mims, but I'm up to the eyes in cooking for this dinner tonight.'

'It's OK. Give Nessa my love. Tell her I'll see her later.'

'Let me know what the doctor says.'

'I will, if she lets him near her. She still hankers after Dr Mitchell, the old lecher. Says he was the only doctor who ever understood her.'

All morning she kept asking for him. 'When is Dr Mitchell coming, Mia darling?' She refused to listen when I told her repeatedly that Dr Mitchell had been retired for five years and how much she'd liked his successor, Dr Shah, the last time he'd called. Tears rolled down her cheeks. The rest of her was ominously still.

'I'm frightened Mia,' she said. 'Do you think I'll ever move again?'

'Of course Mum. You'll get better. I'm sure you will.'

She looked as though she'd shrunk in the night and her sheets smelled of urine and I wasn't sure at all. I cleaned her as best I could and we waited. And waited. The morning was endless. I sat in the room watching shadows and listening to the sounds of an empty house. Dying sounds. Joseph had offered to stay in and help look after his grandma.

'No, don't worry, I'll be here. I couldn't possibly go to work and leave her like this. But don't forget tonight. It's Vanessa's birthday dinner. I said we'd be there at eight.'

Joseph had been accepted at a seminary in Newcastle. He was going to be a rabbi. His destiny. Had this been my mother's destiny – to stare at me with fearful eyes, at last truly helpless in her well-worn bed of helplessness?

And Vanessa? Would it be her destiny to shock her family by seeking fulfilment in the arms of a dangerous stranger? My birthday present to my niece was a silver coin on a chain. On the back of the coin, instead of a ship, I'd had a single word engraved. 'Serendipity'.

But it was to be several months before Vanessa got her present. I couldn't keep my promise to come to her dinner and two days later Gabby called me in distress to say that her daughter had left home, and then Mum died. Ten days after she'd said she was frightened she'd never move again, her coffin was being lowered into a muddy hole at Bushey Cemetery.

Clive Wiseman, as the family's number one male mourner, dropped the first clod of earth on the wooden casket. His features were set in studied solemnity. I remember thinking how affluent he looked in his three-piece suit. Sleek and well-fed and rather pleased with himself despite the deliberate droop. That was how I pictured him, in pinstripes dropping spadefuls of brown mud on to his mother-in-law's coffin, the day Gabby appeared in acute distress at the door of the house I'd inherited in Hendon.

It was eight o'clock in the morning. She'd arrived in her night-gown, her hair uncombed, her face crumpled and blotched with tears and old make-up.

'I loathe him,' she said in a voice I'd never heard her use. It was her own. Hate had finally forced out Gabriella's true voice. 'Clive Wiseman is – the most despicable creature – in the world.'

That was all I could get out of my sister for a long, long time. She told me of her loathing and put her arms round my neck and slid into darkness. I thought she'd stay there for ever.

🍃 17 🍃

The darkness. The blessed darkness. At last it came. She held me and I leaned on her shoulder and felt it drift over me, its wide-open warm mouth swallowing me. And I slid down its soft throat and into its wet warm belly and I wanted to stay there for ever.

'Gabby,' I heard her say. 'Gabby! What is it?' Alarmed. 'What happened? What has Clive done?'

Clive? Who was Clive? Oh, you mean the Messiah with a balding head who bumped into me in Birmingham? The redeemer who offered me salvation and safety and chicken soup in exchange for belief in his household gods? The upright chartered accountant with a fortune and a family and a future? That Clive?

No Mia. I can't talk in this thick heavy darkness but if I could I'd swear to you that Clive Wiseman, my Clive Wiseman, would never, absolutely never, have done anything his mother had forbidden. He was the man who remained the child who still cried when her voice was cross, remember? Didn't he stay forever the small boy who pleased her every day with a clean plate, his sums all ticked and a good bowel movement? And didn't he make sure to find a nice amenable Jewish girl to marry for his mother to mould?

Clive was perfect, Mia. A Blue Ribbon husband. Doing wrong? Certainly not – especially not to Gabby, his ideal little wife. His Gabs who came to him so young and innocent and opened her legs to him 3.4 times a week (when asked) and learnt to make kreplach soup and small talk and to colour co-ordinate his home and never to laugh at him. Ever. Not even when his willy drooped and his constipation stiffened and his lip wobbled when his clients taxed him and his mother disapproved ever so slightly of the shade of the roses he sent for her birthday. 'Poor, poor Clivey,' Gabby would say with a face that was concentrated concern. Again and again and again. Her concentration never flagged.

In fact, if ever there was a wife who deserved the impeccable services of a man like Clive Wiseman, it was his Gabriella. So don't ask questions Mims. Anyway, what gave you the idea that there was anything wrong? I just came for breakfast. To Hendon for my breakfast. For a nice cup of tea and the thinnest slice of toast you can manage. And darkness. Oh Mims let me stay here in your darkness. It's safe. Here, hold my hand and take me upstairs and put me into my old bed and tuck the blankets round me and I'll sleep. Such an expert sleeper. Such a clever girl. Such a cutey-pie. A real charmer. Shh. Shh. Gabby wants to go to sleep . . .

'Wake up Mummy.'

Stop digging your fingers in my eyes you horrid little creature.

'Open your eyes! Please, please, please open your eyes.'

Can't you see your mother's trying to rest? Can't you *see*? Of course you can. You've always seen everything, haven't you Vanessa? Long long before you opened those haunting eyes of yours. There was your mother, sweet Gabby stripped bare, moaning and panting and making wild mating sounds in her marriage bed with her lover, her sister's lover. You saw it. Her deception and his adoration and her remorse and her penance. And her husband. Her righteous husband. The fine husband for whom she'd doused the fireworks and gone to sleep. You knew him too, didn't you Vanessa? Your father. Was he your father?

I'll bet you wouldn't have turned a hair to see him dragging himself into his Garden Suburb home at six this morning, bleeding and whimpering like a battered tom cat. Not you. You've been watching him Nessa. I know you have. Watching him, watching me – and then walking away in disgust.

'Clive,' I called when I heard the door opening. 'Clive, is that you?'

He'd been coming home late, night after night, but never this late. I turned on the light and looked at the time.

'Clive!'

Why didn't he answer? I shivered and waited for footsteps, listening, listening. A cat outside. A car. A whimper. Was that him?

'Clive!'

Huddled in my dressing-gown I crept out on to the oak-panelled landing and looked down the staircase to the hall. The first shafts of daylight shone weakly through the glass-paned door on to a dark heap on the floor. I walked down, one step at a time, stiff with dread. It was his jacket, hastily dropped. There were retching noises from the lavatory. Was he drunk? Imposs-ible. Not him.

'Clive, what happened? What's the matter? Where were you?'

No answer. More retching. Silence. I heard the lavatory flushing and water gurgling down the drain and the door opened and I saw that his shirt was torn and splattered with blood and his face – and his head – oh God. There was a gash across his bald patch. An oozing zigzag-shaped crack. Mia's Ugly Baba. I thought of Mia's Ugly Baba.

'Gabs – I'll explain – someone hit me – beat me up. It hurts, Gabs, it hurts. I'm so sore. So sick.' And he sank down on the bottom step and covered his face and wept. Great self-pitying sobs.

'Who hit you? We'd better report it to the police.'

'No!' He jumped up. 'Not the police. Please Gabs – don't phone the police. Stay here – here, sit down. I'm hurt. Badly hurt.'

'Why? Why not the police?' I refused to sit. Stood over him as he cowered with pain and shame and humiliation. His inquisitor. Waiting. 'Why Clive? What have you done?'

'Nothing bad Gabs. Nothing – criminal. I was beaten up. I – told you.'

'Well then . . .'

'No – wait. I'll tell you. I'l tell you everything.'

And he told me. Slowly, sob by sob. The whole sordid story. Ronald. Ronald's jealous boyfriend. Sleaze. Muck. Disgrace. What would his mother say? No wonder he was vomiting. I wanted to vomit. I wanted to scream. I wanted to yell out my hate and anger and every curse that had ever been mouthed.

223

Not yet though. First I'd stand there, impassive, listening, pretending to give him the absolution he sought.

'Forgive me Gabby, please. This will never happen again. I promise.'

I turned away from him and slowly opened the front door. 'Out!' I'd never heard this voice before. It came from depths I'd never dared plumb. A well of pure icy hatred. 'Get out. I never want to see you again. Never, ever, as long as I live.'

'But – I'm sorry. Gabs, I am sorry . . .'

'Out.'

He went. He crept past me, head bowed, and I shut the door quietly. Trance-like. It wasn't happening. I looked down and saw a bloodstain on the cream carpet that covered the stairs. And from the lavatory came the stench of his vomit. And my hate-well bubbled and bubbled and finally burst in a convulsion of madness that took me from room to room to room, breaking and screaming and ripping and raving. Until I came to his throne. His oak-seated lavatory. And I threw up again and again and then threw in Hippocrates and then, with a final heaving retch, the Song of Solomon. And pain tore through my body. Unbearable pain. Such loss. Such a waste. Such a pitiful waste.

I don't know how I found my way to Hendon. I suppose I must have driven there. To her. To Mia. To the darkness.

Oh Nessa let me sleep. Be a good girl and go away and please let Mummy sleep.

But she didn't. None of them did. They kept pulling the darkness away. The voices, the faces, the laughter. That was the worst. Jeering fingers pointing at me and shrieks of mocking laughter.

'Leave me alone,' I begged. 'I want to sleep. I want to die.'

And they laughed even louder. Their voices rang in my ears.

Vanessa, shrilly: You were asleep before and look what happened to the perfect Mr and Mrs Wiseman, the toast of suburbia. Where are they now?

Bernice, disapprovingly: The least you could have done was to sprinkle salt on the carpet stain. My goodness, Gabby, I thought I'd taught you a thing or two and now I find you knew nothing. Nothing. No wonder my poor Clivey had to do what he did.

Mum, sadly: Oh dear, in the end it was Mia who turned out to be the strong one. You always were rather a flighty little girl, weren't you Gabriella? Never quite to be trusted somehow . . .

Herbert Green, bitterly: . . . No. Not you. And if you think I've forgotten about – you know what – you're mistaken, Gabby Marks/Wiseman. You're a little bitch. That's what you are – a little bitch. You've had this coming to you all your life.

And Seamus O'Reilly: I told you I loved you and you didn't believe me. I knew you and still loved you and you turned me away. For what? For that? For him? Wait for me, Gabby. I'll return one day. Just wait for me.

'I can't,' I screamed out loud. 'I can't. It's too late. Please leave me. All of you. Please let me sleep.'

Mia's voice was soft and mellow, breathing warmth over my cold cheeks. 'Here Gabs, here's something to eat. Please try and eat. You've had nothing for three days. Talk to me Gabby. Tell me what happened.'

'I can't. Mims, let me die.'

She wouldn't. They wouldn't. I felt myself being lifted on to a stretcher, a rush of outdoor air, the rumble of an engine. Voices of strangers. Whiteness. Tubes in my arms, down my throat. 'Leave me.' I gagged and choked on the slime they forced down. 'Leave me alone. I've had enough.' And I tried to get up, to run. But I couldn't. I was weak and tired and heavy with despair. It was easier to submit. To the food, to the electric shocks they jolted through my brain. I didn't care any more. And with the shocks came blissful oblivion. Peace.

'She's getting better,' I heard them say. 'She's improving every day. We're extremely pleased with her progress.'

Was I? Were they?

'Mims,' I said at last, 'are you here?' Perhaps I should open my eyes. Yes, there she was, as ever, sitting at my side. 'Mims, can you take me home?'

'Soon.'

'Mims, have you spoken to – Clive?' I had to know.

'No. Not to Clive. Bernice phoned. She told me that you'd had a – disagreement – and decided to separate. That was all. Clive's with her in Birmingham. Look – she sent flowers. She wishes you well.'

I shut my eyes again. I couldn't bear the sight of her Interflora bouquet, a perfect triangle filled with the most expensive blooms. How many bunches had Bernice sent to mark the milestones of Wisemans up and down the country? Engagements, weddings, anniversaries, births – and this time a floral tribute to an ending. 'With all the best on your breakdown and breakup from a former fairy godmother.'

'Take them away please. I don't want them in my room.'

'I will. Gabs, look at me. Listen. Please listen. If you make an effort to eat, they'll let you come home in a few days. Just try. I'll look after you.'

'Vanessa. Where's Vanessa?'

'I've spoken to her too. She's – fine. Living with a boy – a young man – called James. She wants you to understand. She's frightened of your anger.'

'My anger? And I thought she was so angry with me. Oh Mims, Mims. I'm so tired.'

Gradually the tiredness lifted, limb by weary limb. At last they said I could leave the hospital. Mia came to fetch me and helped me upstairs and tucked me into bed. There'd been no question of returning to Hampstead. Bleak Hendon was my home. Our home. Mine and my sister's.

'Have a good sleep,' she said. And I did. For the first time in months no faces came to haunt me, no voices to taunt me. In the morning I noticed the sky was blue and I heard birds singing and Mia moving downstairs and I smelt toast. Perhaps I'd live after all.

One morning a few weeks later I saw the funny side. Mia was at work and I was about to go shopping. As I opened the front door, I suddenly remembered opening another door and the bleeding, bedraggled creature who'd crept out into the icy dawn and my furious desecration of the kosher kitchen and the destruction of Hippocrates and the silencing of the Song of Solomon, and for the first time in many months I laughed.

Then I thought of the story Clive must have fabricated for his mother and imagined him trying to restore order to his Hampstead palace, cleaning the incriminating bloodspots off the carpet, shining the kitchen to its former gloss and brushing out the lavatories, and I laughed even harder. I couldn't stop.

When Mia came home that evening I was still giggling to myself. At Gabriella, the best little wife and mother in the world, being cuckolded by an articled clerk. At Clive having been cuckolded by his sister-in-law's lover. At everything.

'You seem much happier today,' she said.

'I am,' I said. 'You know, suddenly I'm beginning to believe that things may have happened for the best.'

She nodded doubtfully and cast a disapproving eye on the laden ashtray at my side and I repeated my promise that I'd stop smoking as soon as I could. She nodded again, even more doubtfully.

'Come on Mims, don't spoil things. I told you I'm feeling better, so please don't you get all gloomy now. Let's have a nice evening. We can go to the pictures or something.'

'I'm going upstairs to have a bath. I'll see you in a while.'

I heard the sound of taps gushing, her footsteps across the landing and the shutting of the bathroom door and suddenly I wanted to be there with her. Together in the steamy bathroom, me sitting on the laundry basket, she floating in the soapy water and listening to what I had to tell her. I had so much to say.

'Mims,' I called outside the door. 'Can I come in and talk to you? Please? Like we used to . . .?'

There was a slight hesitation. 'OK.'

I went inside and there we were. I smiled at her. She half-returned it, then looked away and squirmed uncomfortably. Would my sister ever outgrow her self-consciousness?

'Shall I tell you something funny Mims, something hysterically funny?'

'Well?'

'D'you want to know the truth – about Clive?'

'And that's supposed to be funny? You certainly didn't think so when you arrived on my doorstep early one morning a few months ago.'

I shrugged.

'Go ahead. Tell me then.'

I told her. About the late nights in the office. About my suspicions. About the last night that had stretched into morning and Clive's violent battering by his lover's ex-boyfriend. And she listened, rapt. Never has any girlhood club had such a reunion as the one that took place in our warm steamy bathroom that night.

'His lover?' she marvelled. 'Clive had a lover. Who was she?'

'Well might you ask. It wasn't a she. It was a he.'

The damp bathroom rang with our laughter till we cried and added our tears to the dampness and laughed again as the water gurgled down the drain. And Mia stood on the bathmat wrapped in her towel and I, from my perch on the laundry basket which creaked under my adult weight, put out my arms and she bent down and I rested my head on her soft shoulder and we stayed like that in silence until the steam had melted away.

That was the last secret we were to share in our Hendon bathroom. Not long afterwards, we heard about the flat we'd inherited in a small town in Israel called Kfar Tikva. Mia remembered it as the end of the world.

'Sounds ideal,' I said. 'The perfect spot for two screwed-up sisters.'

I was only half-joking. Certainly the present was far from perfect. Mia toiling away for old Mr Goldblatt and me filling in the days and trying to forget. It was half-living. I hovered in the shadow of my darkness and she in the perpetual shade of Mum's death and Joseph's departure and, yes, Seamus whom she never, ever mentioned. Perhaps Kfar Tikva would offer more. At least it would be warm and bright. And far far away.

'How about it Mims?'

We could afford to move. Apart from Mum's quite substantial legacy, Clive had offered a generous divorce settlement in exchange for my discretion. He'd put the house on the market and his pride in his pocket and written me a grovelling letter begging for my forgiveness. The money offer came at the bottom.

Taking everything into consideration, I've decided to give up my London practice and return to Birmingham. I have tried unsuccessfully to make contact with Vanessa. If you see her and speak to her, please try and explain as best you can. I'm counting on your discretion.

Ah well. He could have that. Cheap at the price. I had a vision of a boarded-up marriage and boarded-up houses and a path through the darkness to a light that beckoned in the distance. Yes, I knew that lights were mostly prettier from afar, that glittering stars and Regent Street at Christmas and Sabbath candles and home fires were hot and tawdry and insignificant and really rather boring when one drew too close. Yet I couldn't help the sudden stirring of – possibilities. The feeling, the old-new feeling that perhaps, just perhaps, we should follow this light and something wonderful would happen.

'Why don't the two of us simply pack up and go? Please Mims, let's think about it.'

I could see her struggling. So tired. Such a weary sister. She'd picked up so many pieces in her life. Had my shattered illusions been the splinters that finally broke her endurance? I badly needed her to survive. To be there – for me.

'Mims, listen.' How could I convince her? She'd looked up, caught her breath, when I'd said 'the two of us'. What other bait could I possibly try?

'Don't you think it was fate that we should be offered the place now, just when we're at a – crossroads? It's like a story. A happy accident. You know the word – serendipity?'

There was a pause.

'Yes,' she said very quietly. 'I know the word.'

I'm not quite sure what did it, but I knew then that my sister had been hooked.

After that our days moved with a new purpose towards our departure. A FOR SALE board was planted in the garden and seemed to take root with more vigour than anything we'd ever tried to grow. While Mia went to work (Mr Goldblatt had pleaded with her to stay as long as she could), I sorted our possessions.

There was so much, so many years, so many people. So many things to leave behind. Old shoes, tired furniture, ancient memories. A fat man called Sid with WE CLEAR ANYTHING on his van took the furniture but rejected the shoes so I threw them away. That left the memories. Nobody wanted worn-out memories.

There was nothing for it. They'd have to come along with us.

We'd pack them with the Coronation mugs and family photographs, and quite soon the pictures would fade and the china would crack and the memories would dissolve in the heat. Already they seemed remote.

All except one. A recollection of a single Sabbath afternoon. Its outlines weren't dimming. They were getting sharper all the time. This one I didn't dare pack in the souvenir suitcase, nor could I bear to leave it behind. And it wouldn't go away. Alone in the house, in its emptying echoing rooms, I kept hearing his repeated pleas. 'Gabriella – I love you. You don't seem to understand.' And my 'No, Seamus, no.' The fear. The guilt. I'd been too frightened to tell him that the afternoon had been more than an episode. I wasn't aware how much more – until now.

Perhaps it wasn't too late. Maybe I should write. Put it down, post it, let it fly away – and forget? In a worn notebook I found his address inscribed in Mia's careful italics. Probably long out of date. It didn't matter. I'd have my say and if the letter returned one day marked 'address unknown' I'd be in another life, another country far far away.

Dear Seamus, I began. Then tore it up. And thought. And started again.

Dearest Seamus,

You must be very surprised to be hearing from me after all these years. Or perhaps not. Maybe you've been expecting it. Or could it be that you're one of those people who is never surprised about anything, who lives and loves intensely from moment to moment without projecting the future or dwelling on the past?

I don't know. I don't know anything about you, except what I learnt in one evening and a single afternoon. That you listened to me and my body more intently than anyone had ever done before and that briefly I was happier than I'd believed it possible to be.

Yes, I suppose I was unfaithful to my husband and, worse, a traitor to my sister. But I know now that never was I more true to myself than when I was with you.

I suppose that's what I want to tell you. So much has happened since then. You may have forgotten me completely. I suspect not. You did love me. I knew you were speaking the truth but there was nothing I could do. My marriage has ended and my mother has died and Mia and I are moving to Israel, a town called Kfar Tikva which she says you once saw together. We've inherited a flat described by my sister as the place to go after all else has failed. I think she sees it as an ending. I want it to be a new beginning.

I signed the letter and folded and sealed and posted it, and tried to forget it had ever been written.

We said goodbye to our children in an Italian restaurant in Hendon. I ordered Parma ham and Vanessa looked directly at me for the first time in years and I thought I saw a gleam of amusement in her eyes. I smiled at her and wondered if perhaps one day we'd laugh together. One day.

'I'm glad you came, Nessa,' I said.

'Aunty Mia talked me into it. But yes, I'm glad too. Perhaps one of these days you'll meet James. You'll like him, Mum. I know you will.'

I had the feeling it was something she really wanted. She brushed a strand of long, dark hair from her face and frowned, and her eyes seemed to be searching into the distance. The silver coin that hung from a chain round her neck glinted in the candlelight.

'Wouldn't it be wonderful,' said my daughter dreamily, 'if somehow we could all end up living happily and in peace.'

I laughed. A bitter, solitary laugh. I couldn't help it. Mia and Joseph didn't join me. 'I see we have another fairy-tale freak in the family,' I said. She lowered her eyes and pulled crumbs off a piece of bread. Little crumbs, one by one. She gathered them into a heap and dropped them into the ashtray that was filling with my cigarette ends.

'Is everything packed? Are you both quite ready?' asked Joseph, after an endless moment of silence. Mia replied. I couldn't. I was hating myself for my lack of care. She'd given me something precious and I'd broken it. Again.

Then the waiter emptied the ashtray and poured Chianti and we twisted spaghetti round our forks and forced out conversation and swallowed cassata and sipped coffee and suddenly saw that the restaurant had emptied. We were the only customers left. The proprietor and his wife stood side by side smiling eagerly, waiting for us to go too. We paid and left and they looked relieved and – that was it. The eve of our departure for the promised land. Our last supper.

And no one, not even Joseph, had dared to ask, 'Why is this night different from all other nights?' We were still much too afraid of the answers.

They searched us at the airport. 'A routine procedure, you understand,' said the woman in blue uniform who ran her hands up and down my legs. I didn't dare catch Mia's eye in case I started giggling and people thought I enjoyed being touched by a stranger.

'Thank you madam,' she said. Why was she thanking me? Perhaps she enjoyed touching me? I looked at my sister and we did start giggling and it didn't matter. Nothing mattered.

We followed the sign that said TRANSIT and I thought of the vast endless journeys of planets passing across the face of the sun and our own imminent flea-hop over miniature mountains and droplets of sea. Transit. Transitory. Transition. The passage or change from one place or state or set of circumstances to another.

The loudspeaker crackled. Our flight was announced. 'Will passengers in possession of boarding passes please proceed to gate number 32.'

'That's us,' I said to my sister. My fellow traveller. 'At last we're on our way.'

He pressed the entryphone buzzer marked 405 and was weak with fear. They don't make heroes like they used to, he thought. Not the way they did in the old days when it still helped to have wishes, and animals sometimes talked and gods walked on earth. The days when Prometheus brought fire from the heavens and Jason sailed through Clashing Rocks and Aeneas dived into the underworld and crossed the dreaded river of the dead. And Moses braved Mount Sinai to talk to God. And Christ died on the cross.

No. There were no heroes like that any more. He certainly hadn't been cast in the heroic mould. What had he done after all? Left home to seek adventure, found and fled from love, settled for a compromise and was now coming back. Well, he may have been short on the deeds but at least he was carrying out the resurrection, poised on the threshold. Master of two worlds.

Why weren't they answering? Perhaps he'd got it wrong. They weren't living there. Or they'd had wind of his arrival and were refusing him admission.

And who could blame them? He hadn't come to grant salvation or redemption or even an expenses-paid holiday in Eilat. He was a mere mortal. Most mortal. A flawed man with a death sentence and all he could offer was reality. Humanity. Pity and terror and love. Was that enough?

'Who is it?' A detached voice called out its demand. Who indeed was it? He? Why had he come? What was it/he all about? Perspiration drenched his body. Panic took his voice away and he coughed and it returned.

'Is that – Mia?'

'No. It's Gabby. Gabriella.'

'Gabriella?'

'Who is it? Who were you looking for?'

She'd forgotten. Was there anything left then? He'd always believed that important memories were learnt by heart.

'It's Seamus. Seamus O'Reilly.'

There was a pause that lasted for a second. Or an hour. Or a lifetime. The time it took for God to make a woman out of man. No time at all.

'Well . . . come on upstairs. We're on the fourth floor.'

❧ 18 ❧

'Is that – Mia?' he asked. Me? Had he come for me? At last, at long long last, had my errant knight returned? I stepped back and looked at the pair of candles and two place settings and a crisply fried carp and shut my eyes and imagined two people sitting at the table. A young woman and a man with dark curly hair and navy-blue eyes.

'Heads or tails?' he was asking. 'Come Mia – it's your lucky night. You can choose.'

She was such a young woman, hardly more than a girl, her blonde head filled with love longings and half-formed fairytales and great dreams of an awakening or a magic castle or . . . something. Was it hope?

'Heads.' Her voice was strong and clear. 'I always pick heads.'

I thought I heard mocking laughter and opened my eyes to the mirror above the sideboard and it showed me a dowdy and plump middle-aged woman with a wry smile and damp hair that needed highlights. And there on the table was a battered fish called Herbert. And frozen to the spot where she'd replied to the disembodied voice that had broken the silence of our Sabbath was my sister Gabriella with eyes like dark coins and a tense white band round her tightly pursed mouth.

'Fancy that,' I heard myself exclaiming in the sort of bright way that older people do when they are mildly astonished. I saw my mouth moving in the mirror and thought that nothing would really astonish me again. Was that growing up? How sad. How very sad. 'Imagine – Seamus O'Reilly in this God-forsaken place. What on earth can he be doing here?'

I had to say something, anything to fill the unbearable silence that was pouring into the gap between the announcement of his name and the knock on the door. She started back to life,

234

laughed a brittle laugh. But her halfpenny eyes still looked stunned as they sought the mirror and her hand patted her hair. I watched her examining herself. She saw me watching, for she turned round and asked: 'What indeed?' And suddenly my sister smiled properly. The old wicked gleam had returned.

'Anyway,' she continued, 'at least there's plenty of food. Herbert has more than enough flesh to satisfy me and you – and Seamus O'Reilly. We can ask him to join us for supper.'

'Of course,' I said doubtfully. 'It's the least we can do.'

'Gabriella?' he'd asked. And I'd known. I'd seen the hope that had lit Mia's face when she heard her name. Perhaps he'd come for her? Perhaps, perhaps. But no. His 'Gabriella' had been an intimate caress. My caress. The most intimate. I'd caught my breath and seen sky-rockets and Catherine wheels and bright fountains of light and been unable to move or speak.

'Fancy that,' she'd tutted like an aged crone long past being rescued by a returning hero. 'Imagine – Seamus O'Reilly in this God-forsaken place. What on earth can he be doing here?'

'What indeed?'

What I'd wanted to tell her was that I knew exactly why he'd come – and it wasn't for the sagging, sweating sister that I could see in the mirror. But I hadn't the heart. And then I caught a glimpse of my own reflection and saw a slightly wrinkled, marginally grey little woman with a tightly pinched mouth and scrawny neck, a forty-nine-year-old with fireworks in her head, and I thought – how funny. Weren't we both utterly ridiculous?

I smiled, I couldn't help it, and said something about the three of us feeding off Herbert. And as she replied in her slow puzzled way there was a knocking on the door. A hesitant tap-tap. The Messiah's arrival would be heralded with a fanfare of trumpets and a rolling of drums and extravagant offers of bliss and eternal peace. But Seamus O'Reilly came quietly. He wasn't so sure of his welcome, and who could blame him?

She looked at me and I looked at her and I'm sure she guessed everything in that moment.

Tap-tap. Tap-tap.

Yes. She knew and I thought she'd be angry but instead she seemed sorry.

'Shall I open the door?' she offered. I nodded and stepped

aside gratefully, for suddenly I was terrified. What would he think? I turned away so that he wouldn't see my face immediately. I heard the turning of the key and felt a gentle draught of cooler air and listened to her high-pitched hello. There was a pause.

'Mia,' I heard him say after a while. Then his footsteps came towards me and I faced him and he had the same startling eyes. But I felt older. So much older. And he looked older and smaller and humbler.

'Gabriella.'

At least his voice hadn't changed.

There was an instant when I knew. Seamus was knocking softly and I was imagining us three sharing Herbert, us two sharing Seamus, when suddenly I realized that Gabby had no intention of sharing him at all. I'd suspected, long suspected. There'd been little things that I'd chosen to ignore and big things that were too huge to contemplate. Clues like Vanessa. But now I knew. Somehow I knew it all. And the strange thing, the oddest thing after all the years of waiting and dreaming, was that it didn't matter. I wasn't astonished and I wasn't even sad. Perhaps I was sorry.

I offered to open the door. She was frightened and I thought I'd stopped caring so what the hell. That's what I told myself as I braved the portal to greet a grey-haired stranger.

'Hello,' I managed. Why had my voice come out in such an embarrassing squeak? Didn't maturity shed self-consciousness as well as surprise? Then he said 'Mia' and his voice sounded the same and when he looked at me I recognized his eyes and I realized that even at fifty-two I still had some growing to do.

They greeted one another.

'Gabriella.'

'Seamus.'

He looked at the table set for two. 'Is this a bad time for you?' he asked. Oh Seamus, whatever happened to your honeyed tongue? Was that the best you could come up with?

'No, it's fine,' she answered – too quickly. Was she frightened that he'd go away? 'We were about to have supper. Join us, do. There's plenty of food. Fried carp.'

She looked at me. Over his shoulder and into my eyes and

once again hers had their gleam. She was inviting Seamus to share our meal, and enticing me to share her mockery. Luring me into that magic circle. Together we'd laugh at Herbert, at Seamus, at ourselves. Was that what I wanted? Was *that* growing up?

I turned away. It was tempting, so tempting.

'Thank you very much,' said Seamus. He turned to me. 'Are you sure?'

'Of course,' I smiled – as ever. 'You do eat fish, don't you?'

'Indeed. It looks delicious. My favourite food.'

His favourite food and most fitting for a Friday. Once, when he was a lad, he'd gone fishing with his brothers. They'd cast a net into the river and caught a dead jackass, a broken pitcher full of sand and mud and weeds – and a copper vessel that had long lost its shine.

'It's magic,' he had said, for he believed in magic then. 'Let's rub it and make a wish. Three wishes. One each.'

His brothers had wished for fame and fortune but Seamus had wanted a fish. That's what he'd desired more than anything that day. He could have asked for the world but he'd chosen to be a fisherman.

Nothing was caught that day and he'd felt cheated and been furious and decided never to go fishing again – until now. And here he was on his second and final expedition. A man – a fisher of men – who'd long stopped believing in wishes and was being offered fried carp. His favourite food. How lucky and how appropriate. Especially on a Friday.

'Have some more,' I insisted. 'It's good for you.' Why was I sounding more and more like my former fairy godmother? Next I'd be checking whether his bowels were moving nicely and if his sinuses were clear.

'C or D, Seamus?' I'd be asking. That was the way Bee's Birmingham breakfasts began. The morning lottery. 'Constipation or diarrhoea?' For C there were prunes and D called for dry white toast. For Seamus there was fish. 'Brain food,' Bernice had always said.

I reminded myself that the middle-aged man who was concentrating hard as he chewed on succulent pieces of Herbert's flesh had been my lover. My Tristan. My bringer of fire. I should be panting for him to ravish me and instead I was feeding him brain food.

'Mims,' I said. She was also intent on devouring poor Herbert. Slowly, systematically and almost wordlessly, she was reducing him to ribs and a spine. She looked up reluctantly. It was much safer to eat than to talk.

'Mmm?'

'Would you like a little more?'

'No. No thanks. I'm fine.' She placed her knife and fork together and suddenly, decisively, sat up. 'How is your wife?'

At long last a question that mattered. He stopped eating and looked from me to her and back to me, and I nodded. 'Yes — how is she?' I echoed.

'My – late wife,' he said after a pause. 'We weren't married long. She died. In childbirth. It would have been a boy.'

We both said how sorry, how terribly sorry we were. And then we looked at one another and there was a silent pact as I noticed her right eyebrow slightly raised. Ever so slightly. I raised mine in response.

Dead. He said his Mary, his Virgin Mary on a silver cloud, the Mary of his destiny, had died giving birth to their son. A terrible tragedy. So why did I only half-believe him? I looked at Gabby, this treacherous sister whom I should have doubted more than anyone. And when she raised her eyebrow I knew that my suspicion was apparent and almost smiled but stopped myself. I'd withheld my smile and had stopped believing in fairy-tales, but I knew then that I'd never learn to resist the lure of Gabby's magic circle. In the end, God help me, it was us. The two of us and Seamus.

'How's Joseph?' he hesitated. How had he gathered the courage to make this pilgrimage? How had he dared to face us? The two of us?

I told him about his son and Gabby told him about her daughter.

'She has wonderful blue eyes,' I put in. 'They're rather like – yours.'

After that, not much was said until we'd cleared the plates and poured the coffee and made dislocated remarks about the heat and the clear starry sky and the exchange rate of the pound and everybody's health.

'Be especially careful when you next have a cold,' said Gabby. We laughed. The two of us who shared secrets. And Seamus drained his cup and then sat back, eyes shut, exhausted. He didn't look comfortable. He didn't look well.

'Why did you come?' I asked. I had to know. Gabby sat very still for she too had to know.

He sighed. Sagged.

'I came to be with you,' he said slowly, 'to say goodbye.' We exchanged glances, my sister and I. But this time I didn't think of smiling.

They'd told him the fish was called Herbert. It was after he'd nibbled at the flesh, sucked at the bones, watched the plates being cleared away and the leftovers tipped into the bin. 'That's that,' Gabriella had said. 'Farewell to Herbert.'

'What? What did you say?'

They'd laughed, the two of them. Laughed quite hysterically until he'd felt uncomfortable. An outsider. Was this what he'd come all this way for? To be humiliated?

He didn't quite get it, even after they'd explained.

'We buy fish every Friday,' said Mia. 'A carp for our Sabbath supper. We choose it live from the tank. It's a – sort of – game. This one reminded us of someone we once knew. An old friend.'

'I see,' he said. He didn't. They were laughing again and he smiled as though asking if he could play too and they looked at one another, considering, and he knew that his future – what was left of it – was hanging in the balance.

He watched as they consulted with one another wordlessly. Why was he hoping so hard that they'd ask him to stay? After all, hadn't Gabriella written to him longingly? Hadn't they both loved him? Weren't they clearly so, so happy to see him?

He had a sudden vision of himself pushing a supermarket trolley and watching them choose a fish they'd call Seamus. No, no, he told himself. It wouldn't be like that.

'I've an idea,' said Mia. And he might have imagined it but he was sure he saw her wink at her sister. She rose, left the room, and returned with a silver shekel. She tossed it into the air and it landed on the coffee table beneath a spider-plant that seemed to be wilting for lack of water.

239

Parched yellow leaves and a shining coin. They were looking at him expectantly.

'Heads or tails, Seamus? This time you must choose.'

They were shouting the odds in heaven that night. God looked on indulgently as his angels placed their bets. They'd returned from their Sabbath soul-vending and should have been doing some serious soul-searching, but God could hardly deny them the odd flutter. Heads or tails? C or D? Chance or destiny? The way humans carried on gambling for happy endings kept him and his angels constantly amused.

'Serendipity,' called Gabriel. 'I put my money on serendipity.'

'Back heads,' cried Raphael. 'She always picks heads.'

The earth stopped turning for a minute while Seamus considered. In heaven there was silence as they waited. And God smiled as he remembered a meeting on a wet pavement in Birmingham and a coin that fell in the King's Arms and an angel that miscounted spare souls. Accidents? Happy accidents?

'Tails,' said Seamus. Heaven held its breath and the earth trembled in the firmament as Mia removed the hand that covered the coin. She looked at Gabriella and they smiled for they knew it didn't matter. They would decide his fate. The two of them.

And God laughed out loud. They thought they'd decide.